THE SUMMONER

THE SUMMONER

Book One of the
CHRONICLES OF THE NECROMANCER

GAIL Z. MARTIN

SOLARIS

First published 2007 by Solaris
an imprint of Rebellion Publishing Ltd,
Riverside House, Osney Mead,
Oxford, OX1 0ES, UK

www.solarisbooks.com

ISBN-13: 978 1 84416 468 4
ISBN-10: 1 84416 468 3

Map by Kirk Caldwell

20 19 18 17 16 15 14 13 12

A CIP catalogue record for this book is available from the
British Library.

Designed & typeset by Rebellion Publishing
Printed in the USA.

This book would not have happened without the patience, support and belief of family, friends and colleagues. I'm deeply grateful to my husband, Larry, and to my children – Kyrie, Chandler and Cody – for encouraging, proofreading, and enabling my work. Thanks also to family and friends who proofed and made suggestions though many drafts. And special thanks to Ethan Ellenberg, my agent, and to Christian Dunn and Mark Newton at Solaris, for believing.

THE WINTER KINGDOMS

CHAPTER ONE

"WALK CAREFULLY, MY prince," the ghost warned. "You are in great danger this night."

Outside the mullioned windows, Martris Drayke could hear the revelry of the feast day crowds. Torchlight glittered beyond the glass, and costumed figures danced, singing and cat-calling, past the castle tower. Dressed in the four aspects of the One Goddess, Margolan's sacred Lady, the partygoers lurched behind an effigy of the Crone Mother, far more intent, this Feast of the Departed, on appeasing their appetite for ale than memorializing the dead.

"From whom?" Tris returned his attention to his spectral visitor. The ghosts of the palace Shekerishet were so numerous that he could not recall having ever seen this particular spirit before, a thin-faced man with heavy-lidded eyes, whose antiquated costume marked him as a member of the court one hundred years past.

The specter flickered and tried to say more, but no sound came.

Tris leaned closer. Now of any time the ghost should be the easiest to see, for on Haunts, as the feast day was commonly known, spirits walk openly abroad and even skeptics cannot refuse to see. The palace ghosts had been Tris's friends since childhood, long before he came to understand that his insubstantial companions were not so easily seen by those around him.

"Spirits... banished," the fading ghost managed. "Beware... the Soulcatcher."

Tris had to strain for the last words as the revenant faded into nothing. Puzzled, he sat back on his heels, his sword clattering against the hard stone floor. The rap at the door nearly made him lose his footing.

"What are you doing in there, or aren't you alone?" teased Ban Soterius through the door. The latch lifted and the sturdy captain of the guards strode in. Nothing in the young man's manner corroborated the strong smell of ale on his breath, save for his mussed brown hair and the slight rumpling of his fine tunic.

"I'm alone now," Tris said, with a glance back to where the ghost had been.

Soterius looked from Tris to the empty wall. "I keep telling you, Tris," the guardsman said, "you've got to get out more. Me, I don't care if I ever talk to a ghost... unless she's a good looking lass with a pint of ale!"

Tris managed a smile. "Have you seen the spirits tonight?"

Soterius thought for a moment. "Not as much as usual, now that you mention it, especially for Haunts." He brightened. "But you know how they love a good story. They're probably down listening to Carroway tell his tales." He pulled at Tris's sleeve. "Come on. There's no law that says princes can't have fun, too, and while I'm standing up here with you, I could be missing the love of my life down in the greatroom!"

Soterius's good humor made Tris chuckle. The captain of the guards was a favorite with the court's noble daughters. Soterius's light brown hair was cut short, for a battle helm. He was of medium build, fit and tanned from training with the guards. Everything about his bearing and his manner bespoke his military background, but the mischievous twinkle in his dark eyes softened his features, and seemed to make the marriageable maidens flock to him.

Tris was just as happy to have those same young girls and their ambitious mothers distracted. He stood a head taller than Soterius, with a lean, rangy build. He had been told often that his angular features and high cheekbones took after the best of both his parents, but the white-blond hair that framed his face and fell to his shoulders was clearly from Queen Serae's side, as were the green eyes that matched those of his grandmother, the famed sorceress Bava K'aa. It was a combination the ladies of the court found quite attractive.

"I promise I'll be down right behind you," Tris said, and Soterius raised an eyebrow skeptically. "I just want to light a candle and put a gift in grandmother's room before I go. Then you can take me on that tour of alehouses you've been promising."

Soterius grinned. "I'll hold you to that, Prince Drayke," he laughed. "Get moving. The way the festival's going tonight, they'll run out of ale and you know that brandy doesn't agree with me."

Tris heard his friend's boot steps fade down the corridor as he made his way to the family rooms. The silent stares from a row of paintings and tapestries seemed to follow him, the long-dead kings of Margolan, King Bricen's forebears. Bricen's lineage was one of the longest unbroken monarchies in the Winter Kingdoms. Glancing at their solemn visages and knowing the stories of what they had endured to secure their thrones, Tris was glad the crown would not pass to him. He picked up a torch from the sconce on the wall and opened the door into his grandmother's room. The smell of incense and potions still clung to the sorceress's chamber, five years after her death. Tris shut the door behind him. It was an indication of the awe with which even her own family regarded her that, even now, no one disturbed the spirit mage's possessions, Tris thought. But the sorceress Bava K'aa earned that kind of awe, and though he remembered her most clearly as an indulgent grandmother, the legends of her power were enough to make him hesitate, just an instant, before stepping further into the room.

"Grandmother?" Tris whispered. He set a candle on the table in the center of the room and lit it with a straw from the torch. Then, he set out a token gift of honey cakes and a small cup of ale, over which he made the sign of the Goddess in blessing. And then, with a glance to assure himself that the door was shut and he would not be discovered, he stepped onto the braided rug in the center of the room. Plaited from her sorceress's cords, the rug matched the warded circle of his grandmother's workspace, and Tris felt the familiar tingle of her magic, like the residue of old perfume. With his sword as his athame, Tris walked the perimeter of the rug as his grandmother taught him, feeling the circle of protection rise around him. Its blue-white light was clear in his mind, though invisible. Tris closed his eyes and stretched out his right hand.

"Grandmother, I call you," he murmured, stretching out his senses for her familiar presence. "I invite you to the feast. Join me within the Circle." Tris paused. But for the first time since her death, no response came. He tried once more.

"Bava K'aa, your kinsman invites you to the feast. I have brought you a gift. Walk with me." Nothing in the room stirred and Tris opened his eyes, concerned.

And then, a glimmer of light caught his eye. It seemed far beyond the circle, struggling and flickering as if trapped within gauze, but as he strained to make it out, he recognized the form of his grandmother, standing at a great distance obscured by fog.

"Grandmother!" he called, but the apparition came no further. Her lips moved, but no sound reached him, yet a chill ran down his back. He did not need words to recognize a warning in his grandmother's manner. Though Tris could not hear Bava K'aa's voice, the indication of danger was clear enough.

Without warning, a cold wind howled through the shuttered chamber, guttering the torch and extinguishing the candle. It buffeted the circle Tris cast, and the image of his grandmother winked out. Two porcelain figures crashed to the floor and the bed curtains fluttered as the gust tore scrolls from the desk and knocked a chair to the ground. Tris gritted his teeth and strained to keep his warding in place, but he felt the gooseflesh rise on his arms as the chill permeated even the area within the cord and circle. Like a glimpse of something there and gone, impressions formed in his mind. Something evil, something old and strong, lost, hunting, dangerous.

Then, as quickly as it came, the wind was gone and with it Tris's sense of foreboding. When he felt sure that nothing stirred in the room, Tris raised his shaking hand to silently thank the Four Faces of the Goddess, and then closed the circle, shivering as the magic light faded in his mind. He looked around the room. Only the torn parchments, shattered figurines and overturned chair testified that anything was amiss. More troubled than before, Tris turned to leave.

From the corridor, a woman screamed. Tris bounded for the door, his sword already in hand.

In the shadows of the hallway, Tris could make out a grappling pair, the dark figure of a man looming over one of the chambermaids who struggled to escape.

"Release her!" Tris raised his sword in challenge. Seizing the moment, the terrified woman sank her teeth into her attacker's arm and wrenched free, running down the corridor for her life. Tris felt his throat tighten as the assailant straightened and turned, recognizing the form even before the thin gold circlet on the man's brow glinted in the torchlight.

"Once again, you've spoiled my fun, brother," Jared Drayke glowered, his eyes narrowing. King Bricen's eldest son started down the hallway, and Tris could tell by his brother's gait that Jared was well into his cups this feast night. Tris stood his ground, though he felt his heart in his throat. Ale never compromised Jared's swing nor blunted his swordsmanship, and Tris had taken enough bruises at his brother's hand to know just what kind of a mood Jared was in tonight.

"You're drunk," Tris grated.

"Sober enough to whip your ass," Jared retorted, already beginning to turn up the sleeves of his tunic.

"You can try."

"You dare to raise steel against me?" Jared roared. "I could have you hanged. No one threatens the future king of Margolan!"

"While father rules, I doubt I'll hang," Tris replied, feeling his heart thud. "Why don't you bed one of the nobles' daughters, instead of raping the servants? Or would it be too expensive to pay off their families when they disappeared?"

"I'll teach you respect," Jared growled, close enough for Tris to smell the rancid brew on Jared's breath. And with a movement almost too quick to see, Jared drew his sword and charged forward.

Tris parried, needing both hands to deflect the thrust that, he had no doubt, was meant to score. He fell back a step as Jared drove on, barely countering his brother's enraged attack. Jared pressed forward, and the anger that burned in his eyes was past reasoning. Tris fought for his life, knowing that he could not hold off Jared's press much longer as Jared forced him back into the glow of the torch sconce.

In the distance, boot steps sounded on the stone. "Prince Jared?" Zachar, the seneschal called. "My prince, are you there? Your father desires your attendance."

With an oath, Jared freed his sword from Tris's parry and stepped back several paces. "Prince Jared?" Zachar called again, closer now and more insistent.

"I heard you," Jared shouted in return, watching Tris carefully. Warily, Tris lowered his sword but did not sheath it until Jared first replaced his own weapon.

"Don't think it's settled, brother," Jared snarled. "You'll pay. Before the dawn, you'll pay!" Jared promised. Zachar's footsteps were much closer now and Jared turned to meet the seneschal before Zachar could happen upon them.

Tris stood where he was for a moment until his heart slowed and he caught his breath, shaking from the confrontation. When he regained his composure, he headed for the greatroom, slowing only when the sounds and smells of the festival reached him as he neared the doors to the banquet hall.

Soterius looked skeptically at him as Tris joined his friend. "What's your hurry?"

The armsman was far too observant to overlook the sweat that glistened on Tris's forehead on a chill autumn night, or the obvious flush of the fight. "Just a little conversation with Jared," Tris replied, knowing from long acquaintance that Soterius would fill in the rest.

"Can't your father—?" Soterius asked below his breath.

Tris shook his head. "Father can't... or won't... admit what a monster he sired. Even good kings have their blind spots."

"Good feast to you, brother." A girl's laughing voice sounded behind them just then, and Tris turned. Behind him stood his sister, Kait, her prized falcon perched on her gauntlet. A dozen summers old, at an age when most princesses gloried in mincing steps and elaborate gowns, Kait was radiant in the costume of a falconer, its loose tunic and knickers hiding her budding curves. Her hair was dark, like Bricen's, plaited in a practical braid, which only accentuated how much she resembled both Tris and Jared. Dark-eyed like her father, with her mother's grace, Kait was likely to catch the eye of potential suitors before too long, Tris thought with a protective pang.

"Didn't anyone tell you you're supposed to get a costume for Haunts?" Tris teased, and even the events in the corridor could not keep a smile from his face as Kait favored him with a sour look.

"You know very well, brother dear, that this is the one night of the year I can wear sensible clothes without completely scandalizing mother and the good ladies of the court," she retorted. The falcon, one of the dozen that she tended like children, stepped nervously in its traces, restless at the noise of the boisterous crowd.

"Are you going to take that bird with you on your wedding day?" Tris bantered.

Kait wrinkled her nose as if she smelled spoiled meat. "Don't rush me. Maybe I'll take him with me on my wedding night, and not have to start birthing brats immediately!"

"Kaity, Kaity, what would mother say?" Tris clucked in mock astonishment, as Soterius laughed and Kait swung a lighthearted punch at Tris's shoulder.

"She'd say what she usually says," Kait returned unfazed. "That she had better find me a suitor before I've scandalized the entire court." She shrugged. "The race is on."

"You know," Soterius said with a wink, "she might find you someone you actually like."

Kait raised an eyebrow. "Like you?" she replied with such a withering tone that both Tris and Soterius chuckled once more.

Soterius raised his hand in appeasement. "You know that's not what I mean."

Kait looked about to make another rejoinder when she glanced at Tris, who had fallen silent. "You're quiet, Tris."

Tris and Soterius exchanged glances. "Had a bit of a run-in with Jared," Tris said. "Stay out of his way tonight, Kaity. He's in an awful temper."

Kait's banter dropped, and Tris saw complete understanding in eyes that suddenly appeared much older than her dozen years. "I'd heard," she said with a grimace. "There's talk at the stables. He thrashed a stable hand down there half to death for not having his horse ready." She rolled her eyes. "At least I've managed to stay away from him for a few days."

Tris looked at her and frowned. "Where'd you get that bruise on your arm?"

Kait felt for it self-consciously. "It's not bad," she said, looking away.

"That isn't what I asked, Kaity," Tris pressed. He could feel his anger burning already, for this welt and all the others over the years.

Kait still did not meet his eyes. "I earned it," she sighed. "Jared was taking it out on one of the kitchen dogs, and I clipped a loaf of bread at his head to let the pup get away." She winced. "He wasn't very happy with me."

"Damn him!" Tris swore. "Don't worry, Kaity. I'll make sure he stays away from you," he promised, though they both knew past attempts had only limited success.

Kait managed a wan smile. "After the party, think you could do up one of your poultices? It does smart a little."

Tris ruffled her hair, feeling such a mixture of anger for Jared and love for Kait that he thought his heart might break. "Of course. I don't even have to sneak the herbs out of the kitchen any more."

Long ago when they were children, Tris had dared night runs to the kitchens to get the herbs he needed to bind up the bruises and cuts Jared inflicted. Though he was only eight years Kait's senior, he was her self-appointed guardian since the day she was born. Maybe he had been stirred by how small and lonely she had looked in the nursemaid's arms. Or perhaps it was Tris's fear that a baby would prove a more amusing target for Jared's cruel humor than the ill-fated cats and dogs that disappeared from the nursery with distressing regularity.

They stuck together, and he frequently took the brunt of Jared's tempers for her. Jared drove off one nursemaid after another with his outbursts. As Kait got older, she and Tris found safety in banding together against Jared, able to make him back off when they no longer made such an easy mark.

"Father's got to listen soon," Kait said wistfully, breaking into his thoughts.

Tris shook his head. "Not yet he won't," he said. "He won't hear a word I say, even though he and Jared argue more and more. Some days, I think they argue about saying 'good morning.'"

Kait sighed, and the bird on her gauntlet fidgeted. "Maybe mother—?"

Again, Tris indicated the negative. "Every time she tries to say something, father accuses her of favoring her children over Jared. I don't think he's ever quite gotten over Eldra's death," he added. Jared's mother died giving birth to Bricen's firstborn, and it took the king nearly ten years to find the will to wed again, a decade in which young prince Jared had little supervision and less correction as his father retreated into despair.

"Mother won't even bring it up anymore," Tris added. "She just tries to keep you out of his way."

"Uh oh," Kait whispered under her breath. "More trouble." Tris followed her gaze across the crowded greatroom, to the red-robed figure that stood in the hall's entrance. A hush fell over the room. Clad in the flowing blood-colored robes of a Fireclan mage, Foor Arontala, Jared's chief advisor, made his way through the crowd. The throng parted in front of him in a desperate haste to get out of his way, yet the fine-boned, porcelain-pale face that peered from beneath a heavy hood and long dark hair did not even acknowledge their presence.

"I hate him," Kait whispered in a voice that only Tris and Soterius could hear. "I wish grandmother were here. She'd squash him like a flea," she added, with a little stamping motion for good measure.

"Grandmother's gone," Tris replied tonelessly, thinking of his unsuccessful attempt to contact

Bava K'aa's spirit earlier in the evening. He moved to tell Kait what had happened, and then, out of long habit, stopped. Bava K'aa always kept his training such an elaborate secret that even now, he was unwilling to put it into words.

"I wish your father had been quicker to bring a new mage of his own to Shekerishet," Soterius added in a whisper. "Even a grannywitch would be better than that," he said with carefully shielded distaste.

Foor Arontala passed among the hushed partygoers as if he did not notice their existence, gliding with preternatural smoothness through the crowd to exit on the other side of the hall, but it took several minutes before the revelry began again, and even longer before it began to sound wholehearted.

"Crone take him," Tris swore under his breath.

"He looks like She already has," Kait giggled.

Soterius took it upon himself to lighten the mood. "Do I have to remind both of you that there's a party going on?" he reprimanded with mock sternness. "Carroway's been telling tales for most of a candlemark over there," he said, gesturing, "and you've missed it."

"Is he still there?" Kait said with sudden interest. "Is there room?"

"Let's go find out," Tris said, hoping that the diversion would break his heavy mood.

Carroway, Margolan's master bard, sat in the center of a rapt audience. It was evident by the press of partygoers around him that the storyteller was building to the climax of his tale.

Carroway leaned forward, recounting the adventure from the time of Tris's great, great grandfather's rule in a hushed voice that forced his listeners to lean closer. "The Eastmark raiders pressed on, cutting their way toward the palace. Valiant men tried and failed to push them back, but still the raiders came. The palace gates were in sight! Blood ran ankle-deep on the stones and all around, the moans of the dying cried for justice." As Carroway spoke, he leaned to the side and casually lit two gray candles.

"King Hotten fought with all his might as all around him, swords clashed and the battle raged. Twice, assassins closed around him. Twice, hurled daggers nearly found their mark." With lazy grace, Carroway's arm snapped up and *thunk, thunk*, two daggers appeared from nowhere, thudding into the woodwork behind the rearmost listener. The children screamed, then giggled at Carroway's sleight of hand.

"But the weary defenders had no more troops to spare," Carroway went on. "Now it was the eve of the Feast of the Departed—Haunts as we call it—when spirits walk most boldly among us. They say that on Haunts, the spirits can make themselves solid if they choose, and cast illusions so real that mortals cannot sense or feel the deception until—" he paused, and a well-timed small *poof* and a puff of smoke appeared by sleight of hand, "—everything so solid the night before vanishes with the morning. Knowing this, King Hotten begged his mage to do anything that would stop the invaders. The mage was nearly spent himself, and he knew that summoning a major spell would probably be his death, but he harnessed all the power he possessed and called out to the spirit of the land itself, to the Avenger Goddess, and to the souls of the dead. And with his dying breath, the fog began to change.

"From the blood-soaked stones, a mist began to rise. At first, it hovered above the street, swirling around the raiders' legs, but it grew higher and denser, until it reached the horses' bridles. Soon, it was a howling wind, and as the terrified raiders watched, it took on faces and shapes, distorted by the tempest. And on that feast night so long ago, the spirits chose to take on form, to manifest themselves completely, to seem as real and solid as you or me." A thin fog was rising from Carroway's candles, swirling along the floor of the castle, sending its tendrils among the listeners who startled as they noticed it and stared at Carroway, eyes wide. As they watched, the thin veil of smoke formed itself into the figures of the story, phantom wisps in the shapes of rearing horses and fleeting ghosts.

"The spirits of Shekerishet rose to defend it from the raiders, by the power of the dead and the will of every valiant fighter who ever died to defend king and kingdom. A howl rose above the wind, the shrieks and warning wails of the rising ghosts; and the fog was so thick that it separated the attackers from each other." Carroway's wrist flicked and two small pellets scattered from his hand, screeching and wailing as they hit the hard floor. His audience jumped out of their seats, wide-eyed with fright.

"Confounded and terrified, the attackers ran," Carroway went on. In his gray bard's robes, dimly lit by the flickering torches, he looked like something out of legend. "The wall of spirits drove them back, onto the waiting blades of the Margolan army. The ghostly guardians of the palace pushed back the enemy, pursuing the raiders until they scattered beyond the gates," he said, stretching out his hand. His audience shrieked in good-natured fright as the smoke rose at Carroway's command, shaping itself into a man-sized apparition of a skeletal fighter, poised to draw his sword from the scabbard that hung against his bony leg.

"They say that the ghosts still protect Shekerishet," Carroway said with a grin. "They say that the spirits of the castle defend it from intruders and will let no harm come to those within. They say that the curse of King Hotten's mage still carries power, and that every king's mage since then has added to it with his dying breath."

"And that," Carroway said, sitting back with satisfaction, "is the story of the Battle of Court Gate."

Tris chuckled as the wide-eyed children filed away, leaving their costumed storyteller to gather his belongings. Kait danced up to Carroway and blew him a teasing kiss. "I loved it!" She piped up enthusiastically. "But you've got to make it scarier." She winked at the bard. "If I hadn't already sworn never to get married, I'd pick you," she added. Tris suspected that Kait was only partly jesting, though she had known Tris's childhood friend for so long that Carroway was like a brother.

"You're going to give her nightmares," Tris joked, rescuing the blushing minstrel.

Carroway grinned. "I hope so. That's what Haunts is all about." He stood, shaking out the folds of his cloak. A group of costumed revelers passed them, arms entwined, singing loudly and badly off-key.

"Good Haunts to you, bard and all," one of them called out, tossing a golden coin to Carroway, which the storyteller caught in midair.

"Good Haunts to you, sir!" Carroway called in acknowledgment, holding up the coin and then, with a flourish, making it disappear, to the delight of the partygoers. Carroway was as tall as Tris but thinner, with a dancer's grace. His long, blue-black hair framed features so handsome that they veered toward beauty. Light blue eyes, with long lashes, sparkled with intelligence and a keen wit.

Ban Soterius appeared at Carroway's side. "Don't let the priestesses hear you call it that," their friend warned in mock seriousness. "It's Feast of the Departed, young man." Soterius grinned and rubbed his knuckles. "I got reminded of that more than once when I was in school."

Carroway grinned. "Haunts is a lot easier to say," he replied archly. "Besides, what else are you supposed to call a holiday for dead people?"

"I suspect you're missing some deeper point on that," Tris laughed.

"I'll see you three later," Kait said, reaching up to calm her falcon as a noisy group of revelers passed by. "Good Feast to you," she called. "Don't get into too much trouble."

"Easy for you to say," Tris rejoined. He turned to Carroway as Kait blended into the departing crowd. "Come on, or we'll be late for the feast." The three young men were easily Margolan's most eligible bachelors, not yet twenty summers old, and were the targets of the court's ambitious mothers. While Soterius relished the attention, and was rarely without a lady on his arm, Carroway was more likely to choose his partners from among the castle's entertainers, singers or musicians whose talent he respected, and who were less star-struck over his court position and friendship with Tris.

To the chagrin of many of the court mothers, and even, sometimes Tris suspected, his mother Serae, Tris had successfully evaded the matchmakers. Jared's escapades made Tris wary, and he had yet to meet any of the local nobles' daughters with whom he could carry on an interesting conversation more than once. His self-imposed solitude was in sharp contrast to Jared's wantonness, and Tris was well aware that some of the court wags invented their own, less flattering explanations for his unwillingness to choose and discard consorts with the same regularity as the rest of the court. Let them talk, he thought. He had no intention of bringing a bride into

Shekerishet with Jared nearby, and even less desire to subject children of his own to Jared's cruelties.

Perhaps some day, he thought wistfully, watching as Soterius and Carroway bantered easily with the costumed girls who passed them. Some day, when I'm safely out of Shekerishet, in permanent residence at father's country manor, far from court, far from parties, far from Jared.

"Tell your fortunes?" a voice rasped from behind them. Tris turned, startled, to find a bent old woman in an alcove, gesturing with a gnarled finger. He knew at once that she was one of the palace's ghosts, although this night, the spirits walked openly, seemingly solid. "For you, Prince Drayke, and your friends, there is no charge."

"Where did she come from?" Soterius murmured.

Carroway shrugged. "Let's go see what our fortunes hold."

"I'm not really sure I want to know," Soterius balked, but Carroway was already dragging Tris by the sleeve.

"Come on," Carroway teased. "I want to know how famous a bard I'm going to become."

"Speak for yourself," Soterius muttered under his breath. "Really, I'm not sure—"

"I'm with Ban," Tris murmured.

"No spirit of adventure. Come on," the bard insisted.

The crone looked up as they approached, and her jaw worked a wad of dreamweed. A bit of spit dribbled down her stubbly chin as she pushed back a lock of greasy hair and nodded, taking in everything with piercing green eyes that seemed to see through them. Her dress was made of faded silk, expensive once but now long past its glory; and she smelled of spice and musk.

The seer sat before a low, intricately carved table, its worn surface wrought with complicated runes. In the center of the table was a crystal globe, set atop a golden stand. Both the globe and its stand were of much greater quality than Tris had anticipated, and he looked more closely at the crone.

She raised a bony finger and leveled it at the bard's chest. "You first, minstrel," she rasped, and motioned for Carroway to kneel. She looked up at Tris and Soterius, and her eyes narrowed. "Wait in silence."

She hummed a raspy chant, ancient and strange, intoned just below Tris's ability to catch the words. Her gnarled hands caressed the crystal, brushing its surface, shaping themselves around it gently, hovering just above its smooth contours.

The globe began to glow, a cold, swirling blue that began at its nexus and gradually filled the whole crystal with a brilliant flare. The crone closed her eyes, humming and swaying.

When she spoke, it was in the clear tones of a young girl, without a trace of the smoky rasp they'd heard before. "You are the maker of tales and the taker of lives," said the girl's voice, bell-like and preternatural. "Your tales will be the greatest Margolan has ever known, but sorrow, yes, great sorrow will teach you your songs. Take heed, dreamspinner," the voice warned. "Your journey lies among the immortals. Guard well your soul."

Tris realized he was holding his breath. Soterius stared, unmoving. Carroway, eyes wide, watched the swaying seer with amazement. The seer's face relaxed, as if a curtain had fallen, and the voice went silent.

"Let's get out of here," Soterius said.

"Stay," the crone commanded, and while she did not raise her rasping voice, the grated command froze Soterius in place. "You will come, soldier," she said as Carroway, still dazed, scrambled to his feet. Ashen, Soterius obeyed.

From the voluminous pockets of her frayed robe, the hag withdrew a well-worn pack of cards. Jalbet cards. Tris recognized the stock-in-trade of roadside oracles and the parlor amusement of ladies at court. Deftly, the crone laid down four cards.

"The Ox," the crone grated, naming the cards. "The Black River. The Coin. The Dark Lady." The crone gave a harsh laugh. "These speak for the Goddess," she rasped. "Look with care."

"I don't understand—"

"Silence!" Her twisted finger stroked the first worn card. "The Ox is the card of strength. Your health and strength will serve you well, soldier. Together with the Black River, the cards speak of war." She spoke as if to herself, her dry voice taking on a singsong quality. "You will prosper. That is the tale of the coin. But," she hissed, as one broken nail quivered above the last card, "beware. For your journey shall be taken along dark roads, in the company of the dead and the undead. You will be among the servants of the Dark Lady. Guard well your soul."

Soterius swallowed hard, staring at the cards. He gave a nervous glance at the globe, which remained clear and unremarkable. The crone looked up at Tris, and beckoned wordlessly. His heart thudding, Tris obeyed, settling nervously into his seat as Soterius hurried out of the way.

"Give me your hand," the crone commanded, reaching across the table. Slowly, Tris extended his hand, turning it palm up as the witch drew it toward her.

"A great quest will come to you, Son of the Lady," the crone whispered, tracing a barely visible line on Tris's palm with her nail. "Who can see its end?" she mumbled, her nail tracing the folds of Tris's palm. "Many souls hang in the balance. Your way lies in shadow." She caught her breath, her finger trembling.

"What is it?" Tris breathed, afraid to speak above a whisper.

"You are indeed the Lady's own," the crone rasped. "Your hand betrays no time of dying."

"Everyone dies."

"As the Lady sees fit. Your time is of her making. You are truly in the Lady's hands," she whispered. "Guard well your soul, or all is lost." Then, before their eyes, the crone's image wavered, and while her mouth moved, they could not hear her words. Tris could feel a strange power pulling at the spirit, a force he could not identify. The spirit seemed to disintegrate, fading first to haze and then to nothing.

Soterius tugged at Tris's shirt, nearly pulling him to his feet. "Come on!" the soldier urged, his voice just shy of panic. "Let's go."

The smell of roasting meat wafted from the banquet hall. A roaring fire crackled in the huge hearth and musicians played a lively tune as the guests hustled in. With a grin, Carroway joined his companion minstrels, eagerly accepting the lute that one of his friends pressed into his hands. Tris could see Jared at the front of the room near the king's table, angrily berating a servant. Tris saw the studied control in the seneschal's face as Zachar struggled to show neither his disapproval nor his embarrassment. Kait motioned Tris towards two seats next to her, and he and Soterius slipped through the crowd to take their places. Kait's falcon shifted, nervously, and Kait signaled to the falconer, who accepted her bird onto his gauntleted arm and whisked the predator away to quieter mews.

"Your father's never allowed falcons at the table in the manor," Soterius whispered to Kait. "I'll have to tell him how it's done at court."

Kait gave him a bantering look of disappointment. "Another fashion you can share with the rural nobility," she said with feigned ennui.

Tris glanced at Soterius, aware that the other tensed. "What's wrong," Tris asked, scanning the crowd that awaited King Bricen's arrival.

Soterius shook his head, and while his expression was neutral, his eyes showed their concern.

"The guards assigned to the feast aren't the ones I ordered," he said barely above a whisper. "I'm going to have a word with the lieutenant over there," he said. But just as Soterius moved to leave the dais, a trumpet's herald announced the arrival of King Bricen of Margolan.

"Later," he murmured, frustrated at the delay. Tris watched Bricen and Queen Serae process through the throng, stopping to greet the well-wishers who pressed around them. His father's ruddy exuberance told Tris that the king had enjoyed a few pints of ale in his private rooms before joining in the celebration. Serae, always so coolly self-possessed, seemed to glide across the floor, graciously accepting the curtsies and bows of the ladies and nobles who formed an aisle among the tables. Bricen assisted Serae onto the dais just as Jared concluded haranguing the servant, and Bricen glowered at his eldest son, whose mute glare in return made no pretense to shield the tensions between father and son from onlookers.

"Good gentles," the king boomed. "Tonight, let both the living and the dead make merry! As we are now, so once were they. And by the Goddess, as they are now, so we shall someday be, so best we eat and drink while we may!"

The king took his seat and washed his hands in the proffered bowl. The cupbearers began their work and a procession of kitchen staff followed the steward to the king's table, bearing steaming trenchers of roasted game. Carroway and his fellow musicians struck up a jolly tune, and the buzz of conversation, interrupted by the king's arrival, resumed its din. But despite the festive atmosphere, Tris felt a chill settle over him. The ghost's cryptic warning repeated in his mind. Glancing around the greatroom, Tris could see none of the palace spirits that were usually so evident, even to those without a trace of magical talent. Never could he recall the ghosts' absence from such a feast, especially on Haunts.

As dinner wore on, Tris could sense Soterius's increasing tension. At the first opportunity, Soterius excused himself and slipped over to speak with the ranking lieutenant. In a few moments, he returned, looking no less concerned. "What's going on?" Tris murmured.

"I don't like it. The lieutenant said he was ordered to change the guards by Jared." Soterius gave a barely perceptible shake of his head. "Look around. They're all new guards, the younger ones who fancy Jared's talk of a bigger army. I'd ordered more of the seasoned men, whose loyalty to the king I don't doubt."

Tris looked out over the crowd. Soterius was correct. For months, Jared had been visiting the barracks. To "raise the spirits" of the guards, the prince had replied in answer to his father's questions. Bricen, perhaps tired of the incessant arguments with his heir, had let it go at that. Now, Tris felt his misgivings renewed about Jared's sudden interest. Of equal concern, he noted, scanning the guests, were the faces he saw—and did not see—among the partygoers. Few of the older nobles were in attendance, lords and barons whose loyalty to the crown was absolute. Those who figured among the guests looked ill at ease, a rarity at one of Bricen's legendary fetes. Instead, Tris saw many of the newer nobles, landowners whose first-generation status had been won on the field of combat or bestowed by recent favor. And like the guards, Tris knew that these newly titled men looked favorably on Jared's fiery rhetoric of expansion and conquest, finding it much more exciting than Bricen's stable statesmanship.

On pretext of returning a poor goblet of wine, Tris signaled to Zachar. A whispered question and confirmation gave Tris his answer, though it did nothing to allay his concern.

"Zachar says that many of the older nobles responded late to the invitation, as if they hadn't received notice in time," Tris related to Soterius under his breath. "Very strange. And there seemed to be some pressing reason in each case why they couldn't attend."

"You think they know something we should?"

Tris stole a glance toward Jared's end of the table, where Foor Arontala sat next to Jared, toying with the food on his trencher but consuming nothing. "Maybe there was some 'help' creating those pressing reasons," Tris said, looking away as Arontala's unblinking gaze leveled in his direction.

"So what do we do about it?" Soterius asked, his words muffled by a bite of venison.

Tris paused. "I want to get a look at what's going on in Arontala's workshop."

Soterius choked on his meat, and the servant behind him had to pound on his back. "You want to do what?" he rasped after he took a sip of wine. "Are you crazy?"

Tris did not reply for a moment, mindful that Jared's eyes were on them. When Jared resumed his conversation with the red-robed mage, Tris glanced again at Soterius. "If Jared's up to something, you can bet Arontala's behind it. And we won't know what it is until we get a look in that workshop." Although he was not prepared to recount the ghost's warning, Tris already concluded that if such a thing as a "soulcatcher" posed a threat, then the first place to go looking for it was the library of the Fireclan mage.

"You know I'm not much for magic," Soterius retorted under his breath. "But I believe my guards when they tell me that the doors to Arontala's rooms are spelled tight. No one comes or goes without him."

Tris chewed thoughtfully on a leg of mutton. "Then let's try the window."

Soterius bit into his bread. "No. Uh huh. Not a good idea. Besides, I thought you hated heights."

"I do," Tris admitted. "But it's for a good cause. Come on, you've been dying to get me back up in your climbing rig ever since last year. And you know you always like to try some stunt on Haunts, just to give Zachar a few more gray hairs." He chuckled. "One year you decided we should rappel from the tower and we nearly got shot by the guards. The next year you decided to try to swing from the sleeping rooms to the other side of the courtyard, but you landed in the stable instead."

"Thank the Mother and Childe it was hay and not manure," Soterius replied dryly. "You're serious about this, aren't you?"

Tris nodded. "Too many things aren't what they should be. We'll get our chance when dinner is over and the festival moves down into the town."

The rest of the long feast went uneventfully, with a series of jugglers, acrobats and magicians that even lifted even Tris's mood. Carroway, the mastermind behind the evening's festivities, looked quite pleased with himself as he fussed over his actor friends, adjusting the elaborate costumes and makeup in the far corner of the feast hall and watching with pride as one group of performers after another strove to outdo themselves before the king. As Carroway finished a long, haunting ballad, which was among Serae's favorites, Bricen, showing the same gusto in his feasting for which he was legendary on the hunt, clapped and roared his approval, prompting even louder accolades from the guests. But Tris thought his mother looked distracted, as if she might be marking time until she could make her exit to the private rooms. That was unusual, he thought with concern, for his mother—though never as boisterous as Bricen—was known for her graciousness as a hostess and was usually quite partial to Carroway's ballads.

As the bells in the tower tolled midnight, the outer doors to the greatroom swung open. A black-robed figure, its face shrouded by a deep cowl, stood in the doorway bearing a glittering chalice. Soundlessly, the figure bowed in deference to Bricen, who stood, playing his role in the drama.

"Greetings, Grandmother Spirit," the king intoned. "We are ready for the march." From behind the robed figure of the Crone emerged three costumed actors, each in one of the other faces of the quartern Goddess: Mother, Childe and Lover. Four faces of one goddess, the light aspects of a single deity. The king offered his arm to Serae, and together they led the procession down the aisle toward the waiting players, the tables emptying as the other guests filed in behind them. Tris saw Soterius catch Carroway's eye and make a slight gesture; the minstrel nodded in acknowledgment as the procession left the feast hall.

Tris pulled Soterius into a side corridor, letting the rowdy supper guests push past. Carroway dodged into the hallway a few minutes later. "What's going on?" the bard asked as the last of the revelers passed. The three friends moved further into the shadows, and Tris cast an anxious glance toward the torchlit main hall to make sure they were alone.

"Father and the rest of the family will take leave of the guests at the main gates," he hissed. "As late as it is, they should all head up to bed. Once it's quiet, we can head for the tower and climb down from there."

Soterius looked askance at Tris. "Let's be clear about royal prerogative here," he objected. "Tris has a hare-brained idea that's likely to get us all charred into bits or turned into frogs," the guard complained, his expression resigned as Tris explained the night's work to Carroway.

"I'm game," the minstrel chimed in when Tris was finished. "We bards are quite accepting of magic," he said with mock snootiness aimed at Soterius, who scowled. "Unlike those plebeian military types who only believe in what they see. Count me in."

"What I see worries me enough," Soterius groused. "Wait here. I'll go get my gear."

CHAPTER TWO

SOTERIUS RETRIEVED A large bag from his quarters, and together, the three made their way through the passageways of Shekerishet. It was already the wee hours of the morning and the night's revelry was winding down inside the castle. Most of the partygoers had departed. A few costumed stragglers made their way across the courtyards as Tris and his friends climbed the steps to the upper chambers.

They headed for the section above the audience rooms of the king. Tris tried his best to push aside his earlier foreboding. Despite the warnings of the ghost, and his grandmother's apparition, no danger presented itself. Under other circumstances, tonight's adventure might have been fun, harking back to the escapades he and the others had shared when they returned from fostering. They had been high-spirited boys back then,

Zachar's private curse, the seneschal was fond of telling them. Tris might be the second son of the king, but it didn't exempt him from a tongue-lashing if things got out of hand.

"You're quiet," Soterius prompted.

Tris shrugged. "Maybe I'm festivalled out. It's been a long week." He paused. "Carroway," he said, turning to the bard, "have you seen any of the palace spirits since the fortune-teller?"

Carroway shook his head. "Now that you mention it, no. Funny, especially on Haunts. I've seen lots of people dressed as spirits, but the real ghosts are nowhere to be seen."

Tris nodded, uneasy. "There's something wrong. Did you see the way the fortune-teller disappeared, how she seemed pulled away? And where are the rest of the ghosts? There're always as many ghosts as mortals at the festival. The palace ghosts are always most visible on Haunts."

"Could that be why it bears the name, do you think?" Carroway smiled. "It's strange, I'll give you that." He shrugged. "Maybe they're all entertaining the guests in the courtyard. Or maybe even they celebrated a little too much and they've gone back to wherever ghosts go to rest."

"Maybe," Tris said, unconvinced.

Carroway sobered. "That's one more thing that's got you thinking there's trouble?" he asked, with a look that Tris knew read more into the statement. While Tris always self-consciously downplayed what magic talent he possessed to Soterius, Carroway was a willing helper when

Bava K'aa would ask the boys to help her with a minor working. Carroway was also comfortable with Tris's odd ability to speak to spirits at any time of the year—not just on Haunts—and drew some of his best tales and songs from the stories of these long-dead courtiers. It was a talent Tris had learned early to hide from nearly everyone else, although Kait and Bava K'aa quietly encouraged him. Instinctively, Tris knew not to let Jared suspect that he had any magic talent. He was glad to avoid another reason for the palace wags to talk.

"Hurry up!" Soterius whispered, holding open a door. They followed him into the darkened room. Carroway lit a torch.

"So what's the plan?" Tris asked.

Soterius grinned as he unpacked his bag. Two large, heavy coils of rope tumbled to the floor. As Soterius laid it out, Tris could see two climbers' harnesses of leather straps and buckles. Soterius wriggled into one harness and passed the other to Tris. "Help me with this, will you?" he hissed.

"Now what?" Carroway asked skeptically. "Men aren't supposed to walk down walls like flies."

"Back in my father's lands, everybody climbs down walls like this," Soterius pointed out.

"Everybody?" Tris teased.

"Well, all right, mostly just the mountain people, because the cliffs are so sharp they'd never go anywhere otherwise. But we have a lot of mountain people and a lot of cliffs, so it's almost everybody!" Soterius replied. "Help me get this anchored before we get caught. If I'm going to get another tongue-lashing from Zachar, I want to earn it!"

"You have a pretty strange hobby," Carroway muttered as he cinched the rope tight around its anchor.

"Coming from a grown man who makes smoke ghosts for a living, I'll take that as a compliment," Soterius shot back. Now that he had secured his own harness, he turned his attention to Tris, double-checking the sturdy leather and testing the buckles. When both men were satisfied with the climbing gear, they secured the ropes to iron rings sunk deep in the stone walls near the fireplace. Soterius opened the window and leaned out to look around. He sat on the wide stone of the window ledge and swung his legs over the castle wall, then looked down to the flagstones four stories below. This was the tallest part of Shekerishet, with the lowest floors carved into the cliffside against which the palace stood.

The oldest sections of Shekerishet were carved from the cliffside almost five hundred years ago. Made of the same gray granite as the cliffs, the old palace was an unadorned fortress, square and foreboding, with archers' slits and crenellations. Over generations, Margolan's kings built on to the old castle, adding whole wings and new towers, so that now, Shekerishet sprawled against the base of the mountain's sharp crags, a brooding presence above the city and farms below.

With a grin, Soterius patted the ledge for Tris to join him. Tris fought a moment of vertigo as he looked down into the courtyard.

"All right, here goes." Soterius pushed off, spinning for a moment until he oriented himself with his back to the courtyard and his feet against the stone wall.

"We should have painted a bullseye on your back to make it easier for the archers," Carroway hissed.

"Funny," Soterius muttered. "Just keep that flag of yours handy, Tris, in case someone gets ideas."

Tris patted the pennon of the king's second son in his pocket. It was meant to identify him in battle, but tonight, if a guard spotted them, letting the flag unfurl might make the archer hold his fire long enough to identify the bearer.

"All right, Tris. Your turn."

Swallowing hard, Tris let himself over the ledge. "I just remembered how much I hate heights." He caught his breath sharply as he spun for a moment in the chill fall air, and fought the urge to close his eyes. Aware that his friends were watching, Tris nodded his readiness.

Soterius worked his way carefully down the smooth stone wall of the castle. Tris followed, trying not to constantly reassure himself by jerking on the rope. Although he and Soterius climbed the cliffs around Shekerishet frequently during good weather, Tris had not been out since summer's end, and he felt the lapse in his aching muscles.

It was colder than he expected, and the chill nipped at his face. Tris glanced at Soterius, but the guardsman grinned as the wind whipped his dark hair into his eyes. If the king were to look out of one of those windows just now, they would all have some explaining to do, but that was the beauty of Haunts. Nearly everything could be forgiven in the name of the night's revelry.

As he drew close to the windows of the second floor, Tris frowned. There was a light in the window, a strange, red glow that did not look like firelight. The light glowed from Foor Arontala's chambers, pulsing like a heartbeat. Ignoring Soterius's concerned glance, Tris worked his way over.

Tris eased closer to the window and felt the familiar prickle at the edges of his senses that signaled magic close by. But the magic here felt different from his grandmother's power, Tris thought, his breath steaming in the cold night air. Even an arm's breadth away from the window, there was an aura of dread that almost drove him back. He pressed on, though the foreboding was almost palpable, and while no physical barrier slowed him, he had the feeling of wading through deep, ice-cold water the closer he got to his goal.

Forcing himself past his fear, Tris leaned in to get a glimpse through the window. The room was dark, but the embers in the fireplace made enough light for him to recognize the trappings of a wizard's workplace. Chalices and athames, cords braided from materials of all descriptions, a scrying bowl, chits and bones—the stuff of divination—and clusters of dried herbs crowded for space with vials of powders and potions. But

only one thing in the sorcerer's room commanded his attention, transfixing him as if it knew he
was there. On a pedestal in the corner of the
room sat a crystal globe the size of a man's head,
and from the globe pulsed light the color of
blood. As Tris stared, the light seemed to focus,
and for an instant, Tris could have sworn it oriented itself on him, like one bloody eye, aware of
his presence. Tris's heart hammered in his throat,
and he was suddenly unsure he could tear himself
away.

"Have you lost your mind?" Soterius hissed
from beside him, making him jump.

"Can't you feel it?" Tris murmured, backing
away from the window.

Soterius looked at him skeptically. "I can feel
my rump freezing, if that's what you mean."
They heard angry men's voices from just outside
the door to the wizard's room, and both Tris and
Soterius swung back, flattening themselves
against the wall as torchlight flared in the room
and the voices drew closer. Jared and the king,
Tris thought with a sinking heart. And this time,
whatever the topic of their argument, it was more
heated than usual, with Bricen almost apoplectic
in his anger, though Tris could not catch the
words over the din of revelry in the village.
Edging his way close enough to see into the
room, Tris caught his breath in horror.

It was magelight, not torchlight that lit the
room. Something was wrong, terribly wrong.
Blue magelight glowed from Arontala's hands,
pinning the king against the rough stone wall.

Although Tris could hear none of what was said, the expression on King Bricen's face needed no explanation, nor did the leer that distorted Jared's features as the heir closed the distance between himself and his father, his dagger raised.

Commonsense and terror finally won out over shock. Soterius began to jerk at his rope with all the fright of a first climber, signaling for Carroway to begin winching them up. Tris's heart thudded in his throat as Jared sank the dagger deep into Bricen's chest. Just as Tris readied himself to kick through the panes, Soterius swung against him, slamming him into the wall hard enough for him to lose his breath.

"Are you crazy?" Soterius hissed. "You don't have a chance. We've got to get the guards," he argued, fighting against Tris's struggles with all his might. Just then, Carroway heeded his signal and began to hoist them skyward. Fighting shock, Tris found the presence of mind to begin to climb on his own the last few lengths and dove more than crawled into the window, gasping in fright.

"You look like you've seen the Avenger herself!" said Carroway, helping Soterius to his feet.

"The king!" Soterius stammered, numb with fear and cold. "They've killed the king!"

"That's not funny," Carroway said, glancing out the window once more to make sure they had avoided the guards' attention. His voice trailed off as he looked at Tris, and he paled.

"It's true," Tris gasped, leaning forward and steadying himself on his knees. His heart was thudding so hard he could hardly speak. "I saw Jared—"

"You couldn't have seen anything very well," Carroway said, shooting an uncertain look at Soterius. "You weren't down there very long."

Soterius started freeing himself from the climbing gear as fast as his cold fingers would go. "It was the king and it was Jared," he repeated as if he were speaking with a slow child. "And Arontala. There was blue light pinning the king to the wall. Then Jared came closer and, dear Goddess, stabbed King Bricen, over and over." he said, shutting his eyes to escape the memory.

Tris started past him for the door toward the servants' steps. "I've got to warn Mother and Kait."

"Tris!" Soterius cried, catching Tris by the arm. "If Jared's killed the king, he's going to want you, too. We've got to get you out of here," Soterius grated with military calm. "With Bricen dead, the crown is at stake. Jared's going to want to eliminate loose ends. We've got to get you to safety."

"Not without Kait and Mother," Tris snapped as shock gave way to anger. He shook free and wrenched the back stairs door open.

"All right, then we're coming too," Soterius said, and tossed the rope to Carroway. "Here. Carry this. I've got a sword and you don't." He barred the door to their chamber and drew his sword. "At least if they come looking for us, it will hold them for a while."

He turned toward Carroway, but the bard had already drawn a small dagger from the folds of his tunic. "You thought it was just for the stories?" Carroway asked. "Some of your army friends like to rough up bards now and again."

Soterius slipped past Tris and led the way down the stairs. He tried the handle on the door at the bottom, and eased the unlocked door open. The bedchamber was in a shambles. Queen Serae lay in a heap near the door, her party gown stained crimson with blood.

"Mother!" Tris called, feeling the panic rise in his voice as he shouldered past Soterius and scrambled across the room.

"Dear Goddess Bright," Carroway breathed. "Jared's raised a coup!" Soterius was already at the door to the corridor, which hung broken and useless on its hinges.

Please, please no, Tris begged the Goddess as he reached Serae. Her body was still warm to the touch, still loose-limbed as he stifled a cry and rolled her to face him. The dagger that had ended her life protruded from her chest as her head lolled on Tris's arm. His throat tightened and his eyes swam as he listened in vain for a heartbeat. *She's gone.*

A sob tore from his throat as he cradled Serae, squeezing his eyes shut as unbidden tears streamed down his face. Gasping for breath, Tris dragged a sleeve across his eyes and scanned the room once more. He laid Serae's body gently on the floor, passed a hand across her staring eyes to close them, and whispered a prayer to the Lady.

A groan startled Tris and Soterius wheeled, his sword drawn. Almost hidden among the shambles of an overturned bed lay Kait. Tris and Carroway ran to her, shoving aside debris and the body of a fallen guardsman, and freed her from the tangle of blankets. Kait lay pale and still, her bloodstained tunic warning Tris not to expect too much.

"Kait, can you hear me?" Tris whispered, gathering her into his arms against his tunic stained with Serae's blood. Dark Lady, please, he begged silently. Not both of them. Please, spare her.

"What happened?" he asked quietly, as a spasm of pain crossed Kait's face. Her lips were tinged with blue, and her breathing was rapid and shallow. Her blood stained his hand, seeping between his fingers as he tried to compress the deep gash on her belly. There was too much damage for any but the most experienced battle healer, and no such healers at hand.

Kait's eyes opened. She focused, and managed a weak smile. "I knew you'd come, Tris. Are you dead, too?"

Tris stifled a sob, unashamed of the tears that streaked down his face. He struggled to find his voice as he shook his head. "No, Kaity," he managed to rasp. "At least, not yet. Neither are you."

"Soon. I've seen the Goddess. She's waiting."

"Who did this?" Tris urged as gently as he could, grasping her hand as if to bind her spirit closer.

Kait coughed, and blood flecked her lips. "Jared's men," she whispered. "They were waiting for us. I tried to protect Mother. You'd have been proud."

"I am proud," Tris whispered, blinking back tears.

"Should have seen me, big brother. I think I got one of them."

Tris glanced back at the guardsman's body. "You did, Kaity. You did."

"I've got to go."

"Kaity, stay with me!"

Her eyes opened wider. "Tris—you're here, too. Like grandma." She coughed harder, and Tris thought she was gone. "If you will it, I can stay," she murmured as her eyes fluttered shut. "I'll just take your hand on this side."

The image burned bright in Tris's mind as he clutched her to him, of Kait taking his hand and holding on. With everything in his being, he willed it be so. Yet even as he struggled to hold on to the fleeting spirit, something else, something strong, struggled to pull her away.

Kait shuddered in his arms and went limp. Tris buried his head on her shoulder and wept, rocking on his heels, cradling her lifeless form.

Tris, you've got to go, the voice said in his mind, Kait's voice, far away. Tris looked up and frowned. Kait stood in front of him, real but insubstantial, with the same faint luminescence of the palace ghosts.

"Kaity?" Tris rasped in a raw voice.

The ghost shimmered. "You did it, Tris. You kept me here. You've got grandma's power," Kait said. The image wavered once more, nearly blinking out, and a look of distress, then fear crossed her face as her ghost appeared to be pulled away, like smoke caught in a draft. "There's a spell on the palace ghosts. Arontala... Help me, Tris," she begged as her apparition disappeared.

It was Carroway's gasp that told Tris the apparition was visible to the others. Soterius looked shaken, never having seen Tris work any kind of magic. Carroway stared at the empty space where Kait's ghost had been, his ashen face witness that he had just seen far more powerful magecraft than he had ever expected of Tris. Gently, Tris laid Kait's body down among the blankets and covered her with a sheet.

"Before we join her, let's get out of here," the minstrel said gently.

Tris felt grief and shock throb through his body, filling him with rage. "Damn Jared!" he cried, lurching to his feet. His sword was already in hand as he started toward the hallway door at a dead run. Soterius blocked him.

"Let me go!" Tris grated. "Damn it, let me pass!" The blood pounded in his ears as he tried to fight his way past Soterius, who parried and drove him back from the doorway. Carroway tackled him from behind, taking him to the ground and struggling to wrest away his sword while Tris swung wildly with his free hand, blinded with tears and gasping for air. Soterius joined the fray, helping Carroway as he fought to keep Tris back from the door.

With a sharp flick of his blade, Soterius sent Tris's sword skittering out of reach, and lunged, pinning him against the floor. "You won't get within sight of Jared before his mage gigs you like a frog," Soterius snapped, struggling to keep his hold on Tris. "You can't help your mother or Kait. But you can still save Margolan by getting clear of here and coming back with an army of your own."

"And can we do it soon?" hissed Carroway, who had taken Soterius's watch at the door. Breathing hard, Tris closed his eyes and conceded defeat.

"Down the back stairs," Soterius returned, letting up on his grip and tossing Tris his fallen sword. "They come down in the servants' area. We'll run for the stables. Go."

They ran down the narrow back stairs and burst into the kitchen, swords drawn, terrifying the scullery maids who shrieked and ran from the room. Outside in the corridor, Tris heard the pounding of boot steps and, hard after it, the clang of steel. The doors from the feast hall banged open as three soldiers wearing the king's livery charged after two men who were fighting for their lives. Tris and the others flattened themselves against the side of the fireplace, cut off by the battle from their only escape. Tris had only the barest glimpse of the fighters, but he recognized one of the men on the defense as Harrtuck, a sergeant-at-arms, a stocky, barrel-chested man with a full dark beard and olive skin who often guarded Bricen.

"I'll not give up this palace without a fight!" Harrtuck swore as he dodged and parried. His companion, another of the king's guard, thrust and scored. Tris and the others exchanged glances and raised their weapons. With a cry, both Tris and Soterius launched themselves into the fray beside Harrtuck, driving the attackers back by surprise.

"Nice to see you," Harrtuck panted, pressing their sudden advantage.

"Watch out!" Carroway shouted, and Tris whirled, blade ready, in time to see one of the guardsmen clasp his hands to his chest in surprise and slowly topple to the floor. A growing red stain surrounded Carroway's dagger, hilt deep between the man's ribs.

With a cry, Tris engaged the dead man's partner. "You'll soon be as dead as the king," the soldier taunted, driving Tris back a step. Engulfed by grief and rage, Tris struck back with all his might, wielding his sword with a two-handed grip. Startled by the ferocity of Tris's attack, the traitor fell back, then pressed forward again, a murderous gleam in his eyes as three more guards raced in to join him. Out of the corner of his eye, Tris saw Carroway grab a torch stand as a staff to hold off one of their attackers. Soterius and Harrtuck focused on the other two newcomers, leaving Tris to circle the grinning guard in a deadly dance of swordplay.

A burst of red light exploded in the fireplace, and Tris lunged forward, recognizing one of Carroway's parlor tricks. It was just enough of a distraction for him to slip inside the soldier's guard and drive his blade home. The guard sagged forward, and Tris staggered as the dying man's weight nearly wrenched his sword from his grip.

A glint of steel in the firelight was the only warning Tris had as a new opponent dove forward, scything a dagger in one hand as Tris parried the guardsman's sword. Tris staggered as the guard sank his dagger into Tris's side. The guard arched and stiffened, dropping to his knees as his hands clawed at his back, revealing a shiv in his back and Carroway standing with grim satisfaction over the dying traitor.

Tris pressed his hands against his side as both Carroway and Soterius sprinted toward him. Harrtuck made short work of the remaining attackers. His ally lay dead on the floor. Carroway rolled Tris's assailant over with his boot, bending over to withdraw his dagger and wiping it clean in two quick movements on the dead man's tunic as he dropped to his knees beside Tris.

"There'll be more soldiers," Soterius warned.

"They've killed the king, Prince Martris," panted Harrtuck. "None of us could save him. You have to flee!"

Tris gasped as Carroway struggled to lift him to a sitting position. Soterius knelt beside Tris and Carroway moved back to let the experienced swordsman examine Tris's wound. Without a word, Tris knew from the look on Soterius's face how nasty a gash he had taken.

"We've got to get you to a healer," Soterius said tersely as he nodded for Carroway to move to Tris's other side and together they lifted Tris to his feet.

"Aye, but first, we've got to get out of Shekerishet," Harrtuck agreed.

As if on cue, boot steps sounded on the back stairs. With a motion, Harrtuck signaled Carroway to cover Tris while he and Soterius took the newcomers. A burly guardsman in the bloodstained livery of the king stepped into view. Two more guardsmen flanked him. Harrtuck waited in silence until all three were within range.

"Now!" the armsmaster cried, springing forth, sword lowered, to run through the guardsman. There was a whistle of air and then a dull thwack, and the lead guard tumbled forward, his hands grasping at Carroway's dagger as Soterius's sword sliced down from the shadows, neatly cleaving the third man from shoulder to hip.

"Come on!" Soterius cried. He returned to where Tris and Carroway waited, pausing just long enough to regain the bard's dagger, and helped Tris to his feet once more. The blood pounded in Tris's ears and his knees threatened to buckle under him.

"We're not going to get out easily," Carroway hissed as they started toward the door.

"Got any better ideas?" Soterius growled.

"Actually, yes," the minstrel snapped. "In here."

Carroway pulled, rather than led, Tris and the others into a storage room under the back stairs. Strewn about were cloaks and tunics, masks and costumes from the night's revelry. "Here, see if this fits," he said, snatching up a black tunic, cape and mask from the floor and thrusting them toward Soterius.

"You've got to be crazy," the swordsman said in disbelief. "We're running for our lives, and you want to—"

"Just do it," Carroway snapped, plucking more outfits from the jumble and tossing them toward Tris and Harrtuck.

"What in the Winter Kingdoms—" Harrtuck wondered.

"It's where the entertainers change before going to the feast," Carroway explained breathlessly as he shed his own cloak and ripped more than pulled his tunic over his head. "They'll come back tomorrow to fetch their things, but tonight, there's too much to do to worry about being neat. Thank the Goddess."

But as Carroway moved toward him, a voluminous cape in hand, Tris felt the rush of blood to his head as his legs gave way beneath him. Dimly, he heard the worried cries of his companions as he sank to the floor. Then, the room went dark.

Tris was jostled awake to find himself staring at the stars. The cold fall air stung his face and around him pressed a crowd that smelled of ale and sweat, their rowdy songs far overshadowing the more subdued chants of the priestesses.

Tris struggled to sit up, and felt a hand press him down. "Lie still," Soterius hissed. "We're in the procession, on our way to the city gates."

The pain in his side threatened to make him pass out once more, but Tris set his jaw and fought the wave of darkness. A gray robe with a heavy cowl covered his body and obscured his face. His hands were covered with black paint. A wisp of hair that struggled from beneath the hood was sable brown, not the usual striking blond of his own shoulder-length queue.

"Relax," Soterius warned. "Carroway improvised some disguises. Yours was the best we could do, given the circumstances," he apologized. Tris realized that he lay on a bier, one of the many effigies of departed loved ones carried in the ceremony toward the river, where a steady procession of figures, tokens and flowers would make their way down the waters toward the sea. Tucked in with the offerings were pleas for favors from the Goddess or departed loved ones, prayers for intercession or the righting of some wrong, or heartfelt expressions of longing for those who rested with the Lady.

Yet despite its more serious side, Haunts was a night for revelry in the town, and this year appeared to be no exception, regardless of what had transpired at the castle. Banners hung from every window, snapping on the cold night wind. Vendors' carts crowded the streets and costumed revelers elbowed their way through the congested passageways. The city smelled of sausages and ale, candles and incense. From somewhere in the walled city, bells pealed and Tris could hear the plaintive wail of flutes and the beat of drums.

With any luck, Tris thought, they could blend into the crowd and meld into the procession most of the way to the Merchant Gate. From the high spirits of the crowd, Tris was certain no word of the treachery at the palace had reached the city. And it might not, ever.

Jared was clever, and so was his mage. No one but Tris, Soterius and a few guards had witnessed the actual attack. Jared could invent a tale of assassins, and blame the dead guards. Arontala's magic could probably manufacture evidence, or blur the eyes of those who might see otherwise.

Bricen was a popular king, because he did not commandeer the harvest and his troops neither looted the local farms nor raped the farmers' daughters. Of the royal family, Serae had won the good will of the nobility, her gentle manner a stark contrast to Eldra's tempers. In return, the court lavished much more interest and favor on Tris and Kait than on Jared, whose brooding manner and dark habits fed the gossips' talk. Even so, Bava K'aa told Tris once that to commoners, one king was the same as the next so long as the taxes didn't change. No one might even care about the manner of Bricen's death, although Tris was sure that Jared's rule would not be as benign.

It was impossible to distinguish the parade from the crowd. The throng pressed through the main street of the city, flowing toward the outer gates and the burial grounds beyond. In its center, large litters carried statues of the four Light aspects of the Goddess. Drummers pounded, pipers played and the shimmer of tambourines sounded above the din of the revelers. The litters and their statues bobbed above the crowd, held aloft by the press of people

The costumes rivaled any Tris had ever seen. There were "nobles" and gaudy ladies, river merchants and legendary heroes, together with no few revelers costumed as the Lady's aspects; grown women as well as children in the flowing white robes of the Childe; revelers of both sexes in the seductive garb of the Lover; others, male or female, in matronly attire as the beneficent Mother. And dark-cowled specters in the scarlet robes of Chenne, Avenger Goddess. But Haunts was a night for the Dark Aspects as well, and on this night, darkness held sway. Even more partygoers preferred the painted finery of the bitch Goddess, Luck, and they tossed candy coins and painted cards to the crowd. Others swaggered through the streets in the tawdry glamour of Athira the Whore, needing no skill to mimic the rolling, drunken gait. Like dark shadows in the torchlight, gray-cloaked partygoers played the role of Istra, the Demon Goddess, appearing insubstantial as wraiths in the wavering light and wafting smoke. Hunched figures old and young took on the visage and tattered rags of Sinha the Crone.

One goddess, eight aspects—four Light and four Dark. Tris had always suspected that the aspect a person venerated said as much about the person as it did the kingdom and traditions from which they came. Margolan was partial to the Mother, although many within its borders also worshipped the Childe aspect. Isencroft, on Margolan's eastern border, gave homage to Chenne, the warrior. Principality, to the northeast, home to caravans and mercenary companies, traders and roustabouts, was partial to the Lover. Eastmark, Principality's southern neighbor, venerated the Whore, a favorite of gamblers and paid soldiers. Dhasson, to Margolan's west, encouraged adoration of all of the Lady's faces, save for that of the Crone. Dhasson's reluctance to embrace Crone worshippers was natural, given its southern neighbor, Nargi, whose sour-faced priests ruthlessly enforced the Crone's ascetic doctrines. Trevath, Margolan's southern neighbor and frequent rival, shared Nargi's veneration of the Crone, but in Trevath, known for its mines and fine carpets, such worship was much more practical, serving to enhance the power of the king.

The Dark Lady was the patron of the vayash moru, the undead who walk the night. Few mortals gave homage to the Dark Lady, though her name was a frequent oath. Of the eighth aspect, the Childe's dark mirror aspect, even fewer spoke. Worship of the Formless One had ceased generations ago, and now, if the most terrible of the aspects was mentioned at all, it was with a nervous glance and a sign of warding. Nearly all of the residents of the Winter Kingdoms made at least nominal reverence to one or more of the aspects, although Tris heard that some followed the old ways in secret, the belief in the spirit and power of the rocks and trees, the streams and dark places under the ground.

Those ways, it was said, were the ways of the Winter Kingdoms a millennium past, before

Grethor Long Arm invaded from the eastern steppes, spreading his influence as his reign in Margolan prospered and his power grew. His mages were more powerful, and his wealth and power seductive enough for belief in the One Goddess of Many Faces to gradually supplant the old ways, though elements of the superstition and blood sacrifice of those ways lived on, in the cruel worship of the Nargi, thinly overlaid with the trappings of the Crone.

As Tris watched from his bier, a young girl costumed as the Childe Goddess emerged from the crowd by the side of the road. She was playing her role to the hilt, tossing colored rags and straw instead of the Childe's fabled profusion of flowers to those on whom she showed favor. As Tris passed by, the young girl looked up, and her eyes met Tris's.

You are my chosen weapon, Tris heard a voice ring in his mind, disorientingly clear, coming from everywhere and nowhere at once, and as he stared into the eyes of the young girl, he thought for an instant that he saw them glow amber as the face now seemed not that of a mortal child, but of the Childe Goddess Herself. *Die not until I call for thee. Thy time is not yet come.* And as the girl's eyes stared into his, Tris felt a sudden fire touch the wound in his side, as if a red-hot poker were laid against the torn flesh. He stiffened and arched, biting into his lip to keep from crying out.

The voice was gone as quickly as it came, and when Tris looked around, the girl had vanished.

Shaken, Tris closed his eyes. I'm seeing things, he thought, swallowing hard. Goddess help me, I must be dying.

"If Harrtuck's found us horses," Soterius whispered, "he'll be down the next alley with them."

Carroway veered off from the procession at the dark maw of the next street, and they made their way down the cluttered, twisted thoroughfare that was barely wider than two riders abreast. Harrtuck appeared from the shadows and motioned for them. Carroway and Soterius followed the soldier to where four sturdy horses waited impatiently, tethered to a rickety hitching post. Carefully, Harrtuck helped them rest Tris's litter on the ground.

"Can you ride, my liege?" Harrtuck asked as he bent over Tris.

Tris nodded. "There's no choice," he said, and gritted his teeth as he started to rise. To his amazement, no answering pain throbbed through his side. Tris accepted Harrtuck's assistance in swinging up to his nervous mount. Cautiously, the four made their way back to the procession.

"Damn the Fates," Soterius hissed as they ventured out among the pilgrims and revelers.

A handful of palace guards milled at the gate, far from their usual station. They were unmounted, but their horses were saddled and waiting nearby. Tris and Harrtuck exchanged worried glances.

"Are we ready?" Soterius's flat voice cut through the confusion.

"We're going to have to bluff our way through," Harrtuck appraised. "If we get separated, head for the road north."

"Give the signal," Tris assented, never taking his eyes from the guards at the gate.

They waited until the procession swung wide to round a bend, taking the stream of revelers as close as possible to the gate. They were still at least twenty yards away, and while the gates were open, anyone who entered or left had to pass between the guards.

"Now!" Soterius shouted, wheeling his horse from the procession and driving straight for the gates. The others did the same, as nearby revelers scrambled to get out of the way. The gates seemed a lifetime away as Tris leaned low over his mount and spurred the horse into an all-out gallop.

The move caught the guardsmen by surprise and the fugitives took the advantage, driving through their line. Soterius and Harrtuck charged first, freeing their swords and cutting past the guards who blocked the gates. Tris could almost feel the breath of Carroway's mount behind him as their horses plunged into the darkness just beyond the city gate. Behind them came the cries of the guardsmen giving chase.

"Almost there," Soterius shouted.

The horses pounded down the slope from the city to the road below. As he reached the thoroughfare, Tris felt a dizzying lurch, as if he had passed through an unseen boundary. He clung to his reins as a fog swelled around them, rising from the road as their pursuers closed the gap.

The fog thickened and swirled up to the horses' bridles. In the mist, something solid and cold brushed against Tris's leg. Their terrified horses screamed in fright, bucking and lurching. From the forest itself, a ghastly moan filled the darkness. Tris clutched his reins, his heart pounding, as all around them, the fog writhed and twisted. The mist became wraiths, gaping-mouthed and wailing, as more and more of the ghostly fog swept toward them from the dark forest. Whisps of mist became clutching tendrils and puffs of smoke stretched and spread into fearsome, hollow-eyed faces. A multitude of howling spirits swept past Tris and the others, clawed ethereal hands outstretched, moaning the cries of the damned. The air was clammy as they passed and Tris shivered. He clung to the reins, straining to control his panicked mount.

"Look!" Soterius shouted as they continued their headlong run for safety. Tris stole a glance over his shoulder. The spirits massed around the guardsmen as the fog thickened and swirled. The revenants' wails caterwauled above the screams of the guardsmen.

"Let's get out of here!" Harrtuck yelled above the infernal din, setting his horse in a headlong gallop down the road. The others followed close behind, but it was at least a mile before they could no longer hear the screams of the guardsmen or the wails of the dead.

"What the hell was that?" Soterius demanded when they finally brought their panting mounts to a halt at the crossroads.

"We finally found the palace ghosts," Tris replied with an uncertain glance over his shoulder. The night around them was quiet and cold.

"What were the palace ghosts doing outside the city?" Carroway asked, his breath steaming in the chill.

"I don't know, but thank the Childe for them," Harrtuck rasped.

"We hadn't seen the spirits most of the night, remember?" Tris said, staring back into the darkness.

"Yeah, Tris is right," Soterius replied, watching the night around them carefully. "There wasn't a ghost to be seen after we saw the fortune-teller, and that's never the way it is around the palace—especially not on Feast night."

"What if Arontala banished them?" Tris theorized, unwilling to tell the group just yet about his encounter with his grandmother's ghost. "The ghosts are sworn to protect the king, right? Remember Carroway's story? If Arontala could banish the ghosts, Father had one less level of protection," he went on, his voice catching.

"You are correct, Prince Drayke," a deep voice said from the crossroads, startling the four men. Tris's horse shied, and he struggled for a moment to rein in the frightened animal. They wheeled round to see a man on a gray steed almost obscured by the darkness, a few paces away from them on the forest road. Although his face was partially hidden by shadows, Tris recognized Comar Hassad, one of his father's most trusted men-at-arms. Tris's senses prickled as they moved closer, and although his companions seemed to note nothing amiss, Tris realized that their new guide was a spirit.

"Comar, what's happened?" Tris asked, still trying to calm his panicked horse.

"Time is short, my prince. Follow me and I will lead you to safety," Hassad said, wheeling his mount soundlessly and heading off down the forest road at a gallop.

Tris had to spur his mount to catch sight of Hassad. They rode single file, with Hassad in the lead, then Tris, followed by Carroway. Harrtuck and Soterius brought up the rear. Tris had to strain his eyes to follow their guide in the nearly total darkness of the forest. Only hoof beats broke the stillness of the night. The moon above was hidden by the dense trees, and the horses picked their way with care. Hassad led the way, keeping a steady pace despite the darkness.

Moonlight streamed down through a rare break in the trees. Hassad was already on the other side of the clearing, waiting in the shadows. Tris felt the hair on the back of his neck stand on end. As they re-entered the shadows of the forest, he listened more closely to the hoof beats around him. The sound of four horses rose clearly above the silence of the night and as Tris stared at their guide, he realized that the soldier's mount gave off none of the sweaty mist of the other heaving horses.

The coldness of the air around them had nothing to do with the growing numbness he felt inside, as he wrestled with pain and fear and grief. The simple mechanics of urging his horse forward helped him stave off the feelings that threatened to overwhelm him.

They followed their guide for most of a candle-mark, until Shekerishet and the palace city were far behind them and they were nearly through the pitch-black forest. Finally, Hassad slowed and then stopped.

"I can go no further, my liege," the man said, almost hidden in the shadows. "But I have a gift for you. Take it," he said, withdrawing a long, slim package wrapped in cloth, and passing it reverently to Tris. "It is the sword of your father's father. May it guide you home to rule Margolan as a good and true king," he said solemnly as Tris received the package.

"You are nearly through the woods," Hassad continued, looking up to the others. "On the other side is a small village. There is a tavern called the Lamb's Eye. Stay there tonight. You will be safe. Those who keep the tavern will provision you for your journey."

"The Lamb's Eye?" Harrtuck repeated from behind Tris. "When did they rebuild that? It burned last year."

"Seek your shelter in the inn. There you will be safe," Hassad repeated.

The leaves rustled behind them as an animal scurried for cover. When Tris turned again to question their guide, the road ahead was empty. "He's gone," Carroway said quietly, looking around them.

"He didn't just vanish," Soterius protested, reining in his skittish mount. A dozen paces ahead, he stopped. "I think you need to see this," he said, gesturing for the others to follow.

Tris, Harrtuck and Carroway closed the distance, sidling up to where Soterius's horse stood restlessly. A dead horse with the livery of a Margolan man-at-arms lay in the roadway felled by a crossbow bolt. Its hapless rider, half pinned beneath the dead beast, lay still, his armor no protection against the crossbow bolt that pierced his chest.

"It's him, isn't it?" Carroway croaked. "And that didn't just happen a moment ago, did it?"

"Uh uh," Harrtuck said uneasily, taking in the scene with battle-practiced detachment. "Been dead several hours, I reckon."

"I was afraid you were going to say that," Carroway whispered.

Soterius glanced sideways at the bard. "More grist for your stories, minstrel—if we live that long. You'll hold them in awe with this one."

"If we live that long," Tris repeated, looking out over the dark forest around them.

Carroway's expression clearly reflected his terror. "Those stories, about the spirits being able to be solid on Haunts, I never really thought—"

"The sooner we get off the road, the better," Soterius broke in. He looked no less comfortable than the others felt, but his battle training won out over fear. "We'd better get going."

"Where?" Carroway asked, his voice nearly a whisper. Tris glanced back at the minstrel, to see the young man's face pale and his eyes wide. Tris doubted he looked much better, from the way his own heart was pounding.

"To the Lamb's Eye," Tris shrugged and nudged his horse into a canter. "Unless someone has a better idea."

They came to the edge of the woods at the top of a hill. Below them, the fires of the village cast a reassuring glow in the darkness. Even the country folk celebrated Haunts, although with less abandon than their city cousins. There was sure to be no shortage of ale and wenching going on in the streets below, while the more pious made a candlelit pilgrimage to the barrows. In the distance, Tris saw a single-file line of walkers heading for the burial grounds. The pious appeared to be in the minority, as the sounds of music and revelry rose above the cold, still darkness.

"There, that must be the inn," Carroway said, pointing to a lone structure that squatted near the road on the outskirts of town. Its windows glowed and smoke rose from its chimney, and even at this distance, Tris could smell roasting meat.

"Looks pretty solid for a place that's not there any more," Soterius said, glancing skeptically at Harrtuck, who shrugged.

"I haven't been this way in quite a while. If it made enough money for the innkeeper, I imagine he rebuilt it."

"Or else, it's one of those illusions, like in the tales," Carroway whispered.

"Do your tales give any helpful hints for telling the real thing from the illusion?" Soterius grated.

"Not that I know of," Carroway replied, his voice a few tones higher and more pinched than usual.

"I try not to disobey a ghost," Tris observed dryly, urging his horse down the steep road. "If it was important enough for Hassad to send us there, he had a reason. Let's go."

A very solid wooden door gave reassuringly to Tris's touch. The common room was empty, but the air was heavy with the smell of roasting meat mingled with tobacco smoke. Despite a log fire glowing in the hearth, a chill hung in the room.

"Awfully quiet place for a feast night, isn't it?" Soterius murmured, his hand on the pommel of his sword.

"Considering how we must look, maybe that's lucky," Tris replied under his breath with a glance at their disheveled costumes. They approached the empty bar warily, and Tris thudded his fist against the wood to call the innkeeper.

"We'd like a room for the night," Harrtuck rasped as the innkeeper appeared in the kitchen doorway, a florid, heavy-set man whose ample apron was stained with ale and meat.

"Ah yes," the man said flatly from the shadows, gesturing for them to enter. "Two coppers a person. Find a room for yourselves upstairs."

Tris stretched out his senses, feeling the warning tingle of nearby spirits. It was strong here, but wordlessly reassuring. He eyed the silent innkeeper, extending his mage-sense. The image, seemingly solid, wavered and blurred to Tris's sight, and the revenant bowed his head in acknowledgement. *On my soul and by the Lady, you and yours are safe here tonight,* Tris heard in his mind. Tris glanced at his companions, who were edgy from the fight and unnerved from the ride, but who did not seem to sense anything other-worldly about their host. He said nothing as they climbed the steps, noting that neither of the fighters took their hands far from their swords, and even Carroway kept his hand near the shiv in his belt.

"Bed for four here," Soterius said, opening the first door. A candle was already burning on the nightstand as they entered. On the table lay a platter with sausages, cheese and hard biscuits, and two full buckets of ale with four mugs.

"Nothing but dried meat and cheese," Carroway groused, collapsing into a chair. "Can't tell me that's not venison stew I smell."

"Yeah, well, it's food and we're off the road," Soterius growled, walking around the perimeter of the room like a caged thing. "I'm just as glad to eat up here." He stood to the side of the single window and glanced down at the street below, but only a few travelers made their way through the night.

"Not exactly the friendly types, are they?" Harrtuck muttered as Carroway passed around the tray of food and began to fill the mugs. "This whole place feels wrong," he said. "Morning can't come fast enough for me."

"I've had my fill of adventure for one night," replied Carroway, downing a mug of ale. "But

Soterius was right. After tonight, I'll have ballads they'll pay gold to hear!"

Tris let them talk. He could feel the reassurance of the spirits in this place, promising their watchfulness and protection. And something else, a pervasiveness of magic that seemed to surround them, like a warding. He started to say something to his companions, to explain the spectral nature of their host, then reconsidered. He saw too clearly the discomfort on Soterius's face and the fear in Carroway's expression back at the palace, when they saw him speak with Kait's spirit and they glimpsed what his power might truly mean. They won't stay if I tell them, he knew. We're safer here than on the road, I'll stake my soul on it, but I'll never convince them. Too weary to argue, unwilling to feel the weight of incredulous glances, Tris resigned himself to silence.

He was chilled through from the night's ride and bone weary, too overwhelmed to take in the evening's events. The king, dead. His family, slaughtered. Jared, a traitor. And now, he and his friends were wanted men, running for their lives. He struggled against the images of Serae's and Kait's bodies, of Bricen's murder. The cold numbness that tingled in his fingers and chilled him had as much to do with the ache in his soul as it did the chill night outside. They were gone. All gone.

"Let's get a look at that gash," Soterius said. A pot of water already boiled on the fire.

"Look there," Harrtuck said, his voice wary. On the scarred mantel lay a packet of healer's herbs and two vials of oil, along with a pile of torn cloth bandages. "I don't like this at all, for what it counts," he murmured. "Too damn strange."

Soterius knelt next to Tris and gently lifted up the ripped, blood-soaked shirt. "By the Whore!" he stammered, looking up uncomprehendingly at Tris. "What happened to your wound?"

Tris glanced down. Where an open gash should have been was unmarked flesh.

Carroway exchanged astonished glances with Soterius and Harrtuck. "Before I decide I've lost my mind," the bard said incredulously, "someone please tell me they saw a knife gash here? Ban? Tov?"

Soterius and Harrtuck nodded wordlessly. "Aye, and a bad wound, too," Soterius murmured.

Carroway and Harrtuck crowded closer, and Tris felt Soterius's uncompromising stare. "Lady and Childe," Harrtuck swore. "I've never seen anything like it." Carroway met Tris's eyes, levelly awaiting an explanation.

Certain of just how mad the story sounded, Tris recounted what had happened in the procession. Soterius continued to stare at the site of the wound, and Tris knew that the explanation sorely tested his practical friend's credulity. Harrtuck frowned, but faced with the evidence of his own eyes, could do nothing but shake his head in wonder. Carroway's eyes were alight at the thought of true intervention by the Goddess, and Tris guessed that it was only with great effort and out of respect for the tragedy of the evening that Carroway refrained from grilling him mercilessly about the experience.

They ate their cold dinner in silence. Out in the street, someone was playing the lute and drunken voices rose in chorus as boots pounded time. The inn itself was silent, and Tris gathered his cloak around him.

"Coldest damn inn I've ever stayed in," Harrtuck said with a mouthful of sausage. "The sooner we're out of here, the happier I'll be."

Secure in the knowledge that Soterius stood the first watch, Carroway and Harrtuck retired for the evening, with the bard moving a bench closer to the fire and Harrtuck settling himself into a chair. When they were asleep, Tris paced to the window.

For the first time since the tragedy, Tris felt despair finally overwhelm him, and he sagged against the window frame, sobbing silently. The enormity of what had happened, the finality of the loss, the growing awareness of the danger now surrounding him rushed over him in waves. Roused finally from his grief by the chill draft that slipped through the closed window, Tris looked up at the clear stars outside. He caught his breath. There, auguring for all to see, a faint ring burned around the full moon, testimony that a king was dead this night. Eyes still fixed on the stars, Tris sank to one knee, placing his sword flat across his open palms.

Chenne, Avenger of Wrongs, hear me! By all the magic of Margolan, on the souls of my grandmother and my family, let me be the instrument of your judgment. Take my life, my soul, whatever you require, but let me put right what has been done this night.

From everywhere at once and nowhere at all, came a woman's voice so beautiful that it pierced Tris to his soul, and so powerful that his heart thudded in his throat at the sound of it.

Like your grandmother before you, I accept your vow, the voice said, and Tris felt an unseen presence far more powerful than any of the ghosts of Shekerishet brush past him, though nothing save the wind stirred in the darkness. Then, as quickly as the presence came, it was gone.

"Are you all right?" a very human voice said from behind him.

Tris startled, and turned to see Soterius, standing with his hands on his hips. While his face showed concern, there was nothing to suggest to Tris that his friend heard the voice that still echoed in his own ears, the vow of the Lady. Tris lowered his sword and resheathed it without explanation, rising to his feet.

"I want to know everything you and Harrtuck know about war," Tris said levelly, finding his voice clear and strong. "And I will accept whatever you can teach me about sword skill." His eyes locked with his friend's and he knew that Soterius understood just what treason they were committing, and how high were the stakes. "I know what kind of king Jared will be. I have to stop him."

Soberly, Soterius nodded. "I rather thought you'd come to that conclusion," he said, and to Tris's amazement sank to one knee, taking Tris's hand in fealty. "As I was to your father, so also to you," his friend said, his voice cracking with emotion. "By the Lady, I'll see you on Margolan's throne, my liege," he swore, and when he raised his eyes to Tris, they were bright with tears. "I can't let that monster rule this land."

Overwhelmed, it took Tris a moment to find his voice. "Thank you," he managed, bidding his friend to rise as a shiver ran though him at the chill night wind gusting through the cracked window. "But before we can do all that," he said, "perhaps we'd best get back some sleep or the night air will do what Jared hasn't... yet."

Tris eased his boots off and stretched out fully clothed on his bed, sinking into its blankets, undeterred by Harrtuck's hearty snores. Although he doubted the images of the evening would ever let him sleep, exhaustion won out, providing a reprieve from dark memories.

CHAPTER THREE

TRIS AWOKE TO the sound of a shutter banging in the wind. His eyes snapped open and his heart pounded as he looked around, disoriented. The events of the night before rushed to memory and he sat up groggily, feeling the last night's ride in sore muscles.

He stared at the room around him. A single shutter hung by one broken latch, flapping free in the breeze. Jagged fragments of glass clung to the ruined sash and the morning sun streamed through large holes in the charred roof. Tris shivered and sat up on the bare bed—just a weather-beaten collection of boards. On the other side of the room, he caught a glimpse of his reflection in the broken shards of a mirror, dulled by long exposure to the elements. He stretched out his mage sense. The spirits whose presence he had felt so strongly the night before were gone, and so was the pervasive power he had sensed.

"Harrtuck, wake up," Tris rasped. Harrtuck, asleep in a chair near the fire, responded with a snore and rolled over. "Wake up!" Tris insisted, and with a snort, the stocky guardsman startled awake.

"What? Oh, Tris. Goddess, I was sleeping soundly," Harrtuck muttered as he stretched and rubbed his eyes. He sat up, and stopped.

"What in the name of the Holy Childe is going on?" he croaked, looking at the ruined room around them. Just then, the hallway door creaked open as Soterius pushed his way into the room, his face ashen and bewildered. Carroway crowded behind him, wide-eyed with fear.

"What the hell happened to the inn?" Soterius asked, looking around the room.

"Downstairs is the same?" Tris asked, not surprised when the soldier nodded.

"Yeah. And the pitcher and bowl that I used last night are in pieces on the floor, but I never heard it break," Soterius replied.

"Look there," Harrtuck rasped, pointing to the chair beside the ruined dresser. Neatly folded, four clean traveling outfits lay in a pile, and next to them, a stack of nondescript brown riding cloaks.

"They're solid," Tris verified, crossing to the clothing and examining one of the cloaks. "And Goddess knows, we need them."

They started for the common room, swords drawn. The charred remains of broken tables met their gaze as they made their way carefully down the partially burned stairs. The heavy front door hung askew on its hinges, and dead leaves blew along the ruined bar.

"Over there," Carroway said, pointing. On one of the few tables that were still standing was a stack of provisions. A napkin of hard biscuits, enough dried meat and wrapped cheese to keep each of them for a week, a large pouch of dried fruits and four new, filled wineskins. Next to the wineskins was a bag of silver coins, easily enough to keep them in food and shelter for a fortnight.

"Look at the coins," Harrtuck rasped as Tris emptied out the purse into his hand. Tris lifted one of the coins and held it up the light. "Look at the date." In the early morning light, Tris could just make out the date stamped on the coin below the imprint of his father's visage. Twenty-five years past.

Wordlessly, the four men exchanged glances. Fear shone clearly in Carroway's eyes, and Tris saw that Soterius and Harrtuck barely masked their own uneasiness. Even in Margolan, where the spirits moved often and openly among the living, such a display went far beyond the usual encounters, feast day or not. Carroway's hands were shaking as they gathered the provisions. Silently, Tris mulled over the decision he had made the night before, to remain quiet about the true nature of their benefactors. He walked slowly behind the others as they headed toward the stables, as he thought about what to do next. *If I tell them what I saw, what I can see, will they be too afraid to go on? But if I hide what I can do, what that makes me—and Lady knows, I'm not* sure just what that is—if I don't tell them, then they're following a lie. They have a right to know, he concluded, although the thought of making himself more of a stranger to his companions made him feel even gloomier than before.

To their relief, their horses were waiting where they had left them, wide-eyed and skittish. "They've been curried and blanketed," Soterius observed uneasily, looking up at the half-burned stable roof and the sky that showed clearly through its gaping holes.

"Aye, fed and watered, too," Harrtuck added, shaking his head. "Never seen the like in all my years." He looked at Tris. "Looks like your palace ghosts are looking out for you," he said.

It was just the opening Tris needed. "I owe you all an apology," he said, forcing himself to meet Soterius's skeptical gaze. "Last night, when we reached the inn, I realized that the innkeeper was a spirit. I swear by the Lady I didn't know the inn was like this," he said with a sweep of his hand toward the tumbledown ruin. He paused, feeling their eyes on him.

"I was afraid that you wouldn't stay the night if you knew. I could sense that the spirits meant us well. I knew we would be safer here than on the road, but I didn't know if I could convince you. And I wasn't sure... whether you would want to stay... if you knew what I can do." He took a deep breath.

"I've always been able to see the ghosts when others couldn't—talk to them, call them.

Grandmother taught me a little bit of magic." He steeled himself and raised his head. "But the things that happened yesterday, last night, go far beyond what we did... anchoring Kait's spirit, sensing ghosts outside the palace. I can sense things, feel things, see things that I've never seen before. I don't think Grandmother told me everything, told me the truth about what I could do. I don't know myself. And I bear no grudge if you do not want to ride further with me," he finished soberly.

"You're a Summoner," Carroway breathed, eyes wide, but with awe, Tris thought in amazement, not fear. "They say every great mage has an heir, someone trained to take on the power when the mage dies. In the stories, sometimes the power passes at the time the wizard dies. But sometimes," he said, his voice growing stronger as he warmed to the tale, "sometimes it takes a shock, a tragedy, to open the heir to his inheritance." He looked at Tris with growing excitement. "You're the mage heir of Bava K'aa," he said reverently. "And if Arontala suspects that, he's going to want you dead even more than Jared does."

Tris could see warring emotions in the eyes of the two soldiers. He was barely acquainted with Harrtuck, but he knew Soterius well. Ban Soterius was a practical man, accustomed to dealing with what he could see and touch and fight. Soldiers were notoriously distrustful of mages, Tris thought, watching the struggle in his friend's face. Then, to his surprise, Harrtuck slowly bent to one knee, followed a second later by Soterius.

"You're still Martris Drayke," Harrtuck said. "And you're still the only hope Margolan has. Maybe the Lady knows that only a mage can win against that demon in the palace. Where you go, I go, my liege."

"Tris," Tris corrected absently, still over-whelmed by the morning's revelation. "Just Tris." He smiled ruefully at Harrtuck. "There's nothing left to be 'liege' of."

"I can't say I understand magic, or even trust it," said Soterius haltingly, "but I trust you. Count me in."

Embarrassed but relieved, Tris bid them rise. "Thank you," he said and Carroway bowed low, then stood and clasped his hand as well. "Thank you all."

Harrtuck slapped him on the shoulder. "Leave it to the Goddess, Tris. She has her ways."

"And we'll be seeing Her sooner than we like if we don't get out of here," Soterius added impatiently. "Let's ride before we get company."

"Ride where?" Carroway asked, absently stroking his horse's muzzle. "Last night we were just trying to get away. But we have to head somewhere."

Tris realized they were all looking at him. "North," he said finally. What little time there was for thinking last night, he'd spent trying to answer that same question. "To Dhasson, my uncle's kingdom. King Harrol is married to father's sister. We'll be safe there."

"It's as good a plan as any," Soterius agreed. "King Harrol is a fair king, and I think well of his army, so if that's where I'm to end up, it's not too bad."

"He's got a good court for minstrels, too," Carroway added, patting his horse. "Or so they say."

"Then north it is," Harrtuck agreed. "But that's two months' ride and we're wanted men," the grizzled soldier added. "No doubt your brother's put quite a price on your head, Tris. Probably has you wanted for king killing, which is more than a hanging offense. With enough of a bounty, we'll have no chance to tell our story if we're caught.

"And the road north is the worst one, especially at this time of year, coming on toward winter," Harrtuck went on. "Can't do it without a guide. Wouldn't hurt to have an extra sword, either, since the closer we get to the mountains, the more bandits we're likely to see."

"We don't have enough money to hire a guide," Soterius argued, cinching the belts on his saddle and arranging his steed's bridle.

"That's true," Harrtuck mused, and looked at Tris. "Could we promise payment once we reach Dhasson?"

Tris thought for a moment, and then nodded. "Unless we hire a whole army, that's a small favor to ask. But where do we find a guide? And how do we know he won't sell us out for the bounty?"

Harrtuck smiled as he swung up into his saddle. "If we can find the man I'm thinking of, he

won't. I've fought beside him. He's no traitor.
Damn good guide, too, if he hasn't managed to
get himself killed with his business deals."

"Where do we find this miracle worker?"
Soterius asked dryly as he settled into his saddle.

Harrtuck scratched his head. "Last I heard,
Vahanian was doing some trading up near the
river. He was running Principality silks and
brandy into Nargi."

Soterius looked sideways at the guardsman.
"Brandy and silk into Nargi? Their priests take a
dim view of drinking and with their women clois-
tered off, I can't think of much use for silk."

Harrtuck chuckled. "That's the point, m'boy.
The priests take a dim view—but it's not shared
by many of the 'faithful.' A man can get quite
rich giving them what they want, providing the
priests don't find out." He clucked his tongue
and shook his head. "Of course, if they do, they
make an example of you. There aren't many
worse ways to die, from what I've heard."

"Nice," Soterius muttered. "Either he's a rich
madman, or dead."

"Can't imagine wanting to go to Nargi,"
Carroway said as he mounted his horse and took
a backward glance toward the ruined inn. "Their
priests ran the minstrels out years ago. Now
there's only the temple bards, and since they're
devoted to the Crone, I can't think that there's
much that's pleasant to sing about."

"Maybe that's why they need the silks and
brandy," Soterius rejoined, pressing his heels to
his mount. "Let's get going."

They stayed to the less traveled roads, keeping to the forest whenever possible. With the ending of the Feast days, travel was tapering off as winter grew closer. The weather was turning colder, and Tris was grateful for his heavy cloak. He rode in silence, letting the others keep up the banter around him.

It was all almost too much to take in. An icy resolve settled over Tris as he lifted his head to the wind, still finding it difficult to believe that he was now a fugitive, without king or country, a mark for bounty hunters and hired assassins. Just as humbling was the knowledge that Soterius, Harrtuck and Carroway had left everything to come with him.

Tris had no doubt how Jared would rule. Jared argued on more than one occasion against what he considered Bricen's "weak" kingship. An iron-fisted king, mage spies and the taxes to support a large army, those were the things in which Jared trusted. Goddess help any who got in his way, or the merchants and farmers from whom the taxes must be extracted.

And there was no one who could do anything about it, except him. The thought made his mouth dry. Tris enjoyed his role as the second son, out of the public's eye. He'd had the same lessons in law, history and the rule of kings as Jared did, since eldest sons did not always live to claim their crowns. But for Tris, there was never the pressure that was part of the heir's birthright. He would have been quite content to live out his life on one of his father's country estates, surrounded by his books and his dogs, away from the intrigues of court. Now, that possibility was closed forever. It had died with King Bricen, and Tris found that he mourned that loss as much as he grieved for his family.

A slow, cold rain pelted off his cloak and made traveling miserable. On top of everything else, more questions. What had Kait meant when she said he was both alive and in the realm of the dead? Or that to her spirit eyes, he looked like their grandmother, the sorceress Bava K'aa? Tris shivered. A few possibilities tugged at the back of his mind, half-remembered conversations and dreams too real to forget. But at the moment, he was too miserable to ponder them, and so he let his thoughts wander, settling finally on nothing more important than the sound of hoof beats on the cold, wet road.

When they reached their stopping point for the night, a down-at-the-heels inn, Tris caught Harrtuck's sleeve before the soldier had a chance to unpack his horse.

"I need you to teach me to fight," Tris said levelly, meeting Harrtuck's eyes in earnest.

Harrtuck chuckled. "You've studied with Jaquard, my liege—Tris," he corrected himself. "He's as good an armsmaster as any."

"Not out here. Not with what I have to do," he insisted. "Jared almost cut me down in the hallway, drunk and half out of his mind in a rage. That's not good enough if I'm to take back Margolan."

Harrtuck nodded, as if the reality of what lay behind Tris's proposal was becoming clear for the first time. "Aye, you're right," he said finally. "As you wish. Let's get the horses seen to and we'll have a go-round right here. No time like the present to get started."

Later, when Tris could push Soterius and Harrtuck no further for lessons, they went back to the common room for dinner. Sweating and out of breath, the three men were sure they looked as if they'd just come from a wild ride. Carroway was already by the fire, amusing the inn's few other patrons with romantic ballads and tales of heroes from Margolan's past. Although almost unrecognizable with his dyed hair and unfashionable tunic, Carroway's talent still certainly made him the most accomplished bard the inn had seen in quite some time, Tris guessed, gauging by the interest of the serving staff and the innkeeper. The minstrel refrained from his flamboyant sleight-of-hand and was deliberately limiting his repertoire to the older songs any wandering performer might know. Grateful patrons tossed a few coins toward Carroway, which the bard acknowledged graciously.

The innkeeper, a haggard man with stooped shoulders, brought hearty trenchers of venison and leeks to Tris and his companions, together with a large pitcher of ale. The man winced at the crash of breaking pottery in the tavern's kitchen, and shook his head.

"Always happens right about now," he muttered.

"Sounds like you've got a problem with your serving girl," Harrtuck commiserated, downing half of his ale in a gulp.

The beleaguered tavernkeeper sighed. "I wish to the Goddess it were." Overhead, a door slammed and heavy boot steps clunked across the floor. The thin man wiped his hands on his stained apron and scurried back to the kitchen.

Tris shivered, feeling a sudden cold. He looked up, as a familiar prickle started to raise the hair on his neck. Though he saw nothing, he could feel a spirit's presence, an angry ghost flitting just beyond his sight.

"Thin crowd for a cold night," Soterius observed over the rim of his tankard.

"Aye, and it's not the fault of other inns," Harrtuck replied. "Naught else for at least another hour's ride."

"It's not as bad a place as some," Tris mused. "I wonder why—"

The crash overhead made the tavern guests jump. Either several travelers were having a row upstairs, or part of the roof just caved in. Tris glanced toward the innkeeper, but the man merely rolled his eyes in resignation, muttered something to himself and went on with his work, determined to ignore the noise. Out of the corner of his eye, Tris caught a slight movement, like a shadow there and gone.

"Damn!" Harrtuck exclaimed, jumping to his feet to escape the cascade of ale that spilled from his overturned tankard. A serving girl appeared at his side with a cloth, gushing apologies and wiping up the spill. "Never saw my elbow anywhere near the damn thing," Harrtuck mumbled as he daubed the ale from his cloak.

"No problem at all, my lord," the innkeeper assured him, pressing another tankard into his hand. "Don't trouble yourself about it. I'll take the first one off your tab," he fussed, bustling away with the empty mug.

Tris and Soterius exchanged glances. "Odd fellow," Soterius said, glancing toward the bar where the innkeeper conversed with the cook in hushed tones. "Unless the guests upstairs settle down," he added, "we may not be getting much rest tonight."

Carroway finished his songs and accepted a tankard passed to him from one of the appreciative guests. With a disingenuous smile, the minstrel struck up a conversation with his benefactor, one that Tris was certain would provide far more information to Carroway than the bard would share. The other guests, realizing that the entertainment was over, rushed to finish their meals and take their leave. Carroway's companion, seeing the others about to depart, hurried to join them, leaving the four refugees the only remaining guests in the common room.

"They look like they're in a hurry to go somewhere for so late at night," Harrtuck commented.

Tris glanced toward the dark windows. "Should we be concerned?" he asked under his breath as Carroway propped his borrowed lute in the corner and came to join them. Once again, a fleeting shadow flickered in Tris's side vision. The bard had made it only halfway across the room before the instrument slid to the floor with a twang and a disconcerting crunch.

With a pained expression, Carroway ran back to retrieve the instrument. "I don't understand," he said, puzzled, as he lifted the lute and turned it in his hands. He turned back toward Tris and the others. "I set it down carefully—it shouldn't have fallen," he said, looking down at the ruined instrument, its broken neck hanging by its strings.

"I'm sorry," he said ruefully to the innkeeper, carrying the instrument toward the bar. The innkeeper snatched the lute. "Accidents happen," he said quickly. "If you're finished with your meal, I'll show you to your rooms."

Just then a young boy burst through the door and ran toward the innkeeper. "Papa, come quick!" he huffed. The innkeeper bent to listen to the boy's hurried, whispered account, leaving Tris and his friends to exchange worried glances. After a moment, the innkeeper straightened.

"My son tells me there are three Margolan guardsmen riding this way," the thin man said. "They're stopping folks to see if any's seen four fugitives from the city." He paused, then seemed to make up his mind. "If you've no mind to go back that way soon, come with me," he said abruptly, gesturing for them to follow him.

Tris could guess Soterius's thoughts by the look in the guardsman's eyes and the ready way his hand dropped to the pommel of his sword. They had little choice but to accept the innkeeper's offer, unless they wished to fight the guards here and now. Still, the innkeeper's sudden willingness to hide four total strangers was odd enough to raise suspicion. "Hurry," the innkeeper urged. With an eye toward the door, Tris and his friends followed the man into the kitchen, where a plump woman stood near a cookfire and a rangy girl—the serving wench—brushed back a sweaty lock from her face. They were, Tris guessed, the rest of the innkeeper's family, all the help he could afford for such a meager clientele. The boy preceded them, and the others moved aside wordlessly as the innkeeper led Tris and the others to a small storage shed.

As if he guessed their thoughts, the innkeeper managed a wan smile. "There's a door out the back, if that's what you're worried about. You could kick the thing apart, if you needed to. But I'll not lead them to you," he assured them. "Been shaken down by enough of their lot. Whatever you did that has them looking for you, Goddess bless," he said, gesturing for them to hurry.

The door shut behind them, leaving them with the scant light that seeped through the cracks between the boards. The four men drew their weapons and hid behind barrels of provisions and wine casks. They heard muffled conversation, then a series of crashes and bangs as if the inn were being torn apart. Tris shied back into the shadows as the heavy boot steps drew closer to their hiding place. The door rattled, then opened a handsbreadth before a crash of crockery sounded and the soldier turned with an oath.

"Nothing here," the soldier called back.

"Nobody upstairs, either," a second voice said.

"You there, innkeeper," a third speaker barked. "There's gold in it for you if you see them and turn them in. You look like you could use some gold."

"Most everyone could use some gold," the innkeeper replied off-handedly. "I'll remember what you've said."

"Let's move on," the third speaker clipped. The boot steps receded. There was the sound of a tankard clanging against a wall, as if it had been thrown with full force, and the boot steps drew near once more.

"What's the meaning of this!"

"Please sir, it slipped," the serving girl apologized.

"Slipped!" the outraged guard shouted. "It nearly hit me on the head!"

"Must have been put back too close to the edge of that shelf," the innkeeper interjected. "So sorry. No harm done. Can I get a wineskin for you gentlemen to take with you?"

That seemed to appease the guard, for the footsteps receded and did not return. Tris could barely make out the outlines of his companions in the darkness, but his own thoughts whirled at the overheard conversation. How could the upstairs be empty, when it sounded as if a pitched brawl were going on? He wondered. But before he could puzzle long, the light tread of the innkeeper came their way, stopping to unlatch the door to their hiding place.

"They're gone," he whispered, gesturing for them to emerge. Cautiously, blinking as their eyes adjusted to the relative brightness of the kitchen, Tris and the others stepped out, their weapons still at the ready.

"What was all that about?" Soterius questioned.

The innkeeper shrugged. "We're a natural place for them to stop if they're looking for fugitives," he said, with a sideways glance to his wife that gave Tris the impression the innkeeper was purposefully answering only part of Soterius's question.

"Whatever your reason, thank you," Tris said, as Soterius moved to the common room door, glanced out and signaled an all clear.

"With them gone, you're welcome to stay the night," the tavern master offered nervously.

Tris looked to Harrtuck, who shrugged. "Might be safest," the armsman mused, stroking his chin as if the newly shaven whiskers remained. "We know the guards have already been here. So there's no reason for them to come back. And there's nowhere else close tonight."

Tris looked back to the innkeeper. "We are grateful for your hospitality."

"One thing I don't understand," Carroway remarked as the innkeeper began to lead them from the kitchen. "If there's no one upstairs, who was making all the racket?"

The innkeeper froze, then exchanged a worried glance with the squat cook. Finally, as if resigned to losing his guests one way or the other, the haggard man turned. "There's nothing human up there, no," he admitted slowly. "But there's a ghost with a fearsome temper that has ruined this inn, and me with it," he lamented, and at that, he sagged against the wall and covered his face with his hands.

"I won this inn fair and square in a card game last summer's feast," he went on miserably. "Should have known nothing good could come that way. Found out that the haunting started just before that, driving out the travelers, breaking up the crockery, making it hard for a body to sleep, if you know what I mean." He sighed. "Driven us to the brink of ruin," he continued. "Every night, same thing. Sounds like an army tearing the place apart upstairs, but when I go up to look, nothing's been touched. Don't even bother any more. Then it moves to the common room, playing tricks, like the lute tonight, and your friend's ale." He shrugged. "Likes to bother the girls in the kitchen, too." He sighed. "There's naught can help except a Summoner, and there's been no Summoner in Margolan since Bava K'aa went to the Lady."

Dejectedly, the innkeeper led them to their rooms. "It's always like this," the innkeeper lamented. "Cold as a tomb. Hard to keep a lantern lit. But no one's ever seen anything, just heard footsteps and bumps."

As the innkeeper talked, Tris strained to look into the darkness. His heart pounded, though he felt no fear in the presence of the spirit, just a rise of the blood in anticipation of the contact. He peered down the hallway, and frowned. Near the end, he saw a faint glow, like sunlight catching a mist. He took a step toward it, and the glow started to fade. On instinct, Tris closed his eyes and called out in his mind to the haze.

You there! Stand fast!

The glow hesitated, then grew brighter. Emboldened, Tris reached out his hand, his eyes still closed. *Show yourself! We mean you no harm.*

Gradually, the mist coalesced, taking on shape without mass until at last an outline of a man stood before them. Behind Tris, the cook gasped, and the innkeeper muttered a curse, making it clear that the specter was visible to all. Tris studied the silent shape. It was a young man, perhaps a few seasons older than himself, with the strong, rangy build of a plowman and the homespun clothes of a farmer. But what struck Tris most was the anger that radiated from the revenant, in face and stance and feel.

"Good sir," Tris said carefully, daring to open his eyes. The spirit stood as real before him as it had taken shape in his mind. "We bid you peace," he said with a gesture of welcome. "Why do you harm this inn?"

At first, Tris could hear nothing as the specter began to speak. Closing his eyes to concentrate once more, Tris strained to hear, and began to make out the voice, as if from a great distance. "—just last planting season," the spirit was saying. "I had a bag of coins, all that my family owned, to buy two cows at market. Out back," the spirit recounted, with a gesture behind him, "a brigand overtook me." The shade's hand went to its ghostly throat. "He slit my throat and took my coins and dumped me in the woods. I want my coins back," he stated simply. "And a stone raised over my body."

"Sweet Mother and Childe," the innkeeper gasped behind Tris. There was a soft thud, and Tris guessed that either the cook or the serving wench had fainted.

Tris took another step toward the spirit, and moved slowly to take four coins from the purse at his belt, money from the first tavern. "If the boy took these back to your family, they would buy your cows and more beside," Tris offered, holding the coins on his outstretched hand toward the spirit. "And my companions and I can raise a cairn in the woods, if you like." He paused. "If we do that, will you rest and not trouble this good man any longer?"

The spirit hesitated as if he were considering the bargain, then slowly nodded. "It is a good offer," he said, nodding. "I will rest."

Tris gestured for the boy to come forward, and to his credit, though trembling, the lad did as he was told. Tris bid the spirit give directions to his family's home, and had the boy repeat them. "At daybreak, as soon as it is safe for the boy to travel, he will take the coins where you bid," Tris said evenly, and once more, the spirit nodded.

"Now," Tris said, gesturing behind him for the others to begin descending the stairs, "will you show us where you lie, so that we can give you peace?"

The spirit winked out. "Where did he go?" the innkeeper gasped, backing toward the stairs.

"Out back, I suppose," Carroway guessed. He shrugged as the others turned to stare at him. "Well, he hardly needs to use the stairs!"

Sure enough, when the group reached the back of the inn, the spirit stood waiting for them at the edge of the woods. Motioning his companions to join him, Tris led the others after the ghost, who stopped just a few feet from the path. The shade pointed, and Tris took several steps to the right until the ghost nodded in satisfaction.

"Give me a hand," Tris said, bending to lift a stone the size of a melon that lay nearby. His foot kicked at something partially hidden beneath the leaves, and in the dappled moonlight, he glimpsed the yellow-white of a weathered bone. Gently, Tris laid the stone over it and turned to accept another from Carroway. Within a quarter hour, they had built a small cairn, and Tris made over it the sign of the Goddess. He looked back to the spirit. The anger was gone from the young man's stance, a wistful expression on his plain features.

"Go to your rest in peace, good sir," Tris said solemnly, raising one hand, palm outstretched.

The ghost began to fade, growing dimmer and dimmer until it was once more nothing but mist, and then the mist itself was lost in the moonlight.

Tris stared after the apparition, feeling a mix of satisfaction at having been able to free the ghost's spirit, and chagrin that it had been witnessed so openly.

"I'll go see to the horses," Soterius said, turning away. Tris frowned as he watched his friend stride off, but Harrtuck stepped closer and laid a hand on Tris's arm.

"Don't worry about him," Harrtuck rasped. "Like as not, it'll take him a bit to think this all through. After all," the armsman said with a chuckle, "we soldiers don't have much trust in mages. Me, I'd rather trust in cold, hard steel than a lot of mumbo jumbo." He paused. "Until now."

Tris stared after Soterius. What in the name of the Four Faces is happening to me? he wondered, feeling an uneasy mixture of pride and fear. Calling hand fire, lighting candles without a reed, doing a little hedge magic, that's one thing. Being Grandmother's mage heir, controlling the kind of power she had, that just can't be true! And if it is true, if Carroway's right, if I'm a Summoner, a mage—by the Lady, what does that mean? But before he could think further, Carroway plucked at his sleeve.

"The woods are no place for the living at night," the bard cautioned. "Let's go back to the fire. You look like you could use some brandy, and I think I'll have a bite of that cheese I saw on the bar."

Reluctantly, Tris let his companions lead him back to the welcome lights of the inn. The innkeeper and his family were waiting for them, greeting him with the honor due to a king, so that Tris flushed with embarrassment.

"Anything you want is on the house," the relieved innkeeper gushed. "Your food, your drink, your beds, and food for your horses." He beamed, and seemed to stand a bit straighter. "Now perhaps we can make a decent living from this pile of boards!" he cried, and did a little jig with the plump cook that left the dough-faced woman flushed and out of breath.

With a sigh, Tris accepted their gifts of food and beverage, though all he yearned for was a stiff drink of brandy and a bed for the night. He entreated the innkeeper to tell no one, and he and his wife swore silence. Tris realized that his unthinking reaction to the troubled spirit put them in even greater danger should Arontala hear the tale. Harrtuck sat beside him by the fire, saying nothing, yet by his presence, reassuring him that the events of the night had not in any way compromised his loyalties. *Sweet Lady, it can't help but change the way they see me,* Tris thought as the brandy burned its way down his throat. *I don't know what it means myself.*

The brandy did its work, and Tris found that he could barely keep his eyes open. He fended off more offers of bread and dried fruits, protesting that the grateful family had already done quite enough as he stumbled up the stairs to bed.

CHAPTER FOUR

A DAY LATER, when they left the innkeeper and his unhaunted tavern behind them, Tris sat with the others around a small fire at a makeshift campsite, surrounded by the noises of wild things and the darkness of the forest. He was still sweating from a thorough bout of sword practice with Soterius and Harrtuck, and he smiled to himself, recalling their praise at his growing skill. Tonight, the travelers roasted what game they had snared and sat in silence, watching the flames. They were still a day's ride from Ghorbal, a bustling trade city on a tributary of the Nu River, upstream from where that swift current grew to its mighty rush toward the sea.

Finally, Tris looked up at Harrtuck. "Tell me again what happened, out in the barracks," he said, and although effort made his voice flat, he guessed that Harrtuck could easily read the emotion in his eyes. Tris clasped his hands, staring at the flames, hoping he could maintain his composure.

"Everyone knew that there was bad blood between Jared and your father," Harrtuck began quietly, looking into the fire. "Your brother made no secret of it in the barracks, and those of us loyal to your father tried to warn Bricen. But many of the soldiers liked Jared," Harrtuck continued, "because he had simple ideas they could follow.

"After a while, some of the soldiers started to like the idea of having a young fighting man to lead the kingdom, as I'm sure Jared always intended." He paused. "Although I'm not sure the idea was completely theirs," he added, with a watchful look at Tris.

"Arontala," Tris muttered the name of the mage like a curse. "I should have guessed."

"One of Jared's men burst into the barracks and announced that the king was dead," Harrtuck went on. "A dozen of us who were loyal to the king headed for the palace, hoping that we could save you and the Queen and Kait, but we failed—except for you, my liege."

"And the others you came with?" Tris asked softly.

"All dead," Harrtuck reported. "As I would have been. You know the rest."

"Thank you," Tris said in a voice just above a whisper. He stared into the flames, trying to push away the memories. It was no use. They haunted his dreams and lingered behind every conscious thought. *If only I had found a way to get father* to listen, he thought miserably, clenching his fists. I should have done more, tried harder to get him to see how dangerous Arontala was, to see what Jared was really like. His nails dug into his palms until he drew blood. But then, father wouldn't listen to Kait and me when we tried to tell him how Jared beat the servants… or us. Mother tried. He wouldn't hear her either. Maybe I didn't try hard enough, often enough. I could have done more. And now, because I didn't, Kait and mother are dead.

"Tris," Carroway said softly, and Tris realized that the other had been addressing him without response for several minutes. "Don't blame yourself. You did all anyone could do."

Tris started to his feet like a snapped spring. "If I had done everything I could, we wouldn't be here," he said thickly. "Mother and Kait wouldn't be dead. I should have made father see. I should have challenged Jared. By the Whore, if I'm a mage, I should have tried to stop Arontala when he first came. He was weaker then."

"And you were just a boy," Carroway said quietly. "Your father never got around to finding a new court mage when your grandmother died. Maybe he didn't know how. Maybe he didn't want to share the power. When Jared took the initiative, I think your father was relieved. I always thought he hoped it was a sign Jared was growing out of his brawls and wenching."

"What if grandmother trained me just for that reason?" Tris cried, the words tearing hoarsely from his throat. "What if she foresaw something like this, and trained me in order to stop it? If I had studied more, practiced more, maybe the power would have come on me before this, maybe I was supposed to stop Arontala, and I failed."

"Men go mad on maybes," Harrtuck observed, watching compassionately as Tris dragged a sleeve across his eyes. "What's done is done. And it seems to me, we need to put as much distance between you and Margolan as we can. Once we're in Dhasson, we can figure out the best way to take the bastard down. But there's naught to be done tonight, except live to see morning."

Tris nodded, although sleep seemed far from likely. "I know," he said, his voice raw. "But running away doesn't seem like the most noble thing."

Harrtuck regarded him cynically. "Dead is better?" When Tris turned away, back toward the fire, Harrtuck shrugged and began helping Soterius drag some pine boughs closer to the fire for them to bed down. Carroway watched Tris in silence for a few minutes as the latter paced at the edge of the forest, deep in silent argument with himself.

When Soterius and Harrtuck went to see to the horses, Carroway ventured closer. "There really hasn't been a chance to tell you how sorry I am, about Kait and everything," he said.

"Thanks," Tris murmured in a strangled voice. "It seems like a nightmare that I'm going to wake up from any minute now, and I'll find Kait, and tell her how much I love her." He squeezed his eyes closed against the tears that came anyway, making further words impossible.

"The worst thing is, I know she's out there," Tris rasped when he could find his voice again. "I can feel it, but I can't bring her to me. There's something holding her back." His eyes met Carroway's, and Tris knew that his friend could clearly read his pain. "She's trapped, she's terrified, and I can't help her," he admitted, his voice raw. "What good is being able to talk to spirits if you can't help the ones you love the most? I can't fail her again, but I don't know how to help her."

Carroway laid a comforting hand on his shoulder. "I don't know how, but I know you. And if you were of a mind to listen, I'd tell you that there was nothing you could have done differently back at Shekerishet, but I know you won't hear a word I say."

Tris shook his head. "No, I won't, but thank you for saying so."

"Get some sleep," Carroway instructed. "Ban's got the first watch."

IN TRIS'S DREAMS, Bava K'aa still stood as straight and uncompromising as she had in life, a dark-haired woman for whom the years added little gray and few lines. Bava K'aa had an aura of power, even without the gray robes and charcoal mantle that marked her as a spirit sorceress or Summoner.

"Tris," the dream figure summoned.

"Here, grandmother."

"The time has come," Bava K'aa said.

"For what, grandmother?"

"For you to remember my lessons," Bava K'aa replied. She reached out to take his hand, and he felt her warm flesh close around his fingers. "You must remember what you have learned. Do not be afraid. The power will come to you, Tris. I have prepared you."

"For what?" he asked again. Bava K'aa's image seemed so real and her touch so firm that it was hard to remind himself this was only a dream. He reached toward her on instinct, hungry for the comfort of her touch, and the spirit's eyes acknowledged his pain as her expression softened, then grew worried once more.

"There is a threat to Margolan and the Winter Kingdoms that is greater than Jared," the ghost-figure of his grandmother said, with the perfect assurance her tone always carried when she advised kings. "An old evil has arisen. The Obsidian King is stirring once more. Arontala seeks to free him from where we imprisoned him, long before you were born. You must stop him," she said with a gaze that seemed to stare through him and into his soul. "Seek your teachers well."

"Why didn't the power come before... before they died?" Tris demanded. "I could have stopped Arontala—"

"You were not yet ready," the ghost replied. "Power knows when the vessel is ready. I knew from your birth that you were my mage-heir, Tris," his grandmother said. "To protect you from... others... it was not safe to tell you, until the power came upon you." Her gaze was uncompromising. "I have taught you many things, and taught you to forget them, until the time was ready," she said, with a faint smile. "Now, you must remember."

"Grandmother!" Tris called. "What is the Soulcatcher?"

The spirit stopped as if stung, and great concern filled her eyes. "What do you know of the Soulcatcher?"

Tris told her about the ghost's warning. Bava K'aa listened gravely, then nodded. "I should have seen this," she said with a sigh. "When the Obsidian King was vanquished, we were too few and too worn to destroy him completely. So we bound his soul in an ancient orb, a portal to the abyss. An orb called 'Soulcatcher.' We believed it safe, but perhaps we were too confident, too anxious to be done," she mused. "If Arontala can release the Obsidian King's soul, all we labored for is lost. The Obsidian King will combine his power with Arontala's, take Arontala's body for his own, and return to rule the world." The image wavered, and Tris feared it would disappear altogether. "There are no longer enough powerful mages to defeat him, as we did, should he rise again. It would take another generation, and he would ensure that all who could threaten him would be destroyed."

Her gaze turned once more on Tris. "You must defeat Arontala. You must find a way to destroy completely the soul of the Obsidian King. All hope rests with you, my child." And before he could ask her any of the questions that echoed in his mind, the apparition vanished, and with it, the dream, leaving him startled and awake, chilled with sweat.

The fire was out, and a light frost clung to the ground. But the morning cold was not the only reason for the chill Tris felt. Never in his life had a dream felt so real. Tris realized he was shaking, and let out a breath that misted in the morning air.

While Carroway rounded out the last watch, Tris gathered wood and rebuilt the fire. The chill of the dream had still not left him, and he could hear Bava K'aa's voice ringing in his ears. Gratefully, he accepted a cup of the strong hot drink Harrtuck brewed over the fire.

"We're not too far from the last place I'd heard Vahanian was doing business," Harrtuck said, leaning against a tree, his face wreathed with the steam that rose from his mug. What the ghosts at the inn had not left for them, Harrtuck had obtained at the last village. The goods were minimal, but more than sufficient to keep body and soul together until better could be earned. Tris stretched, more saddle-sore than he had been in his life, ruefully becoming aware that a prince's life during peacetime made one painfully out of training.

Harrtuck noticed his discomfort and flashed him a wicked grin. "Give it a week, Tris," he chuckled. "You'll harden up." Tris took cold comfort that even Soterius looked stiff and sore. Harrtuck, however, seemed none the worse for the past few days' adventures though he was a dozen years older than Tris and his friends, tribute to hard years on the road with the king's army.

"Why would Vahanian agree to be our guide?" Soterius asked, seating himself slowly by the fire and gratefully accepting the warmed rations Harrtuck dispensed. Soterius looked more dour than Tris could recall, and kept a bit more distance.

"Because we're going to pay him, for one thing," Harrtuck replied. "Because he owes me a few rather large favors, for another."

"Large enough to die for? We're rather dangerous to know these days."

Harrtuck shrugged. "I wasn't planning to announce who you were when we were introduced, if that's what you mean. Vahanian's used to running questionable cargo. There are things you ask, and things you don't. It won't be the first time he's run contraband that could get him killed." He paused. "I know you don't care for hired swords, Soterius, but sometimes, they're a necessary evil. And Jonmarc Vahanian can be trusted. That's more than can be said for some."

"He'll probably want us to travel with a caravan, at least part of the way," Harrtuck went on, chewing at a piece of roasted meat. "Most caravans are always looking for hired swords. Good mercenaries don't want to wander around waiting for action with a bunch of rug merchants, and since even wealthy caravans pay less than noble Houses, what swordsmen a caravan gets usually leave as soon as they've gotten a little experience."

"Hired swords, huh," Tris replied skeptically.

"Not such a bad life, given the alternatives," Harrtuck replied, pausing to sip his steaming drink. "Your meals are free, for one thing. That's nice when you're out on your own. And caravans are full of interesting types," he added dryly.

"It will make for a little slower progress than traveling alone," Harrtuck continued, "but we won't be as clear a target. Jared's likely to guess that you'll head for your uncle's kingdom, and he'll send people to look for you. As part of the caravan, you'll have safety in numbers. And if you can keep the bandits away, it's not a bad way to see real life in the kingdoms," Harrtuck added, finishing his drink and setting it aside on a stump. "That might be most interesting to you, my prince."

It was true, Tris thought. He knew little of the common life. He had had the classic royal training, fostered out to his uncle's for several years in his teens, been coached and prodded by a herd of tutors and advisors. But of the people themselves, he knew little. It might, as Harrtuck said, be interesting indeed.

"At least, that's what I think he'll recommend," Harrtuck said, stretching. "But with Vahanian, who knows?"

"So where do we find this legendary adventurer?" Soterius asked acidly.

Harrtuck shrugged. "Well, that's the hard part. Last I heard, he was trading near Ghorbal, on the river. We'll start there. Of course, there's no guarantee he's still there." He spat. "Hell, there's no guarantee he's still alive."

"That's a day's ride, at least," Soterius objected.

"Most likely," Harrtuck agreed. "But it's in the right general direction, so if we can't find him, we'll have lost no time."

"Sounds reasonable to me," Tris replied.

"I'm for anything that raises our chances of making it north alive," Carroway put in. "I've got far too many ideas for stories to die just yet."

GHORBAL WAS A thriving small city, at the crossroads of the main routes between Margolan, Principality, the river and roads east through Eastmark and Nargi. Caravans made Ghorbal their resupply stop before heading north into the very profitable territories of Principality, or to unload the "unorthodox" supplies banned by the sour-faced Nargi priests before heading into the eastern theocracy. A thriving black market existed in the Nargi borderlands near Ghorbal, where knowing the right people and paying the right bribe made it safer for smugglers to double their profits by moving contraband into the unfriendly kingdom. Further south, the river was watched by Nargi garrisons, and traders foolish enough to venture past those borders never returned.

The Tordassian Mountains lay between Ghorbal and Principality to the north, a place of treacherous passes and dark forests. That combination had served to discourage unwanted incursions from its northern neighbor, though the gems and gold of Principality and the wealthy markets of Eastmark drew intrepid traders despite the hardship. A major trade route wound north just above

Ghorbal, to the best river crossing into Dhasson in over a month's ride, and through the passes into Principality with its rich mines and then to Eastmark's fabled court. That made Ghorbal a popular supply outpost. The Nargi, on the eastern banks of the Nu River downstream and to the east of Ghorbal, had no official interest in Ghorbal's wares, though smugglers found the northern border of Nargi to be a profitable market—trade to which Margolan patrols turned a blind eye. Although patrols were frequent south of Ghorbal along the river border with Nargi, above Ghorbal, they were few, leaving the flatland to the traders and the mountains to the outlaws.

Ghorbal nestled in a curve of the Nu River's largest tributary. The Nu was the wide, swift trade artery for points south and west. Although further north the Nu would become wild and nearly unnavigable, between Ghorbal and the Southern Sea, it was a trader's dream.

They left their horses tethered in a copse on the northern side of the city, as a precaution, Harrtuck explained, which permitted them to make their way through the city on foot and have a ready escape should one be needed. Ghorbal stretched out across the river plains, a tumble of low, white buildings and vast open market areas. They could hear its bustle even before they entered the city, and the morning air smelled of horses and incense, market animals and cooking meat.

"Busy place," Soterius observed as they squeezed between a trader leading a loaded cart and an obese merchant with a donkey laden with Cartelasian rugs.

"Keep your wits about you," Harrtuck warned under his breath. "Ghorbal is not a place for the timid."

"Great," Carroway muttered. He glanced around, then brightened as he saw a minstrel performing not far away. "On the other hand," he added, not taking his eyes from the bard, "this might not be such a bad place after all."

"Assuming Vahanian is even here," Tris asked, uneasy in the press of people, "Where is he likely to be?" Although Carroway had reapplied the dark dye, which masked his white-blond hair, Tris still felt vulnerable, as if the four of them stood out in the crowd, an easy mark. The sooner they left Ghorbal, the happier he would be.

Harrtuck shrugged. "Might not even be in town any more, for all I know. He doesn't make his money standing still," he chuckled. "Actually, given the ways he's made his money, he doesn't stay alive standing still." The older man stopped to get his bearings. "Been a while since I've been in Ghorbal," he rasped, looking around. "But there are two good places to start. One's the marketplace, just over that way," he said, gesturing north. "And the other's the Dragon's Bane Inn, over in the East Quarter," he added.

"Where do we start?" Soterius questioned.

"We start with both," Harrtuck replied. "You and Carroway head for the Inn. There won't be anything remarkable about a soldier and a minstrel going to the Bane, unless they arrive together," he said, glancing skeptically at Carroway. "Separate, but stay in sight of each other. Soterius, you follow Carroway. Carroway, keep your eyes open.

"Tris and I will head for the market. We'll rendezvous back at the horses at dusk. This may take a few days," Harrtuck warned. "If you find Vahanian, tell him Harrtuck has an offer for him and tell him that there's gold in it for him," he added with a grin.

"We just walk into the Inn and ask for him?" Carroway asked, perplexed.

Harrtuck raised an eyebrow. "There's few in Ghorbal don't know Jonmarc Vahanian, for good or bad. Those at the Inn were rather fond of him, last I knew, since he paid his bills and didn't often break the place up."

"Sounds like a great guy," Soterius muttered.

Harrtuck ignored the comment. "Time's wasting, boys," the armsman growled. "Wouldn't be surprised if Jared's sent troops as far east as this, looking."

"This just keeps getting better and better," Carroway replied darkly, as he and Soterius headed off for the Inn.

THE CLOSER TRIS and Harrtuck got to the market, the tighter the press of bodies became in the winding streets of the city. Finally, the streets opened on to a large market area, a forest of vendors' carts, flags waving with pictures of their wares, smelling of leather and spices and roasting meat. All around them, vendors haggled with patrons, their voices rising. Other merchants hawked their wares, calling out to passers-by and holding up their goods for inspection. The cacophony of voices mingled with the clatter of carts and the staccato of hoof beats. From somewhere in the market, the sound of a minstrel rose above the din.

"Where do we look?" Tris asked, uneasy in the crowd.

Harrtuck shrugged. "Could be anywhere. Might not be here at all. If the fates are fair, he's in a Nargi prison. Or dead from a bad business deal," he added.

"What does he look like?" Tris asked, scanning the crowd, his senses at high alert.

Harrtuck shrugged once more. "You'd guess he's good with a sword by his walk. He's a Borderlander by birth, but he's spent enough time on the river that he can speak their jabber like a native. Dark hair, dark eyes," Harrtuck continued. "Can charm birds out of the sky, but more often than not, he can't leave well enough alone and annoys the hell out of someone."

Tris looked out over the crowded marketplace. None of the merchants he could see came close to Vahanian's description. Too old, too tall, too heavy. They searched the marketplace for over three candlemarks, but each time Harrtuck emerged from a trader's stall, he shook his head.

"Thinks he saw him a fortnight ago, hasn't seen him since," Harrtuck reported from his last enquiry, and rubbed his chin where his beard ought to be. "The last one I talked to said he saw him just last week. I think we need to find a place to stay the night. It sounds like Jonmarc comes through here regularly, so if we don't find him today, we might be luckier tomorrow."

Tris frowned. "Unless the Margolan guards catch up with us in the meantime."

Harrtuck shrugged. "Possible. But there are a lot of roads out of Margolan. More than a few roads north don't come through Ghorbal. And unless the entire army is looking, it will take them a while to look in all the villages along the way. Besides, it's the best plan we've got."

"I know," Tris replied nervously, "but it doesn't mean I like it."

On the second day, they worked their way down more of the narrow, winding streets of Ghorbal. On a tip, they lingered for two candle-marks near the entrance to a silk merchant's warehouse where the man said he thought he saw Vahanian just that morning. But before anyone emerged from the warehouse, Tris spotted three guards in the livery of Margolan on horseback.

"We've got company," he whispered to Harrtuck. They retreated into an alehouse until the guardsmen moved on, but the encounter made Tris feel even more vulnerable.

"We're not going to be able to wait here forever," he murmured to Harrtuck, as they sat in the shade of a kerif vendor's shop and sipped the hot, bitter drink while they watched passers-by.

"Patience," Harrtuck counseled. "He's here. I'm sure of it. He's got his own reasons to lay low. But there are too many people who've spotted him recently. He'll be back."

They repeated their inquiries the next several days, piecing together more clues about Vahanian's movements. Finally, on the seventh day since their arrival in Ghorbal, Harrtuck veered toward the stall of a rug merchant who was hawking his wares in the thick river patois of the Cartelasian traders.

Tris hung back, watching for any sign that he and Harrtuck might be attracting undue interest. So far, the traders and buyers seemed intent on their business, unfazed by a few more strangers among them.

"We're looking for a trader," Harrtuck began, but once he lapsed into the unintelligible patois, Tris could not follow his conversation. After a few minutes, he returned to where Tris stood, and planted his hands on his hips.

"Well, he says that wagon over there belongs to Vahanian, but he hasn't seen him around all morning," Harrtuck said, gesturing to a sturdy wagon filled with bolts of cloth. The wagon was still hitched to a strong horse, tethered near the entrance to three branching side streets. Just the right spot for a quick getaway, Tris thought. "So assuming he hasn't been hauled in by the authorities, if we keep his wagon in sight, we should find him."

"Eventually," Tris added. He was uncomfortable out in the open. Carroway had altered their appearances, dying Tris's white-blond hair an unremarkable shade of brown, and chopping his own fashionable court style into a more common style. Soterius's hair was lightened to a muddy blond, and Harrtuck had shaved off his beard. Still, there was only so much that the disguises could do to hide them from anyone truly searching.

A commotion erupted, and Tris strained to see more. At least a dozen Nargi priests were clustered around a row of merchants near the wharf, gesturing angrily and shouting in their clipped, staccato language. It was starting to get ugly, as their voices rose and the priests began to ransack the traders' wares, shouting even louder as they held up goods and shook them for emphasis. Tris took a step closer to get a better look when Harrtuck grabbed his arm and pulled him into an alcove.

"We've got trouble, m'boy," the armsmaster breathed. "Those Margolan guards are back, and they're coming this way. Don't turn," he hissed.

"We've got to warn the others."

"No time. They're smart enough to get back to safety," Harrtuck growled, stepping behind a stack of baskets.

"Those guards aren't just wandering around, they're looking for someone," Tris added, keeping an eye on the three guardsmen, who made their way through the crowd, asking questions. From behind the pile of baskets, Tris watched as the guards approached a woman in a blue robe who nodded as they talked with her and gestured toward where he and Harrtuck had stood moments before. "They're coming our way."

"Over here," Harrtuck rasped, dragging Tris by the sleeve toward Vahanian's wagon. The large cart overflowed with rolls of Cartelasian rugs and bolts of fine Kourdish silks. With the cart between them and the street, Harrtuck nudged Tris. "Climb in, m'boy," Harrtuck whispered. "Unless the guards mean to search every merchant, we can wait for Vahanian here."

They no sooner burrowed beneath the carpets and silks before the voices of the Nargi priests reached them, even louder and more strident. Chaos erupted as the arguments turned to shouts and stacks of goods crashed to the ground. From their hiding place, Tris and Harrtuck could see little, but the sound of running footsteps pounded closer.

Suddenly, the cart lurched forward, then began to roll faster, straight toward the Margolan guardsmen. Behind them, the angry priests came almost within reach of the cart's back gate.

"You there, stop!" the guardsmen ordered, but the wagonmaster paid no heed, driving his cart and horse at breakneck speed.

With a cry, the wagonmaster rode straight for the hapless guards, giving them no choice but to throw themselves out of the way or be ridden down. The tangle of angry priests gave chase, plowing past the guardsmen and knocking them back as the desperate priests lunged toward the escaping cart.

Tris and Harrtuck struggled to hold on as the cart lurched down the rutted street. The rolls of carpet and bolts of silk pummeled them as the wares bounced and shifted. "Hang on!" Harrtuck hissed as the cart cornered on two wheels, spilling some of its precious cargo behind it. The Nargi priests, unable to run any longer, hefted the spilled silks and carpets in the air, still shouting curses and threats.

Heedless of the crowd, the wagon's driver careened through the streets. "Where is he going?" Tris managed through clenched teeth as he struggled to hold on. A roll of carpet whacked him in the head from behind as two more slippery bolts of silk slid down on him from the front, burying him. Some of the loose silks flew behind them on the breeze like richly colored flags.

"Don't know, but he's riding like the Avenger herself is behind us," Harrtuck rejoined, struggling for a handhold and being pummeled by falling carpets.

Their driver gave a cry of exultation as the wagon shot out of the city gates and onto the open road. "We're going to have a long walk back," Tris muttered, hanging on with all his might, his arms aching from the strain. There was no choice but to stay with the wagon, wherever it was headed, at least until it slowed. Finally, at least a half a candlemark after they left the city, the wagon reduced its breakneck pace, then stopped near a small grove of trees.

"Where are we?" Tris whispered. Harrtuck shrugged. "Do you think he knows we're here?"

Harrtuck shook his head. "Can't. Whoever it was wasn't even in sight when we—"

Just then, a crossbow bolt thudded into the carpet a handsbreadth from Harrtuck's shoulder.

"I would advise you to move real slowly," a man drawled. "My aim gets better on the second shot."

Harrtuck broke into a broad grin. "By the Whore!" he spat. "That was your best shot," the armsman rejoined. Tris looked at the soldier as if he were mad, but Harrtuck's grin broadened further.

"Come out!" the wagonmaster ordered, but Tris could hear a shade less certainty in their captor's tone. Slowly, hands raised, Tris and Harrtuck pushed off the bolts of silk and rolls of carpets that covered them and stood.

Their captor's crossbow was notched and leveled at their chests. He was young, perhaps ten seasons Tris's senior, with chestnut brown hair that fell shoulder length in a neat queue. His dark eyes glinted with a quick intelligence, and his tan spoke of seasons spent outdoors. A scar ran from below his right ear down into his collar. But what struck Tris most was the self-assurance in the way he held the crossbow, and in the solid, fighter's stance that told his captives that his marksmanship was no bluff.

"Vahanian?" Tris breathed, his hands still raised in surrender.

"Would you put that toy away, Jonmarc?" Harrtuck groused good-naturedly. "The blood is running out of my fingertips."

Jonmarc Vahanian looked at Harrtuck in astonishment for a heartbeat, and then slowly unnotched and lowered his bow. After another instant, a broad, lopsided grin broke across his handsome features. "Harrtuck, you old devil," he laughed, stepping forward.

Harrtuck embraced him, and slapped him hard on the back. "You're still alive, Jonmarc," he greeted. "Business must be good."

Vahanian dismissed the remark with a shrug. "You know me, Tov. I get by."

"Who were your friends back at the market-place?" Harrtuck asked. "Never saw you near so many priests before in my life. I thought for sure the Crone would strike you dead."

Vahanian laughed. "I was just getting a friendly lecture from the local, ah, merchants' guild," he said, but his expression made it plain that he relished the altercation.

"Since when are priests interested in what you have to offer?" Harrtuck asked skeptically. "Don't tell me you've taken a vocation?" he joked.

Vahanian guffawed. "Not likely, unless it's with the Dark Lady," he laughed. "I probably owe her more than a lifetime's service." He sobered. "I've been running some goods into Nargi," he added. "Cartelasian carpets and the like."

Harrtuck stared at him, perplexed. "Why would carpets get a reaction like that from the priests?"

Vahanian stared at the sky in mock innocence. "Couldn't say. Except that somewhere along the line, someone stuffed the carpet rolls with Mussa silks and Tordassian brandy."

Tris watched the entire exchange mutely, trying to get a sense of the adventurer-merchant. If

Vahanian had survived smuggling past the Nargi for long, he must certainly be as good as Harrtuck boasted. But if he were as motivated by profit as he appeared, Tris thought with concern, the sizable bounty Jared almost certainly placed by now might win out over any friendship that Harrtuck presumed. He watched the two men banter and tried to relax, but kept one hand close to his sword.

"You haven't explained yet why you were hiding in my cart, Tov," Vahanian said.

Harrtuck drew a deep breath. "I've got a business proposition for you, Jonmarc. We need a guide."

Vahanian looked from Harrtuck to Tris and back again. "We?"

"Myself, this young man, and two others," Harrtuck replied, sidestepping introductions. "We need to go north, to Dhasson."

"So go," Vahanian countered. "Lots of people do it without a guide."

Harrtuck shook his head. "It's a bit more complicated than that, Jonmarc. You know what the roads north are like come winter, and we're nearly on the storm season. A guide is the difference between making it through and freezing to death, and I've no mind to cheat the Goddess on this one." He paused. "And there's another small aspect I haven't mentioned," he said slowly. "We've got a rather hot cargo to deliver."

Vahanian grinned. "Now you're speaking my language." He frowned. "But Dhasson has open borders. There's not much to smuggle that they won't trade openly, besides dreamweed and you know I don't handle dreamweed."

Harrtuck fixed him with a hard stare. "I don't anticipate trouble getting into Dhasson, Jonmarc. It's getting out of Margolan," he said evenly. "And the cargo is human."

Vahanian looked at Tris with a long, even stare before looking back at Harrtuck. "Say on," he said, his voice skeptical.

Harrtuck shrugged. "I have three friends who witnessed an indiscretion on the part of a rather important nobleman," he lied. "They saw him murder another noble. They managed to get away, but the murderer knows they witnessed the crime. He's placed a bounty to make sure they die before they have the chance to tell the dead man's friends. The three young men have other plans," Harrtuck said drolly.

Vahanian's face was an unreadable mask, and his dark eyes looked skeptical. "Ah, you know you're a good friend of mine, Tov," he hedged, a hint of the river patois coming into his voice. "But I don't usually run people as cargo for a very good reason. I'm rather fond of my neck."

"I happen to know for a fact, Jonmarc, that you'll run anything except slaves and dreamweed for the right price."

"It would have to be pretty damn high."

"Twice the bounty, once we reach Dhasson safely," Harrtuck offered, his scarred, boxer's face taking on a cagey expression.

Vahanian looked skeptical. "In gold?"

"In gold," Harrtuck promised.

"And who's going to be so glad to get these witnesses that he'll pay such an outrageous sum?"

"King Harrol."

Vahanian was silent for a moment and looked hard at Tris as if trying to decode the last few minutes' conversation. "The king, huh," he said uncertainly after a pause. "So when you said 'hot,' you might have been understating it?" he asked dryly.

"Perhaps just a wee bit," Harrtuck admitted.

"And how well-heeled is the noble who wants these two?"

"He's got an ample treasury," Harrtuck replied. "Enough to hire scouts and bounty hunters, and pay spies from here to the border."

"Uh huh," Vahanian replied. He looked at Harrtuck. "And what's to keep me from seeing if this noble's willing to up the ante?" the mercenary asked.

Harrtuck shrugged. "Nothing. Except that he's got a blood mage keeping him in power and keeping the people under his thumb." Harrtuck raised his eyes to fix Vahanian's gaze, and Tris had a feeling that much more was being communicated between the two than what was said. "The same one you ran into back in Chauvrenne," he added, his eyes narrowing.

For an instant, before Vahanian's impassive mask slipped back into place, Tris thought he saw a reaction in the smuggler's eyes. Vahanian gave another appraising glance at Tris, and then his jaw set. "I don't like it, Tov, but I'll do it,"

Vahanian said. "But you knew that before you ever found me."

Harrtuck grinned. "I suspected, but I didn't know. You're a good man, Jonmarc."

"I'm a fool in a business where fools die young," Vahanian snapped. "Don't forget for a moment that I expect to be paid well."

"I wouldn't dream of it, Jonmarc," Harrtuck replied blithely. "Now, let's find a place to stay the night and unhitch this nag of yours so I can ride back to Ghorbal for the other two members of my party."

WHEN SOTERIUS FOLLOWED Harrtuck and Carroway into a roadside tavern upriver from Ghorbal, they found Tris waiting with Vahanian. "And this is the last member of the party," Harrtuck introduced as Soterius joined them. "Ban, former captain of arms for our dubious noble," he added, with a meaningful glance to Soterius.

Vahanian looked Soterius over with a practiced eye. "Captain of arms, huh," he said, his voice making it clear that he was not impressed. "You pretty good with that thing?" he said, nodding toward the sword that hung at Soterius's belt.

Soterius met his gaze and his challenge. "I didn't get to be captain by accident," he replied levelly. "I could outfight any of my men, and they were all trained by a master."

"Uh huh," Vahanian replied, looking away distractedly, as if he had already reached his conclusions. "Well, I'm your guide now, which means you're paying me to get you to Dhasson alive, so it's my rules." He turned back toward the fire. "Rule number one, kill the bastard or get the hell out of the way."

Soterius bristled, but a warning glance from Harrtuck tempered his reply. "And rule number two?" he asked, not attempting to hide the insolence in his tone.

Vahanian glanced back at him with a hint of wry amusement. "Give me plenty of leg room," he replied cryptically.

"Who does that guy think he is?" Soterius muttered later, when he and Tris headed up the stairs together toward their rooms.

Tris chuckled. "Apparently Harrtuck thinks Vahanian's opinion of himself is deserved," Tris said, amused at Soterius's reaction. "For what Harrtuck agreed to pay him, it had better be."

They entered the room that the five of them had paid extra to have for themselves, and Soterius nodded toward Vahanian, who was looking out the window onto the street below. "How much did Harrtuck tell him?" he asked in a whisper.

"Not much," Tris replied. "Gave him the basic story, left a few things out. Offered to pay him twice the bounty once we reach the palace at Dhasson alive. So Vahanian knows we're hot, but not who we are."

"Or quite how hot," Soterius added, looking toward the fighter once more. "Do you trust him?"

Tris shrugged. "No. At least, not yet. If he's an honest mercenary, he won't change sides in the middle of a war. Harrtuck's fought beside him, so that's something. But I don't think he stays alive by being overly sentimental."

"Then we're thinking alike," Soterius replied. "I'll keep an eye on him."

CHAPTER FIVE

THE SWORD GLINTED in the sunlight as it struck for its mark. Teeth gritted, the auburn-haired young woman parried, her arms aching at the jarring blow.

"Good, get in closer, closer," the instructor hissed, and she drove forward, slashing determinedly, her jaw set resolutely. And then, the opening she was watching for came. With a cry, she dove forward, beneath his guard, to score on the shoulder of his padded practice jacket. Overhead, a little greens-caled gyregon, Jae, fluttered its leathery wings and rasped its excitement, a spectator with an aerial view.

"Well done, your Highness, well done!" the instructor congratulated her, out of breath but pleased.

Kiara Sharsequin, princess of Isencroft, grinned tiredly and wiped the sweat from her brow with her padded sleeve. Her auburn hair was caught back in a knot, framing features that showed both her mother's Eastmark blood and her father's Isencroft heritage. Dark, almond-shaped eyes and a slightly duskier complexion gave an exotic look to the northern features she had inherited from her father, along with her height and high cheekbones. The little gyregon fluttered to land on her shoulder, and she reached up to stroke its scales.

"By the Mistress, you made me work for that, Darry!" she exclaimed, catching her breath.

"That's enough for today," Darry replied, still grinning at her triumph. "But your parry has gotten much better and you're taking the offensive more vigorously of late. Working out frustrations?"

Kiara reached up to loosen the knot that held back her hair, and shook her head as the auburn waves cascaded around her face. "You've guessed it. Some days, I think you and these sessions are the only things keeping me sane."

Darry sobered. "So I guessed, Kiara. But you are the Goddess Blessed," he reminded her. "The Holy Lady watches over you."

Kiara sighed and sheathed her sword, dropping down on a bench to unlace her padded gear. "I hope so, Darry. With the way my luck's been going, She's lost interest, or forgotten me altogether."

"Not likely, my princess," Darry replied, his weathered face softening with a smile as he ran one hand back through thick hair well streaked with gray. "I remember when She appeared to you, lady, everyone who was living then remembers! No, She has a purpose for you," he repeated with conviction. "But, like you, I pray it bodes well for Isencroft."

Kiara set aside her padded jacket. "So do I, Darry," she said pensively. "Of late, nothing bodes well for Isencroft, I fear."

"You are tired, my princess," the salle master replied. "Perhaps things will not loom so large in the morning," he said, reaching out to touch her chin affectionately. She smiled, but it was forced, and the smile did not reach her eyes. "Or, if not, perhaps you will feel more their equal." He paused. "At the least, you can give thanks that another day has passed without you being Chosen for your Journey."

Kiara shook her head and looked up at the salle roof. "One more thing to worry about," she said resignedly. "Trouble on the northern border, Cam and Carina gone these weeks and no word, Father..." Her voice drifted off. "And now, at any time, to be called by the Sisterhood for my Journey—"

"You are finding, perhaps, that to rule is not so easy, hmmm, my little falcon?" he said, sheathing his own sword. "But trust the Sisterhood. They do not choose these things lightly. And for you, Goddess Blessed, I expect that your coming-of-age Journey will not be ordinary."

"I'm not sure that's comforting, if you were trying to reassure me," Kiara said, already feeling her aching muscles protest as she rose. Once more, to no one in particular, she cursed Isencroft's tradition of insisting that all of its nobility, male or female, excel at the swordsmanship which distinguished the realm. She knew better than to let Darry hear her, since the armsmaster was wont to remind her that even the peasant folk, except for women with suckling babes and children too young to wield a weapon, were expected to drill with the homeliest of arms. To be of Isencroft was to know the sword. She prayed that her people's preparations might be enough.

She feared otherwise. Broad and vast, Isencroft was populated more by herds than people; scattered pockets of townspeople staked a hard-won home on Isencroft's flat plains of fertile ground and good pastureland. There had been no famine in Isencroft for longer than anyone could remember. But in generations past, wars came almost as regularly as the rains, as one neighbor or another advanced, hungry for Isencroft's land and access to the Northern Sea.

Kiara no longer trusted in the skill at arms of her people. The threat that lurked beyond the borders was of magic, not of men. "And then, there's Margolan," she sighed, helping Darry pick up the weapons strewn around from their practice.

"I heard there was a messenger," Darry replied noncommittally.

Kiara gave an undignified snort. "Messenger indeed. A little overstuffed hedgeweasel arrived with an invitation from His Majesty, Jared of

Margolan, bearing royal greetings and an invitation to visit the palace. And a reminder of a betrothal contract signed when I was born." She grimaced as she helped Darry replace the weapons. "His Majesty," she repeated derisively. "All our spies report the same thing, that he murdered his family to seize the throne—"

"Dangerous words, my princess," Darry cautioned, "even if true."

"Of course they're true!" she retorted, resting her hand on her hip and fixing Darry with a glare. "And now he wants to enlarge his empire. By marriage."

"Your father would never force you—"

"But my father is not himself," Kiara replied, dropping into a dispirited slump on the salle bench. "We both know that. And if Jared has any spies at all—let alone the dark mages that are supposed to be at his bidding—he knows that. If he didn't cause it," she added darkly. "That demon of his, Arontala, could probably create a curse at least as strong as the one on Father, before breakfast, no doubt."

"You worry too much, Goddess Blessed," Darry said gently, resting one foot on the bench beside her and leaning on his knee. "Our people will hardly let you be carried off into a marriage against your will."

Kiara shrugged. "You've told me enough times yourself that we of the blood royal often have less choice about our lives than the poorest peasant. So many things hang by a thread right now, Darry," she said, pulling her knees up to her chest like a child and wrapping her arms around them, hugging herself tight. "The nobles must suspect that father's not well. He can't even keep up appearances now, and the longer he's 'indisposed,' the more they'll talk. Two poor harvests in a row plus foul weather this year, and we may have famine on our hands come winter. Margolan used to be a trusted ally. But now, weak as Isencroft has become, all it might take is a threat from the east, or magicked beasts from the north, to give us no choice. Give me no choice," she whispered, "except to buy Isencroft's safety with myself."

"By the Childe and Crone, you're gloomy today!" Darry exclaimed. "Any other disasters you would care to consider? Plague? Flood? Locusts?" He grinned wickedly. "Perhaps extra practice sessions for a morbid princess would turn her mind to more useful things?"

Kiara lifted her head just far enough to glare balefully above her folded arms. "There's a penalty for killing a princess with too much arms practice. There has to be. And if there isn't, I'll see that Allestyr creates one right away."

Darry laughed. "Since Carina's gone away, you brood too much, my princess," he chided. "Trust the Bright Lady. One day Isencroft, and you, will see happier days."

With a sigh, Kiara uncurled and stretched, standing. She patted the instructor on the shoulder affectionately. "I hope you're right, Darry. For all of us," she said, painfully aware of her aching muscles and knowing that, even with a hot bath, she would feel their session in her bones come morning.

THE MUCH-COVETED hot bath was over far too soon, and the night's work that awaited her gave Kiara far more concern than her sore muscles. In the private parlor outside her sleeping rooms, Kiara's closest advisors waited for her arrival. She slipped into the room and greeted the group. Their reserve gave her an indication of their concern.

"Is everything ready, Tice?" Kiara asked the thin, white-haired man.

Tice nodded. "All is ready, Your Highness. But I beg you, please reconsider. The risk is just too great."

"You know as well as I do that there is no other way," Kiara replied stubbornly, and reached out to accept the small velvet pouch in Tice's hand. From it she drew out a finely worked necklace, set with stones that glimmered in the candlelight. Pressing her candle into his hand, Kiara secured the clasp around her throat and lifted her head

"You are too young for such great responsibilities," Tice clucked.

Kiara gave him a sidelong look. "You coddle me, Tice," she chided gently. "Hasn't father told you that I'm already almost too old to make a 'suitable' bride? By this age, almost twenty summers old, in the farmlands, a girl has already whelped four brats, five if she starts young and keeps at it each year," she said with a wicked grin.

"Your Highness," Tice said with a "tsk tsk" that did little to hide his amusement. "I hope you restrain your language in public."

Kiara chuckled. "That all depends. I'd like the Margolan ambassador to convince his king that I'm not at all suitable for such a great ruler," she replied, her voice thick with sarcasm.

"Another scrying might not be necessary," Tice argued. "You should conserve your strength. You're driving yourself too hard."

Kiara fingered the intricate designs of the ancient pendant. It was set with oval stones in each of the five gems sacred to the Goddess: diamond, the stone of the deepest caverns; ruby, the color of fire; emerald, green as the seas; sapphire, blue as the skies; and amber like the Lady's eyes. Its metal was worn smooth from the years, and its power made her fingers tingle. "Really, Tice," Kiara said, touching his arm gently, "you worry too much." She smiled her most engaging smile and Tice shook his head in resignation.

"You have always gotten your way with me, Kiara," Tice replied. "And I don't imagine that is going to change. I just beg of you to conserve your strength. Isencroft needs you."

"Everyone is here, Your Highness," said Kellen, a trusted guard. Although the man-at-arms had been at every Ritual since the start, he still looked decidedly ill at ease.

Kiara looked at the small, anxious group. Her five closest advisors awaited the Working, apprehensive yet committed. Allestyr, the king's seneschal, nodded in silent greeting, as did Brother Felix, an acolyte to the Oracle.

"I'll begin the warding." Cerise, healer to Kiara's late mother, took her place, stepping forward and taking up a chalice from the altar in the center of the room. Even her healing talents could not overcome the hunching back and slight limp that age inflicted.

The others formed the circle. Kiara stepped into the center. Jae made his perch this time on Tice's shoulder. Brother Felix reverently raised his hands, revealing another chalice, cradled gently between his roughened palms. This one was low and wide, filled with still water. Kiara took the glass chalice from Brother Felix and held it in front of her. Then, taking a deep breath, she began.

"Powers that be, hear me! Goddess of Light, attend!" Kiara recited, her eyes closed in concentration. "I am the Chosen of Isencroft, the line of the blood. We gather to invoke the ancient Powers. I claim the Powers by the blood of my family and the title of the crown. In the name of the aspects of the Holy One, protect this kingdom. May the Mother defend it like a firstborn and the Avenger guard its borders. May the Dark Lady cherish it like a lover and the Childe in all her innocence preserve it as a beloved. I will it be so!"

The chalice flared, lighting Kiara's face with its eerie blue glow. Kiara gasped as the air in the chamber began to stir, sweeping around them. Gentle at first, its strength grew until it rushed around them with a howl, and Kiara imagined that she glimpsed faces in the magewind. "Spirits of the Land, hear me!" Kiara began again. "Winds of the North, obey! Waters of the Southlands, bend your course to the will of the Chosen. Fires of the Eastern Sun, be bound by my command. Land of our fathers under the sun of the west, I compel you by the right of the heirs of Isencroft to reveal what is hidden and find what is dear. Let it be so!"

A glow began deep within the still waters. Kiara stared into the chalice and its swirling mist.

The image within was nearly complete. "Cam and Carina," Cerise reported as the images of Kiara's journeying cousins filled the chalice. The mists shifted and the image blurred. When the waters cleared once more, Cerise gasped.

The images shifted again, flashing fragments of scenes so brief it was just barely possible to identify them, of flames and the flash of swords. Kiara saw images flicker in the amber mist. Carina was in danger, and Cam's face was grim, his hair sodden with sweat, as he set about with his sword. Then, a gray mist obliterated the picture.

Kiara sagged to her knees and the image disappeared.

"Break the circle!" Cerise hissed. "We can't help you until you break the circle!"

"Wind and Fire, Land and Sea, I release you!" Kiara whispered. The chalice's light dimmed, then faded into darkness. Tice and Allestyr rushed forward as Kellen wrapped Kiara in his

arms and gently lifted her from the floor. Brother
Felix took the chalice from Cerise.

"What did she see?" asked Allestyr.

Cerise shook her head. "Nothing good, I fear.
Cam and Carina are in danger, but the waters are
unclear. Whether our vision was, or is to come,
or may be changed, is not certain."

"Thank you," Kiara whispered, still leaning
heavily on Kellen. She could feel the last vestiges
of the powers they had summoned tingling
around them.

Kellen shouldered open the heavy door to
Kiara's bedchamber and Cerise helped the
princess into bed. Brother Felix stepped up to
attend her as Tice and the others stood back
along the walls of the room, waiting.

"Well?" Tice asked.

Cerise looked up and brushed a strand of gray
hair from her eyes. "She'll be all right," the healer reassured. "But each scrying drains her."

Kiara rolled her head to look at the old healer.
"You know I hate it when you talk about me like
I'm not here," she reproved, a tired smile softening her complaint. Cerise patted her hand and
pressed a cup to Kiara's lips. They had their
answer for tonight, Kiara thought. Cam and
Carina, King's Champion and King's Healer,
were in danger, their quest to seek the Sisterhood
and find a solution to the king's illness still uncertain.

Cerise ended her ministrations and stood. The
princess fought back sleep, determined to remain
alert while the others were near. Jae left his perch

on Tice's shoulder and flew to the top of Kiara's headboard like a sentry.

Allestyr took a kettle from the fire and poured them each a cup of mulled wine. Cerise cradled her cup in her hands and sank into a chair, staring at the fire.

"She's pushing herself too hard, taking her father's place and training for her Journey. Carina's absence only makes it worse." Cerise said.

"Perhaps the Oracle—" Allestyr began.

"You know that the king is impatient with the Oracle," Cerise replied tiredly. "The Goddess too often keeps her own counsel about Isencroft's troubles."

"We need an answer soon," Kellen said, draining his cup.

"I know, Kellen," Cerise whispered. "I know." They may have said more after that, but the mulled wine, the warmth of the fire and the fatigue of the evening finally overcame even Kiara's will, and despite her best efforts, she drifted into sleep.

CHAPTER SIX

JARED DRAYKE DRUMMED his fingers. "He's not telling everything he knows," the king growled. Foor Arontala gestured to the black-robed torturer, and the subject of Jared's irritation screamed once more as the red-hot iron burned into his flesh.

"Please, no more!" the soldier begged. "Master, I swear I have told you all!"

Jared's mood soured by the minute. "Where is my brother?" Jared growled.

The soldier's face was white with terror. "No one knows, sire, I swear I am telling you the truth. We lost his trail in Ghorbal, when he escaped with the mercenary Vahanian. It's as if they were swallowed up whole. I can tell no more. Mercy, my liege, I beg you," the scout whimpered. Hog-bound with chains and forced to kneel before his king, the man was barely coherent, and a row of fresh, seeping burns along his face and arm attested to Jared's frustration.

Jared exploded into a string of expletives. "No, of course you can't tell me. You failed." Jared nodded once more to the torturer, who set aside his poker and lifted an axe. "You know the consequence for failure." Before the scout could twist to see, the torturer swung the axe, neatly cleaving the scout's head from his shoulders. The body, still pumping blood, fell to the side of the interrogation dais, and the blood ran along the narrow gutter along its edge, into the ornate bowl at its lip. Jared looked away in disgust.

"Display his body outside the barracks," Jared ordered. "Let him serve as an example. Perhaps the next scout will be more diligent." Jared turned his glare pointedly to the red-robed mage who stood silently by the cold hearth. "Not that my mage has done much better," he said dryly after the executioner dragged the corpse and its head from the room.

Foor Arontala was a thin man, his shoulders slightly rounded, with lank brown hair that fell unkempt around his pale, youthful face. His robes, the color of dried blood, only heightened his pallor. Arontala's pale blue eyes hinted at his true age, centuries instead of mere decades, and his thin lips hid incisors that confirmed the rumors that said he was among the Deathless Ones. Arontala's expression was unreadable as always. "I'm not sure what you are saying, sire."

Jared made a contemptuous noise. "The hell you aren't. You assured me this would go smoothly."

"It did," the mage replied, unmoved by Jared's temper. "You have the throne of Margolan and any who resisted you were silenced."

"My brother lives," Jared snapped. "He can rally discontent, challenge my throne—"

"Your brother has never shown the slightest interest in ruling."

"He doesn't have to," Jared fumed. "All he has to do is live long enough to reach Dhasson and others will make him a rallying point."

"Then we have to make sure he never reaches Dhasson."

Jared stood and walked to the window of his chamber. It was autumn and only the thick stone walls of the palace kept a chill from the room. His sable brown hair fell in soft waves to his shoulders, framing a face that would have been handsome but for the arrogant turn of his lip and the hard glint in his brown eyes. The resemblance between Jared and his younger half-brother was unmistakable, though Tris was as fair in coloring as Jared was dark. "What do you suggest?"

"You are certain he is heading north. Only a few roads lead there. Hire a tracker to find him and reward him well for the hunt."

Jared wheeled on the mage. "That's it? I could have come up with that. Can't a mage do better than that?"

Arontala fixed him with a cool stare. "There are uses for magic and uses for men. My magic confirms that your brother is alive and heading north. But without more precise information, I cannot summon harm without laying waste to a good bit of the population along the northern route."

"Then do it!"

Arontala looked faintly amused. "That would not be wise, sire," he replied, moving away from the wall. "Even you rule by consent of the people. My power can't alter that should enough of them seek to change it. There are still whisperings about your father's death. And about your suspicious dark mage," he added with a hint of irony. "They fear you, but they do not hate you. Yet. Wait until your brother is dead before you make your presence more onerous to them, or you will provide him the opening you wish to avoid."

Jared turned back to look out the window. "Then hire your assassins and pay them well. I want Tris dead."

"As you wish, my lord."

Jared looked back at him over his shoulder. "And the other matter? Did you secure it?"

Arontala crossed the room, but Jared did not see him move. It was an annoying habit and Jared suspected that was precisely why the mage continued to do it. Arontala lifted the bowl with the soldier's blood and let his finger run along its rim. The mage's tongue wet his lips as he raised the bowl and began to drink, Jared saw a flash of white teeth that made him shiver.

"Feed your filthy habit elsewhere," Jared snapped. "A mage that can only go about in darkness is only half of use to me."

Arontala ignored the command and set the empty bowl aside, his mouth immaculately clean.

"You should not speak of what you do not comprehend, my liege," the mage said dryly. "If you prefer, I can feed otherwise, but I am not sure that even you are strong enough... yet... to harbor a rogue vayash moru with impunity."

"Your precious dark gift has done me little good," Jared growled. "And as for rumors, do you think the commoners would believe I would give safety to one of your kind... after we've gone to such pains to exterminate the others?" He paused. "I still think they could have been turned to be... useful to us."

"Ah yes," Arontala said in that smooth voice Jared found so mocking. "Jared Drayke, slayer of vayash moru, defender of the kingdom. Even I could not turn and retain control of so many of... as you put it... my kind."

"Even you?" Jared sneered.

Arontala made a dismissive wave.

"There are still the palace ghosts."

"The dagger which slew your father was spelled to destroy the soul as well as the body. His body was burned, and the ashes mingled with dryroot and scattered under a full moon. There is no magic that can bring him back," Arontala replied.

"And the others?"

"Some of the spirits were banished," Arontala replied. "They cannot return unless I bid them come. As for your stepmother and her brat, their spirits are still here under my watchful eye," he said with a lethal smile as he walked around the pulsing, red orb in the center of the room. "They await the Feeding," he said, his hand hovering just above the surface of the orb. "They are quite safe in my Soulcatcher," he smiled.

"There is still Bava K'aa," Jared snapped. "I saw what she could do."

"Bava K'aa is dead."

Jared turned toward the mage and shook his head. "She was a mage. A strong one. She could will her spirit to remain."

"That was why we set the warding around the throne room when your father fell," Arontala replied. "And why I set the spell to banish the castle ghosts. If her spirit is here, which I do not sense, she did not come to Bricen's aid."

Jared began to pace. "No, she didn't," he replied softly, as if answering himself instead of Arontala. "But she always favored Serae's brats. And I think she always meant for Serae's son to rule." He looked up at the mage. "I want you to find her body and destroy it."

Arontala returned a skeptical look. "Bava K'aa was buried within a citadel of the Sisterhood. Nothing short of war could breach their protections."

"Why are you so clear on what can't be done and not on what can?" Jared exploded. "You're supposed to make sure that nothing interferes. If you can't do that, perhaps there's a stronger mage who can!"

Arontala looked faintly amused. "Perhaps. But I sense that you fear something more than Bava K'aa's ghost."

Jared stopped pacing in front of the empty hearth and stared into the darkness of the opening. "I've always heard that sorcerers must have a mage heir." He turned to face Arontala and forced himself to meet those mocking, dark eyes. "What if my cursèd brother is her heir?"

As usual, Arontala's eyes revealed nothing. "You have no reason to believe that. Your brother has shown less interest in magic than he has in ruling. Really, Jared, if you thought him to be such a threat, why didn't you kill him yourself? You had plenty of opportunities."

"If he has Bava K'aa's power," Jared continued doggedly, "do you realize what that means? He could summon her spirit to fight me, use her powers against me and take the throne. If he becomes a Summoner, if he inherited grandmother's gift, then both the spirits and the undead heed his command."

"You are worried about children's tales and ghost stories."

"Then prove me wrong," Jared hissed, turning on the mage. "Drive out the Sisterhood. Make sure Bava K'aa can't return from the dead. And find my brother!"

"As you wish, sire," Arontala answered with a low bow Jared was not altogether sure was respectful. "But there are a few more details in which you might be interested."

"Speak."

"I have set a barrier spell on the border with Dhasson," Arontala reported, a smile at his own cleverness touching the corners of his thin lips. "It is particular to your brother. It will summon every dark thing in the Northern Lands as soon as he breaches the border." Arontala smiled his pleasure. "No one could withstand those... things... and live."

"No one but a mage," Jared muttered darkly. "My brother has the lives of a cat." He paced. "And while you tell me you are the strongest mage in the Winter Kingdoms, you have not told me who made those dark beasts, since they are more than you can conjure."

It was the first time Jared scored against Arontala, and the mage turned with a dismissive gesture. "It does not matter who made them," he said. "What matters is that we have made them useful."

"It doesn't matter who made them," Jared echoed dryly, "until that mage appears and demands his due."

"There are more pressing matters to worry about," Arontala responded impatiently.

"Like my brother."

"He is only an average swordsman, my liege," Arontala replied with patronizing mildness. "Even with help, there are too many of the creatures to fight. He will not survive crossing the border. Not for long."

"Your assurances are hollow," Jared snapped. "I can't rest until he is dead."

"You will not wait long, your majesty," Arontala answered, gliding to the window. "Have you so little faith?"

"Yes," Jared returned. "You have not delivered Isencroft to me, let alone rid me of my brother. If such a simple matter eludes you…"

"Only a weak king uses magic when statecraft will do," Arontala replied impatiently, turning from the window. "You have the covenant, signed by your father and King Donelan of Isencroft, sealing the betrothal of a princess of Isencroft with the ruling son of Margolan. I have already arranged for Catoril to travel there and bring Princess Kiara back to visit. You need only impress her. I should think even you can handle that."

Jared glared at the mage. "You were supposed to have solved the Donelan problem by now," Jared replied, beginning to pace. "The possibility still exists that he may forbid the marriage. Kill him and she has no choice. Isencroft is on the brink of famine. Even our proud warrior princess must see that there are no alternatives to Margolan's… protection."

Arontala watched Jared with dry amusement. "It has been said that those for whom magic is most addicting are not mages. I have fixed Donelan in a wasting spell. He resists. To do more, over this distance, is a waste of my power."

"I'll judge that!" Jared snapped. "You were told to see him dead."

"Patience, my liege," Arontala said smoothly. "Patience. It is not wise to make too great a show of our powers. Not yet. Donelan has not been seen in months. If it were not for my scrying, one could assume his death already. And Kiara Sharsequin is not another of your empty-headed mistresses. She is Goddess Blessed and a skillful warrior. You will have to win her consent to the marriage with your own abilities." He smiled coldly. "Once the wedding is over, I will assure her death."

"More promises," Jared muttered. "Leave me. I'm tired of your prattle. Bring me news when your spies reach the northern roads. I want to know when my brother crosses the border."

Arontala bowed low with exaggerated grace. "As you wish, my liege," he murmured, but the glance with which he fixed the king gave Jared no doubt that the wizard's show of servitude was merely one more dangerous game.

He watched the mage leave and shuddered. The sorcerer could make all the reassurances he wished, Jared thought, but he was underestimating Bava K'aa.

Despite his heavy robes, Jared shivered. As for ghosts, the palace had more than its share. Now, despite Arontala's warding, he swore he could feel their presence, waiting, mocking, angry. He must make sure Tris could never draw on their power, never turn them against him as they had savaged the attackers of King Hotten generations ago.

Arontala says he's banished them, but maybe they're just beyond the gates, he thought. And they're waiting.

He looked back outside, struggling to calm his thudding heart. The living he could master, but the dead were another matter entirely.

CHAPTER SEVEN

TRIS AND THE others made camp at the edge of a small forest, just far enough within the tree line to hide themselves from the village below. There were many people on the road, returning from festival or taking goods to the last fairs before winter, and so Harrtuck made a small fire without concern.

"Now what?" Tris asked Vahanian as the mercenary sat next to the fire, a hot mug of watered ale gripped in his hands against the cold.

Vahanian glanced up at him. "Now, we find some cover for going north," he said, draining his mug and setting it aside. He clasped his hands and looked into the fire. "A caravan's good cover," he said after a pause. "Lots of people for camouflage and they still make decent time on the road."

"Won't that be slow?" Carroway asked, finishing his dinner. "I mean, they have to stop a lot to sell their wares and give their shows."

"Beats four fugitives and a guide trying not to look obvious," Vahanian said, never taking his eyes off the fire.

"So what are we going to do?" Soterius asked, setting his plate aside. "Just walk up and say, 'Hello there, we want to be your hired swords?'"

Harrtuck laughed and even Vahanian smiled. "A little like that," Vahanian said. "If they're passing anywhere near here, there's a caravan I have in mind. An old friend of mine named Maynard Linton owns it. Maynard will take us on, no questions asked, and keep his theories to himself if our guards seem overly well-bred," he said, with a pointed glance toward Tris and Soterius.

"How do we find him?" Tris asked.

Vahanian shrugged. "There's a settlement on the other side of the forest. I'll go down to the tavern. Tavern keepers always know where the caravans are."

He left within the hour, heading down the slope into the village while Tris and the others stayed hidden in the forest. Vahanian paused at the outskirts of the village to take stock. It looked quiet enough. Some of the banners from the holiday remained aloft from the corners of buildings, fluttering cold and forlorn on the autumn breeze.

The tavern was on the edge of the settlement, its broken sign askew and unreadable. Vahanian made his way up the sagging steps, toeing a drunk out of the way, and pushed open the greasy door. Something skittered across his boot as he entered. The tavern was full, testimony to a lack of competing facilities, Vahanian was sure, rather than to the food and ale. He sized up the clientele—third-rate merchants, petty cut-throats, fewer and uglier whores than usual, and one or two freelance fighters who appeared to be nothing more than common thugs.

He took a place at the bar so that his back was to a wall, and casually rested his boot on the rail of a chair as the barkeeper brought him a mug of ale. For a candlemark, he listened silently as the patrons grumbled about taxes and guardsmen, muddy roads and too much rain. He listened more closely when the talk turned to trouble in the north, but heard nothing more specific than rumors of dark magic and fierce beasts. As he listened, he watched the crowd. There were few enough inns on the way north, making it likely for those who traveled frequently to spot one another. That included bounty hunters, whom Vahanian wanted to avoid more fervently than ever.

"Heard anything about caravans coming this way?" he asked, draining his mug. He slid his coin across the sticky wood.

The barkeeper shrugged, bit the coin, and threw it into his apron pocket. "I hear there's some coming," he replied in a voice that suggested that he sampled too many of his own goods.

"Any in particular?"

"Maybe. Heard something about Couras's caravan passing through here going south in a few weeks," the barkeeper added, wiping out a glass and setting it back to be used again. "Heard tell that Linton's caravan was heading north, might be here in two or three days."

Vahanian nodded and sipped his drink. He froze as he recognized a squat man with oily blond hair, rising from a table in the back. He had an inkling the man had been looking for him, back in Ghorbal. When it came to tracking prey, bounty hunters seemed to have all the time in the world. If the hunter made a calculated guess about Vahanian's direction, he would check out the inns first. Bad enough if Vahanian were about his usual business, but with the fugitives in tow, it made the risk unacceptably high. He would have to do something about it. As Vahanian watched, the bounty hunter made his way among the crowded tables toward the door. Vahanian turned slightly so that his face was hidden as the man passed, then set his drink aside when the door closed behind the man and followed him into the night.

In the darkness of the alley behind the inn, Vahanian tackled the squat bounty hunter from behind, locking his arm around the man's throat. "So, Chessis, you're still in business," Vahanian said, tightening his grip.

"Let me go, Vahanian. I'm not looking for you."

"Right," Vahanian replied, maintaining his pressure on Chessis's throat. "And I'm not worth a lot of money to you dead."

"That was a long time ago," Chessis croaked. "They've probably retired the purse by now."

"Somehow, I doubt it. What are you doing here?"

The bounty hunter twisted slightly, enough to bring his boot around, and Vahanian realized almost too late that there was a blade set in its toe. The knife sliced his pantleg as he released his hold and jumped back, pulling his own blade. Chessis dropped into a defensive squat, circling and looking for an opening. In the narrow alleyway with its tangle of overhead laundry lines, drawing a sword would be impossible. Instead, Vahanian crouched, knife in hand, ready to spring.

Chessis lunged. Vahanian parried. Chessis feinted, then lunged again, his knife scoring against Vahanian's arm. With an oath, Vahanian pivoted, his left foot snapping out towards the surprised bounty hunter, letting his boot connect hard against the man's knife hand and sending the weapon skittering down the alleyway. Before Chessis could recover, Vahanian spun, slipping within the bounty hunter's guard and burying his knife deep in the man's chest. With a groan, the oily-haired man clutched at the spreading stain on his shirt and sagged to the ground, just as Vahanian felt the point of a sword in his back.

"It may be too close to fight with this," a gravelly voice said, "but I have plenty of room to run you through, Jonmarc."

Vahanian dropped his knife and raised his hands. "Hello, Vakkis."

"Some day, before I kill you, you're going to have to teach me that footwork," Vakkis remarked coolly. "You're really a marvel, Jonmarc. I may miss you when you're dead. Escaping from the Nargi is feat enough. Learning their ancient fighting skills is another." Vakkis made a *tsk tsk* in the back of his throat. "It's going to be much quieter for me after you're gone, Jonmarc."

"I never knew you cared, Vakkis," Vahanian replied. "I'll be glad to give you your first lesson now, if you want." The jab of the sword's point between his shoulder blades was his reply.

"You know, Chessis was telling the truth," the bounty hunter went on. "We aren't looking for you, at least, right now. I've got another client."

"Slime spreads," Vahanian remarked, and this time, the sword jab drew blood.

"Where is Martris Drayke?"

"How in the hell would I know?"

"Turn around, slowly, and keep your hands up," Vakkis replied, keeping the point of his sword against Vahanian's flesh as the fighter turned, and bringing the sword to bear above his heart. "Now, I'll ask again. Where is Martris Drayke?"

"You're getting old, Vakkis," Vahanian replied. "Hearing's going. I don't know what the hell you're talking about."

A slow smile crept over Vakkis face. "You actually don't, do you?" the bounty hunter chuckled. "This is more satisfying than I'd dreamed. Jonmarc Vahanian, played for a fool."

"I'm glad one of us is having fun. Mind letting me in on the joke?"

A cold smile made Vakkis's pointed features even harsher in the moonlight. "They managed to elude me in Ghorbal, but I heard they'd teamed up with you. Our little kingslayer, Martris Drayke of Margolan and his friends, seem to have bought themselves a guide," Vakkis said, watching Vahanian with amusement. "You really didn't know, did you?"

"I don't know what you're talking about."

To Vahanian's astonishment, Vakkis reached into his cloak and withdrew a small purse filled with coins, which he dropped at Vahanian's feet. "Even by your standards, there's fair compensation in there for information," Vakkis said, stepping back a pace and lowering his sword. "Now, where is Martris Drayke?"

"Go to hell."

"Loyalty from you, Jonmarc? I'm surprised," Vakkis clucked. "I thought you unburdened yourself of that along with your commission."

"Go screw the goddess."

"In time," Vakkis said with a cold smile. "Think about my offer. I'm easy to find. That purse is only a down-payment. Jared of Margolan has promised to make a rich man of anyone who delivers his brother alive. And you've never let king, honor or country stand in the way when money's involved."

The bounty hunter took another step backward, into the shadows of the alley, so that his face and form were barely visible. "Think about it, Jonmarc," Vakkis said, his voice carrying in the chill night air. "More money than you can imagine. Pay me a cut and I'll stop hunting you. Wealth and freedom, just for delivering the goods. What businessman could resist?" Vakkis said as he faded into the darkness.

Vahanian did not move for several minutes, until he was sure that Vakkis was actually gone. Only then did he realize just how hard his heart was thudding. Wealth and freedom. He looked down at the purse at his feet. There's only one thing worse than a bounty hunter, a voice said in the back of his mind. And that's the snitch he pays for the kill. The cold night air seared his lungs. He paused and then, surprising himself, stepped over the purse and walked toward the end of the alley, stopping only to snatch up his fallen blade.

Vahanian found Tris at the edge of the camp when he returned, skinning the rabbits Harrtuck brought down for their dinner. "I killed a man for you tonight, Prince Drayke," Vahanian grated. Tris stiffened and rose to his feet as Vahanian continued. "You didn't think it was important enough to tell me the truth, even though it's my neck you're risking to get you to Dhasson."

"Jonmarc, I—"

"Let's get something straight right now," Vahanian continued. "I am not expendable. We don't move from here until I know what's going on. The whole story. If I like what I hear, and believe it, I'll take you to Dhasson. If not, I leave right now, and you can find another fool. And, Your Highness, I'm nobody's liegeman. If I take you to Dhasson, and that's a very big 'if' right now, it's on my terms, my way. Do you understand?"

Tris took a deep breath and nodded. "Good," Vahanian said. "That means you're smarter than most royals. Now, let's hear your story—all of it."

"Vahanian, you're back," bustled Harrtuck. Harrtuck ambled toward them from the fires of the camp, coming up behind Vahanian. With one fluid movement, Vahanian wheeled, bringing his fist to connect soundly with Harrtuck's jaw.

"What the hell was that for?" Harrtuck shouted.

"I found out from a bounty hunter who your 'cargo' really was," Vahanian snapped. "He could have slit my throat and I'd have never seen it coming."

"Jonmarc, you don't understand—"

"I understand that my life is as important as your three nobles," Vahanian grated, still standing over the stout armsmaster. "And that I can't decide what risks are worth taking if I don't know the game." Glaring, Vahanian turned away and Harrtuck scrambled to his feet.

"In fact, I can't think of one reason right now—even your money—why I should take you to Dhasson."

"Arontala's back. And he's got a king this time, not just a general at his command," Harrtuck said quietly from behind Vahanian, who stiffened at the name.

"How do you know?"

Harrtuck gave a short, harsh laugh. "Know? How we know is the reason we're in the forest freezing our rumps off instead of toasting by a nice palace fire," he said, and together, he and Tris told their tale. This time, the only thing Tris omitted was what happened with Kait in the bed-chamber and his subsequent dreams of his sister and his sorceress grandmother.

Vahanian sat in silence for several minutes after they finished, staring at his hands, his face unread-able. "I take you to Dhasson, and then what?"

"Then you collect your money from King Harrol and leave," Harrtuck snapped. "At that point, your jewels are out of the fire."

"And the rest of you?"

"I'm going back," Tris said evenly. "Someone has to stop Jared. I'm the only one who can."

"You're going to stop Foor Arontala? Look, prince, even with King Harrol's entire army, it just ain't enough," Vahanian said, shaking his head.

"Don't underestimate him," Harrtuck said qui-etly. "His grandmother was Bava K'aa. He's a Summoner."

"He's a mage?" Vahanian asked sharply, look-ing through narrowed eyes from Tris to Harrtuck. "You didn't tell me he was a mage."

"I'm not a full mage," Tris said, "at least, not yet."

"Yeah, well, I hate mages."

"Right now, I'm not even a mage student."

"Well, prince, if you're going up against Arontala and expect to live through it, you'd better be a damn good mage," Vahanian said. "Glad I won't be there to see it."

"I told you a hired sword was a bad idea," Soterius snapped, coming up from the campsite. "You can't trust them further than you can throw their money."

"Young pups bark the loudest," Vahanian returned with a shrug. "You know so much, you guide them. I've got other ways to earn as much gold as I want."

"You've wanted to get Arontala for ten years now," Harrtuck objected. "After what happened at Chauvrenne, you ought to be glad for an opportunity."

A cynical, lopsided smile drew over Vahanian's features. "You can't enjoy revenge if you're dead," he replied. "Save your breath. I'll take you to Dhasson. After that, you're on your own." He walked away, leaving the others in the glow of the fire.

Tris looked at Harrtuck. "Now what?"

The armsmaster gestured to the sky in frustration and spat. "Let him cool off," he said finally, and raised one hand to stroke his absent beard. "By the Whore, I miss my whiskers! Damn thing itches all the time."

"I don't like it," Soterius began, with a baleful glance toward where Vahanian had disappeared.

"You wouldn't like any hired sword if he were led here by the Childe, vouched for by the Virgin herself, and brought on the wings of the Avenger," Harrtuck snapped. "Really, Ban, I know what guardsmen think of them. But I've hired out my sword and you trust me, don't you?"

"You know I do."

"Then trust me on this," Harrtuck pressed. "Jonmarc will come around." He looked after the angry mercenary, who was barely visible in the darkness. "Just give him some time."

Tris bent down to pick up the empty bucket that lay with their gear. "While that happens, I'll get some water," he said eager for the chance to do something other than sit and wait. The evenings were the hardest time. He headed down the slope toward the village well. During the daylight, with the ride to think about, he could push away the grief that threatened to overwhelm him. But come night, the loss grew almost too great to bear. Of everything he left behind, he missed Kait the most. At times, the loss ached as if someone had broken off a sword tip, deep inside him. At other times, it hurt too much to feel anything at all. Only the knowledge that he might have to outride Margolan troops kept him from seeking relief in the flask of brandy Harrtuck carried, and so he wrestled with the dull ache that made it impossible for him to focus on much else, and wondered when, if ever, it would lessen.

The wooden handle of the well's crank creaked in protest as Tris drew up a bucketful of water. Just as it neared the top, he felt an insistent tap on his shoulder. He spun to look, losing his grip on the crank as he drew his sword, but the roadway around the well was empty. The autumn wind stung his face, and Tris realized that the night was suddenly colder. He felt gooseflesh rise on his neck, and looked around once more as the sense of a spirit's presence tingled in his mind.

"Show yourself," he whispered to the darkness. He waited. When nothing stirred, he turned and began to draw water, only to feel the tap on his shoulder once more. This time, he pulled the bucket up to the edge of the stone well before he turned. Closing his eyes, he focused on the tingle and stretched out his will, summoning the presence. When he opened his eyes, the apparition of a young woman stood before him. She wore a scullery maid's dress that was at least a generation out of date. She had the ample, sturdy build of a milkmaid, but her eyes were filled with such a great sadness that Tris reflexively stepped toward her in comfort.

"Please sir, have you seen my baby?"

Tris shook his head, and the girl's sad eyes grew fearful. "He was here a moment ago," she said, stepping toward the well. "I just ran back for another bucket." She turned toward the well, and looked down, then cried out in horror. "Oh sweet Goddess, there's his hat!" she wailed, tearing at her hair and launching herself toward the water far below before Tris could start toward her. Though insubstantial as she was, there was no way for him to prevent the tragic reenactment.

Tris's heart thudded as he stared at the silent well, guessing at the tragedy that bound the girl's spirit to this place. She no doubt left her small son unattended for a moment, only to find when she returned that he had climbed to peer into the well and had fallen to his death. In her grief, she threw herself after him, doomed to repeat the awful moment for eternity.

Or perhaps not, Tris thought. He laid a hand on the cold stone of the well and shut his eyes. He felt a thrill of challenge as he decided to try something that he could only barely frame in his mind. Trusting to instinct more than thought, he stretched out with his thoughts, reaching out to the doomed girl in the silent spirit realm where he glimpsed Kait at the palace. After a moment, he felt a tug in response, growing stronger as he focused on it, willing it into substance. When he opened his eyes, she stood before him, transparent but visible.

"I want to help you," he said gently. Maybe, he thought, if I can keep Kait's spirit here, I can help this spirit pass over, though how he might accomplish that, he had no idea.

"I will not leave without my son."

"You have proved your love by staying with your son. You have paid your debt. You may rest."

Once more, she fixed him with a gaze half-mad with grief. "Not without my son."

At that, Tris turned back to the well and stared down into its black waters. He shut his eyes, concentrating, and stretched out a hand toward the water. Nothing stirred. Although he could feel himself tiring quickly, he tried once more, and again, felt nothing in response. The third time, he stretched out his hand toward the darkness, he felt a gentle tug in reply, and pulling with all the strength of his will, he gradually sensed another spirit's presence, small and faint. When he opened his eyes, the ghost of a tiny child sat atop the well, and the woman spirit gasped in recognition and rushed forward, clasping him to her breast.

"Lost," the boy cried, clinging to his mother. "Lost in the dark."

Tris felt his throat tighten watching the two shades hold each other tightly. Finally, he raised his hand in farewell. "It is time for you to go."

The woman looked up at him, her eyes peaceful as she clasped her child against her. "I do not know by what power you can do these things, but I thank you," she said with an awkward curtsey. "You must be the chosen of the Lady."

"Would you pass over to Her now?" Tris asked, and the spirit woman nodded.

"We are tired," she said, holding her child tight. "Now that we are together, it is time to rest."

Tris stretched out his hand as his grandmother did over those who were about to die. He struggled to remember what Bava K'aa said at those times, doing the best he could to match the idea, if not the exact words. His head throbbed from the exertion, painful enough to blur his vision.

"Sleep, sister," he said in a voice just above a whisper. "Let the winds carry you to your rest. Let the river guide you and the warm soil welcome you. You are welcome in the arms of the Lady. Let it be so." As he spoke, the image of an old woman stirring a deep cauldron flashed through his mind, and when he opened his eyes, the outline of the mother and child was beginning to blur. The woman held her son against the hollow of her throat, her hand upraised in parting, and the small boy waved a farewell.

"What in the hell is going on?" a rough voice said from behind him. Tris wheeled to find Vahanian standing on the other side of the well, his hands planted on his hips, his face a mixture of anger, disbelief and uncertainty.

Tris swallowed hard and turned toward his bucket. "I came for some water," he said, hoping his voice sounded steady. The implications of what just transpired made his head swim.

"That's not what I meant," Vahanian grated. "You're standing out here in the dark, talking to ghosts. Your friend was telling the truth, wasn't he? You are a mage," he pressed, the last word clearly an indictment.

Tris squared his shoulders and turned toward the mercenary. "I don't know what I am," he snapped. "I'm a prince without a kingdom, a son without a family, a fugitive and a beggar. Why do you care?"

"Like I said, I'm either in on everything, or I walk away," Vahanian replied, his voice icy. "I'm not going to ask again, but I may pound it out of you. What the hell did you do?"

Tris licked his lips nervously. "I'm... not really sure," he admitted. "I've always been able to see ghosts, talk to them, not just on Haunts, but all the time. Even ghosts that nobody else sees." He shrugged. "Just lucky, I guess. But I never saw them outside of the palace. Now, since the... murders," he forced himself to go on, "I see the ghosts outside Shekerishet just as easily as I saw the palace ghosts."

"There hasn't been a Summoner since the sorceress in Margolan died," Vahanian replied, chewing on his lip. "That's been five, maybe six years ago. No one to lay them to rest, nobody but the seers and frauds to pass a message over to the other side, no way for anyone to get their blessing and know for sure it was real." He looked thoughtfully at Tris. "If you're as good as Harrtuck thinks, you really are the deadliest thing in Margolan. I imagine Arontala and that new king would love to get their hands on you."

Before Tris could reply, Vahanian snatched up the bucket. "Tomorrow, we'll talk about not making a target of yourself," the mercenary grated, striding off toward the camp so that Tris had to hurry to follow. "I doubt your uncle will pay me if you're dead."

AT DINNER AROUND their campfire, Vahanian gave his report to the others. "We're in luck. Linton's caravan is coming this way, bound north—right where we want to go."

Soterius bolted down his food and went to check on the horses, making an obvious effort to stay out of Vahanian's way. Tris sat quietly on the other side of the fire, in no hurry to answer more of the mercenary's questions, or think about the implications of what had happened at the well.

Vahanian didn't seem to notice. He looked back down the slope toward the quiet town. It was just after dusk, and the villagers were gathering in their herds, securing their flocks for the night. The glow of cooking fires warmed each of the small houses as whisps of smoke rose from the chimneys and on the still night air, they could smell roasting meat.

"We should have no problem being hired on as extra guards," Vahanian reported. "There's been 'trouble' in the north, although no one would say exactly what. Bandits, for sure, that's part of it." He shook his head, pausing to bite into the rabbit Tris offered him. "But there's something more. Wouldn't be surprised if there was border trouble. There are some pretty wild clans out beyond the northern ridge who have always been hard to keep at bay."

He paused and stared at the fire. Harrtuck looked at him skeptically. "There's more you're not saying," the other soldier prodded. Vahanian shrugged.

"Just a funny feeling about what they did say," Vahanian admitted finally. "People are afraid, and some of the people in the tavern weren't the type who scare easily. I had the feeling there's some dark magic involved, or at least," he added, "people suspect it."

"That's just great," Soterius replied as he returned from the horses. "Bandits you can fight. We're not going to be any protection against magic."

Tris shifted uncomfortably as Vahanian gave him a pointed glance.

"If the tavern information was right," Vahanian continued, "the caravan's heading our way. We can wait for them to catch up to us," he said, "but our rations are running a little thin. Or," he added, "we can ride toward them. We'll backtrack, but once we find them we won't have to forage for provisions." He paused. "We'll just have to watch for guardsmen."

"Since I always vote with my stomach," Carroway said, "I say go looking for them."

Tris grinned at his friend's quick analysis. "It sounds reasonable."

"I'm glad you said that," Vahanian replied as Harrtuck chuckled. "Because riding suits me better than sitting around. We'll leave in the morning."

LATE THAT NIGHT, when the fire burned down to embers, Tris wrapped his cloak closer around himself, ready for his turn on watch. It was unseasonably cold, and frost covered the leaves, chilling him to the bone. Despite the late hour and his aching muscles, Tris was wide awake as he awaited Vahanian's return from walking the camp perimeter. Finally, he came into view and Tris mustered his nerve as he rose to meet the mercenary.

"Goddess take anyone fool enough to be out on a night like this," Vahanian cursed, stomping wet leaves from his boots. His breath fogged in the chill air. "I don't envy you the next turn."

"You look like you were in a fight."

Vahanian shrugged. "There was someone out there. Tackled him once but he got loose, damn his soul." Vahanian shook his head. "Might have just been a bandit, but then again, could be a spy." He looked pointedly at Tris. "Keep your eyes open. He might be back."

"There's something I need to ask you, Jonmarc," Tris said as Vahanian turned back toward the camp.

"How about tomorrow, huh? I doubt I can get warm tonight, but I'd at least like to lie down."

"Teach me to fight."

Vahanian looked up at him, then paused a moment before answering. "Yeah, sure. You're going to have to learn if we're gonna earn our keep with a caravan."

"That's not what I mean. I need your help. Harrtuck says you're the best."

"Does he, now?" Vahanian chuckled. "Don't believe everything you hear." He paused. "Although, in this case, Harrtuck is right."

"Then you'll do it?"

Vahanian laughed harshly. "This isn't some high-priced salle and I'm not your fencing instructor. If I weren't this good, I'd have been dead a long time ago. I learned what I know one fight at a time. I can't teach that, and you can't learn it any other way."

"I want to kill the man who killed my family," Tris said, surprised how flat the words sounded when he actually brought himself to say them.

"And that will bring them back, right? Forget it. Nothing brings them back. Forget it and move on."

"I can't bring them back, but I can stop Jared, make him pay for what he's done."

"All by yourself," Vahanian mocked. "Kill the beast, save the princess, be a real hero."

"That's not what I said."

"I've known a lot of heroes," Vahanian returned. "Buried them myself."

"I'd like a fighting chance. If you're so good, you could give me that."

"I don't give anything," Vahanian replied, turning away. "I'm paid. Well."

"Then I'll pay you. Double."

"Double?"

"Yeah, double. As soon as we get to Dhasson."

"Dhasson's a long way away," Vahanian replied skeptically. "You could be dead by then."

"So could you. Guess we'll both have to take our chances."

Vahanian smiled coldly. "Then you have a teacher. Be ready at dawn. Miss one day and the deal's off."

Tris nodded, feeling his stomach tighten. "Good enough."

"Now let me get some sleep, will you?" Vahanian grumbled, heading toward the bed of pine branches he had fashioned earlier. "I've had enough for one day."

Tris watched him go, then drew a deep breath and headed out on his own patrol. He had the uneasy sensation that things were starting to come together, like being swept up in a swift current. *Oh Kait*, he thought. *I'm sorry I let you down.* He reached out in his mind in the darkness and felt a tingle of her familiar spirit, far away. Kait's spirit blurred, as if something powerful were holding it back. He felt a glimmer of her presence, and sensed her terror. The image was gone as quickly as it came, like a heavy door sealing out the light. Tris opened his eyes, shaking at the contact.

Something imprisoned Kait's spirit, something strong enough to keep her from coming at his summons, evil enough to frighten even the dead. The image of the glowing orb in Arontala's chambers flashed into his mind. The only way to free Kait's spirit would be to find the Soulcatcher and destroy the Obsidian King's soul. And the only way to do that lay in destroying Arontala.

At dawn, Tris nudged Vahanian with his boot.

"Go away," Vahanian grumbled, rolling over.

Tris nudged again, and Vahanian opened one eye and groaned. "It's dawn," Tris said, taking perverse delight in the mercenary's reaction. "Let's go."

With a curse, Vahanian grimaced and sat up. "All right, all right," he muttered. "There's a clearing over there," he said, pointing. "Let's go."

Tris followed him to the clearing, his hand already on his sword. When they reached the open space, Vahanian stopped, and folded his arms across his chest. "Draw your sword," the mercenary said, all traces of sleep gone. "Let me see your stance and grip."

Tris complied, and Vahanian circled him, appraising. "Not bad," the fighter said after a moment. "At least you've had some training."

"I need to know more than what they teach at the salle."

"Well, if you've figured that out, you're smarter by half than most of the aristocrats I've met," Vahanian muttered from behind him.

Tris had only the briefest warning, a rush of a sword slicing through the air. His reaction was more instinct than cunning as he wheeled, deflecting the blade at the last second, barely averting a nasty gash. The intensity of Vahanian's attack made Tris wonder if the mercenary truly meant to harm him, as Tris parried blow after blow. But the determination in Vahanian's eyes told Tris that the lessons had begun.

At the first clash of steel, a cry went up from the camp. Before Tris and Jonmarc had traded half a dozen blows, the others joined them at a run. While Vahanian's advance absorbed Tris's complete attention, out of the corner of his eye, he noted that Soterius's sword was at the ready, suspecting the worst.

"Just an early lesson," Vahanian called to them, and Tris realized as he wheeled to parry that Vahanian was not even out of breath. On the other hand, Tris thought ruefully, it was taking his complete concentration to avoid getting hurt.

Vahanian's sword whistled past Tris's ear. Tris felt his heart pounding as he parried, knocking the blade away. If I live through my first lesson, I might learn something, Tris thought, clearing sweat-soaked hair from his eyes.

Instinct warned Tris to duck. He swung his sword upward to clash his blade against Vahanian's, deflecting but not stopping the point of his weapon. Tris cried out as the blade gashed his arm.

"Enough!" Vahanian shouted, lowering his sword. Breathing hard, Tris lowered his weapon, awaiting a trick. But Vahanian sheathed his sword and approached, frowning in real concern as Tris's hand went to his injured shoulder.

"Let me see," the fighter commanded, and Tris removed his hand, sticky with blood. "Not too bad," Vahanian pronounced, examining the wound. "Wash it out with some of Harrtuck's herb tea and bind it up. It'll be gone in a few days."

"You're good," Tris panted, cursing himself for being out of breath. Vahanian regarded him with amusement.

"Yeah. I've had to be," Vahanian replied, standing back. "Whoever trained you did well on the basics," he added. "But he played by the rules. Rule one out here is that there are no rules."

"I noticed," Tris answered ruefully, his hand covering his injured shoulder once more. Though the wound was not deep and would not impair his ability to fight, Jaquard, the palace armsmaster, would never have intentionally inflicted such an injury. Vahanian's would be a rougher school.

"You got one good defense in, right at the end," Vahanian continued. "Just before you lost your focus. Do it again next time."

CHAPTER EIGHT

THE CARAVAN WAS ahead of the tavern's report, and they caught up with it in less than a day. Tris and the others dismounted and led their horses into the bustle of the fair. Caravans were popular because they brought both entertainment and trade. Far from the cities, the caravans carried gossip about the court and fashion the rural women could discuss if not mimic.

This caravan came up from Trevath in the south. As Tris and the others made their way through the crowd looking for Maynard Linton, Tris wondered at the number of people involved in setting up the fair and moving the goods and animals. He had attended many fairs in Margolan, but always long after they were set up, never amid the bustle of the workers and entertainers behind the scenes.

"Some setup, huh?" Harrtuck elbowed him, guessing his thoughts.

"A different view of things," Tris admitted. "Amazing that everyone knows where to go."

"Comes with practice," Harrtuck shrugged. "I spent a while with a caravan out west a few years back. If there's not much trouble about it's a decent enough living, although the more peaceful it is, the more boring for types like us."

Tris smiled at the swordsman's casual acceptance. As if he knew what Tris was thinking, Harrtuck grinned. "Oh, Vahanian will toughen you up, never fear," Harrtuck assured him with a laugh. "We'll make sure you earn your keep." He paused. "Wait here," he said to Tris and the others. "I'm going to check some things out while Vahanian's making our introductions. Stay out of trouble."

"Do you think we're in danger here?" Carroway whispered.

"Question is," Soterius snorted, "can we possibly be in more danger?"

"Come on," Vahanian called to them from near a large, weathered tent. "And be quick about it. I want you to meet the caravan master." Before Vahanian could reach to draw back the tent flap, angry voices carried on the crisp air.

"Kaine, I've told you before," an older man argued. "We are expected in Dhasson. If I let every rumor steer this caravan, we'd have never left our southern base."

"How can you pay no mind?" an angry voice countered. "Traveler after traveler from the north tells of magicked beasts in Dhasson, yet you lead this caravan like you're going to a summer picnic!"

"Foolish tales don't pay for our food and horses," the first voice returned. "We've survived war, flood and locusts. We cannot run from shadows."

"You'll see these shadows," the second voice argued. "And you'll see what they'll make of your precious caravan if you go to Dhasson!"

Vahanian drew back from the tent flap as angry boot steps neared from inside. A young, red-haired man shouldered his way through them without looking up. Tris and his friends exchanged glances, and watched as the man stomped off angrily into the fray of the caravan.

"You find a little bit of everything, even lunatics, in a caravan," said Vahanian, dismissing the event breezily. "Follow me."

Vahanian entered first, followed by Soterius, then Tris, Carroway and Harrtuck. The inside of the tent was furnished as comfortably as any room at court, Tris noted, although all of the furnishings and decorations were easily transportable. By the look of the rugs on the ground and the tapestries that hung from the tent's sides, this caravan did a profitable business.

"Jonmarc, this is a surprise," greeted a booming voice. A short, round man with a coppery tan rose from behind a portable counting table and bustled over to meet them, grinning broadly. He clasped Vahanian's hand in a firm handshake and slapped the mercenary on the shoulder, although Vahanian stood a head taller.

"Hello, Maynard," Vahanian returned. "How's business?"

"Adequate," the fat trader returned, moving with nervous energy. "The south was good to us. Took in some spices and silks that will trade well north. Been a while since they had a caravan through, so they were hungry for entertainment, too," he added with a grin.

Vahanian chuckled. "I'm sure your people kept them well supplied."

"Nothing but the best," Linton boasted. He turned his attention to Tris and the others. "But you've never been the caravan type, Jonmarc."

"We're looking to sign on, at least until you reach Dhasson."

Linton's eyes narrowed as he appraised the rest of the group, stopped at Tris, then looked back skeptically at the fighter. "I don't suppose you'd tell me why?"

Vahanian shrugged. "Things change. Now it's a good time to head north."

"So you want somewhere to hide?"

Vahanian smiled. "Uh huh."

"Who's looking for you?"

"No one important. Jared of Margolan."

Linton stepped forward, stopping in front of Tris. "These three look too saddle sore to be real hired swords," the caravan master said. Vahanian raised an eyebrow, waiting for the rest of Linton's postulation. "Their hands aren't rough enough to have done much real work."

Beside him, Tris could feel Soterius start to bristle. Carroway looked tense, his gaze flickering around the room. Harrtuck seemed unruffled. Tris began to wonder if Vahanian's idea was a good one. *If we stand out so obviously...*

"Let's just say one goal is to remedy both those problems as quickly as possible," Vahanian said blandly. "Calluses come fast on the road. You'll get your money's worth out of them setting up camp, even if we don't see any bandits."

Linton looked at Vahanian once more, as if weighing the danger against their friendship. Then, with a shrug, the trader broke into a broad smile. "You're welcome to stay as long as you'd like, Jonmarc," Linton offered, heading back to his counting table. "If word from the road is true, a few more hired swords—even marginal ones— may be very welcome."

Vahanian crossed his arms. "What did you hear, Maynard?"

The fat caravan master shrugged. "Wild stories that get bigger with each retelling," he replied. "I've heard that some of the boarder clans may be restless, out on Dhasson's outer fringes. And if that's true," he said, grinning, "then the good people of Dhasson may need some entertainment to ease their minds."

"Is that all they're saying?"

Linton frowned and looked down. "No, it's not," he said finally. "There's talk of dark magic. Monsters. You know the country folk, Jonmarc," Linton said. "They blame magic for a cloudy day."

Vahanian smiled. "Or a poor hand of cards," he agreed. "Me, personally, I blame it for flat ale." He paused and cleared his throat. "Maynard, we couldn't help overhearing your last, um, guest..."

Linton's face darkened, and he turned away. "Kaine. Devil Bitch take him! Signed on a week ago, and it's been the longest week I can remember."

"So get rid of him."

Linton began to pace. "Goddess knows, I would like to. But he's the best rigger we have, and my old rigger fell and broke his back. Might be able to sign on another one in Dhasson, but we won't find one out here," he said with a sweep of his arm, "in the middle of nowhere."

Vahanian frowned. "Pretty convenient timing, wouldn't you say, Maynard?"

The weathered caravan master looked up, and shook his head. "You've always been cautious to a fault, Jonmarc and, the Lady and Childe knows, it's kept you alive. But sometimes, bad luck is just bad luck."

Just then, the tent flap whisked back. "Maynard, are you here?" A dark-haired woman strode into the room, stopping toe to toe with the stocky caravan master.

"What can I do for you, Carina?" Linton asked, unperturbed by the woman's abrupt entrance. She wore healer's robes that hung loosely on her thin frame, and was no taller than the squat caravan master. Short, dark hair framed a pretty face with a determined expression. She had the pale skin of the clans near the

Northern Sea. Her green eyes glinted with fire and intelligence, and the set of her jaw made it clear that she would not be ignored. While it was equally clear that Carina had not noticed their presence, Tris could tell that Vahanian certainly noticed hers.

"Taking on clerics, Maynard?" Vahanian quipped.

"You've got to do something about Kaine," Carina demanded, ignoring Vahanian's comment.

"What now?"

"He's got the riggers in an uproar," Carina continued. "When he isn't filling them full of ghost stories, he's got them convinced that we'll be snowed under on the northern route long before we get to Dhasson. He's even got half of them believing that there are monsters waiting to eat them once we cross the border." She sighed in complete exasperation. "Both my assistants quit this morning, just walked away muttering about monsters. They're not the only ones you'll lose unless you shut Kaine up."

"Maybe I can help," Vahanian interposed, stepping forward.

Carina appraised him coolly. "How?"

Vahanian managed his most charming smile. "I've run into Kaine's type before. I can take him aside, talk some sense into him."

By the expression on Carina's face, the healer had no doubt as to just how that conversation would occur. "No thanks. Whatever bones you break, I just have to fix, and I've got more than

enough work to do already." She turned pointedly back to Linton. "If there's something between
ignoring Kaine and having him mashed to a pulp,
I'd advise you to do it soon."

Linton clucked appeasingly. "I'm sure Jonmarc
had something less unfriendly in mind," he said
with a warning glance at Vahanian, who
shrugged. "I'll talk with Kaine. It's just that he's
the only rigger we have."

Soterius spoke up. "I'm from the mountains,"
he said, conveniently omitting just which mountains. "Everybody up there climbs. I don't know
much about tents, but there's no problem getting
to the top of one."

"You're just full of surprises," Vahanian murmured under his breath to Tris.

"That could be useful," Linton said, brightening. He put an arm around Carina's shoulders as
he walked the healer out. "I promise you," he
said to her, "I'll take care of it." With a look that
said she was not completely convinced, Carina
nodded and went her way. Linton turned back to
Tris and his friends. "Go see the caravan for
yourself," Linton offered. "It may not be the
biggest in the Winter Kingdoms, but you won't
go away disappointed." He paused. "And don't
mind Carina. She's a spitfire, but she's the best
damn healer I've ever had. Lucky to have her.
Just happened to be heading north, like you," he
added.

"Where do we go for a tent and some provisions?" Vahanian asked. "There wasn't time to
pack for the road."

Linton gave him a skeptical look. "That bad, huh? Go see my provisioner. Tell him I sent you to him and he'll see to your needs."

"Thanks, Maynard," Vahanian said as they moved toward the tent flap.

"It'll be thanks enough if you don't get me run out of town this time, Jonmarc."

"I promise," Vahanian replied with a roguish grin.

"Uh huh," Linton muttered skeptically. "We'll see."

They filed out of the tent and into the bright mid-morning sun. The air was crisp. Heading north would bring winter sooner, Tris thought as they joined the bustle of the caravan. Tris could see the traders setting up dozens of brightly tinted booths with gaily-colored flags picturing their wares. The babble of voices carried in the clear air as work teams raised the large tents. Already, the air carried the smell of roasting meat and cooking vegetables, and Tris realized how hungry he was. "We've got a lot to do before there's time for food," Vahanian said.

On one side of the caravan grounds were the animal handlers, with their collection of exotic beasts. There was a great leathery stawar from the southern jungles, swishing its huge tail in boredom. In their cages, two adult maccons padded from side to side, their exquisite coats rippling and their dark eyes disquietingly intelligent. Beasts of every kind populated the cages, along with hundreds of squawking birds with brilliant plumages. Even at this distance, the smell was overpowering.

To the other side were the traders, setting out their wares: spices from Trevath, beautifully wrought jewelry and gems from the mines of Margolan, exquisite fabrics from the east, trinkets and pottery and hundreds of other desirables from the Winter Kingdoms. One merchant snapped out a small Noorish carpet from its packing, draping it on his booth with others in a casual display of wealth. Even the small rugs were far too expensive for any but the lesser nobility, Tris knew, although many such tapestries hung at Shekerishet. That had never seemed remarkable, but now Tris realized just how fabulously expensive even one such carpet must be.

The glint of gemstones came from another booth as a leathery old man bent over his tables. Whether they were real or just clever fakes, Tris did not know, but the stones glittered with fire in the bright sun. The next booth offered the buttery leather of the western plains, tanned and worked by skilled artisans. Boots and sheaths, saddles and packs, or well-worked leather armor all hung from the display. The merchant looked as preserved as his wares, his dark, dry brown skin tight over hawk-like bones. He regarded the four newcomers for a moment, then looked back to his work.

"Not a bad place if you've got money to spend," Harrtuck observed, sticking his hands in his pockets.

"Well, well, there's our 'friend,'" Soterius said, as Tris followed his stare. At a cooking pit not far ahead of them, Carina the healer talked with an old woman who was turning a spitted roast. "You know, Carina's not bad looking, if you don't mind a little temper."

"She's a healer, Ban," Tris replied dryly. "I doubt she's been waiting for you to liven up her life."

Soterius grinned. "You never know. Practicing the healing arts could be a lonely business."

Just then a huge, dark-haired man came from between the tents and sauntered over to the cooking pit. Although he did not touch Carina, his stance and his proximity made it clear that they were a pair. He stood taller than Vahanian and was twice his bulk, with large hands and thick arms. A cloud of wild, dark curls framed his face, shadowing green eyes. He looked as if he could raise one of the largest caravan tents by himself, Tris thought. Carina spoke gently to him, and the giant smiled. There's something odd about those two, Tris decided. Something that doesn't fit here any better than we do. His speculations were interrupted as Vahanian called to them to follow.

The afternoon passed quickly setting up tents and booths. Soterius used his climbing skills to lend a hand with the rigging, while Carroway joined up with the bards and minstrels, and was soon laughing and trading stories with the group. Tris stretched and winced at sore muscles. Lacking Soterius's climbing expertise or Carroway's talespinning talents, he joined Vahanian and Harrtuck in setting up camp. It was a vivid revelation that training to be a prince meant no training at all outside the court, and Tris was chagrined at his lack of skill in the simplest tasks. Harrtuck stuck close to him, whispering instructions and fending off the curious, but Tris intercepted enough questioning glances and condescending instructions from the workmen to have a realistic appreciation of his skills.

The few muscles that were not already sore from the road would be aching in the morning, Tris thought as he and the others lifted, steadied, pulled and pushed to ready the caravan for the night's audiences. The other camp workers asked no questions. Harrtuck took to the activity effortlessly, though Vahanian remained watchful. Tris doubted that the fighter ever looked at ease. When the last ropes were tightened and the final stakes driven, Tris straightened painfully. He wondered just how long it would take to harden to the demands of his new life, and whether he would survive that long.

Harrtuck stopped beside him and grinned. "And you thought supper was free. We'll loosen you up with some sword practice," Harrtuck promised, his grin broadening at the look on Tris's face. "Best way I know to relax after a long day. Not a bad way to meet some of the other hired swords around here, either," he added, glancing around them. "I don't mind the idea of knowing how good the other escorts are before we get into a tricky situation."

"My thought exactly," Vahanian said from behind Tris. Tris turned. The fighter's dark hair was windblown and his sleeves were rolled up for work. Sweat glinted on his brow as he dragged an arm across his forehead. But other than that, Vahanian looked as comfortable as he ever did, Tris thought, relaxing a little. If he felt safe here, it was probably all right, Tris told himself. Soterius joined them.

"Talk is thick with the ropers," Soterius confided under his breath. "No one believes the old rigger's accident was accidental. Watch your back around Kaine. He's as well liked as a trapped skunk." He paused. "And one more thing. He went out of his way to try to talk with me. Maybe he's just nosy. But he tried his best to find out who I was and where I'd been. So, keep your guard up. I'll bet a purse of gold he'll try the same with each of you," Soterius warned.

Vahanian shrugged. "His kind is in every caravan. The less said, the better."

"Do you think he's a spy?" Tris asked.

Harrtuck snorted. "Anything's possible. Best to keep your head up and your eyes open."

When the supper fires were lit and dusk was just an hour away, Vahanian led Tris and the others to an open field not far from the edges of the camp. "Let's start to put a little edge on your swordsmanship," Vahanian said, unsheathing his sword. Soterius stepped forward, meeting the challenge.

"I think you're underestimating what Jaquard taught us," Soterius said, warily advancing.

A faint smile grew at the corners of Vahanian's mouth. "Not really," he said, raising his blade and beginning to circle. He thrust forward and Soterius parried, their swords clashing. Soterius wheeled and swung his blade, going high. There was a crash of steel and a blur as Vahanian dove and tumbled and Soterius's eyes widened as he swung around, looking for his opponent. Vahanian parried and ducked, dropping below Soterius's guard and moved in, then Soterius gasped and dropped his weapon, clutching at his shoulder in surprise. Vahanian stepped back and opened the fist of his free hand to reveal a small dagger.

"Your armsmaster taught you the rules," Vahanian said evenly as Soterius examined his shoulder and found only a scratch, although the cloth of his shirt was cut. "Out here, there aren't any rules. And the sooner you learn that, the longer you'll live."

"You drew blood!" Soterius said in amazement.

Harrtuck made a disparaging noise. "He could've had your heart, boy! Takes skill to score so lightly. Jonmarc's right. Alley skills, not tournament rules, are what keep you alive out here."

"Up to the challenge?" Vahanian said to Tris with a grin. Tris smiled warily in return and took up a fighting stance. He held few illusions about how the bout would turn out, but he set his jaw and sprang forward with a cry, taking the offensive. He saw a glimmer of surprise in Vahanian's eyes. Vahanian met Tris's blade in mid-swing, deflecting it. Tris thrust forward and Vahanian sidestepped, bringing his own blade around so quickly that Tris relied more on instinct and peripheral vision than sight to parry the blow. The blades clattered and slid along each other for an instant, and then Tris freed his weapon and pressed forward.

He sensed more than saw Vahanian drop and roll and wheeled to counter. Although the tip of his sword snagged on Vahanian's sleeve, Tris felt a rush of air behind his right leg and then saw Vahanian spring to his feet, grinning widely, sword lowered.

"Nice job, Tris!" Soterius cheered.

Harrtuck guffawed. Tris lowered his sword and looked at Vahanian, not attempting to hide his chagrin. "I think you'd have hamstrung me if you'd made that blade connect, wouldn't you?" Tris asked.

Vahanian jabbed the point of his sword into the soft ground and rested both hands on the pommel. He wasn't even breathing hard, Tris noted sourly. "Right you are," the mercenary replied. "And it's a good move if you're fast enough, because you're assured they won't be coming after you."

"That's cheating," Soterius replied with a knowing grin.

Vahanian shrugged. "When would you rather learn moves like these, now—or when some son of a whore clips you in a fight?"

Soterius raised a hand in appeasement. "No contest from me on that one, Jonmarc," he conceded. "I've spent enough time around the barracks to be a little dubious about chivalry and honor."

Vahanian raised an eyebrow. "Chivalry, yes. Honor is another thing entirely."

"That's not a beginner's move," a rough voice said. They looked up to see the burly giant who had been with Carina.

"I'm not a beginner," Vahanian replied neutrally. Tris noted that the fighter neither raised nor sheathed his sword, and he guessed that the mercenary sensed no threat.

"Obviously," the large man answered. His unruly dark hair sat like a storm cloud around his face, and his skin was bronzed from a season out of doors. He was dressed in a simple tunic and pants, but the sword belt that hung from his ample waist was finely worked, and if the blade in the scabbard lived up to its pommel, it was well crafted, a working piece and not for show.

There's more here than meets the eye, Tris thought.

"I'm Cam," the dark-haired fighter introduced himself, directing his comments to Vahanian but taking in the rest of them with a sweep of his glance. "I watched you practice. I'd like to join you if I could, for a few rounds."

"Sure," Vahanian agreed amiably. Maybe with luck, Tris thought, the big man would be a good source of information. At the least they should be able to learn something more about the other guards who attached themselves to the caravan.

Cam was surprisingly agile for his size, Tris found after a round with the giant, and good with his sword, too. Although seeing the blade in action gave little opportunity to appreciate the artistry of its forging, Tris thought he glimpsed runes etched in the side of the blade, and a complex and foreign inscription on the guard. An unusual weapon for a hired fighter. He watched from a distance as Cam sparred with Harrtuck. Either the weapon was stolen or, like themselves, there was a story unwilling to be told.

The smells of dinner reached them on the crisp night air as Tris and Vahanian ended another round. Tris dragged a sleeve across his face and wiped back his hair from his forehead. More than a candlemark of hard practice worked up a sweat, even in the cool fall air. He was just about to suggest that they head for dinner when a man ran up from the camp.

"Cam! Come quickly!" the runner shouted while he was still a distance away. "You're needed!"

Without a word the giant sheathed his sword and with a nod toward the group, started out at a run for the camp.

"That's it for tonight, anyhow," Vahanian said, putting up his own weapon. "Let's see what all the excitement is about."

It was not hard to keep Cam in view, even when following at a more leisurely pace. The burly fighter stood a head taller than many in the camp, and was twice the bulk of all but a few. Cam slowed to a jog as he reached the more crowded section of the caravan's midway, then took off again at a run as the messenger pointed to the left.

Sure enough, there was trouble, Tris noted. But not the sort for which he imagined Cam would be summoned. He had expected a brawl or a thief. One of the large tents where the caravan performers held shows in the evening collapsed. A crowd of caravaners gathered, and Tris and the others worked their way toward the front.

"What happened?" Tris asked one of the men who was nearest the front.

"Damn pole snapped clean in two," the man replied. "Kraveck was setting the last of the rigging when it went down, and so did he."

Carina knelt beside the fallen rigger. As Cam approached, she stretched out her hand to the big man, who took it, paused for a moment as they spoke in low tones, and then settled into place on the other side of the man. Cam raised his massive hand for quiet, and the crowd hushed immediately, stepping back a few paces.

Carina reached out once more for Cam with her left hand, and placed her right hand gently on Kraveck. She shut her eyes and let her hand begin to slide gently down the length of his body, slowly, hovering just above his skin. As Tris watched, her face twitched with pain, and her eyes pinched shut with the suffering she shared.

When she had followed the full course of his form once, she shifted toward his head, and gently laid her hand on his forehead, retaining her contact with Cam with her other hand. Cam looked as if he were in a trance, his eyes shut and his face slack, completely open to Carina's working.

She's drawing strength from him for her healing, Tris realised. Kraveck must be in bad shape.

Carina's hand remained over Kraveck's forehead for a quarter of a candlemark. Then, slowly, she began to move once more, slowing this time over his chest. Her face contorted and it seemed to Tris that Kraveck breathed more easily.

Just below Kraveck's ribcage, Carina stopped. She swallowed hard and leaned forward, and it seemed to Tris that the thin healer was willing every ounce of her strength into her effort. For nearly half a candlemark, she labored, her lips moving in concentration, her body tight with effort. Then suddenly she slumped and would have collapsed but for Cam's quick reflexes, as he caught Carina and tenderly lifted her into his arms. She raised her head and lifted one hand, giving direction that only Cam could hear.

"You there," Cam hailed one of the riggers standing near. "She's done all she can for him, and she wants to get him to the building where he'll be easier to watch. She says to slip a board under his back so you don't undo what she's done, and take him there directly. She'll be there as soon as she's rested."

Two of the riggers sprang to do as Cam ordered, and Tris noticed that the big man looked drained and tired himself. Cam waited, Carina cradled in his arms, until the riggers did as he asked. Satisfied that Carina's wishes were carried out, Cam turned toward the healer's tent, followed by the crowd as if he were a prophet.

"I've seen healers before," Vahanian said. "But not like her. Curious why a healer with that kind of talent is here, wouldn't you say?"

"Maybe they were dismissed from a noble house."

Vahanian shook his head, still staring after them. "I doubt it. That kind of talent is too rare."

"Easy on the eyes, too, if you ask me," Soterius offered from behind them.

Vahanian shrugged. "Friends and lovers are just hostages to fate, waiting to be taken," he replied. "When you're out on the road long enough, you learn that," he said, and turned away, walking back toward the fallen tent where workers were already swarming to ready the area for the night's crowds.

"Leave it to our friend to have a sour comment on everything," Soterius said darkly, watching Vahanian leave. "I've never spent much time with a mercenary before. Guess I haven't missed much, if they're all like him."

"Only the ones who stay alive very long, m'boy," Harrtuck commented, joining them from behind. "When you've survived as many tight spots as Jonmarc has, you'll have rough edges of your own, I wager."

"We can't reach Dhasson soon enough for me," Soterius returned.

THAT NIGHT, THE dreams came. Tris heard Kait calling his name so plainly that he expected to see her standing in his tent. She called again, more distant now, so plaintively that it made his heart ache.

"Kait, are you here?" he asked quietly, unsure whether he was awake or asleep.

"Help me, Tris," Kait's voice called, muffled and far away. Tris concentrated, allowing himself to fall into a light trance. Kait's spirit remained distant.

"Kait, where are you?" he called after her. She gave no sign of hearing him. Her voice grew more desperate, her pleas more anguished, but try as he might, Tris could neither bring her spirit to him, nor let his spirit be drawn to hers. It was as if a thick window separated them, on the edge of a gulf, so that he could see her, but nothing he could do could break the transparent prison, or bridge the gap.

"Help me, Tris. Help me."

Tris woke shaking, covered in sweat. His heart raced and as he lifted a hand to wipe a sodden lock of hair from his eyes, he saw that his fingers shook. *I'm going mad,* he thought. He forced himself to breathe deeply, willing the shaking to stop, and attempted the centering exercises his grandmother had taught him. He failed miserably.

Tris covered his face with his hands, as close to weeping as he had been since the night of the murders. I'm coming for you, Kait, he vowed. Living or dead, I'm coming for you. I'll get you out, I swear!

"Are you all right?" a voice sounded outside the tent. Soterius popped his head through the flap.

"Just a bad dream," Tris said, hoping his voice sounded stronger than he felt.

"I guess you're entitled to a few of those," Soterius allowed. "Me, I just keep dreaming about all those pretty wenches back home. Stood one up, you know, the night we left."

Tris looked up, barely able to make out his friend's face in the moonlight. "I'm sorry," he said quietly. "I've ruined everything for all of you."

Soterius managed a tired grin. "It's a little late for second thoughts," he quipped. "And you didn't ask us to come, we came on our own." He shrugged. "I didn't leave anyone special behind, just a string of broken hearts." He grinned. "Harrtuck never said anything about a family. I think the barracks was home to him. Carroway had his eye on that pretty flute player, but I don't think she knew it," he added, "so don't lose sleep on our account. I look at it as a chance to see the world."

Tris stretched an aching muscle in his back. "Move the world, you mean," he said. "I'm so sore from setting up tents I probably couldn't sleep anyway."

"I know what you mean," Soterius replied. "And what doesn't hurt from rigging tents hurts from Vahanian's damn training. I wasn't this sore when I first joined the guards!" He paused. "Are you going to be all right?"

"I'll be fine." By the doubt on Soterius's face, Tris knew the other took the lie for what it was worth, but with a nod, Soterius left. Tris ducked his head out of the tent flap and stared at the full moon. Kait's voice, more distant now, still called to him. He would not sleep again tonight, he knew, staring at the moon. Not now; maybe not ever again.

CHAPTER NINE

THE SOUND OF arguing reached Tris as he arrived to take over Vahanian's watch. Sure enough, as Tris rounded the corner, he spotted Vahanian and Carina locked in a pitched argument that seemed to stop just short of a toe-to-toe confrontation.

"He was one of my patients!" Carina defended hotly.

"He wasn't too sick to loot the other poor bastards' pockets," Vahanian retorted. "Look, lady, when I'm on watch, I watch. And when I see something, I take care of it."

"That doesn't include dragging a man out of his sick bed and hauling him over to Linton!" she snapped. "He had a fever."

"He felt pretty cool when I grabbed him," Vahanian replied. "Bit of wormroot under the tongue can give you hot flashes. So can a little dryfleck in a glass of wine. Ask Linton. He spent time in Noor. He knows all about drugs... and poisons. Takes a little widow's heart each day, mixed with brandy, to make him harder to poison. Builds resistance."

"That doesn't change anything," Carina argued stubbornly. "You hauled a sick man out of my hospital, dragged him across camp, and accused him of stealing. When something concerns one of my patients, I want to know about it, before you toss him out on his ear on the road and send him packing."

Vahanian swore and rolled his eyes skyward. "I caught him wrist-deep in one of your other patient's pockets. All due respect, priestess, but why don't you do your job and let me do mine?"

"I'd be happy to," she grated, red-faced, "if doing your job didn't make more injured patients for me to fix." She threw her hands in the air in resignation just as Tris came within a few steps of the pair. "I don't know why I'm bothering. You won't listen. And I'm not a priestess," she added. Shaking her head, she turned back toward the makeshift building that served as her healer's shelter.

"Don't disillusion me," Vahanian called after her. "You're so sure you're right, I figured you heard it from the Lady herself."

In reply, a crockery mug flew from the shelter's door, sailing close enough to Vahanian's head to make the mercenary duck.

"You have a real way with women," Tris observed dryly.

Vahanian chuckled. "I don't think Carina likes any man who isn't on a stretcher."

"You really caught a thief?"

Vahanian shrugged. "Yeah. That's not what worries me. I think it might have been the prowler I tackled snooping around our camp on the way here. He had an old bruise exactly where I thumped that guy on the jaw. Can't say for certain."

"Why would the same prowler be here?"

"Good question. All I can come up with are ugly answers. Maybe he's found what he's looking for, and he's keeping an eye on it," he said with a pointed look at Tris. "Or maybe he's not interested in you at all. Maybe he's scouting the caravan and other travelers for bandits. He might have just gone looking for an easy purse to cut when he found us."

Tris was quiet for a few moments. "I'll be extra careful," he said finally. "You look tired. Go get some sleep."

Vahanian cracked a smile. "First some ale and chow, then some sleep. But you've got the right idea," he said veering off toward the cook tent.

Despite Vahanian's foreboding, Tris's watch passed uneventfully, and he was happy to pass the shift to Harrtuck as evening fell.

"Heard Vahanian had another run-in with the healer," Harrtuck observed.

Tris shrugged. "I'm not sure it upset him as much as it did Carina," Tris shrugged. "I rather thought he was enjoying the whole thing."

Harrtuck chuckled. "That's Vahanian. He can be a real pain in the ass when he feels like it." He lifted his face to the wind and fell silent for a moment.

"What's wrong?" Tris asked.

Harrtuck shook his head, frowning. "Can't say. Just a feeling. Something's not quite the way it should be. Eyes on us, watching." He shrugged. "I think I'll make an extra pass along the perimeter tonight." He paused. "In fact, why don't you send Soterius out here? Might be nothing, but I'd welcome an extra sword tonight."

Tris nodded. "Sure. I'll get him." What he didn't add was confirmation of the same groundless foreboding. He had dismissed it as nerves before Harrtuck's observation, but now he was not so easily persuaded. Still, he thought, looking around at the fires that glowed against the cold autumn sky, there was nothing of concern… yet. But he did not expect to turn in early tonight—just in case.

THE SOUND OF hoofbeats thundered from the forest just as the supper fires burned low. Breaking from the woods at a headlong pace rode more than two dozen tattered riders, screeching a bloodcurdling battle keen, their battered weapons raised. The camp erupted in confusion, as men and women fled the attackers or ran for their weapons. Caught unprepared, the caravan cook hoisted what remained in his kettle of soup and with an oath, let fly the steaming liquid, scalding the nearest rider who flailed madly and dropped from his bucking mount.

"Bandits!" Vahanian shouted, drawing his sword. From out of the night came a hail of flaming arrows, and around them, the caravan tents and wagons burst into flames as the wagoners ran cursing to extinguish the fires.

Men on horseback ringed the camp. From their motley armor and the haphazard tack of their horses, Tris guessed that their attackers came together by chance more than design. No doubt more ranged in the forest, responsible for the hail of arrows. As the bandits charged, Tris ran for a place on the line, sword drawn and ready.

An arrow grazed his shoulder. Some of the caravaners charged forward with a cry, while others began to pull the wagons together for defense or ran to protect the horses. Just at the edge of his sight, Tris glimpsed a fleeting spirit, and a moment later, another and a third.

Sweet Chenne, I can see them dying! he thought, fighting down panic. As his gift had strengthened in the weeks since they fled the palace, sighting the spirits came easier and easier, until now it was almost impossible for him to block out the hum of the revenants that invisibly surrounded the living. But even that, outside the heat of battle, was far different from sensing spirits fresh-torn from their bodies, feeling the sundering of soul and body.

One of the bandits was riding right for Tris, his foam-flecked horse wild with battle. Struggling to keep his wits about him, Tris ducked under the rider's swing and parried as the horse nearly rode him down. The attacker wheeled and charged again. This time, Tris stood his ground, dropping low and scything his sword along the grass to catch the rider's mount.

The screaming horse flailed to the ground, throwing its rider clear. With a sword's stroke, Tris dispatched the hapless beast, then closed on his rider as the bandit climbed to his feet, eyes dark with rage. With a cry and upraised sword, he ran at Tris. The prince lunged, slipping inside the man's guard and sinking his weapon deep into the man's chest. The bandit gasped and fell to his knees, clutching his chest. His eyes widened as he cursed in surprise and then, blood flowing from between his fingers, fell over dead.

Tris felt a sudden, disorienting lurch as if he had been slammed hard from behind. He shook his head to clear it, and stared at the dying bandit. As he watched, the man's form shifted, and two identical bodies lay one on top the other. The second form grew more and more transparent, then rose, barely visible, and fixed Tris with a sad and knowing gaze before fading into the air completely. Before Tris could shake the image from his mind, he heard the rush of hoofbeats behind him and a sharp, heavy thump on the side of his head sent him reeling, then turned the world to black.

When he came around, the situation did not look good. The bandits fought like men possessed. Vahanian waded grimly into the battle, cursing as he swung his sword. Being on horseback gave the bandits an edge they did not deserve, and made the raid doubly costly for the caravaners. Watching Vahanian and Harrtuck, Tris knew their first priority was to take down as many of the bandits' mounts as possible. As Tris staggered to his feet, his head pounding, steel clashed and axes swung as the caravaners held their ground. The clamor of the spirits around him threatened to crowd all reason from Tris's mind, and he murmured a warding spell Bava K'aa had taught him. It did not silence the spirits, but it pushed them just far enough from his thoughts to make action possible.

Tris could see that Vahanian's opponent was fixed on reaching the centre of the battle, and worse, the bandit was damnably skilled with his weapon. Flames rose at the centre of the battle, diverting at least half of the caravaners from defense as they ran to save the tents and wagons. A glance told Tris that the bandits chose their targets well, setting ablaze the tents and wagons least likely to contain booty. He reclaimed his fallen sword and headed toward the action.

To his right, Tris could see the old grannywitch swinging an axe with two-handed determination. Wild-eyed, with her gnarled hands white-knuckled on the axe's handle, her lips moved in arcane verse as she kept her opponent at bay. Suddenly, the bandit dropped his sword as if stung, and the pommel of the weapon glowed red hot. The bent old crone seized the opening her spell made to swing her axe without remorse.

Tris headed for the battle at a run, resolutely ignoring his pounding head and the revenants rising from the newly dead on the battlefield. Carroway joined him halfway across the open area, appearing from the smoke that shrouded the burning camp. "Look there!" Tris said, pointing.

The shell of the house Carina had converted into a makeshift hospital attracted the attention of one of the brigands, who was single-mindedly attempting to enter. Carina, armed only with a long stave, barred the door. Out of the corner of his eye, Tris saw Vahanian dispatch his opponent and head for the healer's shelter at a dead run.

"Maybe I can help," Carroway muttered, digging into the pouches at his belt for one of the pellets he used in his storytelling. A flare of green light startled the bandit, giving Vahanian an opening. As Vahanian cut down the bandit, Tris looked up to see another streak of green light rise in a flare from the minstrel's hand.

"Parlor tricks," Carroway said with a wicked grin. His right hand twitched and a blade flew, dispatching one of the bandits as it stuck neatly between his shoulder blades. The bard's tunic was soot streaked and bloodstained. Carroway ran over to the fallen bandit and matter-of-factly retrieved his blade. Tris staggered, feeling the sundered spirits wrench free of their dying flesh. *Lady save me, there are so many!* he thought, struggling to renew the warding that offered some protection for his sanity.

Carina was still engaged grimly in protecting the patients in her sickroom as another bandit charged. The bandit slashed at her and Carina parried his blows with the stave, but it was obvious that she was tiring.

"You don't get in without the price of admission," Vahanian called to the bandit from behind and the brigand turned.

"And what might that be?" the bandit sneered, his blade raised.

"You've got to need a healer," Vahanian returned, swinging his blade hard. He cut through the bandit's parry as Carina swung her stave, full force, at the bandit's knees. Cleaved shoulder to hip by Vahanian's blade, the brigand fell to the ground just as Tris and Carroway arrived, swords raised. Tris stumbled at the jarring impact he felt in his mage senses, caused by the bandit's swift death, and he clung to the warding with all of his waning might.

"That was a fair defense you put up," Vahanian said to Carina. Carina was breathing hard and her tunic clung sweat-soaked to her form. Her short, dark hair hung in her eyes and as she pushed it back, her hand trembled. "Are you all right?"

"I'll be fine," she assured him, although her words sounded more certain than her tone. Footsteps from behind gave him no time to argue, and as Vahanian turned to meet his next opponent, Carina retrieved her stave and withdrew into the shadows of the ruined building. Tris took up a guard post outside.

A crash like thunder sounded behind Tris. One of the main caravan tent posts snapped and fell across the roof to the makeshift hospital, dragging the burning tent with it. He wheeled in time to see the blazing tent set the roof of the healer's shack afire.

"The roof's on fire!" Tris shouted above the fray.

Vahanian and Soterius were close enough to hear. "Leave the bandits, come with me," Vahanian shouted to Soterius as Tris covered his face with his tunic and ducked inside.

The sagging canvas of the ruined tent crackled with flames. Fire spread quickly to the dilapidated thatch of the building's roof, and smoke billowed from its doorway. As Tris fought his way through the smoke, Carina was already dragging one man from the burning building, though it took all her might to move his heavy body. Although the smoke made his aching head even worse, Tris helped Carina drag the man to safety.

Vahanian and Soterius pounded up as Tris and Carina reached the open air, and Vahanian caught Carina's shoulders as she turned back toward the burning building.

"Stay out here," he shouted. "We'll get the rest."

"My patients, my risk," Carina snapped back, shaking free. "There are still more in there." Before any of them could stop her, Carina shouldered past and headed at a dead run back for the smoking building. Soterius charged through the doorway, only to retreat gasping for breath. Ripping the cloak from the injured man, Vahanian plunged the cloth into a nearby bucket and ran with the soaked rags to the doorway.

"Here, use this," Vahanian said, as he the tore the sopping cloth in broad strips. Tris and Soterius snatched them from his hands.

"We're only going to get one chance," Soterius said, muffled through the rag.

"Let's go," Tris agreed, pressing the soaking cloth against his face.

The three men charged into the smoke together then dropped to their knees, nearly blinded. Soterius crawled toward the back corner, where the outline of a patient was barely visible. Not far inside the opening, Vahanian's hand connected with a pant leg. Tris saw Vahanian feel for the man's shoulders and heft the injured man onto his back. Gasping for breath, his eyes stinging with the smoke, Vahanian crawled as fast as he could, trying to balance the helpless man. Heaving his burden just beyond the doorway, Vahanian turned back into the smoke as Tris crawled on, and in the near darkness, he could see Carina struggling with her patient. A crack like thunder sounded overhead, and Tris turned in horror.

"Carina!" Vahanian shouted, diving toward the healer as the beam above Carina's head gave way in a shower of sparks. Tris saw the beam begin to break, felt Carina's shock and terror, and reacted as power and fear filled him.

"No!" The rasped command tore from his throat as Tris struggled to his knees, one hand outstretched toward the beam. Tris felt his power rise, felt it strike from his hand to throw the beam aside.

"Run!" Vahanian panted as he pushed Carina toward the doorway, dragging the last patient toward the door. Tris started toward them and fell forward, gasping for breath in the searing heat. Just as Tris felt the world around him begin to darken, strong hands gripped his shoulders and half carried, half-dragged him, pulling him out onto the grass. Behind him, the building's timbers groaned like a dying man, and then collapsed with a burst of flame and sparks.

Someone pitched a bucket of water onto him. Slowly, Tris roused, his lungs aching, hacking and gasping. He was dimly aware of the burns on his arms and calves. He struggled to see, blinded by the ash and smoke.

The hospital building lay in ruins, burning fast. Along the perimeter of the camp, the screams of horses and the clash of blades rang in the night air. But the fight was further away, no longer in the heart of the camp, and as Tris gasped for breath, he saw Vahanian nod.

"They've pushed the bandits back. Good thing. I can't breathe, let alone fight," Vahanian rasped.

At Tris's elbow, the old grannywitch emerged from the smoke bearing a rough-hewn cup. "Drink this," she said, pressing a mug into his hands. Tris drank it gratefully, feeling the liquid burn down his raw throat. Whatever the potion was, it began to work immediately, clearing his head and fortifying him enough to stand.

Carina dragged herself to her knees and bent over one of the patients they had pulled from the burning building. She hammered on his chest with all her strength. "By the Lady, breathe, damn it, breathe!" she sobbed.

Vahanian made his way over to where she knelt. "Carina—"

"He was breathing fine just before the fire," Carina argued with no one in particular. Her soot-covered robes were scorched and her arms were dotted with burns from falling embers. Tears streaked through the ashes on her face, and her hair fell limply into her eyes as she bent across her charge. "Breathe, dammit!"

Vahanian reached down to take her by the shoulders, but she struggled free. "No!" she cried, reaching toward her patient. "I have to help him."

"He's gone," Vahanian said gently. "Look at him. It's too late."

Carina sat back on her haunches and buried her face in her hands. "It's not your fault," Vahanian said quietly. "Look at where his wound was, right through his ribs. Would have been hard for him to breathe anyway, even with healing, but then the smoke..."

She lifted her head enough to glare at him. "You don't understand what it is to lose a patient."

"No," he conceded quietly. "Just soldiers under my command."

"You must have the eye of the Lady on you, to have made it out alive," the grannywitch observed, taking the cup from Tris. She filled it once more and offered it to Soterius, who accepted it gratefully. Tris could see the burns that peppered Soterius's arms and face, and imagined he was in no better shape himself.

"Thanks for dragging me out of there," Tris said.

Soterius looked at him for a moment without saying anything, and Tris knew his friend saw him use magic to hurl aside the beam. "Glad to do it," Soterius said, and while his tone was sincere, he looked away. He doesn't know what to think of me any more, Tris thought, still feeling the witch's potion burning in his throat. He never bargained to be liegeman to a mage.

The old crone took back the cup and offered it to Vahanian, who waved it away, gesturing for her to attend to Carina. The crone knelt beside Carina and took her in her arms, letting the healer sob against her shoulder like a brokenhearted child.

Vahanian was looking at Tris. Ashen and shaking, Tris met his eyes. They both knew the beam had changed its course at Tris's command. He hates magic even more than Soterius does, Tris thought at the look in Vahanian's eyes. His outlaw prince is an untrained mageling. One more thing to worry about.

"If you'd have taken my advice, none of this would have happened," a voice cut caustically through the smoke. Tris looked up to see Kaine dogging Maynard Linton as the caravan master picked his way through the ruins.

"Where's the healer?" Kaine demanded, stopping where they rested. "I've been wounded."

"The lady's busy. Go away," Vahanian said, interposing himself between Kaine and Carina.

Kaine moved to shoulder past him. "She's a healer, let her heal," Kaine snapped. This time, Vahanian's blade blocked Kaine's path.

"I said, the lady's busy," Vahanian rasped. He looked as if he were beginning to feel the day's battle in every aching muscle and was considering taking it out on Kaine. "Go away."

"You're a fine protector, Jonmarc Vahanian," Kaine shot back. "Like as not 'twas bandit friends of yours what did this," Kaine sneered, but he backed up a step from the glinting blade. "I told Linton that taking you on would mean trouble. None of this would have happened if we hadn't taken on your thieving hide."

Vahanian took a step toward Kaine, his blade raised higher. "I still have the strength to run you through, Kaine, and I'll do it if you're here by the time I count to five. One…"

"See what I mean?" Kaine whined, taking another step back. "Cut me down in cold blood, he would—"

"Two…" Vahanian growled, advancing.

"I've no desire to be run through, Vahanian," Kaine retorted, licking the blood from his split lip. "But mark my words," he said, looking to Tris and the others, "we won't be rid of bad luck until we're rid of him."

"Three…"

With an uncertain glance at the mercenary and his sword, Kaine raised his hands in surrender and backed away, disappearing in the throng as the caravaners returned to their ruined camp.

"I wouldn't have minded seeing that troublemaker run through," Soterius remarked darkly as Vahanian sheathed his sword.

"Not worth the effort," Vahanian replied. Tris glanced back at Carina, who still sobbed in the crone's arms.

"I'll see to her," the old grannywitch said, patting Carina's back. "Be about your business."

Vahanian walked a few paces and stopped. Tris caught up to him and looked down at the dead bandit at Vahanian's feet. Vahanian looked from the dead man to Carina and back again. "That's the same thief I ran out of camp yesterday, the one I thought was our prowler," Vahanian said tonelessly. "Looks like we got him." He swore. "I hate being right some times." Vahanian started to turn away, only to see Carina watching them. The look of loss and regret in her eyes silenced any comment he might have made. "Come on," he said tiredly to the others. "It's clean-up time."

By SUNSET, THE ruined camp was quiet. Groggy with fatigue and still feeling the effects of the smoke, Tris kicked at a charred scrap of wood as he headed up the slope toward the caravan from the worker's tents. His head itched below the bandage that covered his scalp wound, and the wound itself throbbed. Soterius and the others piled the bandits' bodies to burn. The smell of burning flesh made Tris want to retch.

The caravan lay in complete disarray. Charred heaps were all that remained of many wagons. In the center of the clearing, the main tent smoldered, its remaining posts like burned bones thrusting up from the ground. Maynard Linton was wandering among the ruins, shaking his head.

"They cost us most of a season's profit," Linton said sadly, his jowled face the picture of misery. "Whole wagons gone. I don't know how many dead or injured. All this and winter coming on." He shook his head once more. "Not good," he said, worried. "Not good."

Tris spotted Carroway, weighed down by two buckets of water. His tunic was torn, one sleeve ripped shoulder to wrist. Soot-streaked and splashed with blood, the bard smiled tiredly as he spotted Tris. "Good to see you in one piece," Carroway hailed him, stopping. "Why don't you come with me? Carina needs all the help she can get over at the tent."

Tris accepted one of the buckets and headed toward the largest remaining tent. Burns in its roof opened it to the sun. Tris ducked under the sagging tent flap. The tent was a sick ward, with the injured laid out in neat rows on blankets. Of the nearly one hundred caravanners, it appeared that nearly half awaited Carina's ministrations.

Night fell. Tris and Carroway brought in torches to light the healer's work. The old hearth witch, Alyzza, worked alongside Carina, making poultices and mixing healing teas. Both Cam and the old lady kept a protective eye on Carina, forcing the healer to rest, eat and drink. As Tris watched Carina, he realized that she and Cam shared an uncanny resemblance. Brother and sister, perhaps, he thought, not lovers?

By the time the night was well spent, Tris decided that an impromptu healer's lot was nearly as exhausting as a fighter's. Carroway stepped assuredly into the chaos, carrying the wounded, directing others who brought their comrades for healing, splitting wood for splints and crutches and ripping large pieces of cloth into bandages. In the center of the tent, a fire gave Carina the boiling water she required for potions and poultices. Tris followed Carroway's lead, trying not to focus on his own throbbing head, or, in the moments when his head did not ache, on the questions that his battlefield vision raised.

As the first light of dawn streaked above the hills, Carina reached the last of her patients. Her face was drawn with exhaustion and dark circles rimmed her eyes. Tris surmised she was moving on sheer willpower, and his opinion of the healer doubled. Gently, Carina placed a hand over her patient's wound and closed her eyes, leaning against Cam for support. In a few moments, the patient smiled in astonishment as Carina lifted her hand to reveal a wound that was well on its way to healing, normally the work of several weeks. As the man expressed his gratitude, the healer sagged against Cam, utterly exhausted.

A few stragglers pressed forward with minor injuries. "Come back tomorrow," Cam barked, folding Carina in his arms protectively. "She's done everything she can tonight." With a whispered word to Carina and an answering nod, the fighter lifted the healer like a child and with a grim expression that dared anyone to attempt to stop him, strode from the tent.

Maynard Linton followed Cam and laid a hand on his shoulder. "Will she be all right?" Cam nodded, gently rocking the healer in his arms like a tired child. "Almost good as new. Can't say the same for all of them," he said with a jerk of his head toward the tent.

Linton stretched out a hand and gently brushed back the dark hair from the healer's eyes. "Thank her for me when she wakes up, please," he said quietly.

Cam nodded. "That I will," he promised, then shouldered his way through the crowd to the tent opening and disappeared.

Harrtuck and Soterius found Tris and Carroway a few moments later. Soterius offered them both trenchers laden with food. "Here. Eat. No matter how interesting it's been, it doesn't justify missing a meal," Soterius said. For a moment, they were silent as they wolfed down the food.

"Linton always hires on the best cooks he can afford," Harrtuck said, his words slurred by a full mouth. "Looks like it might be the only good thing about this trip," he said, cleaning up the last of his food with a thick slice of bread.

"He must be doing very well to have a first-class healer travel with them," Tris mused. He looked around. "Where's Vahanian?"

Harrtuck shrugged. "Last I saw he was helping burn the bodies. Wouldn't be surprised to find him drinking with Linton in his tent when this is all over."

Tris looked down the caravan midway toward the far end of the fields, where a pyre burned. The dangers of the road were becoming painfully clear. It would take more than a little luck for them to reach Dhasson alive.

Alone in his tent, exhausted and sore, Tris was too tired to sleep. He watched the flickering candle flame. The visions that came over him on the battlefield were disquieting and clear. By the Lady, he thought, if I can't do better than that, I'm no use to anyone. I won't live to get to Dhasson, let alone take back Margolan if I see every ghost on the battlefield! His stomach churned as he thought about his failure. He froze, making himself an easy target. Worse, he was barely useful defending the camp. His mage power seemed more dangerous than defensive.

"Don't be so hard on yourself, Tris," came a voice, and Tris startled, looking around the small tent. Flickering and barely visible, was the image of Bava K'aa. "My time is short," she warned. "I failed to prepare you for the time the power would come upon you. I should have expected... circumstances like these... might have triggered the power. Forgive me."

Tris held out his hand to the apparition, who glided closer and reached out for him. Tris felt a tingle as her insubstantial hand brushed past his outstretched fingers, and he closed his eyes, squeezing back tears. He felt the tingle through his whole body, and the overwhelming sense of his grandmother's presence, as if, for an instant, she shared his mind. He opened his eyes and stared questioningly at the ghost, who smiled sadly.

"I cannot stay," the spirit said regretfully. "Even now, dark power searches for you. Listen well, Tris. You have the power to become a great Summoner, more powerful even than I. But you must learn control." She hesitated, and the image flickered and dimmed. "Already, Jared seeks a way to banish my spirit forever; else, I would train you myself. Go to the Library at Westmarch. There, you will find a teacher for your training."

"But the Library at Westmarch was destroyed in the Mage Wars," he protested. "It doesn't exist anymore."

"So we permitted people to believe," Bava K'aa said with a knowing smile. "For those whom the Sisterhood vouchsafes, the Library will yield its secrets."

"Show me how to control what I see," Tris begged, his fears rising in his throat. "I'm no use to my friends if I can't protect them."

"I must go," the spirit said. "I do not know if I can come again. At Westmarch, you will find a beginning to all that you seek. Ride with the blessing of the Lady," she said, raising a hand in farewell.

"Please, wait," Tris called.

But by then, the ghost had faded to mist and then to nothing at all. Tris stared at the air where the spirit had been for a long time, until the guttering candle reminded him of the hour and he sought fitful sleep as the dawn began to light the sky.

CHAPTER TEN

IT TOOK TWO days after the bandit attack for Tris to find the opportunity to speak with Carina alone. He tried to arrange his tasks so that he could keep the healer's tent in sight, but she did not leave the tent by herself for an exasperating length of time.

When Tris finally saw his chance, Carina was heading toward her tent, coming from the far side of the caravan camp. It was the last day before they moved on, and the crews were already starting to break down tents and booths. Setup and teardown were the times when the most accidents occurred, and when Carina was the busiest. No surprise then, Tris thought, that she was difficult to find.

"I wanted to thank you for what you did," Tris said, catching up with her and touching the gash on his forehead that was well on its way to healing. Carina looked at him tiredly, and frowned slightly as if trying to place him.

"You're one of the hired guards, aren't you?" she asked. "You helped me get the patients out, when the building was on fire." Tris nodded. She looked at him a moment longer, as if trying to put something into words, then looked away.

"My friends call me Tris," he said. There was no hiding his Margolan accent, he knew, but at least the name was common. His mother, Queen Serae, had quickly gained the affection of the people of Margolan, making her name and the names of her children embarrassingly fashionable when he was a boy. No one, it seemed, fancied Eldra or Jared enough to use their names, and that had been one more thing Jared held against Tris and Kait. Now Tris was grateful that it was not remarkable that a laborer might share the same name with a prince.

The healer smiled tentatively. "You saved my life in that building. Thank you."

Tris dismissed the words, embarrassed. "I'd like to talk to you." He paused, then forged on. "I'd like to talk to you… about how you do what you do."

Carina stopped and met his eyes. "That's an unusual request from a swordsman," she said neutrally. "I don't bless swords or curse enemies, and I wouldn't show you how if I could."

"That isn't what I meant."

Carina looked at him closely, as if taking his measure. "What you did… in the fire… using magic to throw that beam… Have you ever done that before?"

"No," Tris replied uncomfortably. "But my granny was a hedge witch." Tris begged the forgiveness of Bava K'aa's spirit for the gross understatement. "I need to learn... to understand... how to control my power before I kill someone, and how to block out the spirits before they drive me mad."

"Come inside," Carina said, gesturing for him to join her in her tent. Her voice was brusque with exhaustion but not unkind, and Tris imagined that she was often besieged by questions from the curious. She motioned him to be seated and nudged a small clay teapot closer to the fire in the center of the tent floor. "Why do you think I can help you?"

"I don't know where else to go," Tris said, forcing himself to meet her eyes. "When I was young, my grandmother taught me some of her magic—like lighting a fire without a spark. But now, it's like a floodgate opened," he said, his growing desperation clear in his voice. "Every time I dream, I remember something else she taught me. I can feel the magic, but when I touch it, I'm not sure whether I'm using it or it's using me." He paused. "Carina, when did you know that you could do what you do?"

Carina paused before answering. "I think at some level, I've always known," she said quietly. "But I didn't start to train for it until after—" She stopped abruptly. "Until I was in my teens."

"But how did you know?" Tris pressed, and she looked at him for a moment before she spoke.

"I just... knew," she answered quietly. "I can't describe it. Maybe it's different for different people. I felt the power, but I didn't know what it was for, or how to make it do anything. Then once, when my favorite horse was hurt, I was caring for him and I was thinking about what it would take to heal him, and things happened." She smiled. "Scared me half to death."

"How did you know where to go, to learn more?"

Carina's face hardened and she looked away. "That wasn't a problem," she answered, her tone cold. "It was taken care of."

"I'm sorry," Tris said gently. "I didn't mean to pry."

Carina shook her head. "It's all right. It's just that, where I come from, people are superstitious. They don't like mages." She gave a sad smile. "In fact, they like them even less than they like twins."

So that was why such a talented healer and an expert swordsman traveled with an obscure caravan, Tris thought.

"Look, Tris, there isn't anything else I can tell you," she said, uncomfortable, as if she'd said too much.

"It's not that simple," Tris said, shaking his head stubbornly. "When the bandits attacked, right before I got hit, I saw the bandits die," he said, the words tumbling out, "I saw their spirits rise up out of their bodies," he confessed in a whisper. "I thought I was going mad. It happened everywhere I looked, until one of the raiders smashed me over the head," he said, ruefully touching his wound.

Carina frowned, and Tris sensed that she was suddenly taking him seriously. "You saw... the spirits rising out of the bodies?" she repeated slowly.

"If you can teach me nothing else, teach me how to block it out," he begged. "Surely, you have to know how to block out pain to do your duties. Otherwise, I am no help to my friends and little use to the caravan."

"Have you spoken of this to anyone else?"

"About the battlefield? No," he said, looking down. "The friends I travel with—they know I have some power, but they have no idea how little I can control it. I haven't said anything else. People would think me mad. I think the hedge witch suspects."

"Yes," Carina said thoughtfully, "Alyzza would suspect," she said. "She was court sorceress for a minor noble when her powers failed to save the noble's only child. The child's death nearly drove her mad and the court no longer wanted her. And so, she is here," Carina said, gesturing to the fair beyond the tent. "Like all of us, somewhere we never expected to be." She was silent again, and just when Tris began to fear she was going to turn him out, she spoke.

"I will help you as much as I can," she said slowly. "I will ask Alyzza to help as well. But you must be careful," she warned. "Say nothing about your magic to anyone else. You might attract more interest than you desire."

"Thank you," Tris said, as he got to his feet.

Carina smiled sadly. "Why don't you wait to thank me until I've helped you?" she said. "Come back after your sword practice, if you have the strength."

Thoughts full of a hundred questions, Tris slipped outside the tent. "Just remember, I saw her first," a voice came at Tris's elbow. Ban Soterius gave him a wry grin. "I'll give you credit for courage, Tris," he added, "considering Cam's size. I wouldn't want to face him to come courting."

Tris gave Soterius a dry look. "With the way you change companions, I'd be scared if I were you, too."

Soterius grinned. "Just my way of spreading sunshine," he replied, slapping Tris on the back. "No reason to overwhelm one and make all the rest miserable. You could take a few pages from my book, you know." He lowered his voice conspiratorially. "And now that you don't have any official entanglements to worry about, you're free to choose for yourself, no one's business but your own," he added.

"Remind me of that if we make it to Dhasson in one piece," Tris replied. "Really, Ban. That's been the furthest thing from my mind."

"I know," Soterius replied. "That's the trouble with you. Too serious. The right woman could lighten you up." He smiled wickedly. "Of course, so could the wrong woman."

Tris gave him a good-natured punch on the arm as they walked toward the main camp area.

Before the supper fires were lit, they were pressed into service on a variety of jobs dismantling the camp, and when Tris finally grabbed a trencher of dinner and found a place near a fire, he dropped wearily onto his log seat.

Harrtuck had promised that life on the road would toughen him up, Tris thought, and rubbed a sore muscle ruefully. Since they joined the caravan, Tris discovered that muscles he did not know existed could ache enough to keep him awake at night—loading and unloading tents, equipment and merchandise, straining with guy-ropes to erect the large tents and sledgehammer the stakes that supported them. And then, after he was already bone weary, sword practice with Vahanian. Tris sipped the mug of ale and wolfed down the rest of his stew. All of this activity might be the making of a swordsman, but it was likely to be the death of a prince.

Carroway joined him looking equally exhausted.

"I'm going to be dead long before we reach Dhasson," the minstrel complained, digging into his food. "If it's not a full day of entertaining for the audiences, it's this bloody sword work at night." Carroway stretched and groaned. "Are you sure Vahanian's not secretly out to get us?"

"Ready for tonight's practice?" Vahanian asked, dropping down beside them with a steaming trencher of food. The mercenary grinned as Tris groaned his reply. "That excited, huh? Must be doing a good job then."

"Couldn't you at least look tired?" Carroway complained as he finished his ale.

"What's the point?" Vahanian replied with his mouth full. "Doesn't make any less work."

"No, but it would give me a lot of satisfaction," Tris answered. "Where are we going next?"

"Further north," came a reply from Tris's other side. "And if you ask me, it's a mistake." Tris turned to see Kaine, looking tired and dirty. "Nothing but trouble up north." Kaine swigged his ale. "'Course, seems to be a lot of that goin' around, if you take my meaning," he said, with a sidelong glance at Vahanian.

"I'm not sure I do," Tris answered carefully.

Kaine snorted. "Where have you been? Dhasson's at war. 'Course, now, they're not saying that, but war's what it is, all the same," he said, dropping his voice. "Some of the people coming through from that direction have some mighty strange tales. Mighty strange," he said, taking another draught.

"How strange is 'strange?'" Tris asked, leaning forward.

Kaine finished his ale and set his mug aside, then tilted his head to look at Tris. "How's unnatural things from out in the Blasted Lands for strange, huh?" he asked. "Word is that there've been some creatures sighted up near Dhasson that aren't the making of the Goddess, if you take my meaning," he said broadly. "'Twas a deserter through here that told some stories would stand your hair on end. Thought Dhasson's army was taking a beating and didn't fancy being eaten, or worse, so he lit off, or so he said," the tent rigger continued, wiping his mouth with his sleeve.

"The tribes' mages couldn't conjure things like that," Vahanian said thoughtfully and Tris turned. By the Lady's breath, Tris thought, he looks like he's taking this seriously!

"Don't know about the past, but they sure seem to now," Kaine replied. "And there were other stories. About day turning to night and lightning that wasn't the right color. About locusts coming up out of nowhere and disappearing just as fast. And about whole plains that were dry as a bone turning into mud right when the army went to cross them, and there weren't no rains for days, either," Kaine added. "Now if that's not magicked, what is it?"

"Certainly sounds like magic to me," Vahanian replied. He got up, headed for the barrel of ale, and scooped up another mugful.

"You're a cautious one," the tent rigger said to Tris as Vahanian walked away. "There're lots that don't hold with magic, but I've been around. I've seen strange things can't be explained no other way. Here's another piece of advice. Watch your back around that one," he said with a barely perceptible nod toward Vahanian, who was out of earshot at the ale barrel. "No count of the men he's killed or betrayed. The Eastmark army doesn't hang men lightly, but there's a death sentence on him. Betrayed a whole platoon, he did, at Chauvrenne."

"I'll certainly keep it in mind," Tris replied, as Vahanian walked back toward them. His thoughts lingered on the reports of magic far more than on Kaine's dark warnings about Vahanian's past. Certainly magic was no stranger to any of the Winter Kingdoms. And the grandson of Bava K'aa ought not to be surprised at arcane works, he thought, remembering the many times he saw his grandmother work spells at the palace. Some of them were workings of convenience, the sorts of things that any hedge witch might have done, like lighting a candle without a spark. But there were other times, Tris recalled, when as a young boy he hid in the shadows of his father's warroom, hoping to be overlooked so he could watch the exciting bustle of preparations for war. Then he saw some of Bava K'aa's true magic, as she scryed for the location of enemies or divined the weather or learned something of an enemy from captured belongings.

So it should not be unusual for magic to be at hand if Dhasson really were at war, he thought. Except that the kind of dark magic the tent rigger gossiped about was unusual. There were legends about a time when dark magic was as common as locusts, and the people of the Winter Kingdoms suffered for it. Then the Light mages banded together and fought the Mage Wars up in the sparsely populated far north.

That was many years ago, when Tris's grandmother was just a young woman. But anyone who ventured into the Blasted Lands did not doubt that strong magic had been loosed. There were creatures and plants that existed nowhere else, nightmare things that survived on the magic left in the area, magic which made it unsuitable for use by normal folk for long. For every story about monsters in the Blasted Lands there was at least one story of some fool who ventured in and never returned. The stories of lost treasures ensured a steady supply of fools, and kept the legends alive.

Dark magic like that was not supposed to still happen, Tris thought, watching the fire. After the Mage Wars, a secret society of the most powerful female witches formed, the Katae Canei. The Katae Canei combined their powers to suppress knowledge of the dark arts, to discover and root out any mage bold enough to try to learn them, and to destroy the runes and spellbooks of the dark masters. For a generation, they were successful. Bava K'aa was rumored to have been the chief of the Katae Canei Sisterhood.

Who had taken the mantle in the years since his grandmother's death, Tris did not know. The Sisterhood did not announce such things. Without a court mage, there was even less such information in Margolan. One thing was certain: if there were magicked creatures loose in the Northern Lands, someone was dabbling in the dark arts. And the return of the dark mages would be a disaster, unless someone could do something to stop it.

Just then, Soterius ambled up and dropped down beside Tris, warming his hands around a hot mug. "So what am I missing?"

Tris glanced from Kaine to where Vahanian stood and back. "Just talking about the trip north. Kaine here doesn't like the idea of crossing into Dhasson."

Carroway made a dismissive gesture. "Dhasson doesn't bother me. But the forest on the way to the border, that's another matter," he said, taking a long draught. "You know, the natives call it Ruune Videya, which means 'ghost trees,'" the minstrel said, warming to his subject.

"Stories say," he recounted, leaning forward, "that Jaq the Damned slaughtered peasants there two hundred years ago over a rebellion." He paused to sip his drink. "They say bodies are buried everywhere, which is why the forest grows so thickly," he added, glancing at Kaine and Tris. "They say that the spirits walk, restless from their unjust deaths, waiting to avenge themselves." He looked pointedly at Tris. "Not that I put much stock in ghost stories."

"Well, if you're too darn lazy to fight tonight, I say we turn in." Vahanian said as he walked back toward the group, draining his mug in one draught. Tris nodded and stood, ignoring Kaine's warning glance.

"If tomorrow's as long as today, I don't imagine there's enough time to rest before Winterstide," Tris replied. "Thanks for the stories," he said as he fell into step beside Vahanian.

"Keep them in mind," Kaine replied darkly. "All of them."

Tris and Vahanian walked halfway across the camp before either spoke. Finally, Tris broke the silence. "I get the feeling you two know each other from somewhere?"

Vahanian snorted. "You could say that. Kaine's a lying son of a whore and always has been. I met him a long time ago, right after he slipped the Nargi border with an angry captain at his heels. Seems Kaine helped himself to the captain's gold. I'm rather surprised he's still alive."

"He seemed a bit surprised to see you, too."

"I hope so," the mercenary replied. Tris heard concern in his voice. "Because otherwise, someone sent him here, looking for me. While there are more than a few people with a reason to find me, only one has a recent grudge. In which case, Kaine's only looking for me because someone told him that I'm with you," Vahanian said, looking out over the dark horizon as if he expected to see more bandits, or worse.

"Good night, Jonmarc," Tris said as they reached their tents.

"Sleep lightly," the mercenary replied. "And keep your sword in reach."

VAHANIAN MADE IT his business each night to check on his traveling party's mounts. They began the journey with better than average horses, and although most places hanged horse thieves, a surprising number of the beasts still managed to go missing. When the horses were accounted for, Vahanian headed back across the camp, shivering in the chill night air. He ducked into Linton's tent and squinted at the light. Several oil lamps set the large tent in a cheerful glow, and a brazier warmed the small space.

"You're looking good, Jonmarc," the caravan leader chuckled as he brought out a tray with a large decanter and two glasses. "Life on the road suits you."

"I'd have been dead a long time ago if it didn't," Vahanian replied, leaning back and propping up his boots on a trunk.

"Your 'contraband' are finally earning their keep," Linton continued, pouring the golden Margolian brandy and setting a glass in front of Vahanian. "Some day you'll have to tell me the full story. It's not like you to rescue the nobility."

Vahanian sipped his glass. "Times change," he said, staring at Linton and past him. "You'd be surprised."

"Probably not," Linton said, dropping heavily into his leather folding chair.

"Get to your point."

"My point, Jonmarc," Linton repeated, stopping long enough to take another sip of the brandy, "is that someone else has figured out as much."

"Who?"

Linton shrugged. "The names they gave, like their reasons, are fabricated, I'm sure. But earlier this evening, two men won a sizable amount at our gaming tables. Large enough to get the attention of the master gamer, and when he came to congratulate them on their winnings—and make sure they weren't cheating—they asked to see the caravan master.

"The gamesmaster brought them to me. They claimed to be rug merchants from the west and said they left their wares back at the inn where they were staying. They also said they'd just been through Margolan and what a pity it was that things weren't as they used to be."

"Do tell," Vahanian replied dryly, taking a long sip of his drink.

Linton leaned back, clomping his heavy boots up onto a sturdy trunk and finishing off his drink. "They went on to say that there was a new king in Margolan and that business wasn't good. New taxes. And there were rumors that not all of King Bricen's family were really dead," Linton said, watching Vahanian carefully.

Vahanian said nothing, but he took another drink of his brandy and met Linton's eyes steadily. "And?"

"And I got the feeling that my two visitors were probably going from one caravan to another, plus all the inns between Margolan and Dhasson, with the same story," Linton said.

"Why Dhasson?" Vahanian asked.

Linton shrugged. "It's well known that King Harrol was kin to Bricen. It's where I'd seek sanctuary if I were Martris Drayke," he added, staring pointedly at Vahanian. "I told them it was an interesting story," Linton continued. "And sent them on their way with a promise to look them up if we were ever in their province and needed rugs to trade."

"So why tell me about this," Vahanian asked, draining his glass.

"Because one of the men bore a striking resemblance to Vakkis," Linton replied, setting his drink aside. "All the way down to the knife crease you put in his cheek."

Now Linton had his full attention. Vahanian laid his empty goblet on Linton's counting table. "How sure are you?" he asked in a voice that could have etched glass.

"Very sure," Linton said. "My casino master tells me that the traveler was unusually skilled at contre dice and fond of Valiquestran whiskey and that he never, ever had his back to the door."

"That's Vakkis." Vahanian cursed. "Any hint that he was still looking for me?"

Linton shook his head. "He didn't mention anything. But he was dressed better than usual and either the bounty business has been good lately or he's on retainer to someone with a lot of money. He was spending Margolan gold."

"Damn."

"Jared Drayke may be a whore's son of a king," Linton said, leaning forward, his voice dropping to a cautious rasp, "but he is a dangerous whore's son. And like as not, he has your number, Jonmarc."

"Where was Vakkis headed?"

Linton's tanned face creased in a grin. "Thought you'd ask. The Boar's Inn in Westerhaven—not far. Of course, since he told me that's where he'd be he won't be totally surprised if he gets company—"

"Only if he sees me coming," Vahanian replied, pushing to his feet.

"Jonmarc..."

"Don't worry, Maynard," Vahanian said as he grabbed his cloak. "I know we're a danger to the caravan. Let me take out Vakkis and we'll be gone in the morning."

"Would you sit down and stop thinking with your sword?" Linton snapped. "Did I say anything about leaving?" He spat loudly into a bronze cuspidor next to his counting table. "I haven't gotten to be a rich old trader by shivering every time a bounty hunter looks in my direction. Do you think you're the only one in my caravan who's got someone looking for him? If you can take Vakkis down, all the better. Why do you think I called you in tonight? And if you can't, we keep our eyes out. He doesn't have anything solid or we'd have been ridden down by King Jared's troops by now. Just warn the others to keep their heads down," the caravan master continued, pouring himself another drink.

A slow grin crept into the edges of Vahanian's mouth. "I knew you were a good man when you didn't water the ale, Maynard," he said.

"And I knew you were an honest mercenary when you paid for it," Linton shot back. "Now get out of here. And good hunting."

CHAPTER ELEVEN

THE SMOKE OF *battle and the smell of blood filled the air. Around her, clashing swords clanged and hoof beats thundered as the struggle for the embattled city wore on toward evening. For Kiara Sharsequin, Princess of Isencroft, nothing mattered except the bearded man gasping for breath on the ground.*

"The king is down!" she heard a man shout. The word passed down the line. She pushed through the knot of armsmen around her fallen father and dropped to her knees beside him, weeping.

"Kiara, you must get free," the injured monarch managed, blood flecking his lips as he struggled to raise a hand. Even that gesture exhausted him, but Kiara dabbed at his lips with her robe.

"I won't leave you."

"You must go," he whispered. His eyes closed and Kiara sobbed, holding his hand. Just behind his head, the flag of Isencroft lay trampled in the mud.

"Your Highness," a guardsman said insistently. "We must get you to safety."

"I won't leave him."

"Look!" a guardsman shouted, pointing, and Kiara raised her head to follow his gesture. Just beyond where the king lay, the air shimmered. The sparkling air took on shape and substance, until the form of a stern, strong woman appeared, her close-cropped, dark hair cut for wearing a battle helm and her arms strong and muscled from wielding a sword. To Kiara's open-mouthed amazement, she found herself not an arm's length from Chenne, the Avenger Goddess.

"Kiara," the apparition said.

"Yes," the girl stammered, her eyes wide.

"Take up the flag, Kiara. This is not yet your father's hour, nor yours," Chenne said, fixing Kiara with her amber eyes. "Darkness is coming, and you hold a key which can dispel it. Lift that sword," the goddess commanded. Trembling, Kiara reached for her father's bloody sword and wrapped her hands around its pommel. Chenne stretched out her ethereal hand and touched the sword's point, sending a wave of white fire down the length of the weapon.

Kiara gasped. The blade glowed with an inner blue fire, as if first taken from the forge. Chenne withdrew her hand and looked appraisingly at Kiara.

"Raise this sword in my name and know that the armies of Isencroft will follow you in any just cause," the Avenger Goddess said, transfixing Kiara with that amber gaze. "Your role will become clear. Only believe," the Goddess said, her shape becoming more insubstantial as Kiara watched in astonishment. "Only believe."

The air shimmered once more and then the image was gone, leaving Kiara sword in hand and open-mouthed. The men-at-arms around her knelt in fealty, even as her father groaned and lost consciousness.

"We are yours to command, Princess," the armsman closest to her said reverently.

Still trembling, Kiara swallowed, then grasped the sword firmly with both hands and lifted it high overhead as a rallying point. It seemed weightless in her hands, still tingling with power, more a relic than a weapon. "In the name of the Goddess, we'll drive back the invaders!" she swore, feeling the sword alive with supernatural fire. A soldier raised the flag aloft as two more came to bear the injured monarch away, and yet another brought Kiara a battle steed. And then they were cheering, shouting the name of the Goddess, chanting Kiara's name...

"Your Highness," the voice said again, more insistently. "Please, wake up."

Kiara Sharsequin found herself in a tangle of sweat-soaked bedclothes under the worried eyes of Malae, her lady-in-waiting. "I'm awake, I'm awake," she managed, still blinking at the light and attempting to convince herself that the memories of the dream were long in the past.

"You must get ready," Malae repeated. "The ambassador will be here within the hour."

With a groan, Kiara nodded, blinked a few more times, and then rolled groggily to her feet. "I can't believe they're sending an ambassador over this," she said, shaking her head. As if in agreement, Jae rasped and hissed animatedly, then hopped onto her wrist and gurgled contentedly as she stroked his scales.

"He's going to be downstairs sooner than you'd like," Malae scolded gently, steering the princess toward a bowl of warmed water and letting her splash the sleep from her eyes as Jae hopped from Kiara's arm to the washstand rail.

"How is father?" Kiara asked as she straightened and reached for a towel.

"The same as ever," Males replied sadly. "Every morning you ask and every day the answer stays the same."

"I know," Kiara replied, setting the towel aside and walking to the wardrobe. "But every morning, I still keep hoping you'll tell me something different."

She flung open the wardrobe doors. "Hmm. I wonder," she said, pondering her choices. "What does one wear when one doesn't want to marry the ambassador's king?" She reached for one gown, shook her head, started to reach for another than changed her mind and ended up planting her hands on her hips once more. From his perch on the washstand, Jae hissed his opinion.

"Perhaps something somber," Malae suggested, reaching for a gray gown that was never one of Kiara's favorites. "Like this. It is not your most flattering gown."

Kiara brightened. "Perfect. We'll make my hair a bit more severe and skip the rouge. We'll play up all his fears of what 'warrior princesses' should be." She sighed. "With any luck, I'll look less appealing than their stories led them to believe."

Malae chuckled. "I'm not sure it's possible to ruin your appeal so easily, Your Highness," she said, helping Kiara remove the gray dress from the wardrobe. "But perhaps we can forestall them once again."

Kiara sighed as she removed her nightgown. "We've got to do more than stall them, Malae," she said, staring at the gown. "I want them to go away altogether."

"I know, Your Highness," Malae replied, offering the princess a robe and leading her to a chair. Malae picked up a brush and began to work on the princess's long auburn hair. "If only King Jared were a more honorable man."

Kiara gave a decidedly un-princesslike snort. "Honorable? Jared? The words don't go together. Not after what our spies tell us."

"Is there any chance that the spies were mistaken?" Malae offered hopefully.

"None. And I know exactly why he's interested. He wants Isencroft. He could raid what's left in the treasury and draw on our men and boys to raise a larger army," she said bitterly. "Plus our crop land, in a good year, could provision a massive army. Absorbing Isencroft would solve their problems."

"You must admit, Your Highness, that it would solve a few of Isencroft's, as well," Malae said gently.

Kiara slumped. "Yes, I know. There's not enough left in the treasury to make it worth raiding. And after three poor harvests, our men and boys might want to leave home for greater adventures."

"I don't think it has reached quite that point," Malae reproved gently. "But still, you must keep him from suspecting how bad things have been here if you wish to avoid his offer."

"And I've got to keep him thinking that father is well," Kiara added as Malae began to braid and twist her hair. "That's the hardest part. If he realizes I've been running the kingdom myself since father took sick, he'll bring an army to take me to Margolan."

"You underestimate yourself, Your Highness," Malae said, her hands flying as she worked Kiara's hair. "And you dismiss the loyalty of this kingdom. You are Goddess Blessed. Chenne came to you. Our army would follow you anywhere, and so would our people."

It was true, Kiara knew. Ever since that day on the battleground a year ago, when she had seen the Avenger Goddess and rallied Isencroft's failing troops, she had been a legend. While the reverence the peasants showed her was mortifying, even many of the nobles treated her with a respect that bordered on awe. It certainly helped over the course of her father's illness, since there was never a question from the nobility about her fitness to rule in his stead until he could recover—if he recovered. Ordinary illnesses were bad enough, but magic ones were worse. First the war, then bad harvests. Donelan was a king with nearly empty coffers, and no likelihood of raising funds from his impoverished people. Even if he recovered, Kiara knew, Isencroft's future was in peril.

"How will you turn him away, Your Highness?" Malae asked, pinning up Kiara's hair.

"I'll think of something," Kiara said, watching Malae slide the ornate hairpins into place. "Although I'm running out of excuses. If it wouldn't compromise my ability to rule, I'd have told him I was entering the service of the Goddess."

Malae chuckled. "That would be a loss for the kingdom, Your Highness. And I doubt the Goddess needs your vows. She's claimed you as her own already."

Whatever that means, Kiara thought gloomily. She looked at herself in the mirror. Six months of hiding her father's illness, taking on the burden of kingship in secret, had taken a toll. To her estimation, her reflection looked tired and worn.

Kiara sighed. "I guess I'm ready," she announced as Jae fluttered to her shoulder. "How long until the ambassador arrives?"

Malae glanced out the window at the courtyard. "That's his coach now," she said, letting the curtain fall close. "He should be announcing his arrival within minutes."

Kiara nodded in thought. "We'll keep him waiting a candlemark," she said. "It won't do to look as if I were waiting for him. And I shall do my best to appear bossy and solemn, as I presume Jared would like it best to have an empty-headed little doxy to follow him around like a lapdog." She grinned wickedly. "At least, that's the plan for starters."

Malae adjusted Kiara's gown. "I'm sure you'll be quite convincing."

Kiara met her eyes. "I hope so, Malae," she said wistfully, staring toward the window. "I hope so."

The dreaded hour came too quickly. Steeling herself, Kiara gathered her skirts and headed for the stairway, preceded by an entourage hand-picked by Malae for its impressiveness. Kiara paced in the back hallway above the stair as she heard the seneschal announce her with as many formal titles as he could apply. Jae fretted on her shoulder. When the time finally came to make her entrance, Kiara lifted her head, squared her shoulders, and reminded herself to appear somber and bossy, then began the descent to the chamber where Jared's emissaries waited.

She took her time, using the long flight of stairs as a pretext to examine the ambassadors. One man was thick set and coarse looking, more like a strongman than a diplomat. His companion looked more the part. He was a distinguished gentleman of perhaps sixty summers, white haired, slender and fine boned. Despite his polish, he seemed nervous, and for an instant, Kiara had a pang of conscience about the ruse she must now play out. She wondered if failure would cost the ambassador his life, and guessed, from the concern she saw in his blue eyes when she met them, that it might indeed. I have no choice, she thought as she inclined her head in greeting. And neither does he. Princess or liegeman, we're both pawns. The seneschal stepped up to announce her.

"Esteemed visitors," Allestyr intoned, "I present Her Royal Highness, Kiara Sharsequin, Princess of Isencroft." Kiara met the ambassador's gaze impassively, but watched him closely, gauging his reaction.

"Your Highness," the burly man said with a fumbling attempt at courtliness, "May I present Ambassador Catoril of the Royal Court at Margolan."

Catoril stepped forward and dropped to one knee, then cleared his throat to prompt his guard to do the same. The older man seemed mortified by his companion, but kept his composure. "Your Highness," the ambassador said. "This is a great honor."

"You may rise," Kiara replied stonily, pitying the ambassador for the performance on her part he must now endure.

The ambassador rose gracefully, while his companion shambled to his feet. Bowing low, the ambassador withdrew a small box from a pouch at his belt and held it out to her with a cautious glance at Jae, who seemed determined to make his presence as intrusive as possible and nearly pecked the man's hand. "If it please Your Highness," Catoril said, "a gift from Jared, King of Margolan." He opened the box to reveal a ruby the size of an almond, glowing with inner fire. "It is but a token of our king's esteem," the ambassador said as he offered the gift.

Allestyr stepped forward to receive it for Kiara, who maintained an impassive expression. "Her Highness appreciates the gesture," the seneschal replied, whisking the gift away. "Your king is most generous."

"King Jared is a strong king, respected by all our people," Catoril said, and it seemed to Kiara that the ambassador barely kept himself from glancing nervously back at the oaf beside him as he spoke. So, she thought, the guard is here to assure that the ambassador doesn't speak out of turn. How interesting. She looked at Catoril and wondered just what it might be that the man could say which would warrant a guard.

"We have much to discuss," Kiara said formally. "Come, let us find more suitable quarters." Allestyr led them from the receiving hall into a small parlor where a meal for four was already set on the table, along with a small bowl of diced meat for Jae. As Kiara had researched from court protocol, the foods chosen and their presentation were appropriate to the ambassador's rank but did not suggest any attempt to impress.

Kiara waited until they were all seated before she addressed Catoril once more. "You have come a long way, ambassador," she said as the servants poured wine and brought the first course. "Tell me of your travels."

"Quite uneventful, Your Highness," Catoril replied. "The road from Margolan to Isencroft is straight and safe. We did not anticipate any adventures."

He may be honorable, but he's no fool, Kiara thought. *Whatever his opinions of his king, he's doing his job reminding me that Margolan is close enough to cause trouble, and no barriers exist to stop them.*

"How fortunate," she said impassively. "And how fares your king?" At her elbow, Jae pulled at his meat. *Maybe with luck,* Kiara thought, *they'll think he's my familiar and report that I'm a witch, and unsuitable for marriage. Not likely. King Bricen's second wife was the daughter of Bava K'aa, the most powerful sorceress in the Winter Kingdoms. With my luck,* she thought, *Jared would like a witch-bride.*

Catoril studiously avoided looking at Jae. "King Jared is in fine health, Your Highness," he said, a bit too quickly. "He is quite involved with the hunt these days, as has always been his pleasure." He paused. "King Jared also asked after your father, King Donelan. He is well?"

It was Kiara's turn to remain impassive. "Quite well, yes," she lied, meeting Catoril's eyes. "He, too, is taken with hunting, and sends his regrets that he was not here to meet with you," she continued. "He is in the field a few days' travel from here, and I'm afraid that even affairs of state come second to a chance for a large boar," she said lightly.

"I believe that is a reason King Jared can appreciate," Catoril replied, and if he sensed deception on Kiara's part, the ambassador gave no indication. "I wish King Donelan luck in the hunt."

Kiara inclined her head. "I will pass that on to him. He is usually quite lucky," she said, feeling a pang at the deception. While it was true that Donelan was an excellent huntsman, it was also true that he had not been well enough to hunt all season. Resolutely, Kiara forced her mind from those thoughts as if her guests might read them, and looked back at Catoril, only to find his guard staring at her. Unfazed, she met the rough man's gaze, and the guard looked away. She sipped her wine. The sooner these guests from Margolan were on their way, the better.

The servants set the first course in front of them. It smelled delicious, reminding Kiara how hungry she was. Jae impudently stole a tidbit from the corner of her trencher. "And the royal family, how are they?" Kiara asked, watching Catoril closely. A flash of pain seemed to cross his eyes, although his face remained impassive.

"You did not hear, Your Highness? Several weeks ago, a terrible tragedy struck. Fire broke out in the royal living quarters. I'm afraid no one but King Jared escaped."

"How fortunate," Kiara murmured. Catoril's guard looked decidedly ill at ease and frowned as he watched every move the ambassador made.

Catoril's fine hands fluttered nervously as he spoke, and he dropped his knife.

"But to speak of happier things, Your Highness," Catoril continued, regaining his poise, "I bring you tidings from King Jared. He extends an invitation for you to visit Margolan as his esteemed guest. It would be a great honor to receive you."

"How kind," Kiara replied. "Unfortunately, I must decline until spring," she stalled, watching Catoril closely. "There are religious celebrations here in Isencroft over which the first-born daughter of the king must preside. My father would be inconvenienced were I not to carry out my role, and our people would be offended should I choose to travel from the kingdom at that time."

"King Jared will be quite disappointed," Catoril returned, and Kiara thought she saw a glimmer of nervousness behind those icy blue eyes. "He hoped to show you Margolan's midwinter festival, which is quite impressive."

"I am honored," Kiara replied. "But I must defer to my people."

"Our princess plays a vital role in our own midwinter feasts," supplied Allestyr. "Our people's devotion runs strong," the seneschal added with a meaningful look at Catoril. "You know that Chenne appeared to Kiara on the battlefield and gave Her blessing. There is nothing the people of Isencroft wouldn't do for their princess."

If Catoril registered Allestyr's veiled warning, it did not show in the ambassador's impassive face. "Indeed," the older man murmured. "Our customs differ somewhat, but King Jared respects Isencroft's devotion to the Goddess. We will plan a spring visit, and take the opportunity to show the princess how lovely Margolan is in blossom."

"You are very gracious," Kiara replied, feeling her stomach twist. She had eluded the invitation for now, but it would be twice as difficult to evade come spring. She would have almost nine months to plan, she told herself, finding her appetite completely gone as the servants removed her untouched trencher and placed a new one of steaming game in front of her. Spring was a long time away.

And so the day passed, with each side probing the other through conversation which appeared pleasant and guileless. When at last Kiara could excuse herself and have her servants ready the guests for bed, she made her way back to her own quarters, exhausted by the sham. Malae was waiting for her anxiously.

"So, my Lady, how did it go?" she asked, helping Kiara removed her gown.

Kiara sighed. "We've postponed the trip once more, but I'm afraid that eventually I'm going to run out of excuses."

Malae clucked her tongue. "You've bought yourself time, Your Highness. That is precious in itself. Now you must trust Cam and Carina. You do your duty by giving them more time," the older woman said gently, patting Kiara's hand. "And who knows? Perhaps by spring, the Goddess will have selected you for your Journey."

Kiara managed a tired smile. "That would certainly get me out of going to Margolan, but I'm not sure it would be less of an adventure." She paused. "Do you remember how I used to worry when I was a child and Father would go off with the soldiers?" Kiara asked, wriggling into her nightshirt and dropping onto the bed. Malae smiled.

"I couldn't forget, Your Highness. You usually found your way into my bed and I carried you back to your own room," Malae chuckled.

"I never thought I could worry more about him," Kiara said wistfully.

"The burdens of the crown come young," Malae replied, "as they did for your mother. And I will tell you what I always told her, when she would come to my rooms for a hot cup of tea in the middle of the night. Trust the Goddess."

Kiara smiled sadly at the thought of her mother, Queen Viata, dead now three years. Viata, had been a daughter of the king of Eastmark, an old and proud monarchy, nearly as old as the House of Margolan. Her marriage to Donelan had been something of a scandal. Donelan was only the third king in his line, testimony to Isencroft's troubled history—an interloper to the minds of the more established aristocracy in venerable Eastmark. Worse, theirs was a love match, not even an arranged alliance. So it was with strained goodwill that Eastmark let its princess go to wed the upstart king of a frontier kingdom, a place with a strange, war-like aspect of the One Goddess. Isencroft's court had been equally dubious of their new queen, with her exotic features and heavy accent, and her devotion to an out-land aspect of the Goddess. But the will of a young, determined and utterly love-struck king prevailed, and while Viata had a troubled time with the aristocracy, the love between her and Donelan never wavered, even when their union produced just one child, and that, a girl.

It was from Viata that Kiara learned the Eastmark style of fighting, with its complicated and deadly footwork. Viata's almond-shaped eyes stared back at Kiara from her own reflection, and her mother's duskier skin mingled with Donelan's fair northern blood, made it easy for Kiara to tan as soon as the sun turned warm. And it was, indirectly, because of the sting of the court's chilly reception of Viata, that Kiara found herself betrothed to Jared of Margolan. King Donelan, anxious to legitimize the House of Isencroft, engineered the arranged marriage at Kiara's birth, knowing that the alliance with ancient House of Margolan could further enhance the standing of his lineage in the eyes of the ruling houses of the Winter Kingdoms.

Kiara sighed. "I know. But things have gone so wrong. It seems as if the Lady's forgotten us."

Malae pulled the covers back and beckoned for the weary princess to lie down, then bent over and tucked her in like a child, brushing her hand across Kiara's forehead. "Chenne doesn't forget her Blessed One," the older woman comforted.

Kiara caught Malae's hand for a moment and pressed it against her cheek. "Please, stay with me until I fall asleep."

Malae nodded and crossed to a chair by the fire. "As you wish, my princess," she said, settling into a comfortable seat and cozying a throw around her. "Now, sleep."

Despite the comforting crackle of the fire and the knowledge that Malae was near, it still took more than a candlemark for Kiara to fall into a fitful sleep, filled with troubled dreams.

KIARA AWOKE WITH a start. She blinked, then raised herself on her elbows. The sun was already up, but Malae had drawn her heavy drapes to block its light and let her sleep. Jae dozed in his perch on the headboard of her bed, hissing softly. Kiara could smell a pot of herbal tea already boiling on the fire. Although Kiara thought she moved noiselessly, Malae was awake and beside her by the time she poured herself a cup of tea.

"Allestyr worries about you," Malae said, laying a soft woolen shawl across the princess's shoulders.

"I know," Kiara replied quietly, staring at the dancing flames. "They all do. I'm sorry to be such a bother."

Malae sat down next to her and laid a comforting hand on Kiara's arm. "It's our honor to take care of you, my princess," she said. "But we worry more these days, since there are many strange things afoot."

Kiara nodded glumly. "Something's about to happen, something big. I don't know what it is, but I can... feel it."

"You are Goddess Blessed," Malae replied. "Perhaps the Goddess is about to choose you for your Journey."

Kiara shook her head tiredly and sipped at her tea. "It couldn't come at a worse time." Malae patted her hand. "Perhaps the Oracle could help," the older woman said.

"I have been thinking the same thing myself," Kiara confessed. "But—"

"But you're also thinking that your father was never comfortable with the Oracle's prophecies," Malae finished for her. Kiara nodded and gulped her tea.

"Odd, isn't it? I've been running the kingdom for him for months now, and I'm scared like a kitchen maid to go against his wishes."

Malae chuckled. "Not so odd, my princess. He is still your father, and still the king. But if you recall, he is not opposed to the Oracle. He merely lacks patience with her roundabout prophecies." She smiled. "Your father is a direct man. He does not want to have to figure out advice. I suspect that if the Oracle spoke plainly, your father might take up a good bit of her time."

"I imagine you're right, Malae," Kiara said, cradling her teacup. "I guess I'm just afraid of finding more questions and no answers."

There was a quiet rapping at her door, and Kiara called for the visitor to enter. It was Allestyr, looking as if he had been up and active since dawn.

"My princess," the elderly seneschal said gently. "Your father calls for you."

With a sigh, Kiara finished her tea and set the cup aside. Malae was already on her feet, handing the princess a warm woolen robe. "Perhaps your father will know what you should do," Malae said, helping Kiara into the robe. "The magic that has crippled his body has not touched his mind."

Kiara nodded, squaring her shoulders. "I try not to give him more to worry about," she replied. Jae fluttered into the air with a squawk and landed on her shoulder.

"He is the king," Malae said. "Kings worry, whether you want them to or not."

Kiara smiled. "I think you're right," she said, and followed Allestyr into the hallway.

Her father's rooms, which always smelled of leather, cologne, and spices, now had the odor of a sickroom. His favorite hunting bows hung unstrung along the wall. His riding outfit lay folded in the armoire, next to his robes of state. Even his beloved intricate wooden puzzles lay forgotten on the table, too vexing for him now.

Kiara made her way to the king's massive bed, where her father lay propped up on pillows, a shadow among the furs and blankets. Next to his bedside was a steaming pot of mulled wine laced with the medicines that kept the king alert. King Donelan smiled and gestured for his daughter to join him, making a place for her to sit on the edge of the bed. Kiara smiled and climbed up, sitting cross-legged and wrapping herself in one of the king's sleeping furs.

"Good morning, Little Bird," King Donelan said fondly. Kiara reached out for his hand and pressed it to her cheek. He looked up at Jae, who hopped about on Kiara's shoulder, awaiting attention, and

Donelan reached up to stroke Jae's crest. "And good morning, Jae. Any good hunting lately?" he asked, and the gyregon squawked in excitement.

"Good morning, father. How do you feel today?"

King Donelan coughed and shook his head, gently freeing his hand to reach for his warmed wine and holding the steaming mug in his hands for a moment before he sipped at the medicine. "The same as always, I'm afraid." He paused. "You look a bit worse for wear, Kiara," he said gently. "Tell me about the ambassador's visit."

Kiara recounted the details of Catoril's visit and her evasion while King Donelan listened. When she finished, the king nodded as he thought. "You did well, Kiara. You've bought us time, but you are also correct that it will be more difficult to dissuade him come spring. But there is no other answer which would have satisfied him, so don't fret yourself." Kiara took his mug to keep it from spilling as coughs racked the ailing monarch.

"Thank you," he said, accepting the mug once more when the coughing fit ended. "Now, you haven't told me everything," the king said with a knowing glance at his daughter. "You are too tired for having had a simple dinner with an ambassador. You've done another Working lately, haven't you?"

Sheepishly, Kiara nodded. "Did you know or did Tice tell you?"

King Donelan smiled. "No, Tice kept your secret. But I can feel the regent magic when it is done by one of the blood, whether you work it in my presence or not."

"I don't know what to do, father," Kiara blurted, looking down at her hands. "Your illness hasn't gotten any better, no matter how many mages and physicians we bring in. If they're right, and it's mage-sent, then we still don't know by which mage. Margolan won't stop until we're at war or Jared has me to wife, and the scouts are bringing back more reports that there are dark creatures along the western border, unnatural things that shouldn't be, but are. No matter where I turn, Isencroft is in peril, and it seems as if nothing I can do will help."

She caught her breath, then continued headlong, feeling a little relief as the worries tumbled out in words. "Then in the Working, I saw Cam and Carina in trouble. There was danger, and flames..." Despite herself, a tear made its way down her cheek. "They're not going to make it to the Sisterhood," she said miserably. "So we won't know whether the Sisters know how to heal you, and I can't bear to think of life without Carina—"

"Hush, child," King Donelan said sternly, but his hand was gentle as he reached out to brush away Kiara's tears. "Now listen to me. First of all, remember that a scrying shows what may be, not what must be. So what you've seen, while troubling, isn't certain. Cam and Carina are quite resourceful," the king said with a chuckle. "I wouldn't count them out just yet." He paused, thinking. "But I agree, the other things together are worrisome, even for an old battle horse like me." His eyes saddened. "I never intended for you to take this on yourself just yet, Kiara. I hoped it would be many years before you shouldered these burdens, and that you had a consort to share them with. I am so sorry."

Kiara took his hand and folded it in both of hers. "Oh, father," she said, sniffing back her tears. "I'm made of sterner stuff than that. After all," she said, managing a smile, "I'm your daughter."

The king chuckled. "That indeed you are. But even the king knows to get help when he's outnumbered. So this is what you must do," he said, his voice hardening as it did when he was about to issue a royal decree. "You must go to the Oracle at Chenne's temple. Whatever she tells you, you must do it, even if it means leaving on your Journey."

"But father—" Kiara protested in amazement, eyes wide. "You've never had any patience with the Oracle!"

King Donelan's face was stern as he shook his head, silencing her protests. "No 'buts.' If it means you must leave the palace, then that is what you must do. If it means you must leave Isencroft, then so be it. If this is the time for your Journey, then you will go without protest. Tice and Allestyr have kept the kingdom running while I was out on campaigns long before you were born. They're not so old that they can't do it again, if that's what the Goddess wishes."

Seeing the resolve in his eyes, Kiara swallowed and nodded. "Yes, father," she replied, looking down at her hands again. The king reached out to tip her chin upwards, so that she looked into his blue eyes.

"Kiara, you are very brave. The Goddess did not come to you to have you trapped in a palace by an old man's sickness. I have known since the first moment I held you that there was some great purpose for which you were born. Perhaps this is your time."

Kiara nodded, all tears gone, and clasped his hand firmly. "I'll do what you ask, father. I'll go tonight."

King Donelan nodded. "That's better." He began to cough once more and reached for his wine. "Now leave me to my medicines, my dear. And have them make you a better breakfast than that little bit of fruit you pick at each morning." He smiled at her surprise. "Oh yes, my dear. The king knows even that." He waved his hand at her gently. "Now, be gone. I feel a nap coming on." He watched her as she made her way to the door.

"Kiara," he called after her as she reached the doorway, and she turned.

"Trust the Goddess."

CHAPTER TWELVE

THAT NIGHT, WHEN the moon was full, Kiara
set out. Jae caught up with her as she
reached the stables, alighting on her shoulder and
making questioning hisses as she readied her
mount. She reached up and scratched his scales
just below the crest on his head.

The horse she chose, a midnight stallion,
nickered. The same intuition that made her
select the war horse also nudged her to find a
saddle suitable for a long journey, though the
Oracle was only a candlemark's ride from the
palace.

She left a note for Malae, telling of her journey
to the Oracle, adding a note to Tice that author-
ized the seneschal and Allestyr to assume the
regency in her stead until she returned. Hardly a
note one leaves for a quick ride, she thought, grimacing as she cinched the saddle straps. Then

again, princesses, even in Isencroft, rarely felt moved to take off in the night.

Kiara grabbed a saddlebag and checked her gear. Her sword and belt daggers hung at her side. She wore her drabbest riding gear and her most comfortable boots, along with a heavy cloak. Deep in her packs was a signet ring with the royal seal which would open any border in Isencroft and end any argument.

Under her riding cloak was the leather and light mail bodice she wore whenever she ventured beyond the castle grounds. Had she been more vain, it might have vexed her that the protective gear did nothing for her figure. Now, as she twisted her long hair into a knot and secured it at the nape of her neck, she was glad that she rarely fussed over such things. *Otherwise I'd be sick, since I probably look more like a hired sword than a princess right now,* she thought.

"Your Highness."

Kiara looked up at the voice that came from the shadows. Rall, the late queen's champion, led his horse into the small circle of lantern light. "We are here." With him was Hastart, another of her father's most trusted soldiers. She had sent for each, asking them to outfit themselves for a night journey and meet her in the stables at the twelfth hour. She saw that they took her instructions literally, and were ready for a long and dangerous journey.

"Thank you for coming," she said, as she swung up into her saddle. "I have an urgent request to take to the Oracle. Ride with me to the temple. Perhaps she will have a message for us."

Both men bowed. "As you wish, my princess," said Rall. "We will accompany you wherever you go, for as long as you need us."

Even at this hour, there were travelers leaving the palace grounds. Not wanting to attract attention to her quest or her absence, Kiara slipped past the guards without comment by attaching herself to another group long enough to clear the gates. Once they were out of sight of the palace walls, she urged her horse toward the temple of the Oracle.

The Oracle's temple nestled at the edge of the forest, near the river, where the trees parted to frame the open sky. Its white marble glistened in the moonlight, and a reflecting pool mirrored the stars and the altar fires. On three sides, a ravine-shrine to the goddess ringed the temple, both monument and protection. Stone monuments were silhouetted in the glade, homage to military heroes, favored by Chenne.

The temple was quiet as Kiara hitched her horse to a tree and stepped onto the marble terrace. She motioned for Rall and Hastart to wait with the horses, and started down the pathway toward the grotto. They passed the mews of falcons, sacred to Chenne the warrior, and the birds fluttered and shrieked in alarm. "Well, they've certainly heard us coming now," Kiara muttered to Jae, who eyed the falcons as she jerked his traces lightly in a warning reminder. The little dragon hissed in disappointment and settled down on Kiara's shoulder, his scaled head swiveling as he looked for other late-night morsels.

Kiara looked toward the altar and stopped. A white-robed woman who seemed to appear from nowhere stood just beyond the fire. The Oracle! Kiara thought. Drawing a deep breath for courage, Kiara swallowed and moved closer.

"My apologies, priestess, for disturbing your night," Kiara began, unsure of how to proceed. "I am Kiara of the House Sharsequin, and I—"

"I know who you are," the cowled woman replied. "Why have you sought the Goddess?"

"I've come to pray for my father's health," Kiara replied, hoping her courage didn't desert her. She paused. "And to ask the Lady how to save our kingdom."

The cowled priestess nodded. "Your father is dying," she replied matter-of-factly. "But the illness is mage-sent."

"We recognized that a dark mage sent the illness, my lady," Kiara said.

The priestess nodded slowly. "You have sent your best healer to find a cure, is that correct?"

"Yes, m'lady, but it will be some time before she returns—"

"The Sisterhood may help delay your father's death, but to destroy the spell, you must destroy the caster of the spell."

"Your Grace, we have no mages of such power—"

"From Margolan comes both the spell and the solution," the priestess replied. "The dark hand who cast the spell and He Who Can Restore."

Her voice took on a singsong lilt as she swayed in trance, insubstantial beneath her robes. "Your path lies along a different course. If you wish to save your kingdom, then you must let others save your father." The Oracle paused. "You must play your part in destroying the caster of the spell. What you seek can be found within the Library at Westmarch. The time for your Journey is come. You must go to Westmarch."

"Westmarch!" Kiara breathed. "But it doesn't exist! It's nothing but a children's tale—isn't it?" Her voice trailed off, unsure.

"Behold my servant." At that, the priestess raised her hand and Kiara saw a figure, clad in the brown robes of a land mage, step from the shadow of a marble column. "If you succeed, my Chosen, you will save your king and kingdom," the Oracle continued, her voice becoming more firm and certain, losing the singsong of the priestess. "If you fail, the darkness comes." For an instant, Kiara saw the same flash of otherworldly eyes that she remembered so well from the battlefield of her childhood. "Go with my blessing."

At that, the fiery eyes dimmed suddenly and with a moan, the robed figure slumped, its hood falling back to reveal the mortal priestess through whom the Goddess spoke.

"Come with me, Kiara Sharsequin," a brown-robed figure said from the shadows. "The priestess will be well. She is privileged to serve her Goddess. Now, your turn has come."

"I must let my guards know," Kiara stammered. "I can't just disappear."

"We will announce your Journey to them," the robed figure replied, "and to your father. He has awaited this time. Come." The figure held out a hand, and heart thudding, Kiara stepped forward, despite Jae's hisses. As she neared, the figure reached out to envelop her in a cloak that smelled of herbs and smoke and the wet moss after a new rain, and for an instant, as her head swam, Kiara swore the ground melted from beneath her feet. When the mage lowered the cloak, the temple was gone.

"Where am I?" Kiara asked, her hand moving for her sword.

"In a cloister of the Sisterhood," replied her robed companion, whose hood fell back to reveal an aging woman of medium build, her weathered face handsome, whose blue eyes sparkled with amusement at Kiara's confusion.

"In Dhasson?" Kiara asked, looking around her. "But that's where I sent Carina—it's over two months' ride away!"

The robed woman smiled indulgently. "We are still in Isencroft. The Sisterhood has many cloisters. The one you speak of is one of the few we permit outsiders to recognize. There have been too many over the years who sought to destroy us. This is one of those secret places."

Kiara looked around in silence, reaching up to stroke Jae's talons as the gyregon, shrieking its alarm, clenched painfully on her shoulder. With an unconvinced hiss, the little dragon settled down, gazing balefully at their host.

With a smile, the woman looked at the frightened little dragon and spoke a word that to Kiara sounded like the rush of water on rock. To Kiara's astonishment, the gyregon calmed immediately.

"What did you say to him?"

"Merely that neither he, nor you, had cause for fear," the Sister replied.

"You can talk to Jae?"

"You have much to learn, Goddess-blessed," the sorceress replied. "Come."

Kiara followed the woman down a maze of corridors, carved deep within the rock. The air was fresh and cool, and the pathway was worn smooth. Chambers with heavy wooden doors branched off from their path. Finally, the corridor opened into a great hall. Magelight sparkled from the crystals that coated the rock pillars of the chamber, and in the massive hearth, a magefire gave warmth without smoke.

Four Sisters sat behind a massive oval table wrought from the rock itself. The women wore no ornamentation and were clad in the same plain brown robe as her hostess. Even so, Kiara could sense their power.

"Come closer, Kiara of the House Sharsequin," one of the Sisters said, in a voice that crackled like fire in dry leaves. Kiara was later unsure she heard the voice at all, or whether it sounded, unspoken, in her mind.

"You petitioned the Goddess for the health of the king and the safety of Isencroft. She has told you the source of the bane," the woman continued. "Would you undo this spell to save your kingdom?"

Without hesitation, Kiara nodded. "Yes, Your Grace."

"Would you give up your privilege, your position if that is what the Lady requires?"

"Yes, Your Grace."

"What of your life, Kiara Sharsequin? This spell was not mortal-made. Would you risk your life?"

Kiara swallowed, but nodded once more. "If that is the will of the Goddess," she whispered through a dry throat.

"It may be so, my child," the sorceress replied, blue eyes glinting in the magelight. "Step closer."

Kiara took a deep breath and stepped nearer to the dais. Jae sat like a statue on her shoulder. The speaker stared at her, and she felt a fleeting presence inside her mind. The Sister crossed her arms and leaned back, looking satisfied.

"Chenne has chosen well," the woman said. "Tonight, you begin your Journey."

Kiara nodded silently. The sense she felt at the palace, of following a pathway she could not clearly see, became even stronger, frightening and yet right.

"In the Library at Westmarch, you will indeed find all that is required to break this spell," the sorceress continued. "But a great evil must be cast down before that can happen."

"Your Grace, I do not know where to find the Library at Westmarch," Kiara replied. "I thought it was only a legend."

The Sister nodded, and looked to her fellows. Once again, Kiara sensed other presences, as if a conversation were taking place just on the verge of her hearing, and assumed the four were in conference. Finally, the Speaker leaned back once more. "Your Journey is part of a much larger story, one that began long ago," she said.

"Years ago, a great war was fought among the mages of the Winter Kingdoms, between those who would nurture the currents of magic for the good of all, and those who sought to bend its course for their own gain. In a conflict that nearly destroyed everything, the darkness was driven back, but not defeated. When the Great War ended, the mages of the Light were too spent to pursue the Dark Ones further, and it was our hope that they were damaged even more than we. We were mistaken." Her expression hardened. "They have returned. This time, we must stop them before they rise once more, or there will be no reprieve. Neither we nor the world itself can bear another great conflict."

"But I am not a true mage," Kiara protested weakly. "I have only the blood-line magic of Isencroft's kings. I can do so little. How can it help?"

The sorceress smiled, her eyes distant, as if remembering something from long ago. "There are magicks that have been forgotten, my princess, perhaps even by the Dark Ones themselves." She paused, and once again looked at Kiara as if taking the measure of her soul. "Now, it is time to ready you for your journey. At dawn, you must set out for Westmarch."

Before Kiara could ask the questions that filled her mind, her guide touched her arm. "Come with me," the brown-robed woman said. When Kiara looked back, the speaker and her companions were gone. Weak in the knees, Kiara allowed herself to be led from the audience hall.

She was clearly expected. A stack of new garments lay on the bed—rugged travel clothing that Kiara knew without checking was exactly her size. A worn-looking leather and light mail breastplate lay with them. A sizable purse of gold lay to one side, and on top lay a parchment map, yellowed with years. Next to these, a plain but beautifully worked dagger glittered beside a small velvet pouch and an unremarkable clay oval on a thong, pressed with runes Kiara did not recognize.

Kiara looked to her guide for explanation. The woman nodded toward the provisions. "Here is your first lesson in judgment, princess," her guide said. "What do you see?"

Kiara shook her head. "Ample provisions, more than I would have expected."

"Guard them well," her guide replied. "That riding cloak will hide your magic from those who scry for your power," she said, gesturing with a long, thin finger to the woolen cloak. "Replace your breastplate with the one on the bed." She held up a hand as Kiara began to protest. "It will lessen the impact of magic weapons, such as spelled daggers and arrows, but cannot turn them altogether. And its power can be exhausted, so do not offer yourself foolishly as a target."

Kiara turned the dagger in her hand, admiring its workmanship. "Guard it well, princess," her host said from behind her. "In the hands of a mortal, it will turn the undead. In the hands of a mage, it can destroy the soul."

"Undead?" Kiara whispered.

"You have much to learn," the guide said. "There are some who walk among us neither living nor dead. Some are wizards, who sought such power for themselves. Some are changelings, who by birth or accident lost their mortality. Yet others serve the Dark Lady as vayash moru."

Kiara's eyes widened. "But vampires are only in children's tales."

"Believing in them is beside the point." She reached past Kiara for the clay oval and handed it to the princess, who accepted it in cupped hands. "Guard this carefully, Kiara," she said gravely. "Use it only in a moment of dire need." As the woman turned it to the light, Kiara could see a pattern embossed in its surface. But as Kiara looked closer to examine the pattern, the lines blurred, as if in motion.

"This wafer is spelled with the magic of the Sisterhood," the sorceress said. "Snapped in two, it will transport the bearer and those in immediate contact to the place chosen in the bearer's mind." She replaced it carefully in the bag. "It may only be used once." She anticipated Kiara's objections. "You need not be a mage yourself to use these things. We know your gift, and its limits."

She gestured toward the coin purse that lay on the bed. "There is gold enough for your travels."

She gave an unexpected, mischievous smile. "That, at least, is as it seems." She paused, noting that Kiara remained silent. "There is more you do not say, Goddess-blessed."

"It's just... I sent my closest kinswoman to the Sisterhood in Dhasson. We were told that the Sisterhood's best healers were there. If you were so close, why—"

"Why didn't we just pop in with potions to help?" the Sister finished her sentence with gentle humor. Kiara nodded.

"We are aware of your father's sickness," the sister replied carefully. "And as much as I wish it were so, we do not have a 'magic potion' that can undo the spell. We sent word to our sisters in the Winter Kingdoms to see if any elixir might be found that could help prolong your father's life while you and others destroy the sender of the curse." She paused. "Word travels slowly, even among the Sisterhood. And such marvelous transportation as you experienced can be used only sparingly, for short distances, and at great cost. Otherwise, we are just as constrained by distance and the speed of a horse as non-mages," she said with a sad smile. "As for our cloister here, it is just a small hiding place. We have no healers here."

"But the Sisterhood has the most powerful mages alive," Kiara marveled. "Why would you need to hide?"

The Sister's eyes took on a sad, distant look. "What people do not understand, they either destroy or worship," she said quietly.

"Throughout our history, we have, unfortunately, encountered both. We neither seek worship nor martyrdom. And there is fear among our Sisters—well-founded fear—that now that Jared Drayke rules in Margolan, we may once again be targets."

"Why?"

The sister looked away. "Jared Drayke's mage, Foor Arontala, is well known to us. Now that he controls a king and the resources of a kingdom, his ambition will grow. He will see us as a threat, and rightly so, because his blood magic is the dark stain Bava K'aa and others gave their lives to wipe out."

"Can't you just... tounce him or something?"

The Sister chuckled. "I wish it were so easy. Perhaps no one since the Obsidian King so deserves to be 'trounced' as you put it. But the Sisterhood does not, cannot, intervene directly in the rule of kingdoms. To do so would bring about our destruction. We, too, would be seduced by power, and it would be our ruin. And so, we work behind the scenes. We enable, we guide, we arrange fortuitous coincidences," she said with a knowing smile. "But we cannot become kingmakers. We would be presuming the role of the Lady. Instead, we make it possible for Her will to work."

Kiara considered for a few moments. "If the Sisterhood does not have a potion, Carina's journey is in vain."

The sister shook her head. "We do not know that. Our sisters throughout the kingdoms will search their records and send us word if help can be found." she said. "You are correct that the healers in Dhasson are among our finest. It may well take the length of your kinswoman's journey for them to exhaust their resources and find something that can help. But I do not believe the journey is wasted," she said, meeting Kiara's eyes. "I believe their path is in the hands of the Lady Herself."

A knock at the door startled Kiara but her hostess brightened, expecting the interruption. "Come," she said, and the door opened to admit another robed woman carrying a tray full of food. Kiara's stomach rumbled, reminding her that it was nearly morning. "You must be hungry by now," the guide remarked, and while she did not completely lose her reserve, by comparison, she was now almost friendly. "Please eat well, and take your rest. You have a long journey ahead of you."

"What happens after I wake up?"

"When you awaken you can be on your way," the Sister replied, turning to go.

"Wait!" Kiara called after her. "How am I going to know what to seek at the Library?"

"What you need will come to you." Without additional comment she turned, leaving Kiara and Jae alone.

Kiara watched the door close, then dropped onto the bed as Jae flew a small circle in the room, hissing skeptically.

"I know, I know," she moaned to her companion. "I feel the same way. It's bad enough leaving in the middle of the night and getting assigned a Journey, but, Goddess, we're in a Citadel of the Sisterhood!" she exclaimed while the gyregon gurgled his reply. "We're in the thick of it now, and there's no going back," she said. "Even stopping a dark mage sounds better than marrying Jared!"

With a sigh, Kiara sat up, stirred by the smell of warm biscuits and hot tea. A thick potage simmered under a silver lid. She was delighted to find a bowl filled with bits of meat for a gyregon meal, and Jae settled down across from her on the table to feast, gurgling contentedly as he gulped his bounty. Between mouthfuls, she thought aloud to the little dragon.

"I remember a legend about Westmarch," she murmured. "I think it was supposed to be near the borders of Dhasson and Eastmark, upriver on the Nu," she recalled, spreading out the map between herself and the gyregon.

She frowned. "Cam and Carina went toward the Sisterhood's cloister in Valiquet, the palace city in Dhasson. I'm more than a month behind them." Her finger traced the most likely routes. "Westmarch is almost two months' ride from here," she said thoughtfully. "That's if I take the quick route, right across the top of Margolan, through the Borderlands just below the sea. And pray for good weather." She grimaced. "I don't know which is more dangerous—taking my chances with bandits in the Borderlands or hoping that Jared doesn't notice that I'm sneaking across his kingdom." She thought for a few minutes and looked up at the gyregon, who had finished his meal and rocked back and forth on his hind claws, burbling contentedly.

"That route is still at least three weeks north of Margolan's palace at its closest point," she mused. "And Jared has to suspect I'm there to look for me. The closer we get to Westmarch, the longer it will take his guards to catch up to me, even if he does hear."

She set the map aside and cradled a hot cup of tea. "Maybe Carina will find what she needs from the Sisterhood, and be on the way back to Isencroft before I return," she mused. "Or maybe, the Sisterhood will send her to the Library, too. I don't understand how wizards think! Why can't anything be simple!"

She stood up, stretching, and set the items on the bed to one side, turning down the ample covers. "Well, at least we know we're safe to sleep for tonight," she said to Jae. She climbed into bed and the gyregon made himself comfortable on the chair next to her, wrapping his tail around himself with a contented hiss. "Enjoy it," she said sleepily as she extinguished the candle. "I don't think we'll sleep well until we're home again."

CHAPTER THIRTEEN

Jonmarc Vahanian headed into the Boar's Inn with caution. Inside, a motley clientele packed the greatroom. Toward the hearth, four merchants drank together over steaming trenchers heaped high with food. A small group of priests huddled near the wall, in quiet conversation over a bottle of wine. Three of the local baron's guardsmen laughed raucously near the fire, uproarious over a joke and a large jug of ale.

Altogether unremarkable, he thought, scanning the crowd. Ploughmen and merchants drank together, while near the fire, a bard sang to a small audience. Vakkis was nowhere to be seen. Vahanian ordered his food and a Cartelasian brandy to wash it down. He caught himself tapping his foot, and frowned. Long ago, he'd learned to listen to himself, to the instincts that kept him alive. He was nervous as a cat tonight, without good reason.

Arrestingly blue eyes locked with his. He froze. The blond man had not been there when he first scanned the room. The man was about Vahanian's own age, with an aristocratic mien and hair the color of flax. He was thin, with a pallor that suggested he did not work in the sun. He regarded Vahanian with a mixture of curiosity and jadedness that sent a chill down the mercenary's back.

"Here's your brandy," the barkeeper said, setting down Vahanian's order with a thump. "Five skrivven if you please," he said, pushing a trencher of steaming food next to the heavy glass tumbler. Vahanian dug for his coins and paid the innkeeper, then turned to find a table.

The flaxen-haired man was gone.

Vahanian found a seat with his back to a wall, perfectly positioned to watch the inn's clientele, nodding at the table's other occupants as he squeezed into an open space. He looked back to where the blond man stood just an instant before, to assure himself that the man was indeed gone. Vahanian's misgivings increased as he sipped his brandy. He should have seen the man pass on his way out. Vahanian was facing the stairs to the rooms above, so if the man had simply retired for the evening, Vahanian should have seen him leave by that way, too. The door to the kitchen was behind the bar, and the inn's large windows were shut against the chill night air. The man should still be in the tavern. But he was not.

Forcing his mind away from the flaxen-haired stranger, Vahanian surveyed the room once more. He had purposely chosen a table near the thick of the action, where he could hear as well as see. Three burly guardsmen in nondescript livery finished up their ale at a table near the fire. The red-haired one looked familiar, but Vahanian could not place him. Over the years there had been too many run-ins with too many guards in too many places. By rights, he thought as he sipped his brandy, half the guardsmen in the Winter Kingdoms should look familiar.

He let his attention move from one overheard conversation to the next. The priests at the nearby table were from Nargi, but no arcane religious matters concerned them. The disappearance of a young noblewoman, possibly waylaid by slavers, consumed their conversation, morbid speculation mixing with what appeared to be genuine concern for the young woman's welfare. Not much chance for that, Vahanian thought as he tore off a piece of the warm bread. He had encountered slavers once before, enough to last him for a lifetime. They preferred less traveled byways through disputed territories, where neither king nor noble was likely to bring arms against them. Some mountain passes were nearly unusable because of them, for any but a large armed party.

If slavers were on the prowl again, perhaps a warning to Linton might be in order, Vahanian thought, letting the brandy burn its way down his throat. Across the room, the woeful strains of the bards' songs reached him, a mournful tune about a young woman whose love for an Immortal doomed them both. It was an old tune, with as many variations as there were taverns, and when the guardsmen's laughter drowned out the last chorus, Vahanian found he could fill in the last verse from memory.

"Gettin' so that it's not safe no more, travelin'," his companion to the right commented. "First the bandit gangs, as if common highwaymen weren't bad enough," his tablemate lamented. "Not like the wolves or the weather warn't enough of a problem. But now, it's worth your life to journey north. If the magicked things don't get you, slavers will."

"Maybe the magicked things will get the slavers and save us the bother," Vahanian replied.

His tablemate grunted. "Huh. You'd think so, but there's enough profit to be made, I hear as soon as one slaver disappears there are four more to take his place." He leaned over conspiratorially. "Though I did hear that there were remains found, up on the Joursay Pass, that curdled even slavers' blood," he added in a rum-soaked wheeze. "Naught but pieces of beasts, like they'd torn themselves to bits battling over what was left of some poor Goddess-forsaken group of travelers. Heard tell that the beasts warn't nothing ever seen by nobody round here before, since the Great Wars. Magicked things, bless the Mother and Childe, straight out of the Tales."

"Bound to be bad for business," Vahanian remarked, half-listening as he surveyed the room once more. It was unusually full for early in the evening. Perhaps the rumors were getting credence. If travelers truly feared both slaving gangs and magic monsters, it would be no surprise if they had sought refuge early. Then again, he thought, perhaps both rumors were instigated by tavern owners to boost their business. He did something similar himself, years ago, in his river days. Started the story that one of the tributaries was infested with poisoned eels, and made sure that some dead ones washed up near there. By the time the scare had calmed down, Vahanian had managed to steal most of the business from his upstream rivals, based, not coincidentally, on the ill-fated tributary. Of course, disclosure had resulted in hasty relocation, but such were the realities of business.

"You're right, it's too big a problem for any one man to worry hisself about," Vahanian's tablemate continued, undeterred by the lack of enthusiastic response. "Looks like old Vakkis has bitten off more than his share this time, I'd say."

Vahanian's attention snapped back to the present. "Why do you say that?" he asked casually, glancing down at his food to mask his acute interest. He could feel his heart beginning to pound.

"Why, he's sold his services to King Jared, down in Margolan, to rid the border of slavers and bring back the mage that made the monsters," the tradesman replied, in a tone that told Vahanian that it was no longer fresh news. "Says 'twas the same wizard as killed King Bricen, Goddess rest his soul, and that like as not, kidnapped that noble lady for some awful dark sacrifice." He shook his head, mopping up the last of the juices with his bread. "There's one that's dead for sure, that's a fact," he said ruefully, stuffing the bread into his wide mouth. "More's the pity, since the King of Principality offered a mighty fine sum for her return."

Just like Vakkis, Vahanian thought, feeling his fists clench under the table. He did not doubt that the bounty hunter was using the rumors of trouble in the north to hide his true quest to hunt down Tris. By linking Tris to the dark magic and the young noblewoman's disappearance, Vakkis made it impossible for Vahanian and the others to count on aid from noble houses along the way. Dark Lady take his soul! Vahanian swore under his breath. Now they would have to be doubly careful. Whatever they were going to pay me, I want double, whether or not they bring down Arontala, he thought, finishing off his dinner. Not for the first time, he reconsidered his decision to guide the party to Dhasson.

"He's got a king this time, Jonmarc, not just a general like at Chauvrenne," Harrtuck had said, and Vahanian closed his eyes. A decade's passing did little to cloud the memory of those horrors, or the knowledge of just how terribly a dark mage could twist a man of power and what evil could come of it. It didn't take much to hear the screams of the villagers in his mind, recall their fear. The tavern smells of wood smoke and roasting meat were close enough to the smell of burning shacks and searing flesh that he fought an urge to be sick. He forced the memories back, sure tonight's sleep would not be dreamless. The memories, and the chance to even the score with Arontala, were too powerful to walk away from, even now, even though he'd given up on hopeless causes long ago, at Chauvrenne.

Not yet ready to leave behind the light and warmth of the tavern, Vahanian lingered for a candlemark longer, listening to similar tales and watching the odd assortment of travelers. Finally, he stood. "Good travels to you," Vahanian said to his table companions. He had what he'd come for. Now to ride for the caravan and plan their northbound strategy—and press his employers even more about Arontala and his hold over Jared Drayke.

The three guardsmen emptied their jug of ale and made their way clumsily to the front as Vahanian stood. They pushed their way among the tables as they wended toward the doorway, jostling Vahanian hard as he got to his feet. So hard, that Vahanian took a second look at the red-haired guardsman who pushed him as the loud group passed. Vahanian frowned. Something prickled again in the back of his mind. In his line of work, guardsmen were a necessary part of doing business, whether that involved bribing them or eluding them. Still, for caution's sake, Vahanian settled back into his chair on the pretense of ordering one last ale and waited for half a candlemark to let the guardsmen be on their way before venturing out of the tavern.

The alleyway in front of the inn was quiet when Vahanian finally left the building. He checked the narrow lane with a practiced eye. A beggar leaned on his staff at one end, picking at rags in a heap. In a shadowed doorway on the right, Vahanian could hear the sounds of a strumpet's tryst. Along the street, the darkened stalls of the produce merchants waited for the morning market, with nets of plaster fruit strung above each empty stall and stacks of flat wheeled carts behind, awaiting the next morning's cargo. Cautiously, he ventured down the stairs. His horse stood tethered just beyond the alley's entrance. Vahanian's hand fell to the hilt of the knife in his belt. Something was wrong, an inner sense told him. The sooner he reached his horse and headed for the caravan, the better.

The darkened doorways remained silent as he passed them. Ahead, the beggar shuffled and sang quietly to himself. With the main street only a few paces away, Vahanian began to chide himself. *You're losing your touch. Must be what starts to happen when you go into the guide business instead of real work.*

The only warning Vahanian had was the whistle of the beggar's staff as it swung full force for his shoulder blades. The rod connected hard, driving him to his knees, and behind him, Vahanian could hear the beggar laughing. As Vahanian scrambled to his feet, knife already in hand, two of the guardsmen from the inn appeared at the entrance to the alley, closing the exit. Vahanian wheeled to find the "beggar" peeling off the filthy rags to reveal the red-haired guardsman from the tavern, leering drunkenly as he let the heavy staff bounce in his hands.

"Look, I've got no quarrel with you," Vahanian gasped as he struggled to catch his breath. "Let me pass and we'll just say that none of this ever happened."

The red-haired guardsman shook his head. "I told you he wouldn't even remember," the drunken guard shouted to his friends. His eyes narrowed. "But I remember."

The two guardsmen were slowly advancing, forcing Vahanian to back down the alley. Vahanian glanced past them at his waiting mount. An easy sprint, if he could get an opening. His horse was lightly tethered, important in a business that often required a quick exit.

"Whatever it is, you've got the wrong man," Vahanian stalled, letting the two guardsmen step just a little closer. He dropped to a crouch and wheeled, his left leg arching high as he executed a near-perfect Eastmark kick. Mid-arch, he gasped as pain radiated down his bracing leg and it collapsed under him. He grasped at the knife buried hilt-deep in his thigh.

"None of your tricks this time, Vahanian," the red-haired guardsman grated as Vahanian fought to stand. "I'll have back the money you cheated me, or take my satisfaction out on your useless hide."

Vahanian managed to get to his feet, although it was impossible to use his right leg for more than balance. "Look, I don't know what you're talking about," he gasped. There were too many "dissatisfied customers" over the years, too many places and too many deals.

"Let me help your memory," the red-haired man said. "A card game in Jalwar five years ago."

"Rubies," Vahanian replied, his throat dry. "I paid you in rubies."

The guardsman swung his staff once more, cracking across Vahanian's ribs. "Glass," he hissed as Vahanian gasped for air and staggered backward. "You gave me worthless glass. When I used your 'rubies' to pay my debts, the stinking tax collector arrested me for cheating him." The drunken guard's face hardened. "I worked off that debt in his fields, in his whore-spawned fields, because of you."

"Look, whatever you want, I'm sure we can work something out," Vahanian stalled. Running was out of the question, even if he could get past the guardsman's two friends. He doubted he could make it back to the inn. Shouting for help would elicit no response from the inn's patrons, who were too familiar with the nightly brawls to pay heed.

The guardsmen were trying to back him into one of the vendor's stalls, where they could exact their payment undisturbed. As Vahanian backed toward the melon vendor's table, he caught sight of the pendulous net of plaster fruit hanging overhead. *If only,* he thought, slowing his retreat to let his attackers get a little closer.

Using all the strength in his good leg, Vahanian jumped straight up for the net, slashing at it with his knife. As the heavy plaster fruit fell, he let his momentum carry him toward the table, and as he crashed onto it and slipped off the other side, he upended it, then scrambled for the small flat wagons stacked three high behind the table. Clutching one of the wheeled boards against his aching ribs, Vahanian dove, hitting the rough street with a bone-jarring slam that nearly blacked him out. The wheeled cart skittered toward freedom as his attackers struggled with the fallen netting and the hail of plaster fruit. *Just a little farther,* Vahanian whispered under his breath as he heard boot steps pound. *Just a little farther.*

He heard a cry behind him as one of the guardsmen gave a flying tackle, falling just short of the wagon but grasping both Vahanian's ankles, pulling him from the wagon. The second guardsman closed the distance, hauling Vahanian roughly to his feet and pinning his elbows behind his back. The red-haired guardsman stood before him, letting the staff rise and fall in his hands, his eyes hard.

"Not so easy this time, thief," the guardsman taunted, and the guard behind Vahanian yanked his arms back hard, eliciting a gasp as the cracked ribs protested. "You're going to die tonight."

"Look, I've got money, I can settle this with you," Vahanian bargained as the guardsmen pushed him toward the darkened stalls. His heart thudded. The situation was rapidly moving from very bad to hopeless. "I got cheated on the rubies myself. It was an honest mistake." Snatching an escape out of a dicey situation was his specialty, but this time, no opening presented itself. As they moved toward the shadows, Vahanian feared the guardsman's prediction was quite likely to come true.

"Too late, thief," the guardsman replied tonelessly. "We've had a bad week and you're going to help us work it off."

Vahanian felt a cold rush of air from the shadows, saw the blur of motion instead of the thing itself as something snatched the guardsman on his right and dashed his burly frame against the wall like a child's doll. The other two guardsmen wheeled, swords in hand, to face darkness.

"What kind of trick is this, Vahanian?" the red-haired guardsman cried, searching the darkness in a battle stance.

The rush of wind and the sense of a presence blurred the night again, and the guardsman to Vahanian's left gave a dry wail of terror. There was silence, then boot steps as a dark figure emerged from the shadows, holding the dead guard by his crushed throat with an eerie effortlessness.

"What demon are you?" the red-haired guardsman shouted at the darkness, his voice cracking with terror. The figure continued toward them, until the moonlight illuminated his face.

It was the flaxen-haired man from the tavern.

Vahanian felt elation at his rescue die in a cold lump in his stomach. Nothing human could heft the guardsman by one hand. Cut off from the street, the man was wild-eyed with fear, his sword shaking in his hand and his pale skin ghostly white in the moonlight.

"Stay back, whatever you are," the guardsman menaced with the sword, voice quivering. "This sword was blessed by a priestess. It's good against magic, so stay back now, I'm warning you."

The blond man tossed the second guard aside. A cold, jaded amusement hinted at the corners of his thin lips as he moved relentlessly toward the last guardsman. Vahanian, blocked from escape and knowing himself to be easy prey in his present condition, stepped deeper into the shadows, hoping the blond man would be sated with a third kill.

The guardsman slashed frantically at the blond man, warning him away. Still, the stranger advanced, until with a lightning quick rush he snatched the blade from the guardsman's hand. Eyes wide in terror, sobbing for his life, the red-haired man fell to his knees. The blond man stood before him, his aristocratic face emotionless. Then the stranger reached out one thin, impossibly strong hand to grasp the guardsman by the collar and lift him to his feet, bringing him into his arms. The doomed man fell silent and Vahanian watched in horror as the blond man's lips drew back, revealing sharp, unnatural teeth. In a few moments, the feeding was over, and the vayash moru dropped the dead guardsman like a discarded crust. The flaxen-haired man turned to the darkness where Vahanian hid.

"You are safe now," the man said, with the hint of an accent that Vahanian could not identify.

"Yeah?" Vahanian stepped from the shadows into the moonlight, knowing that he stood no chance against this adversary.

A cold smile touched the stranger's lips. "My name is Gabriel," he said, with a self-assurance Vahanian somehow only expected to find in an immortal. "I have a message for you from the Sisterhood." He licked his lips. "I thought I might find you in the tavern, but the press of... bodies... became uncomfortable for me. When I chose to wait for you outside, I overheard the guardsmen's plan. It became necessary for me to... intervene."

"You have a message for me?"

"Martris Drayke must not cross into Dhasson. Dark magic waits for him there. What you seek from the north will meet you on the journey. He must not cross the border."

"I don't know what you're talking about." Vahanian put on his best wagering face, no small feat considering his heart was hammering so hard he could barely breathe.

Gabriel smiled, a cold grimace that made his teeth far more apparent than Vahanian preferred. "Yes, my mistress informed me you could be difficult."

"And who might that be?" Vahanian returned, managing to get a measure of bravado into his voice.

"I am the servant of the Dark Lady," Gabriel replied, without a hint of sarcasm. "As are you."

"The only goddess I serve is Luck."

Gabriel's eyes held a cold amusement. "Perhaps. Or maybe, you know Her by another name." He paused, an unreadable expression in his eyes, and his tongue darted at the last flecks of blood on his lips. "Now go. And ride a well-used trail. I am not the only one who can smell blood in the darkness."

"Yeah, sure," Vahanian replied uneasily. "Whatever you say." He glanced away to assure himself that his horse still waited at tether, and when he looked back to where Gabriel had been, the blond man was gone. Vahanian shivered. Tonight was too close a call he thought as he limped toward his horse. Apparently, he had seriously underestimated the stakes in this game.

CHAPTER FOURTEEN

"CARINA," TRIS HISSED at the tent flap. He knew that his voice shook, and not entirely from the cold as he stood outside the healer's tent. "Carina!" he rasped, barely above a whisper.

Carina pushed back the tent flap groggily. She pulled a blanket closer around her against the chill, and rubbed her eyes. "Tris, what's wrong? It's the middle of the night."

"I need your help," Tris said, managing as steady a voice as he could. "Please, I can't wait for morning."

Nodding, Carina stepped aside and gestured for Tris to follow. She lit two candles and motioned him to sit. "You look awful."

"I haven't slept for days," Tris confessed. "Every time I drift off, the dreams come back, and I can't block them out."

"What dreams?" Carina asked, wide awake and alert as she settled into her healer's role.

Tris looked away. "My family was murdered," he said softly, swallowing hard. "I... I've tried to call their ghosts," he admitted. "I can't reach them. I can feel them out there, far away, but it's like they're behind a wall, and they want to come, but they can't. Something's holding them back, keeping them prisoner," he finished lamely.

"I keep dreaming about Kait," he added, in a voice just above a whisper. "My sister. She's frightened, she's calling me, and I can't go to her and I can't call her to me. All I can see is her face, pressed against a barrier, calling my name," he said with a shudder, and closed his eyes.

Carina laid a hand on his arm. "Nothing I taught you helps at all?" she asked gently. They had managed to steal a few hours over the last week to help Tris work on shielding, teaching him how to keep from being overwhelmed by the spirits he sensed around him.

Tris shook his head. "Not with the dreams. It keeps the other spirits further away, but it doesn't work with the dreams. I've tried. I've tried everything. Night before last, I even sat up drinking with Soterius and Vahanian until I was sick. Even that didn't help," he said miserably. "I couldn't stop seeing her face." He looked up and met Carina's eyes, feeling they could see right through him. "I let her down once, Carina, when I didn't save her life. I can't let her down again. I swore to her I would come for her, wherever she is, but I can't get through."

Carina chewed on the end of a lock of her hair as she reflected, all traces of sleep gone. "Let's try what I taught you again," she said, and held up a hand to stay his argument. "I need to see what's happening." Her eyes softened and she put a hand on his arm. "There's got to be a way to stop the dreams, Tris," she said earnestly. "I'll help you find it."

Tris held her gaze. "I won't let her down, Carina," he repeated. "And I'm afraid if we stop the dreams, I'll lose the link I have. Can we," he paused, searching for words, "blunt it, like we did with the way I sense the ghosts, so I can pay attention or not, instead of wiping it out completely?"

Carina sat back and regarded him for a moment. "I'm a healer," she said finally, "not a mage. We need Alyzza," she decided. "Wait here." After several minutes, she returned with the crone seer in tow. Alyzza looked no more disheveled for it being the middle of the night than she appeared during the day.

"Bad dreams, m'lad?" she croaked, settling down cross-legged beside him with surprising agility.

Tris nodded. Alyzza took Carina's hand to draw the healer down with them. "Trust an old mad woman to help, do you?" she chuckled. "You must have very bad dreams." She settled into her seat. "Let's see what we can do."

Patiently, Carina and Alyzza led Tris through the basic wardings and the pathworkings. They watched as he raised the mental barriers—

shields, Alyzza called them—that blocked out unwanted thoughts and intrusions. With his wardings and shields in place, Alyzza tested Tris, attempting to break through. Time and time again, he held her at bay while Carina stretched out her healer's awareness to sense the energies and stress within his body.

It was almost dawn when Tris sat back in frustration. "It's not your fault," he said. "I don't think we're getting anywhere. I'm doing everything you've taught me. It's not enough."

"What if you tried to sleep here, where we can watch over you," Carina suggested. "Maybe your shields are holding when you're awake, and you're not able to keep them in place when you sleep."

Tris shook his head in frustration. "It's nearly morning. There'll be no sleeping once the camp is awake. Maybe I just imagined it."

"No," Alyzza rasped. "It was no accident, nor imagining either. There is power in you, great power."

"If there's so much power," Tris snapped exasperatedly, "where is it when I need it?"

"At your fingertips, as you have seen," the old hag replied, nonplussed by his tone. "But it is wild, and so far, it has controlled you. You must learn to control it."

Tris sat back on the rug and ran his hands through his hair. "I don't understand," he said tiredly. "If it comes when I need it, when I'm in danger, isn't that enough?"

Alyzza shook her head. "The more you use your power, the more power flows through you. Power will not be denied. Every mage fights a constant battle to keep his power from controlling him."

"And the dark mages?" Tris asked, staring at the circle of candles on the tent floor.

"The dark mages live an illusion," Alyzza replied. "Consumed by their own power, they believe themselves in control. But they are just the servants of a greater Darkness."

"I'm ready to try again," Tris sighed, sitting up on his knees.

"Focus your thoughts," Carina coached. "See the fire, see the candles burst into light, feel it come from yourself," she said softly as Tris closed his eyes and stretched out his hand.

In his mind's eye, Tris saw the candles, sensed the current of power within himself. Unbidden, he saw Kait's face from the dream, heard her cry out for him, sensed her pain. He felt the power surge and opened his eyes as fire leaped from his outstretched hand, lighting not just the first of the ring of candles, but roaring along the circle until all had burst into flame, nearly consumed. Carina gave a sharp cry and scrambled out of the way, but the crone leapt forward, forcing Tris's hand down.

Shaking, Tris looked first to Alyzza and then to Carina. "What happened?" he asked, staring wide-eyed at the flickering candles. "I was trying so hard, and getting nowhere," he said softly, "and then I thought about Kait, and I felt something so strong flood through me…"

"The dark magic," the crone rasped. "Easy and strong, and more addictive than dreamweed. Your anger called it."

"If it could be harnessed, controlled—"

"It can never be controlled!" Alyzza cried. "Every instant that you draw upon the dark magic places your soul in peril. Even the greatest mages have felt its seduction. There has been no mage so great as the Obsidian King," the crone continued, her voice falling to a whisper, "and even he could not control the darkness. It consumed him, and made him its slave."

"You mean the Obsidian King was once a Light mage?" Tris asked, staring at his hands as if they held a bloodied sword.

"Long ago, yes," the crone replied. "Some say he was possessed by the spirit of an evil one stronger than himself. So believed the greatest mage, Bava K'aa. Others believe he thought that the dark power could be harnessed for good, bent to his will, washed clean. If so, he was wrong. It bent him, over the years, and dulled his mind, so that he could not see the change in himself. Even Bava K'aa could not persuade him to give it up," she went on, and seemed not to notice when Tris started at the mention of his grandmother. "That is how a good man became the greatest evil our world has seen."

Tris felt himself shaking, still staring at his hands. "I was thinking about my family," he said softly, "how they died. And the one who killed them... bringing him to justice."

"Justice was not your thought," Alyzza sniffed. "You were thinking of revenge. You want, more than anything, to be the instrument of his death."

"Yes," Tris whispered, closing his eyes and bowing his head. "You're right. Goddess help me, I do."

"You must decide," Alyzza said archly. "No good can come of vengeance. If that is what you seek, then the dark magic will consume you and you will work such evil that their deaths are trifling by comparison," she said, her hands twitching within her robes. "But there is another way."

"Tell me," Tris begged, raising his head.

"Let go of your family," Alyzza hissed. "Even you cannot bring them back." She placed a hand across his shoulders, and her sleeve brushed his throat. "There is a greater evil at work in the Winter Kingdoms than their deaths. Fight against it. If you permit the darkness to fill you, you will be consumed."

Carina watched wide-eyed as Tris buried his face in his hands. "Goddess Bright," he swore, his voice choked. "Help me," he begged. "I want so badly to punish him... By the Virgin and Whore, if you could have seen how they died." He dragged his sleeve across his eyes. "And now, Kait's spirit..."

"Alyzza, is this necessary?" Carina began, but the crone waved her still.

"In all things there is a time to decide," the witch rasped, her lips almost touching Tris's ear. "All of your roads branch from this moment. Choose."

"Sweet Mother and Childe, help me," Tris gasped. "I cannot... will not... be like that."

"Very good. You speak the truth," Alyzza said, straightening, and as she removed her arm from across Tris's shoulders, he could see the gleam of a knife blade in her palm.

"What?" Carina asked in shock as Tris's eyes widened. "You had that at his throat," the healer whispered.

Alyzza nodded soberly, sheathing the knife once more in the voluminous folds of her robe. "Aye. And even the most powerful mage could not have stopped it from slitting him ear to ear."

"Why?" Carina gasped.

"Because I could not let him live had he chosen darkness," Alyzza replied matter-of-factly. "Now, let's get on with our lessons," she said, settling her robes around her.

CHAPTER FIFTEEN

"IDENTIFY YOURSELF!" SOTERIUS challenged the darkness, as the hoofbeats drew closer at the perimeter of the camp.

"By the Whore," Vahanian cursed as he stopped his horse just within view. "Just let me get to bed." He dismounted and stumbled, nearly falling.

"Let me go," he growled as Cam and Soterius rushed forward. Vahanian knew there was no hiding his injuries. Blood caked his right leg, seeping from beneath a makeshift bandage. His face was bruised, his lip split and, from the feel of it, one eye was beginning to purple. From the way it hurt to breathe, Vahanian knew the guardsman's staff had broken a few ribs.

"I'll get Carina. Help him back to his tent," Cam offered, rousing another guard to take his watch as Soterius slipped his shoulder under Vahanian's arm.

"No, don't do that..." Vahanian protested, his voice trailing into a weak curse as Cam disappeared.

"Not too anxious to be healed, Jonmarc?" Soterius chuckled. Vahanian groaned, resigning himself to his fate and accepting the help Soterius offered.

"I wouldn't mind the healing if it didn't come with an opinion," he muttered darkly.

"You know, Carina doesn't do that to just anyone," Soterius replied. "I've found her to be quite pleasant. And she gets along very well with Tris," he added. "Very well."

"Oh yeah? How did I get so lucky?"

"Don't know. Maybe she likes you."

"You've got a real sense of humor," Vahanian replied, attempting not to limp and then giving up the effort. "That's as likely as a visit by the Goddess herself."

"Stranger things have happened," Soterius laughed. "Of course, it's always possible that you just annoy the hell out of her."

"More likely," Vahanian replied. "Much more likely."

They reached Vahanian's tent and Vahanian eased himself onto his bed. Soterius found a lantern and soon, Vahanian had light sufficient to survey his injuries. "Meet up with an old friend?" Soterius asked.

Vahanian shifted and winced. "An old business acquaintance, if you really want to know," he said, using both hands to straighten out his wounded leg and pulling at the bandage to expose the deep knife gash beneath. Soterius poured water into a pitcher and reached for a clean rag. He wrung it out and handed it to Vahanian, who began to dab gingerly at the wound, cleaning away the worst of the caked blood.

"There are easier ways to settle accounts," Soterius replied, leaning back against a tent post. "Like changing your name, for starters."

"Very funny," Vahanian replied dryly. He tore the cloth back from his wound and dabbed at it again. Soterius reached under the cot, rummaging until he found a flask of brandy and a cup, and poured Vahanian a long draught.

"How'd you know where it was?" Vahanian asked, licking the strong brandy from his lips.

Soterius shrugged. "Didn't figure you'd travel without it, and since I didn't see it, where else would it be?"

Vahanian chuckled. "Has anyone ever told you you're smarter than you look?" he jibed.

"Funny, I've heard the same about you."

From beyond the tent, they could hear footsteps and Carina's voice. "This is what you interrupted us for, Cam?" Carina protested, stopping in front of the tent. "What was it? A tavern brawl? Sell some bad brandy to a guard? Knife in the back from a lady friend?"

"Look, he's hurt bad," Cam said in his most persuasive voice, and without even seeing them, Vahanian could imagine Cam mustering his best boyish grin to win over Carina. He didn't need to see Carina to imagine her response.

"I'll bet Jonmarc sent you because he knew what I'd say if he came himself," Carina said darkly. "Didn't he?"

"Come on, Carina," Cam wheedled engagingly. "I know you two don't always see eye to eye. But look at it this way—you'd heal one of the horses, even if it nipped, wouldn't you?"

"That's going too far," Vahanian muttered. "I've gotten over worse, without help," he said, scowling. Returning his attention to his leg, he dripped a few drops of brandy into the wound, then stiffened, gritting his teeth with an expression that drew a chuckle from Soterius.

"Give up, Jonmarc," Soterius said. "Nothing can save you now."

They heard running bootsteps as a third person joined Cam and Carina. "What happened?" Maynard Linton puffed. "The guard sent word that Jonmarc came in looking like he'd been dragged by a wagon. Oh good, Carina, you're already here. Come on," and with that, Maynard pushed into the tent, pulling Carina by the wrist, with Cam bringing up the rear, a bemused smile on his face.

"Goddess of Light, Jonmarc," Maynard exclaimed, shaking his head as he took in Vahanian's state. "What did you stir up this time?"

"Just a little friendly conversation," Vahanian deadpanned. Even Carina's disapproval softened as she surveyed the extent of his injuries.

"Lie down," she said dryly. He winced as he leaned back on his elbows, then lowered himself onto his back. Carina frowned as she examined the gash in his leg, motioning Cam to bring the lantern closer. Cam handed her the bag of medicines and poultices he carried from her tent, and she rummaged through it, selecting a handful of herbs and a vial of blue liquid.

"What happened, Jonmarc?" Linton asked as Carina began to work on Vahanian's leg.

"Like I said, I ran into someone I knew from a while ago—ouch!" Vahanian replied, stiffening as Carina poured a few drops of the blue liquid onto his wound. "What is that stuff, fire?"

"Not anything a mercenary of your renown should find troubling," Carina replied coolly, and Linton stifled a snicker.

"Anyway," Vahanian continued, "he was... dissatisfied with some business we did. And when he happened to run into me at the tavern, he and his friends decided to even the score."

"Did you learn anything at the tavern—besides about avoiding past customers?" Linton asked.

Vahanian nodded and started to answer, but just then, Carina laid her hands over his wound and Cam motioned them silent. The big man stepped forward to place a hand on Carina's shoulder, and she nodded slightly to acknowledge his presence. Carina closed her eyes, and her features relaxed as she fell into a trance. Gradually, a faint blue light glowed around her hands over the area of the wound. Vahanian stiffened for a moment, then relaxed, and Carina removed her hands, revealing a closed wound that looked as if it had several weeks of good healing behind it.

"How…?" Vahanian asked, completely serious for once. Cam motioned him to be quiet and guided Carina to Vahanian's ribs, opening up what remained of his torn shirt. Vahanian winced as she touched the skin above the broken ribs, then the faint blue light shone once more. Soterius watched the mercenary relax as the healing penetrated the broken bones. Even Linton let out a low whistle of admiration, and Soterius crowded forward to see better.

Carina was tiring, but Cam gently guided her hands to the worst damage remaining—Vahanian's badly swollen nose. Vahanian attempted to watch, then gave up and closed his eyes, as the soft blue light flared again, reducing the swelling and beginning to knit the broken bones. Finally, Carina leaned back against Cam, exhausted.

"I'm afraid you're going to have to get over that lip the old-fashioned way, with a cold rag," she murmured tiredly. "But the rest should be better."

"Thank you," Vahanian said, no sarcasm in his tone this time.

Carina hesitated. "It was nothing," she said, looking down at her hands. "I can help you go to sleep now, if you'd like."

"Can't, just yet," Vahanian said. "Have to tell Maynard something."

"Whatever it is can wait for morning, Jonmarc," the wagonmaster chided gently.

Vahanian shook his head determinedly. "No. There's danger on the road north. Slavers. And some stories about 'magic monsters' that actually sound like there's something behind them."

"The hell I won't!" An angry voice shouted from outside the tent and a moment later, Kaine shouldered his way inside, dragging a large sack behind him.

"Linton, I need to see you," Kaine demanded.

Linton turned to him wearily. "Not now, Kaine. Whatever it is can wait 'til morning."

"No, we need to talk now."

"You can talk elsewhere," Carina said sharply.

Kaine glanced over at Vahanian and barked a coarse laugh. "Marvelous help you hire, Linton. Amazed he wasn't too drunk to find his way back." He gave a patronizing smirk in response to Carina's disapproving glare. "Linton and I have business to discuss. You're dismissed."

Cam growled and took a step forward as Soterius reached for his sword. Vahanian's hand fell to the knife at his belt.

"I'd advise you to apologize to the lady," Vahanian said.

"Enough!" Linton snapped. "Jonmarc, put down the knife. Cam and Soterius, that's enough. And as for you, Kaine, whatever it is we can discuss it in the morning."

"I'm taking half of the caravan down the Karstan Pass in the morning," Kaine retorted, and smiled smugly at Linton's reaction. "You heard me. Those tales about the haunts in the forest aren't just for children. Unnatural beasts are about."

"Those beasts are the stuff and nonsense of the bards," Linton replied.

"Is this real enough for you?" Kaine rejoined, reaching into the sack. He withdrew the severed head of a beast with the jaws of a deep-water fish, protruding eyes and slits for ears. Vahanian looked away, remembering another time long ago, when such a beast had given him the scar that ran from his chin down into his collar.

Linton caught his breath in amazement. "Where did you get that... thing?"

Kaine dropped the head back into his pack and folded his arms across his chest. "One of the scouts found it not a candle's mark from here. Bad enough that such a monster exists, but... where's the beast that killed it?" he said, leaning closer to Linton. "That's why half your caravan is going down the Pass."

"But the Pass leads away from the Dhasson border," Carina protested. "And some of us must get to Dhasson."

"Lady, Dhasson's at war," Kaine retorted. "They're overrun with beasts like that one," he said, toeing the bag. "And to get there, we've got to cross a forest that even the mages avoid. Not me. Think about it, Linton. Head for Dhasson and you arrive with half a caravan. Go with us, and you keep it all."

Linton's face was by now so red with anger that the little man looked ready to explode. "Get out of my sight, Kaine," he roared. "And take the spineless sons of whores with you who want to go. This is my caravan and I'll choose its route.

I've led my caravan through blizzards and deserts, and around army lines. Dark Lady take me if I'm going to be frightened off by granny-witch tales, or the likes of you."

Kaine raised his hands in mock appeasement. "Suit yourself. But Dhasson'll be a mighty scant profit without half your wagons."

"I built this caravan without you, and I can do it again, if I have to, you thieving whore's son!" Linton ranted. "Now get out of my sight and be glad I don't use you as bait for another one of those goddess-damned things," he said with a nod toward the bag on the floor. Cam advanced another step toward the roustabout, who looked from Cam's menacing form and Soterius's sword to Vahanian's knife blade, then to Linton's apoplectic expression. Snatching up his bag, Kaine huffed toward the door.

"Mark my words, Linton, you'll be sorry," Kaine threatened as he pulled back the tent flap. "You'll see." He ducked out just in time as Linton snatched up a goblet and heaved the heavy cup at Kaine's head. The group looked in silence at each other after the roustabout left.

"Don't even say it, Jonmarc," Linton growled.

"I can't imagine what you mean," Vahanian replied with mock innocence. Carina frowned and bent over him once more.

"No more talking tonight," she ordered, with a glare at Linton. "That means you. He needs rest. I have no mind to heal him over again just because you give him no peace. Now, shoo," she commanded, pointing toward the tent opening.

Linton opened his mouth as if he intended to argue, then closed it wordlessly and stalked out. Cam walked to the tent flap and crossed his arms, a human door.

"Thanks for the chivalry," Carina said, making one last inspection of Vahanian's newly healed wounds. "It would have been very impressive... if you could have stood up." She managed a surprisingly mischievous grin. "We'll just let that be our little secret. Cam and Soterius won't tell, will you?"

Cam didn't even try to hide his smile, exchanging a grin with Soterius. "Not us. Your secret is safe."

"Thanks so much," Vahanian replied. "And I might have surprised you," he said tiredly. "I've been thrashed worse than this... more than once."

"Amazing you haven't reconsidered your line of work," Carina rejoined, packing up her kit and shouldering it. "This was a favor to Maynard. I don't usually fix up the damage from bar fights. Just encourages more of them."

She started toward the tent opening. "Carina," Vahanian called after her. She turned. For once, the mercenary's face was completely serious. "Don't change your mind about Kaine's detour. I don't trust him, never have. He's right about the danger ahead on this road. But I've got a gut feeling that there's something he's not telling, something worse in the Pass."

Carina looked as if she were about to make a retort, then reconsidered. "Thanks for the warning," she said. "I had the same feeling myself," she added as she gathered up her shawl and slipped out of the tent.

"For the two of you, that went well," Cam remarked, keeping a careful eye on Carina as she crossed the camp.

Vahanian closed his eyes and groaned. "I didn't end up with more damage than when I started, so I guess you're right. Anyone ever mention that your sister could rile the dead?"

Cam laughed. "She's really rather pleasant around most people, Jonmarc. You bring out the worst in her."

"I have that effect on a lot of people," Vahanian remarked dryly. "Got me where I am today."

"I rather suspected that," Cam said noncommittally.

"You're a very effective doorman," Vahanian replied. "Oh, hell, you're a very effective door."

"Nice of you to say so," Cam chuckled. "Maybe there's a future in it."

"Go to bed," Cam said to Soterius. "I can handle this watch. It's almost dawn."

"Soterius," Vahanian called, and the soldier turned. "Tell Tris I've got a message for him, a warning—from a friend."

Soterius looked puzzled, and nodded. "I'll do that," Soterius agreed, and there was a rustle as he left. Vahanian opened his eyes and glimpsed Carina's tent through the open flap. By candlelight, he could make out the forms of her companions within her tent, Tris and the hedge witch, and he wondered just what it was that Cam interrupted. Bounty hunters and mages, he thought dryly. *The two things I like least. It's got to start getting better,* he thought. But as the flap fell shut and a cold autumn breeze made him shiver, he doubted it.

CHAPTER SIXTEEN

KIARA SHARSEQUIN NUDGED her horse onward and wrapped her cloak closer against the autumn chill. The most dangerous part of the ride was now behind her, the perilous crossing through Margolan's northern reaches.

Kiara avoided taverns, preferring to sleep outside rather than chance an encounter with any of Jared's troops. But staying clear of the taverns had not kept her away from other people, since the roads were thronged with merchants and peasants alike, their horses, mules, wagons and shoulders loaded with all they possessed, seeking to escape the heavy hand of Margolan's new king.

It was impossible to keep to the road and avoid the refugees. They were farmers and traders, and most said little, moving as quickly as they could toward the northeastern border and freedom.

Others tugged livestock and a procession of dirty children, urging on stubborn mules or lugging their own loaded carts. Kiara had still not decided whether she was safer apart from the crowd or hidden in their midst, although she doubted that any among this dispossessed lot held love enough for Jared Drayke to turn in the brown-robed stranger with the gyregon.

Yet Kiara knew that when stakes were high, spies could be anywhere. So she kept to herself, coming to the supper fire only after most of the refugees slept, sleeping lightly within reach of her horse and her sword. It was not easy to avoid the stories of the refugees around her. She caught snatches of conversation as the walkers talked with each other, sharing their tales of mistreatment. If only a third of what she heard was true, then Jared Drayke had indeed managed, in his brief reign, to become one of the vilest kings in the history of the Winter Kingdoms.

She could not doubt her own eyes. They passed a village, burned to the ground, the survivors picking amid the ashes for their belongings. Burned, they said, by Margolan troops, on the order of the king who was displeased with their taxes. Once, she stopped by the side of the road to eat and, as she settled down, discovered bones sticking up from a hastily buried, shallow grave. Then, two days ago, they came upon a copse with oddly swaying branches. As they drew closer, they could see the truth: that the trees were gibbets, and that a dozen unfortunates hung in the fall breeze. Even a cursory glance confirmed a military hand in the matter. The nooses were too regular for it to be a local lynching. It was easy to guess that Margolan troops had taken vengeance for some infraction, real or imagined.

Yesterday's encounter was the one which would stay in her mind forever. They spotted a woman cradling a baby by the side of the road, and called her to join the group. Only then did they see the madness in her eyes and realize that she cradled, not a baby, but a log wrapped in a tattered blanket. She raved wildly about the coming of soldiers, about fire and her family being put to the sword, even the children, she cried, all but her tiny one, she declared, hugging the log fiercely. As the refugees streamed past, she did not join them, but railed on in her grief and madness, stopping only to put the log lovingly to her shoulder, or, with a gentle caress, against her breast.

Kiara was not prepared for how deeply the refugees affected her, nor how her distrust of Jared Drayke could move first to revulsion, and then to white-hot anger. She was taught as heir to Isencroft's throne to rule with firmness, but with genuine caring for her subjects. Although her upbringing gave her limited time among those not of noble birth, her glimpses of peasant life provided an impression of hard work and sparse possessions, but not the wretchedness these souls experienced at Jared's hand.

Your Journey is to find a way to save Isencroft, not to save the world, she reminded herself sternly. But the longer she spent among the refugees, the more moved she was by their plight. And, trained as she was to be a fighter, a part of her longed to see Jared displaced, although she knew that Margolan's affairs were none of her business.

Always, she thought of Cam and Carina, and the frightening scrying she had seen in Isencroft. Had the vision come to pass? Had Cam and Carina survived? If they hadn't, if they weren't on the way back to Isencroft with a cure, would father live to see my Journey completed?

It was nearing sunset when she reached the rolling hills that marked Margolan's northeastern border. Just on the other side of those large stone markers, she thought to herself, and one danger will be behind me. But her relief gave way to concern as the group slowed, then came to a halt, and the refugees began to buzz with conversation. Kiara stood in her stirrups for a better look, then swore and dropped back into her saddle. Two Margolan guards blocked the roadway, extorting passage money from the refugees.

For the better part of a candlemark, the motley stream of émigrés filed past the guards, able to satisfy the demands for something of value in exchange for permission to pass. Kiara readied two gold skrivven, easily a guard's wages for a week, and held them in her glove.

The guards' mood soured after an altercation with an elderly man, nearly coming to blows until the bent old trader anted up two gemstones from the hem of his ragged robe. Now, the guards appeared intent on taking out their bad moods on the next hapless family.

"Please sir," begged a farmer, "I've given you all the coin I own. For the sake of the Lady, please let us pass."

Behind him, his gaunt wife and their half-dozen ill-clad children huddled together. Unlike most of the refugees who led horses or mules laden with packs or harnessed to overloaded carts, the family looked to be traveling with only the clothes on their backs.

"Surely you didn't leave all your coins buried in your field?" one of the guards taunted, stepping closer to the ragged man. "Everyone knows that farmers hide their money. You've only given me enough to get seven people through."

"By the name of the Goddess, sir, it is all I have," the farmer pleaded. One of the guards was already walking past him, toward the huddled family.

"Since you don't have the coin, you can pay for your passage with trade," he leered, and seized the oldest daughter, a child perhaps a dozen summers old. The girl screamed in terror as the guard pressed a knife against her throat.

"I beg you sir, let her go!" The farmer threw himself to his knees and the child's mother prostrated herself at the feet of the other guard as the children began to wail.

"Turn her loose." Kiara drew her sword, and the crowd parted for her warhorse as she advanced on the guards.

The captain regarded her with a snide grin. "Well, well. A doxy on a horse with a bit of steel. Ought to mind your own business, wench. Of course," he added, "you're welcome to mind mine."

"Turn her loose," Kiara repeated. She moved forward until Wraith stood between the guards and the hapless farmer, and she knew that, despite the guard's taunts, he could not help but notice that her horse was a soldier's mount.

The guardsman drew his sword. "This is none of your business. Be gone."

"I'm making it my business," Kiara replied, hoping the girl had the good sense to run if the opportunity presented itself. "Now turn the girl loose and let us pass."

"All we're doing is making a trade," the guardsman said as he moved forward, his sword raised menacingly. "Now leave, before you get hurt."

"You want trade?" Kiara retorted, "then trade this!" Her sword glinted in the sun as she jerked back on Wraith's reins so hard the horse reared. A hand signal sent Jae streaking through the sky as Kiara set her horse riding straight for the guards.

Jae dove at the guard holding the child, and his talons raked across the man's face, lifting eight deep streaks of blood. Cursing in pain and anger, the guard dropped his hold on the girl. She scrambled away, and caught her father's hand, running for all she was worth with her family. Kiara sidestepped her horse toward the guards, knowing how imposing Wraith could be and how obvious his training for battle would appear to a military man. The effect was not lost on the soldiers, who stepped back a pace. From behind her, the refugees cheered and pressed forward, waving their staffs and tools in anger.

"Be gone, woman," he ordered gruffly. "This is none of your affair. Ride past, and be thankful we don't clap you in irons for what your hell-spawned dragon did!"

Kiara did not move. "The way I see it, you're outnumbered," she said evenly. "I think *you'd* best be gone!"

Jae shrieked a warning just as Kiara caught the glint of the dagger out of the corner of her eye. She lurched to one side, deflecting the worst of the dagger's course with her sword, and bit back an oath as the dagger sliced against her shoulder.

The captain drew his sword, expecting an easy win. He was unprepared for the speed of Kiara's strike, or the power with which she wielded her sword. The unwary captain gaped as his sword flew from his hand and landed in the dust. His companion eyed Jae warily as the gyregon circled overhead, screeching menacingly and diving toward the two guards, pulling up just short of making contact with his sharp beak or long talons.

For emphasis, Kiara reared her horse once more, its hooves flailing inches from the captain's head, easily able to crush a man's skull with its heavy iron shoes. Once more, the refugees roared in anger and pressed forward, their staves and hoes no longer waving, but raised as if to strike.

"Whore take you," the captain spat, scrambling to reclaim his sword and holding it lowered in defeat as the two soldiers began to back away. "You'll pay, bitch. I promise you that."

In response, Jae dove full speed at the captain's head. With a cry, the hapless man turned and ran, following his companion. Jae kept up the pursuit, diving and shrieking, until the two soldiers were almost out of sight. Then he flapped contentedly back to Kiara and perched on her shoulder, preening with self-satisfaction.

The refugees thronged around Kiara, exclaiming their thanks and congratulations. Uncomfortably aware that she had lost all hope of traveling unnoticed, she sighed and accepted their thanks quietly, anxious to pass the border without further incident and ride on her way as quickly as possible. As the excited group began to move forward once more, a man threaded his way toward Kiara, and she recognized him as the farmer whom she had rescued.

"Begging your pardon, miss," he said, his tattered cap in hand, "but I'm grateful for what you did back there. We had nothing more to give, but I couldn't have borne to lose Tessa," he said, with a nod to the wide-eyed young girl who followed a pace behind him, looking in awe at Kiara's horse and sword.

"Are you a warrior?" the girl breathed in adulation.

Despite the seriousness of the situation, Kiara found herself smiling. "Not really," she said, letting her cloak cover her scabbard once more. "Where I come from, everyone trains as a fighter, from the time we can hold a sword, so that we never have to suffer from fools like those," she said, with a jerk of her head in the direction the guards had gone.

"We have nothing of value," the farmer said, "but my brother waits for us in the camp just over the border in Principality. Knowing you're high born and all, I've no right to ask, but perhaps you'd share a meal with us, if you be hungry. Sleep well, you could—safe with us—until you're on your way." He smiled self-consciously. "Find a healer for that cut, too," he said, looking toward Kiara's shoulder.

Kiara had almost forgotten the wound until now, but she felt at the ripped cloth, chagrined to find it soaked with blood. Still, not a bad wound, she appraised as she gingerly touched the injury. She had taken worse in practice bouts. But a healer's poultice might still take out the soreness and keep it from going bad.

Kiara smiled at the nervous farmer and his awestruck daughter. "I would be honored to eat with you," she said, and the man brightened in unbelief at his fortune. Shyly, the girl reached out to pet Wraith, shrinking back as the great black horse turned a dark eye to look at her, and then, gaining the courage to gently stroke the horse. "You were very brave back there," Kiara said quietly to the girl, who smiled gratefully and averted her eyes.

"Thank you," the girl said quietly.

"You're welcome," Kiara replied, trying not to wonder how many other young girls the soldiers had encountered, girls who did not have a protector appear out of nowhere.

Kiara worked her way slowly through the throng behind the farmer, who became something of a celebrity. For Kiara, the refugees moved aside with a reverence that made her feel self-conscious, closing behind her with whispered comments about Jae, the warhorse and her sword.

Inwardly, Kiara sighed, torn between her chagrin at making herself so conspicuous, and her knowledge that she could not have sat idle and let the girl be abused. That's what you get for taking yourself so bloody seriously, she thought. Now every bard in Principality will have a new story, and every border guard in Margolan will have a new target. Perhaps, out here, weeks from Margolan's palace, the incident would go unnoticed. Please, she silently beseeched the Goddess. The last thing I need is the Margolan guard on my trail, she thought. Neither she nor the farmer said anything else as the group moved on until they were long past the border and the fires of the refugee camp came into view.

The camp was really a collection of tumbledown lean-tos made from scraps of lumber and tents fashioned from worn blankets. More than fifty fires burned, and Kiara guessed from the bustle around her that each fire easily represented ten to fifteen refugees. The camp smelled of waste and animals, roasting meat and sharp onions. Dogs and pigs ran past her, and only the autumn cold prevented the ground from becoming a fetid pool of mud. She was glad she did not have to experience the smells of the camp in high summer, and was grateful that the steppe flies were dormant for the winter. She sighed as she looked over the makeshift camp. Unless Jared were stopped, and soon, more would experience the misery of the camps, until Jared quelled the flow of refugees or the surrounding nations were forced to close their borders.

The farmer, whose name was Lessel, guided Kiara through the crowded camp until they met his brother, a darker version of himself, who greeted them heartily and invited them to share his fire. Tethering Wraith, Kiara followed Lessel to sit by the fire, jostled by his dozen nieces and nephews who crowded around for a look at the "sword lady." To Kiara's relief, Lessel and his brother asked no questions, happy to have a way to show their gratitude.

"All these people," Kiara asked after she finished a bowl of stew, "are they from Margolan?"

Tadrie, Lessel's brother, nodded grimly. "Aye, ma'am. And until King Bricen's death, we were proud of it. But there's something evil astir in Margolan," he said, "and any that can are running, as a sane man would do."

Kiara frowned. "How could things go so wrong so fast?" she asked. As Tice often pointed out during his interminable history lessons, peasants often lived in miserable situations for generations, uncomplaining even under onerous kings. What degree of oppression must have happened, she wondered, to force so many to leave behind their lands and livelihoods?

"It's almost too big for the telling," Tadrie said. One of his children crawled up onto his lap and a dog scratched his way closer to the fire, teasing a scrap from the dirt. "Whether it be the new king or his whore-spawn mage I can't say, but no sane man can stay in Margolan and keep his life for long." He paused and stroked his daughter's hair absently. "It's not just the taxes, ma'am," Tadrie said, staring at the fire. "We're used to them. And we know that a new king always makes them higher, even if we have no more to give. And it's not just the soldiers, thieving our pigs and busting up a wagon or two to get their payment." He shook his head, but his eyes were hard in the firelight, remembering.

"Never in all the years King Bricen ruled, or his father or his grandfather, did the soldiers of Margolan carry off women from our villages for their own use," he said, his voice rough with anger. "Never once were our homes and crops burned, our animals slaughtered, our men hanged. And never did we see the Dark Things that roam about the woods now, whatever they are, Goddess take them," he said with a shudder.

"Dark Things?" Kiara asked, feeling a sudden chill. Unconsciously, her hand fell to the dagger the Sisterhood had given her. It will turn the undead, the Sister had told her. In the hand of a mage, it will destroy the soul of an Immortal.

"Aye," Tadrie replied. "I've heard them, caught a glimpse, but no one who has seen them close has lived to tell. Once, I found a piece of one," he said with a shudder, "although I can't imagine what could kill one of those," he said, shaking his head. "Oh, the guards told us it was the vayash moru. But it's not."

"How can you be so sure?" Kiara asked, leaning forward, as Lessel's wife approached her tentatively with a steaming mug of watered ale and, with an awkward curtsey, pressed it into her hands before fleeing.

Both Lessel and Tadrie shook their heads once more. "Because in Margolan, we've never feared the vayash moru," he said, and Kiara tried not to show her amazement at how matter-of-factly the two men spoke of the undead among them. "Oh, we've heard tell of other places where they prey on folks, but in all the years my father lived, and his father and grandfather before him, never have we been harmed by them. Fact is," he said, "they seem to know who the bad 'uns are, and if they take a man, he's one about to have his neck stretched for thieving or worse. Most of the time, I guess they live from animals though, of course, we only see them rarely." He managed a half-smile. "They don't mix with our kind, unless they have to."

"You've met one?"

Tadrie nodded seriously. "Aye. They're a solitary sort. The one I met didn't give me aught to fear. Perhaps I didn't meet him when he was hungry," he chuckled, and Lessel laughed with him. Tadrie sobered. "But their kind have it worst in Margolan right now," he continued. "Being blamed for what the soldiers do. A body with any sense ought to know that it's all lies, but some as have been afraid of the vayash moru see a chance to get even, I guess. Soldiers burning them out, putting a stake through them and throwing them out in daylight—worse, too." He sighed. "The soldiers aren't particular when they're hunting, if you take my meaning. Many a regular person's been burned, just on tales folks tell." He shook his head once more. "It's bad, ma'am."

Kiara sipped her drink thoughtfully. If what he said were true, she thought, then two courses were likely. The vayash moru might rise up against Jared Drayke and work their own vengeance or they might forsake their peace with mortal neighbors, and strike back. She shivered. Either way, Tadrie was right. It was a bad time to be in Margolan.

Just then, Lessel leaned forward and gently touched her shoulder, just above her wound. "We must have you see a healer," Lessel said.

"There is a healer who comes to the camp," Tadrie said, rising. "From where, I do not know. He is not one of us. Come. We will look for him."

Kiara rose and followed the brothers, winding through the crowded camp among the makeshift bedrolls and banked fires, stepping over offal and around dogs and chickens, and picking her way over the tangle of sleeping children and idle adults. How Tadrie took his bearings in the chaos, Kiara had no idea. Finally, they reached a tent just within the camp's perimeter. Several small pots steamed on the fire, smelling of herbs and succulents, and more herbs dried on haphazard racks made of sticks. A thin, hollow-cheeked man hunched over the fire, stirring one of the pots.

"Begging your pardon," Tadrie interrupted respectfully, as the man looked up at them, his large dark piercing eyes fixing Kiara as if they could look into her soul. The healer stood, and Kiara realized that beneath his voluminous robes he was slightly built, but his forearms attested to a whipcord strong frame and his hands spoke of hard work. Lank brown hair fell to his shoulders with a slight wave, and around his neck hung several amulets. Just as he was about to speak, he was taken by a paroxysm of coughing that lasted until Kiara feared for him.

"What can I do for you?" the healer asked, when the coughing finally subsided.

"This woman helped my brother on the road from Margolan," Tadrie said. "She stopped two soldiers from hurting his child. She's been cut on her shoulder," he said, gesturing. "Please, can you help her?"

The healer nodded. Tadrie gestured for Kiara to step closer. "This is Sakwi. He will take good care of you." Tadrie looked to the healer again. "Thank you," he said. "We must go back to our family now," Tadrie said to Kiara, "but you are welcome to pass the night with us. You can sleep safely. None here will let anything harm you."

"Thank you," Kiara said. "Save me a place," she added. Tadrie and Lessel nodded, then made their way back to the throng.

"Now let's look at that arm," Sakwi said, moving closer. He gently peeled back the cloth and frowned, then crossed to a pot near the fire and dipped a cloth in its liquid, wringing out the steaming rag as he walked back to her. "First, to clean it," he said, dabbing carefully at the wound until he was satisfied. Then he opened a small leather case and began to rummage through it. He withdrew a vial and dipped a second cloth into another pot, sprinkling it with the contents of the vial and working it in his hands until a paste covered the surface. He returned to Kiara and bandaged her shoulder. The warm poultice felt good, taking the pain from the cut. The pungent scent of herbs cleared her mind.

"How is it that a woman travels alone through Margolan?" Sakwi asked.

Kiara looked toward the fire. "I am on a journey for my father," she replied.

Sakwi met her eyes, studying her. "Show me your sword." Kiara paused, then shrugged and drew her blade, holding the flat of the sword on her open hands for him to see in the firelight, which glittered on the fine engraving of twined roses and thorns.

The healer caught his breath. "You are the one," he said, and as if triggered by the sharp intake, began to cough again. The deep coughs wracked his thin frame.

"It sounds like you need a healer yourself," Kiara observed as she resheathed her sword.

Sakwi shook his head. "It is something no healer may mend. I fear it is the touch of the Goddess, perhaps to keep me humble," he said with a half smile. "Maybe it will take me to her someday, hmm? But not yet I think. Not yet. Come, sit with me by the fire. I have something for you."

Curious, Kiara followed him to a log near the fire, and sat as he motioned her to join him. Jae fluttered to land beside her. Sakwi looked into the fire. "A fortnight ago, I had a dream of the Goddess. She was holding a sword, entwined with roses, and told me to take a message to Margolan. She said to wait among her lost children, for the one for whom the message was sent. I found this camp," he said, gesturing toward the bedraggled refugees around him, "and here I waited. This is the sword from my dream. So the message must be for you."

"And what message is that?" Kiara asked cautiously.

"This," Sakwi replied, reaching under his robe to draw out a star-shaped gem set in silver, about the size of her palm. The pendant hung from a sturdy chain.

"What is that?" she breathed.

Sakwi's deep-set, dark eyes seemed older than his years. "It was given to me for safekeeping, many years ago. I was told to share it with no one until the Goddess herself told me otherwise. Now, you have come. The Library at Westmarch is where you will find that which you seek." The star-shaped amulet in his hand pulsed with a warm glow like the beating of a heart. "The Library at Westmarch was spelled against intruders," Sakwi went on. "I am told that this amulet will allow you to enter."

Sakwi motioned for Kiara to incline her head, and he gently dropped the star pendant's chain around her neck. The gem glowed once more, then went dark.

"What do you know of the Library?"

"For those the Lady sends, it still exists," Sakwi said cryptically. "And to the rest, it might not exist at all. For you, it will give its secrets."

Kiara gingerly lifted the heavy pendant and tucked it carefully into her tunic. "Can you tell me anything more?"

Sakwi shook his head. "About the Library, no. But look," he said with a barely perceptible nod. "Someone else seems to be looking for you."

Kiara looked up and felt her heart sink. On the far edge of the crowd, barely visible in the firelight, were five Margolan guardsmen. *Lady, what have I done?* Kiara groaned inwardly, knowing the guards were looking for her. Or worse—planning a reprisal against the camp and its ragtag inhabitants.

"Don't be afraid," Sakwi said quietly, without taking his eyes from the guards. "It will take them a while to circle the camp. They don't dare cut through. These refugees have nothing to lose." He turned to her. "Go there," he pointed to a thicket just beyond the fire, where several sparse bushes grew beneath a weeping tree. "Hide yourself."

"There?" Kiara wondered aloud. "That couldn't hide a rabbit."

"I will hide you," the healer replied, and something in his tone, his complete confidence, overcame her better instincts. Keeping low, Kiara dodged for the thicket and hunched down, one hand close to her sword and a dagger in the other.

The soldiers circled slowly, eyed in silent defiance by the refugees. Even from her hiding place, Kiara sensed the tension rise, saw a deliberate movement among the stragglers that told her any action by the guards was likely to lead to a fight.

Sweet Chenne, don't let these people die for me! She tensed as the guards came closer. Sakwi tended his fire, paying no heed to the newcomers. But Kiara sensed a change around her. The closer the guards drew to her hiding place, the thicker the bushes appeared, and the lower and denser the weeping fronds of the tree.

"You there," one guard hailed Sakwi. The healer rose unhurriedly, stretched, and looked toward him blankly. "We're looking for a woman, a fighter. She was injured. Have you seen her?"

Sakwi did not speak, and gave an almost imperceptible shake of his head. The guard frowned. "I think we'll just look around," he said in a bullying voice, and took a step toward where Kiara hid. Just then, a flock of bats rose in a flurry of wings, like a living dark cloud. Dozens of bats flew straight toward the guards. Cursing, the guards threw their arms up to shield their faces and backed off quickly, stumbling in their haste. They were still cursing when they reached their horses, and turned at a gallop into the night, swatting at an occasional low-flying bat.

Kiara did not move until Sakwi motioned her to stand. She looked at her hiding place in wonder. It was, once more, a thin thicket of nearly leafless bushes and a spindly weeping tree, poor cover for a fox, let alone a fugitive. "You are a mage," she said.

"A land mage," Sakwi replied. "I will confess that I am not truly a healer," he continued with a self-conscious smile. "My magic does help me grow the herbs," he went on, "but what I know, I have learned to doctor myself," he said, and began coughing once more, so hard that a fleck of blood reddened his lips. He reached into his robe, withdrew a small folded square of paper, and shook a powder under his tongue. Within a few moments, the coughing subsided, and he looked up once more.

"Capsaicin and garlic," he explained, tucking the empty paper away. "Stops bleeding in the lungs. At least, for now."

"Thank you," Kiara said. "I will leave you to your work," she continued, "but one thing more. Can you tell me where we are, so that I can get my bearings from the map?"

Sakwi smiled, and looked at her with an unnerving gaze that seemed to see through her. "I can do better than that," he said, and made a low, strange sound deep in his throat. From the darkness beyond the camp walked a dark gray fox, its head held high and bushy tail gliding behind it, unconcerned at the bustle of humanity or the fires of the camp. A pace from Kiara, the fox stopped.

"Here is your guide," Sakwi said. "His name is quite unpronounceable for you, but you may think of him as Grayfoot."

"You called him?" Kiara said in wonder, looking at the stately animal, which appeared amused at her interest.

Sakwi smiled. "It is part of my gift," he said. "He knows the safest paths to the border. And he is the most cunning of his den, so he will not lead you into ambush or danger."

Jae squawked in protest from where he perched nearby, and in response, Grayfoot made a little noise in the back of his throat. To Kiara's amazement, the gyregon and the fox made several verbal exchanges, which ended with Jae resuming his preening, and Grayfoot looking quite pleased with himself.

"It's almost as if they could..." she stammered.

"All things are possible, my lady," the mage replied. "You can communicate with Grayfoot as you do with Jae," Sakwi continued. "He understands you, and he can make himself understood to you. Trust him, and he will take you to the border."

Kiara was rapidly finding that there was much Tice had not prepared her for. She nodded, humbled that the fox was clearly taking the responsibility for communicating, given her limited skills. "I understand," she said finally. "Thank you," she added, looking first to Sakwi and then glancing to Grayfoot, who inclined his head.

"This is going to take some getting used to," she admitted sheepishly.

Sakwi nodded. "The Goddess chose your quest well, lady swordbearer. Now rest. You will be safe here tonight. In the morning, look for Grayfoot, and he will start you on your way."

Kiara thanked him once more and then followed Jae back through the tangle of the camp to Lessel and Tadrie's fire. She was touched to find that the grateful farmer had indeed saved her the best spot, closest to the fire, and made a bed of pine branches, covered with a ragged sheet. None of them, not even the children, could be persuaded to exchange their places with her, but insisted that she take the spot of honor. Humbled by their gratitude, Kiara gracefully accepted their generosity, but lent her cloak to Lessel's haggard wife to wrap around her two poorly clad youngest ones. Then before she could be the recipient of any further favors Kiara bedded down, and found that sleep came almost immediately.

CHAPTER SEVENTEEN

Tris swallowed hard. "I think that's enough for one day."

"There is very little time," Alyzza replied. "We must make the most of it. Carina, bring us the scrying ball from my bag."

Alyzza pressed the scrying ball into Tris's hands. "Let's see what you can do with this."

Tris turned it. He remembered how accurate a ball like it was at the festival in Margolan, and how dark a future it foresaw. "But I don't know how to scry," he protested.

"You can learn," Alyzza dismissed his hesitation. "Mages of any clan can scry, some better than others. Place the ball in front of you," she instructed. "Clear your mind. Focus. Tell me what you see."

Tris took a deep breath and did as Alyzza instructed. The scrying ball remained dark.

"It's not working."

"You're not concentrating. Try again."

Carina leaned forward, staring into the dark glass ball. Tris took another deep breath and closed his eyes. He tried to ignore the sounds of the caravan beyond the thin tent walls and the dull ache of his muscles from sword practice with Vahanian. Tris pictured the scrying ball in his mind, forcing out all other thoughts, and sought the silent place within himself. As he made his mental descent, the scrying ball in his mind began to glow, faintly at first, and then stronger, a pale yellow light. Hesitantly, he opened his eyes and found the glass ball in his hands glowing like the image in his mind.

Suddenly the scrying ball flared like a captured ray of sunlight, and a tiny picture formed deep within the crystal. A stocky man in his late middle years appeared, his once-dark hair peppered with gray. "My uncle," he whispered. The image shifted, and Tris saw a woman whose resemblance to Bricen raised a lump in his throat. "My father's sister," he murmured. The scrying ball went dark.

Tris looked up at Alyzza questioningly, holding out the darkened glass ball. "What have I seen?" He looked back at the scrying ball as if it would flare once more into life.

"A glimpse of time," the fortune-teller replied. "Much more than I expected. You do indeed have power," she said, a hint of appreciation in her raspy voice. "You knew the figure?"

"My uncle," Tris replied, setting the scrying ball down gently. "The one I'm traveling to meet."

"Interesting," Alyzza mused. "Most pupils are lucky if they can merely make the scrying ball glow on their first try. Some manage an image, but often it is too faint to make out. How is it that you not only call an image, but find kin on your first scrying?" she asked, leaning forward until her wrinkled face was only inches away from Tris's own, and her ale-tainted breath stung in his nostrils. "Very interesting. Try once more."

Tris accepted the scrying ball again and let his hands slide over the smooth, warm surface. He shut his eyes and repeated the calming ritual, slipping into a light trance. He focused his thoughts on the glass ball and stretched out in the darkness.

Something touched his mind immediately. The unfamiliar presence jarred him, nearly causing him to drop the scrying ball. Unlike the warmth Tris had felt before, the presence that touched his mind was cold and malignant. Tris struggled to break the contact, dropping the scrying ball and scrambling backward. He felt the presence follow him. Alyzza lunged for him, wrapping him in arms both thin and strong.

"You must break free, Tris!" Alyzza hissed. "Break the contact!"

Without warning, the presence was gone. A pounding headache took its place. As Alyzza released her hold on him, Tris sank back, one hand covering his eyes. Carina leaned over him worriedly.

"What happened?" the healer asked.

"Something else was looking for him," the old witch replied. "Something evil and very strong."

Carina touched Tris's forehead, easing his pain. Tris's eyes flickered open and he could see the concern in the healer's face.

"Who looks for you, mageling?" Alyzza rasped. "And why is one so strongly gifted a hired caravan hand, I wonder?" she wondered, although by her tone, Tris knew she did not expect an answer.

"What was that?" Tris asked, his palm still pressed against his forehead.

"I do not know," Alyzza said in the singsong tone that indicated her mind was elsewhere. "Something strong, I think, yes. Something evil, very evil. Something knows you are missing and wishes to find you?" she asked. There was nothing of mirth in her toothless grin. "How to hide a mageling as he learns, that is the problem," she mused. "Untrained, you are a danger to us all. But It will be watching for your power. A problem," she muttered. "No matter. You must be trained. We must proceed and hope for time."

Tris looked from Carina to Alyzza. "Can 'it' destroy me?"

"Fie!" Alyzza hissed, "that is the least of your worries." She looked past Tris as if seeing something in her memories. "It does not want to kill.

First, it will consume. It will turn your power and use it for evil. If you are strong enough, you will kill the Master to end the pain but it will have twisted you by then."

"There's no one else to finish my task," Tris said, staring at the darkened scrying ball. "I have to go on."

"Yes, you must go on," Alyzza hissed. "And I will help you as my poor skills allow. But you must find a proper teacher."

"Where?"

"The Library at Westmarch," Alyzza murmured. Tris glanced sharply at Carina as the healer started. "You will find what you seek there, if it still exists anywhere."

"But how—"

"Enough!" Alyzza pronounced suddenly, and climbed to her feet. "I am tired. Tomorrow, when the supper fires are lit, come again. We will work another lesson."

"What if... It... comes looking for me again?"

"Run," the old woman hissed through broken teeth. "Run for your life."

AT THE EDGE of the forest, the night sounds surrounded Tris as he picked his way into the underbrush just beyond the camp. He settled onto a rock and started the pathway to trance. The night sounds grew louder as he concentrated on the pulse of the forest. He could hear the scrabbling of small creatures, the soft rustle of bat wings, the stirring of leaves. He stretched out his senses further, becoming aware of nearby creatures and of the rhythm of the breath of those that huddled deep within their nests and burrows. So far, so good.

Carina and Alyzza worked with him almost every night, improvising a shielding ritual that worked—most of the time—to keep out awareness of the constant cycle of birth and death in the world around him. As Tris gained control over sensing death, he grew better at screening out the endless procession of lost souls that sought him, some seeking rest, others merely attracted to his power like moths to a flame. By trial and error, he grew adept at simple banishing spells and long overdue "passing over" rituals. There seemed no end to the restless ghosts that sought his aid, and he knew he could not accommodate them all without driving himself to exhaustion.

This is what happens with no Summoner in more than five years. Since his grandmother's death, there was no spirit mage in these parts to reconcile the living with the dead, seek the blessing of the departed or send the spirits on their way. Nor had there been any intercessor to set right old grievances that bound souls to this world, he thought. Thank the Goddess that not every soul needs help with the passage.

The dream had not come since the night he had sought out Carina, though its memory never left him and the plaintive sound of Kait's voice echoed constantly in his thoughts. Carina and Alyzza were unwilling to try another scrying after the power that reached out for Tris during their last try. But Tris could not let it rest.

Tonight, he thought grimly, he would try once more to reach past whatever barrier held Kait prisoner, try again to bring Kait to him and end her suffering.

Out of habit, he raised a circle around him for the working. When the wardings were complete, he settled down onto a rock and closed his eyes, stretching out along the spirit plane.

Kaity, are you there?

The image sprang to mind so quickly it jarred him. Kait's face, pressed against the barrier, her cries deadened by a thick pane, desperation clear in her eyes.

Tris, help me!

Before Tris could respond, darkness fell around him, blotting out Kait's face and silencing her cries. Though the darkness made no sound, Tris knew it immediately, recognized it as the silent evil that sought him at the scrying, and struggled to withdraw. Faster and faster the darkness swarmed after him, so that he could feel its chill and its malevolence. He was operating on sheer instinct, and he raced on, desperate to outpace the darkness on his heels, overwhelmed with a primitive terror that transcended words. His power felt wide open, his senses on high alert. Tris's concentration was interrupted as a wood mouse raced past, pursued by a shrieking hawk. With a lurch, Tris felt the mouse's spirit, its hurried pulse and the tiny spark of life that filled it.

With a shriek and the rustle of wings, the hawk dropped from the sky, targeting its kill. Tris felt the mouse's panic like a visceral shock, nearly falling backward with sympathetic impact as the hawk's talons struck. Tris's heart raced as he struggled to break the contact before the mouse's terror moved him beyond reason. He could feel the rodent's fear as the hawk winged higher, felt the awful grip and the sudden, sharp pain as talons dug into the mouse's flesh. Then, with the same wrenching sensation he had experienced on the battlefield, Tris felt the small creature's spirit shudder loose and flicker out.

"No!" The word tore from his throat, deep and guttural, a howl more than a reasoned cry. Startled, the hawk dropped the dead mouse, even as Tris felt his power lash out, unbidden. He saw the animal hit the ground and lie still, and then, to his amazement, saw its savaged body begin to twitch. He stretched out his hand just as a heavy boot came down on the reanimated mouse, snuffing out the glimmer before Tris could react and breaking his contact with the animal with a violent lurch that left him gasping for breath.

Alyzza stood before him, her face a mixture of sternness and fear.

"Why?" Tris croaked, torn between the intensity of the experience and his own wordless loss.

"Don't you know what you have done?" the old crone rasped, and in the moonlight, Tris realized that she was trembling, whether with fear or cold or rage, he could not tell.

Mutely, he shook his head, staring at the spot where the mouse lay.

"I know little of Spirit magic, but this I do know," Alyzza hissed. "Never may you bind a spirit that truly desires to leave. Never may you reanimate the dead. And never may you call the dead against their will."

Tris swallowed hard, still groping for equilibrium after the sudden, violent dissolution of his trance. "But... I don't understand..." he managed. The words tumbled out as Alyzza listened silently, then nodded when he finished.

"A spirit that wishes to remain can be bound to this world without a penalty on your soul," the old witch said, fixing Tris with the intense glare of her mismatched eyes. "Just like a spirit that desires to live may be anchored to its body until the breach be healed, if you have the power," she said. "And the dead that are not free to leave this world may be summoned, so long as you do not seek to bind them to your will or encumber their souls. But," she hissed, leaning toward him for emphasis. "No mage of the Light may reanimate a corpse, nor impose a spirit which is not its own. It is forbidden."

"Why?" Tris asked as Alyzza moved her boot and he stared forlornly at the torn body of the mouse.

"Those mysteries are not mine to know," the crone replied. "But I do know that to defy the Lady is to risk your soul. The Obsidian King breathed another spirit into the dead and bound them as his slaves."

"You knew the Obsidian King?"

The hag cackled. "Those of us who waged war against him will never forget, even in our dreams," she said, a shadow of pain crossing her features. "Did you really think that something less would have driven me mad?"

"Are you mad?"

Alyzza laughed harshly. "Oh yes, quite."

Just then, not far from the forest's edge, they heard a cry and the heavy thud of a body hitting the ground. Straining to see, unwilling to risk his magesight once more, Tris could barely make out the shadows of two men locked in combat, although he could hear their groans of effort and the dull thwack of fist meeting flesh. In a moment, one shadow was victorious, and knelt astride its victim's back, pinning the other to the ground.

"Since you're out there, Tris, could you lend a hand?" Vahanian's sardonic voice cut through the darkness.

Tris snatched up his sword and ran, grateful to leave Alyzza behind. He helped Vahanian keep his struggling prisoner pinned as they bound his wrists, then jerked the man to his feet.

"What happened?" Tris breathed as they began to wrestle their prisoner toward the camp.

"Caught a spy," the mercenary replied tersely. "Has no business sneaking around the camp at night, and I don't like the idea of who might be buying his information," Vahanian added, giving the man a shove toward Linton's tent. "Should I ask why you were out in the woods alone at night?" he asked, an edge in his voice.

Tris looked away. "I—"

"Oh, never mind," Vahanian cut him off. "I probably don't want to know. Here's Linton's tent," he said abruptly. "Let's see what our visitor has to say for himself."

The fat little caravan master groaned as Vahanian bellowed an urgent wakeup. Linton fumbled to light a candle. "Jonmarc, this had better be good," the merchant cursed as he stumbled to the tent flap, then fell silent as he took in their prisoner.

"I was out on guard duty and found this skulking around the edge of camp," Vahanian said, giving the man a push. Vahanian pulled a stool forward and pushed the prisoner to sit.

"Now," Vahanian said, drawing the dagger at his belt and letting it glimmer obviously in the candlelight as he turned it in his hands, "let's see what he has to say for himself."

Their prisoner looked from one to the other, then moved his mouth to speak, but the garbled words were unintelligible. With a curse, Linton turned on Vahanian.

"Wonderful work, Jonmarc. You've broken his jaw."

"Maybe we can heal him enough to get the story. What about Carina?"

"I can't think of many worse ways to get on her wrong side. You'd better let me fetch her," Linton said resignedly. "I imagine I won't be getting more sleep."

Tris and Vahanian waited as Linton left to get the healer. Their captive sat sullenly in his chair.

The signs of his struggle with Vahanian were beginning to show in his face, as one eye was rapidly swelling closed and his cheek purpled. After what seemed like forever, they could hear Linton and Carina arguing as they approached.

"Well, this should make the evening more fun," Vahanian muttered under his breath as Linton reached for the tent flap and held it open for Carina.

"I know that it's an unusual thing to ask of you, Carina, but I would appreciate it if—" Linton was saying. His voice faded as they reached the prisoner and Carina looked from the bound man to Vahanian and then reproachfully, to Tris.

"Let me get this straight," Carina said, lifting her head defiantly and stepping closer in challenge. "You see someone you don't know, beat him to a pulp," she said with a jerk of her head toward the prisoner, "and then you want me to help you interrogate him?"

Tris could see the anger flash in Vahanian's eyes. "I don't need your help to interrogate him. What I need," he said tersely, "is for you to fix his jaw so that he can tell us why he was scouting our camp."

"How do you know he was scouting us?" she argued. "I'm amazed you didn't just run him through and ask questions later."

A muscle in Vahanian's jaw twitched at his effort to remain civil. "I thought about it," he said evenly. "He's been sent here by someone, and I'd like to know why."

With a glare that clearly indicated that the quarrel was not resolved, Carina moved to examine the prisoner. Within moments, she shook her head. "You've broken his jaw," she said, looking up at Vahanian.

"I know that," Vahanian retorted. "Can you fix it?"

Carina looked to Linton. "I'm not going to heal this man just to have your hired muscle work him over again."

"You know we would never ask that of you, Carina," Linton said placatingly. "But it's important. Please, try," he beseeched.

"You understand, don't you, that I can't knit broken bone good as new just like that," she said, snapping her fingers. "I can hurry it along. But even after I'm through, he may not be able to talk for a while."

"Great," Vahanian muttered under his breath, and Carina glared at him.

"Look, if you wanted to talk to him, you should have hit him somewhere else."

"Just try," Vahanian asked evenly. "Please."

Carina looked at him, then glanced back at Linton. "All right," she said finally. "Give me a little room."

After nearly a candlemark, Carina stepped back tiredly from her patient and Linton pressed a hot cup of kerif into her hands, which she accepted gratefully. Their prisoner looked down at the floor, still silent. Tris noticed that in addition to whatever healing Carina had worked on the man's jaw, she had also managed to reduce the swelling over his blackened eye and heal his bruised cheek. Throughout the healing, Vahanian leaned on a tent post, arms folded, his face grim.

"That's the best I can do," Carina finally said.

"Can he talk?" Vahanian grated.

Carina shot the mercenary an angry glance. "You can try," she said.

"Thank you, Carina," Linton interposed, stepping between the two and taking Carina's arm. "Let me walk you back to your tent," he said, gently steering her toward the tent opening. "We are so fortunate to have a healer like you with us, and I apologize coming to you like that in the middle of the night—"

Unmoved by the flattery, Carina paused in the tent entrance to glance warningly back at Vahanian. "Leave him in one piece," she ordered. "I don't want to have to do this again."

"No promises," Vahanian replied evenly, with a measured glance toward the prisoner. "I'm watching out for the camp. Whatever it takes."

"Whatever it takes," Carina repeated, shaking her head. If she had a mind to add more she decided against it, turning instead to accept Linton's arm and head for her tent. Linton shot a look over his shoulder, which plainly cautioned Vahanian to be quiet, and then let the tent flap fall shut behind him, leaving Tris and Vahanian alone with the prisoner.

"Now," Vahanian said, stepping within arm's reach of the prisoner, "let's try the questions again," he said in a dangerous voice. "And you really ought to know," he said to the prisoner, "that I usually don't listen to the lady. So it might be healthy for you to tell me everything I want to know."

The prisoner gave up his story without forcing Vahanian to do more damage. He was looking for food and whatever loot he could carry. Tris could tell by Vahanian's manner that the mercenary suspected more but after a candlemark's questioning, Vahanian finally stepped back with a curse and shook his head.

"Satisfied, Jonmarc?" Linton asked from where the fat little man sat on a hassock, watching the proceedings with folded arms.

"No, but it's all I'm going to get," Vahanian replied tersely.

Just then, Cam stuck his head into the tent. "Excuse me, Maynard," the big man said, with a glance toward Tris and Vahanian, "but there are some people here to see you."

"This fellow was just leaving," Vahanian replied, pulling the prisoner to his feet and walking him to the door. "Would you mind seeing him to the edge of camp, Cam, and heading him away from wherever we're going?"

Cam nodded, taking the prisoner by the arm. "I can do that. I heard you had a restless night," he said non-committally, with a meaningful look at Vahanian.

"Can't imagine who told you that," Vahanian replied. He looked out beyond Cam to where three men on horseback waited, dressed in the robes of Mussa traders. Behind their horses trailed three pack mules, each with a waist-high basket strapped to either side and loaded down with bolts of silks wrapped in protective burlap.

Linton shouldered past Cam and Vahanian to meet the traders. "Greetings, friend traders," the caravan master bustled, managing not to look as if he had been up all night. "Welcome to our caravan. What may we do for you?"

"I don't know about you, but I could use some food and some sleep," Tris murmured under his breath. "Let's go."

Vahanian shook his head, not taking his eyes off the traders. "Not yet. I don't like this. Something's not right. I want to stick around."

The traders dismounted and gave the reins of their mounts to two of the riggers. They walked behind Linton into his tent, not glancing back as Tris and Vahanian followed them inside and took up unobtrusive spots along the tent wall.

Linton motioned the traders to sit and moved to pour them each a mugful of kerif from the pot that boiled on the fire. "So, my friends, what is your business?"

"We are silk traders from Mussa," the taller man replied. He was a strongly built man, with a beard and a tan that testified to a life on the road. "We are traveling toward the south, but we have been on the road for some time, and would appreciate the hospitality of a caravan for the night before we continue on our way."

"Tell me about the road north," Linton asked, drawing up a hassock and ignoring Tris and Vahanian. "We have heard many things."

The tall trader laughed. "I am sure of that. We found the road clear, the weather horrible as usual, and the women happy for new silks."

Linton frowned. "The road was clear?"

"Why yes," the tall trader replied. "As good as can be expected this time of year."

"You found nothing... unusual... on your journey?"

The tall trader shook his head. "No, why do you ask?"

Linton shrugged. "There have been rumors that 'strange things' have been seen on the road north."

The tall trader laughed, revealing a mouth dotted with gold teeth. "I have been on the road for many years, my friend, and seen many strange things. But I saw nothing remarkable on our journey here."

"You are welcome to stay the night here," Linton said, "but we will be on our way in the morning. We hope to reach Dhasson's border before the winter weather makes the road more difficult."

"A wise choice," agreed the tall trader. "We wintered once, not by choice mind you, near here because we lingered too long before the storms. It was not our most pleasant winter." He stood and his companions did the same. "If you will direct us to a place where we can rest, we will not trouble you any longer."

"I'll have someone show you to our trading tent," Linton replied. "We're packing the camp today, so it won't be in use. You can rest there, at least until the riggers take it down."

"You are most kind," the tall trader said with a bow. Tris waited until the men had left the tent and were out of earshot before he looked to Vahanian, but the mercenary was already at the tent flap, looking after the receding traders.

"I suppose I really should ask why you stayed for that, Jonmarc," Linton said tiredly. "Manners have never been your strong point, but you seem determined to be obnoxious."

"They were lying," Vahanian said with conviction. "If he's a Mussa trader, I'm a Nargi priest."

Linton looked at Vahanian for a moment before responding. "Why?"

"I've smuggled Mussa silk for years," Vahanian replied. "The traders aren't on the road this time of year because they've got some sort of festival honoring the silkworm. Silk is their livelihood. The festival is very important to them."

"Maybe these aren't very religious traders," Linton objected.

"And his report about the road," Vahanian continued doggedly. "Every other traveler has told stories that would curl your hair about magic beasts. That trader wanted you to believe he didn't even understand your question."

"Maybe he's not superstitious," Linton snapped. "Honestly, Jonmarc, you've always been cautious, but I can't see the need—"

"Something's wrong. I don't like it."

"You can worry about it all you like," Linton said tiredly. "I'm going back to bed."

CHAPTER EIGHTEEN

Vahanian said nothing when he and Tris left, but the mercenary walked determinedly back to the tent he shared with Harrtuck. "What next?" Tris asked, after attempting in vain to get a word out of the mercenary the entire way across camp.

"We're leaving," Vahanian said resolutely. "Linton can be as stubborn as a mule. That scout wasn't just looking for chickens, and it's mighty suspicious that the 'traders' show up right on his heels." Vahanian shook his head. "Go pack," he said as they reached the tent flap. "We're getting out."

"What's this about packing?" Harrtuck said in a hearty voice. Vahanian stepped into the tent, and Tris followed.

"I caught a spy last night," Vahanian reported tersely. "Then this morning, we get a contingent of 'Mussa traders' who want to stay the night. There's something wrong and I want us out of here."

Harrtuck exchanged glances with Tris, who shrugged. Setting his jaw, Harrtuck took a step toward Vahanian. "Jonmarc—"

"Look," Vahanian retorted, wheeling on the fighter, "you hired me to protect you. I'm doing that. I think we've been scouted for bandits again. Maybe worse. I'm not completely convinced Kaine didn't have something up his sleeve when he split off part of the group. It smells, Tov, and I don't like it."

"We hired you to protect us, that's true," Harrtuck replied evenly, unaffected by Vahanian's temper. "But we've also been hired to protect the caravan. Are you just walking away from that?"

"Yes," Vahanian replied unapologetically, starting to roll up his blankets.

"Well, I'm not," Harrtuck answered, planting his feet and balling his fists on his hips. "I made a promise, and I'm seeing it through, at least until the Dhasson border."

"Nice knowing you," Vahanian clipped. "Because according to the vayash moru who saved my life the night I got thrashed, there's dark magic waiting at the Dhasson border for Tris. Something about 'what you need will find you on the way north,'" he said, still stuffing his things into a saddlebag.

"That's it?" Tris wondered accusingly. "You're leaving, just like that?"

Vahanian turned to look at him. "You're the ones who want to stay. Leave with me and I'll take you to the river crossing, and you can decide whether you're going to Dhasson from there or into Principality. I'll take you that far. But I'm not going to stay here and be a target."

"Have you forgotten what's at stake, Jonmarc, for Goddess's sake?" Harrtuck argued. "Tris is the best chance anyone's had to stop Arontala in ten years. Having that chance should be worth it, especially to you."

Vahanian looked away. "Ten years is a long time," he muttered angrily, turning back to his packing. "What happens in Margolan isn't any of my business."

"No, but what happened at Chauvrenne was," Harrtuck snapped. "Men died for you there, because of Arontala. Or is ten years too long to remember?"

Vahanian turned on Harrtuck with enough speed that Tris thought the mercenary would take a swing at the armsman. "No," Vahanian replied in a low, deadly voice. "Maybe I've put it behind me."

"Did you?" Harrtuck retorted. "And does that go for Shanna too?"

This time Vahanian did swing, connecting a solid punch that bent Harrtuck backward but did not move the fighter from his place. Harrtuck did not return the blow, but rubbed his jaw appreciatively. "Damn good swing," he said. "Damn good. I taught you too well."

Vahanian stared sullenly at Harrtuck, rubbing his fist. "By the Whore, Tov, you deserved that."

"And if Carina hadn't only just healed you, I'd pound some sense into you myself," Harrtuck shot back. "Bandits or no, Jonmarc, we stand a better chance in a group than we do alone on the road, and you ought to know that. You're not running away from the bandits," he said challengingly, lifting his chin as if defying Vahanian to swing again. "You're running from Arontala. Now, do you want your chance at him or not?"

For what seemed like forever, Vahanian and Harrtuck glared at each other. Finally, Vahanian looked away with a curse and shouldered past them toward the tent flap.

"Where are you going?" Harrtuck demanded.

"To shoe the horses," Vahanian snapped over his shoulder. "If we're fool enough to stay here, I want them ready to ride on a moment's notice."

Tris said nothing until Vahanian's boot steps faded. Then he looked at Harrtuck. "That's the second time you've mentioned Chauvrenne," Tris said. "Maybe it's time you told me what happened there."

Harrtuck took a deep breath and looked away. "I made it a rule a long time ago not to talk about Jonmarc, much, anyway," he said, rubbing his jaw.

"You know what's at stake," Tris replied. "I want to know what we're dealing with."

Harrtuck looked back at Tris as if taking his measure. "You're starting to sound like a king, my liege," he said quietly. "Perhaps the road is good for you." He paused, then pursed his lips as he came to a decision.

"I met Jonmarc ten years ago, when we had both signed on with the Eastmark army, out on the border with Dhasson. We were young and good with a sword. It was a good place to be," he said with a sigh, "for a while."

"After about a year, the army got a new commander. And at his heels was a Fireclan mage. You know the opinion fighting men have of mages as a rule," he said, with an apologetic glance at Tris.

"I know."

"The commander, a man of great honor in Cartelasia, began to change," Harrtuck recounted. "He started to use the army for his own gain. Jonmarc was a captain, and he didn't like what he saw. Then one day, his platoon got an order to collect the taxes from a village that refused to pay. He didn't like it, but he went," Harrtuck remembered. "The villagers were a stubborn lot. Marching soldiers into town didn't intimidate them. The order came to burn them out," he said. "Jonmarc refused, and his soldiers followed."

"What happened?" Tris asked quietly.

"They were hunted down and captured by their own army, and brought back in chains for court martial," Harrtuck replied bitterly. "The commander himself ruled on it, with Arontala one step behind him. Had the entire platoon executed for treason while Jonmarc watched, then took Jonmarc out to the village, torched it himself, and left Jonmarc there to die with the villagers." He fell silent for a moment. "Somehow, he escaped. And he's been running ever since." He paused again. "That's why I picked Jonmarc as a guide. He's not only the best damn swordsman I've ever met, but he has as much at stake as you, Tris, in seeing Arontala fall."

"Then why—" Tris began.

Harrtuck shook his head, anticipating his question. "Why isn't he chomping at the bit for revenge? Maybe because the only person he blames more than Arontala is himself. I don't know. All I know is that he was one of the sharpest strategists in the Eastmark army, and he's wasted most of the last ten years running silks and brandy on the river. I guess he just gave up."

"If he's as good as you say, and he smells a rat, maybe we should take him seriously." Tris held up a hand before Harrtuck could argue. "I agree with you about staying with the caravan, at least through the forest. But perhaps we should stay on guard."

Harrtuck chewed his lip, then nodded. "Aye, there's nothing to lose by sleeping with one eye open. I'll talk to Ban and Carroway."

"And Cam," Tris added after a moment's thought. "I have the oddest feeling that he and Carina are bound up in this some way."

"Just pray to the Lady that Jonmarc's being overcautious," Harrtuck replied. "The forest's no place for trouble."

Tris headed for the tent opening. "Where are you going?" Harrtuck asked.

"To shoe some horses," Tris replied without turning. "Just in case."

Tris found Vahanian at work in the makeshift stable, shoeing their horses, checking their gear and readying their provisions, his sword and his crossbow near at hand. If the other stablehands noted the sudden interest, they said nothing, leaving them to their work. For several hours, Tris and Vahanian worked silently, stopping late in the morning for lunch and catching up on lost sleep on the bales of hay. It was not until the afternoon sun lengthened the shadows into night and the stablehands headed for their beds that Vahanian finally spoke beyond a curt order or a pointed instruction.

"So," he said without looking up from the hoof he was inspecting, "I imagine Harrtuck told you about Chauvrenne." It was more a statement than a question, and after a moment's pause, Tris nodded. Vahanian cursed under his breath. "Obviously I didn't hit him hard enough."

"You hit him hard enough to fell a mule."

"Should have been about right, then."

"There's just one thing I want to know," Tris said, looking down at the horse he was handling, and working a new shoe into position.

"What's that?"

"Your friend the vayash moru says I don't dare go to Dhasson. So what happens after we cross the border into Principality?"

Vahanian was silent for a moment, then answered without looking up. "You send a message to your uncle, and I get paid."

"And then?"

There was another pause, more awkward this time, and the sound of Vahanian pounding a horseshoe into place. "Look, Tris, I know what want. You want me to sign on with the great crusade. Well, my crusading days are over. The way I figure, with what you're gonna owe me, I can buy the silk franchise into Nargi. That'll double my profits and I can retire a rich man. Go to the river, get a boat, do some legitimate trading for a change, stop getting beat up—"

"Give up," Tris added. For a moment, before Vahanian's expression slipped back into his familiar mask, Tris thought he saw a flash of something more, but then the fighter's eyes hardened.

"Yeah," Vahanian replied off-handedly. "I guess you can call it that. Harrtuck does. Makes no difference to me."

"Harrtuck says it used to."

"I got over it."

"Did you? Can you?" Tris pressed, letting the horse's hoof down and leaning against the stable wall.

"I was doing just fine until Harrtuck hired me to save your regal ass," Vahanian retorted. "And I have no intention of getting myself killed fighting something you can't possibly beat."

"Someone has to try," Tris replied. "Because he wants it all—all seven Kingdoms. You don't think Arontala will stop with Margolan, do you?" Tris continued. "Where will you run then?" He paused. "I don't have that option," Tris said. "I lost my family."

"There's a lot of that going around."

Tris looked at Vahanian's back for a moment in silence as the fighter moved on to the next horse and began studying its hooves. "Shanna... was family?" Tris asked quietly.

This time, Vahanian was silent long enough so that Tris did not think the mercenary was going to reply. "She was my wife," he said finally without looking at Tris.

"And Arontala... killed her?"

At that, Vahanian looked up, his expression a mixture of anger and pain. "You ask a lot of questions."

"The answers matter."

Again, a long silence, and then a curse and a long exhale, before Vahanian straightened and turned away. "I imagine you'll get it out of Harrtuck anyway," he said, running a hand back through his hair. "Yes, I blame Arontala," he said, his voice low and tight. "I was younger than you are, before I went into the army. Making a good living, or at least getting by, blacksmithing and pulling grave jewelry out of the caves in the Borderlands, from the tombs that everyone forgot about.

"One night, a mage showed up who called himself Foor Arontala. He offered me more money than I could imagine for a talisman he said was down in the caves. All I had to do," Vahanian said with a bitter, mocking tone, "was go get it and bring it back."

Tris waited out the next silence, wondering if Vahanian would go on. Vahanian's gaze was far away. "So I did," he said quietly. "Found it right where the mage said, in a tomb I hadn't seen before. And I brought it back. Slipped it onto a thong around my neck so I'd be sure I didn't lose it. Only that night, the Things came."

"Things?"

Vahanian swallowed hard, remembering. "Things. Like the 'magicked beasts' you keep hearing about. They're real. And they're evil. They came out of nowhere, and all they wanted was death." He paused, and his hand unconsciously rose to a scar that ran from his ear to his collarbone and down under his shirt. "We fought them with everything we had. I ran them through, hacked them to bits, nothing mattered. By dawn, there was no village left, no one but me. And the things disappeared like smoke with the morning light." He turned to Tris, his eyes bright with remembered pain. "The talisman called them," he said tightly. "Arontala had to know that. I brought them to the village. And there wasn't a thing I could do about it when they came."

"Why didn't you die, too?" Tris asked quietly.

Vahanian shook his head. "All I've ever guessed is that the talisman protected the wearer. Arontala probably knew that too."

"What happened then?"

"Then I took the damned thing back to the caves where I found it, made a pyre of the village and ran as far away as I could get. And I never saw the mage again, until he showed up a year later, behind my commanding officer in

Eastmark." Vahanian bowed his head and leaned against the horse. "Is that enough of a story for you, prince?" he said, making no attempt to hide the bitterness in his tone. When Tris said nothing, Vahanian turned to him and shook his head.

"You don't get it, do you?" Vahanian said tiredly. "All the fighting in the world won't bring them back. And if you can't do that, what use is revenge?"

"Someone has to stop him."

Vahanian flung his arms wide in a gesture of hopelessness. "Stop him? You might as well darken the moon. Tame the vayash moru. Raise the dead. It can't be done. You'll be dead, and Arontala will win."

"I have to try."

"Go right ahead," Vahanian muttered darkly, checking his horse's provisions. "I'll ask the bards to tell me the stories. Hopeless causes make great tavern songs."

Beyond the stable walls, there was a dull thud and a muted thump. Before Tris could reply, Vahanian had doused the lantern, grabbed for his sword and crossbow and dropped to the stable floor, pulling Tris down with him.

"What the hell?" Tris rasped, but Vahanian motioned for silence, and gestured for Tris to draw his sword. Carefully getting to their feet, the two made their way to the open stable window.

"Look," Vahanian whispered, his grip tightening on his crossbow. "Out there."

Tris could see several dark shapes making their way through the shadows toward the sleeping camp. "Bandits," Tris said.

Vahanian shook his head grimly. "Uh uh. Slavers."

"How—?"

"Look at how they're moving," Vahanian whispered. "They're too professional for bandits. And that thud was a crossbow bolt. Too expensive for most bandits. We've got trouble."

"We've got to warn the others."

"Head back to camp," Vahanian said, starting to climb over the stable's open sill. "Rouse Harrtuck and Soterius—hell, anyone you can find. I'll cut behind them, see how many I can take out from the back."

Tris glanced questioningly at the mercenary, who scowled as if he could read Tris's mind. "No, I'm not running out on you. If my guess is right, you're going to need all the help you can get. Now get going," Vahanian snapped as Tris headed for the door.

"And kid," Vahanian whispered after him in a hoarse rasp. "Stay low."

CHAPTER NINETEEN

Heeding Vahanian's advice, Tris stayed close to the underbrush, mindful that others prowled the scrub between the tumbledown stable and the caravan's camp. At the sound of footfalls to his right, Tris dropped to his belly, reaching for a dagger. Lying still, with his face pressed against the wet leaves, Tris saw the stranger's boots pass within a hand's breadth of his hiding place. It seemed to Tris that his heart was pounding so hard that the other must hear it, but the slaver continued past.

Breathing a silent prayer to the Goddess, Tris climbed to his knees, dagger still in hand, and made his way in a low crouch toward the camp. Grateful to fate for placing Soterius's tent on the side of camp toward the stables, Tris hugged the shadows until he was close enough to dart into it.

"Ban, wake up!" Tris hissed urgently.

"He can't hear you," a mocking voice said from behind him, and Tris felt a knife press between his shoulder blades. As his eyes adjusted to the darkened tent, he saw Soterius, bound and gagged, looking at him with wide, frightened eyes.

Tris raised his hands in surrender, letting his own knife fall. Then, as the slaver behind him stepped back to reclaim the fallen weapon, Tris lashed out behind him with his foot, praying that for once, he could replicate Vahanian's fighting footwork.

Clumsy as the attempt might have been, it caught his attacker off guard, and the slaver sprawled backward with a curse. Tris lurched for the man, pinning him to the ground, and hitting him hard enough on the chin for the man to fall limp beneath him. Grabbing a leather strap from Soterius's riding gear, Tris bound the unconscious slaver's hands and feet, gagging him with a cloth. He retrieved his own knife and headed to where Soterius made garbled cheers through his gag.

"By the Lady, Tris, you got here at the right time!" Soterius exclaimed in a whisper, rubbing his wrists. "What's going on?"

"Slavers," Tris said tersely, looking back at their prisoner. "Jonmarc's circling behind them, but we saw at least a dozen making their way into camp. We've got to rouse the others."

Just then, they heard the clash of steel in the open area beyond the tents. "Looks like the party's starting," Soterius said with a nervous grin, drawing his sword and heading for the tent door at a dead run. "Let's not keep them waiting." Tris drew his sword, and breathed a hurried prayer for protection as they charged into the fight.

The attackers had chosen the cover of darkness to strike, but someone, friend or foe, had set fire to two bales of straw near the main caravan tent, lighting the night sky. Before they reached the action Tris and Soterius became separated, and while Tris battled two slavers, he glimpsed Soterius engaging a burly slaver almost twice his size.

A dazzling green flame cut through the dark sky, exploding into a million sparkling fragments with a clap like thunder. Seizing the opportunity his opponent's consternation presented, Tris dispatched the hapless slaver before the attacker could recover his wits. Tris chuckled as another red flame shot straight into the night sky, recognizing Carroway's sleight of hand. "Just keep it up, Carroway," he muttered under his breath as he felled a second slaver. He glanced up to glimpse the bard scooting from cover to cover, the better to launch the fireworks.

Vahanian's estimate of a dozen was wrong by at least a factor of three, Tris thought grimly. While the embattled caravan fought bravely, they had already lost half their company—including many of the guards—to the group Kaine led down the pass. Tris wondered just how much of a coincidence Kaine's argument with Linton had been, since it made the caravan that much easier for the taking.

Tris's opponent swung hard, nicking him on the shoulder. Tris could feel himself tiring, but the battle was far from over. By the firelight, Tris saw his assailant's teeth gritted in a victory grin. The fighter stiffened just as he readied another blow, staggering backward. A red stain grew from the dagger lodged between his ribs. Without a word, the slaver stumbled and fell, clutching his chest, and Carroway sprang from the shadows.

"Nice night for it, huh, Tris?" the bard shouted, toeing over the dead man and retrieving his knife. Two more of the slavers were heading for them at a dead run, and Carroway's hand flicked, sending a glimmer of silver through the torchlit night. One of the slavers dropped in his tracks, and Tris stepped forward to meet the challenge, covering Carroway as the bard reached for his own sword.

"Just what I wanted to be doing," Tris replied. In the distance, Tris could see Carina defending the small tent she used as a hospital—no match for the two slavers determined to enter. Just as Tris met his opponent's attack, he saw one of the slavers Carina battled close with his sword, engaging her staff as the other slaver swung a broken board with his full might, catching the healer across the shoulder blades and driving her to her knees. Enraged, Tris cut his way through his attacker's advance, bent on coming to Carina's aid, even as Carroway's opponent drove the bard back until Tris and Carroway were fighting back to back.

"I'm afraid I'm out of tricks," Carroway gasped between parries. Barely fending off his own attacker, Tris saw the slavers pull Carina roughly to her feet as a dark, hooded figure sprang from the shadows, a ball of white light streaming from the folds of its robed sleeves. Alyzza! Tris thought hopefully, and Carina's captors staggered back a pace. But hope died as two other slavers leapt toward the old witch with a heavy cloak, landing hard on the woman and binding her so tightly that Tris wondered if Alyzza would smother.

"I'm afraid we might all be," Tris replied, barely parrying his attacker's blow. Cam, Soterius and Harrtuck were nowhere to be seen in the confusion as the screams and cries of the panicked caravan traders mingled with the battle shouts of the slavers. Tents burned around them, setting the campground aglow in a play of light and shadow.

Just as Tris focused all his energy in beating back his opponent's advance, a sharp thud sounded near his boot and a crossbow bolt buried itself in the ground barely beyond his toes. His opponent took advantage of the instant's distraction and swung with murderous fury, snapping Tris's sword in two. The hope that Vahanian had come to the rescue faded as Tris looked up to find himself ringed by a half dozen cold-eyed slavers with crossbows notched and leveled, aimed squarely at Carroway and him.

"Drop your weapons," the taller slaver shouted. "At this distance, we can't possibly miss. I assure you, you are worth more to us alive than dead."

Feeling sick, Tris dropped what was left of his sword, hearing Carroway's weapon thud to the ground an instant later. Four of the slavers ran forward and forced Tris and Carroway to their knees, roughly removing the remainder of their weapons. Tris exchanged a solemn glance with his friend, whose pale expression mirrored his own dim appraisal of their situation. Within moments, the battle was over and the slavers began gathering their captives in what remained of the camp's main area. Still struggling, Carina was dragged beside Tris, then dropped unceremoniously to the ground. With a muffled curse, the healer managed to score a sharp kick to her captor's ankles. The man gave a cry and wheeled as if to strike her, but a tall slaver barked a reproof.

"No one damages the captives before the captain gets here," the tall slaver snapped. Carina's would-be attacker stopped, and with a growl and a look that promised trouble, limped away.

"Sir," a runner panted, stumbling to a stop an arm's length from the tall slaver. "We have a report from the Pass. The other group has been secured."

The tall slaver smiled coldly and nodded. "Good," he said with satisfaction. "Very good. Kaine has earned his payment," he remarked. "Have them meet us here. We'll take the cargo to the buyers together."

"As you wish." The runner headed for the perimeter, and the tall slaver surveyed his captives.

"I think we're in trouble," Carroway whispered to Tris.

"Looks like it's going to take a while longer to get to Principality."

"You there," the tall slaver barked at Tris. "Quiet."

The slavers secured the camp with professional speed. Tris's spirits sank as he looked over the bound and chained captives. Of the fifty who had stayed with Linton, only two score now remained. The others, Tris presumed, were more likely to have fallen defending the camp than to have fled the attackers. To his bitter disappointment, Cam, Soterius, Harrtuck and Vahanian were among the missing.

"That's all of them, at least, all that's still breathing," a short, pox-faced slaver reported.

"What about the caravan master?" the tall slaver asked.

The pox-faced man shook his head. "Didn't have the heart for it," he said, clucking his tongue. "Found him dead in his bed."

"The men are getting heavy handed," the tall slaver said reproachfully, looking over the wreckage of the camp. "They killed too many this time. Cuts into profits. Next raid, every dead captive is a cut in their ale ration."

"Aye, Tarren," the pox-faced man replied. "That'll get their attention."

Tarren surveyed the captives once more. Smoke lingered over the camp in a dark, noxious cloud.

Behind the wagons, frightened screams mingled with the guards' boorish laughter to reveal the location of the female caravan survivors. Tris clenched his jaw and strained against the ropes that bound his wrists, but even a momentary struggle confirmed that his captors had secured him against any easy escape.

"What have we here?" Tarren said, walking over to where Carina sat, just an arm's length from Tris. The healer's robe was soot-streaked and torn, testimony to her spirited struggle, and her dark hair was tangled. She had not looked up since the guards had dragged her to her spot, and Tris suspected that it was the disappearance of her brother that left Carina bereft of hope, even more than their own dire situation. "Speak, wench. Are you a healer?"

Carina looked up with a glare. "I am," she said tonelessly.

"I wonder," Tarren said, looking at her disheveled appearance. "Healers bring a fine price. Perhaps that's just a healer's belt you've stolen. I must be sure," he said, his eyes narrowing. "If not, I'm sure you have other... talents... we can use," he said, and as if on cue, another terrified scream pierced the night from behind the wagons.

"Tarren, we found him," a slaver hailed, approaching the circle of firelight. As the slaver drew closer, Tris could see that he carried a limp form in his arms.

"Alive?" Tarren asked, frowning.

"Barely," the newcomer replied. "Found him out on the edge of camp. And a dozen of our men, with bolts in their backs, to prove it," he added, joining Tarren in the firelight. With a shrug as if he were unloading a sack of flour, the slaver dropped the body at Tarren's feet.

Tris caught his breath. Vahanian lay pale and still on the ground.

Tarren looked from Vahanian's silent form to Carina and back again. "The bounty's good with him dead, but it's higher if he lives long enough to... question him," Tarren said. "Healer," he said roughly. "A deal. Prove your talent to me with this smuggler, and you remain under my protection." He grinned wolfishly. "Fail, and I place you under the careful eye of my trusted guards."

Tris felt his heart pound. Vahanian was far paler than usual, and a faint blue already tinged his lips. The smuggler's breath was shallow and rapid, and a nasty crimson stain below his ribs soaked his tunic. Tarren stepped forward, drawing a dagger, and Carina shrank back instinctively. The slaver reached down and sliced through her bonds.

"All right," Tarren said, crossing his arms. "He lives and so do you. If he dies... there are plenty of brothels that would be glad for you."

Tris managed as reassuring a glance as he could muster. Carina knelt beside Vahanian and let her right hand glide down the length of the smuggler's body. She moved slowly, beginning with his head, and as her hand moved across his features, the superficial marks of battle—a split lip, a purple bruise on his cheek, a surface cut along his jaw, faded. Tarren watched intently, noting the changes with raised eyebrow.

Tris slowed his breathing and let himself slip into a trance. As if suspended between two realms, he was dimly aware of the slavers' camp, but he also saw the spirit plains, and sensed Carina's healing on a different, life-force level. It was possible to share limited communication, Tris and Carina had found, here in the trance.

Tris, help me! Carina called to him.

Tris breathed deeply and focused his senses on the life force that was Carina, channeling his own energy to her as he had done before in the healer's hut. As he brushed her spirit, he could sense the toll the healing was already taking on her strength.

Carina's hands reached Vahanian's abdomen and she blanched, tearing at the fighter's shirt with both hands to expose a deep belly wound. Tris let the scene in front of him recede further, trying to blunt his own emotions and channel more energy to Carina. He felt a wave of panic in return.

He's dying, Tris! I don't think I can heal this in time.

Tris stretched his mage senses further. He licked his lips with concentration, willing himself deeper still, until he could not smell the smoke or hear the cries of the prisoners, until nothing existed at all except the darkness behind his closed eyes.

And then, he glimpsed it, a thin, evanescent strand of light, so dim that it barely shone above the darkness. It flickered and instinctively Tris dove for it, stretching out with all his will until he reached the glowing strand. He looked back, and saw himself as a second, more brightly glowing strand, as if all the vital strength of his life force could be captured in a single, shining thread. On instinct, he reinforced Vahanian's flickering strand with his own, picturing himself hanging on to the end of a slipping cord with all his strength, hoping that he could lend his strength for long enough for Carina to work her healing.

Unbidden, Alyzza's warning in the glade returned to mind. Never, never can you bind a soul that does not wish to stay, the old witch had warned. Tris held on to the flickering strand with all his might, sensing no desire for the spirit to depart.

He waited forever in the darkness, suspended in unending night. The strand that was Vahanian's fragile life still flickered, but to Tris's relief, did not fade further. Nor did Tris feel the wrenching separation he had experienced at Kait's death, when it was not her life but her spirit he had caused to remain. Perhaps, he hoped, that meant that he was doing what Carina needed him to do, sustaining Vahanian while she worked, and lending his strength to support both the healer and her patient.

The strain began to take its toll as Tris struggled to keep his concentration. Once, the thread flickered dangerously, and Tris lunged for it with all his will. He imagined that he felt the thread surge toward him in response, and clung to the hope of that faint sign of life. Time meant nothing there in the blackness, cut off from all senses but the presence of the clear blue light. Gradually, Tris felt a growing warmth, which began from the very edges of his perception, warming the chill of the blackness as it advanced resolutely.

Just a little longer, Tris heard Carina urge, tired but steady. He redoubled his own flagging efforts, and found, to his relief, that the glimmering thread that was Vahanian no longer flickered, but pulsed a dim, steady blue.

After what seemed like an eternity, Tris heard Carina's voice again. *Break the contact,* she urged. Tris imagined himself gently letting go of the strengthened blue thread, easing his way back through the darkness, which by now had lightened to pale twilight. With a lurch, he came back to himself, and opened his eyes, painfully aware that both his feet had gone to sleep and his back cramped uncomfortably.

Vahanian groaned and heaved a deep breath. Tris dared a look at the swordsman. Vahanian's breathing was measured and deep, and color had returned to his face.

"Well done, healer," Tarren said appraisingly. "You there," he hailed two of the slavers who were among the small crowd that gathered to watch the healing, "tie him up and make sure it's secure," he said with a nod toward Vahanian.

The slavers took a step back, fear plain in their faces. "Vayash moru," they murmured, and the murmur spread among the small crowd.

Tarren looked at them with contempt. "Rubbish. Wives' tales, all of it." He looked levelly at the two again, and the slavers seemed to shrink in on themselves, torn between their fear of Vahanian and their fear of their commander. "Now, tie him and make it tight," Tarren repeated in a voice that threatened worse than any vengeance of the undead. Pale but obedient, the slavers did as they were bid, binding Vahanian to a stake in the ground between Tris and Carina. Carroway, to Tris's right, gave Tris a silent nod of approval. On Carina's left, Alyzza, still hooded, rocked back and forth, humming a haunting melody.

Once Tarren and the others left, Tris glanced over to Carina. The healer slumped against the stake to which she was tied, eyes on the ground. "You were fantastic," Tris praised. "I never believed in miracles, but that was close."

Carina barely managed a wan smile in acknowledgment. "I couldn't have done it without you. Truly," she said in a voice barely above a whisper. The life had gone out of her voice, leaving it flat and tired. He guessed that she was thinking about Cam, and feeling his loss even more potently than before, having lost her healing partner as well as her brother.

"We don't know for sure about Cam and the others," he said as hopefully as he could muster. "Ban and Tov are resourceful. Maybe they were able to slip away, get help," he suggested, although in his heart, he feared the worst.

Carina shook her head. "I want to believe that," she whispered, her voice catching. "But I think we're just fooling ourselves. And we were so close to Dhasson."

"Somehow, we're going to make it," Tris swore, although his resolve far surpassed any ideas of how he might make good his oath. "We have to. I have to."

Carina looked up and held his gaze for a long moment, as if she were taking his measure anew. "I shouldn't dare to hope," she whispered finally. "But I wish I could."

Vahanian roused from his spot between them, then settled back into an uneasy rest. "What about him?" Tris asked, worriedly. He knew how close Vahanian had been to death. Any escape attempt would hinge on the swordsman's recovery.

"I don't know," Carina answered honestly. "He's much better than before, but it was pretty bad. I didn't sense any permanent damage, but then again, there wasn't a lot of time."

Tris nodded. Carroway leaned as close to Tris as the bard could and hissed through his teeth to get Tris's attention. "What's the plan?" Carroway whispered, keeping a wary eye on their distant guards.

Tris grimaced. "Watch and wait, at least for now," he replied with as much of a shrug as his bonds would permit. "And hope for an opening."

"There aren't many of us left," Carroway observed soberly. "Fewer to rescue, but on the other hand, fewer to help fight."

"I know," Tris replied, closing his eyes as the bruises and wounds of the day began to ache in earnest. "It will have to do."

At dawn, the rest of the slavers' camp joined them. Provision wagons rolled noisily into the remains of the caravan grounds, followed by pack mules and finally two wagons filled with another dozen manacled slaves. The slaves on the wagon regarded the new captives with studied disinterest, avoiding eye contact.

They've given up, Tris thought. Not a one of them looks like he's spoiling for a fight. Another omen that any reprieve would have to be of their own making. Tris shut his eyes, willing himself to find a steady center and review his last lessons with Carina. This time he must be ready, he thought. When the time came, his powers—new as they might be—must be under his control. He glanced at Vahanian's slumped form. Sleep well, my friend, Tris thought. I'm going to need time.

Tris watched the slavers closely throughout the next morning. The band appeared to number no more than thirty. They made camp efficiently and were well provisioned. Tris's spirits sank. It was unlikely that these slavers would provide them with an easy opportunity.

He first caught sight of the young girl at breakfast, slipping quickly among the slavers, dodging them like an experienced scullery maid. Just a few years younger than Kait, he thought, but with a glint to her eyes much more worldly than his sister had acquired. Her brown hair was dirty and matted, caught back with a piece of string. The tattered dress might once have been of good cloth, but was now far too ragged and stained to do more than barely protect her from the cold.

Still, there was quickness in her movement that suggested intelligence, Tris thought with curiosity, although during the first two candlemarks that he watched, the girl appeared to be a disaster in action. She spilled hot karif on one slaver, earning herself an incidental cuffing, which she took without a word. She kicked loose two coals from the fire and set a small patch of grass on fire, disrupting breakfast, for which she apologized abjectly, sparing herself another blow.

But when she tripped over a guywire and tipped Tarren's breakfast onto the ground, Tris happened to catch her eye and, to his surprise, caught the barest of winks before she scrambled to clean up the mess. Not inept, he thought, smothering a smile. Intentionally destructive, with an impish humor. Before he could guess more, she disappeared inside the cook's tent.

Just before the breakfast fires were banked, Vahanian stirred. "What hit me?" he moaned to no one in particular, and struggled to open his eyes, then blinked and squinted against the sun.

"From the blood, I imagine the edge of a broadsword," Tris answered dryly.

Vahanian shifted, seemed to become aware of his bonds for the first time and struggled briefly, then leaned back in surrender against the post that secured him. "Let me guess," he murmured. "We lost."

"Uh huh," Tris replied.

Just then, the girl appeared with a loaf of bread under her arm and a pitcher and cup in her other hand. She began to work her way down the line of bound prisoners, giving each an ample slice of the bread and holding the cup for them to drink. She caught Tris's eye knowingly, as if they shared a secret, then moved on to Vahanian.

"How did you get lucky enough to feed the prisoners?" Vahanian asked, licking his lips dryly.

The girl smirked. "Well, for one thing, they sent me to see if you really are vayash moru," she replied. "I guess if I live through it, they might try. Or maybe not," she shrugged.

Vahanian sipped greedily at the water. "I don't understand," he said. She pushed a bite of bread between his lips.

"Half the camp is sure you're back from the dead," she explained in a whisper, with a surreptitious glance over her shoulder. "There were bets on that you'd disappear in a puff of smoke come dawn."

Vahanian swallowed, and bit again at the bread. "I've been accused of a lot of things," he said. "But that's a new one."

"Just promise me something," the girl said, leaning forward as if to press another bite into his mouth. "I know who you are. I've heard them talk about your bounty," she said, her green eyes bright. "When you escape, take me with you."

Vahanian opened his eyes a bit wider at that. "I was dead yesterday," he said, sipping the water she held for him. "What makes you think I'm going anywhere?"

"I've heard Tarren talk about you," she said. "You will."

Vahanian glanced at Tris and back at the girl again. "Fair enough. What's your name?" he asked.

"Berry," the girl replied, giving Vahanian the last of his portion. "I've got to go," she said suddenly, glancing over her shoulder. At that, she moved on to Carina, although she said no more as she fed the remaining prisoners.

The slavers remained at the burned-out caravan site for two days. On the morning of the second day, a rider approached, and Tris looked up to see a dark, thin-faced man on horseback ride into camp.

"We've got company," Tris whispered to his companions. Vahanian looked up, then stiffened, his face tight with anger.

"Vakkis," he muttered, making the name a curse.

"You know him?"

Vahanian nodded grimly. "Too well. Bounty hunter. He's the one I warned Linton about, the one I saw in the tavern. Only this time, I'm not top of his list," he said with a measured glance at Tris. "You are."

Tris digested that piece of news wordlessly, watching the stranger approach. Tarren came out to meet Vakkis personally, and while the tall slaver did not completely sacrifice his reserve in his efforts to please the newcomer, it was apparent, even out of earshot, that Vakkis held the upper hand. After a brief conversation, Vakkis and Tarren headed for where the prisoners were tethered, accompanied by two slavers who walked behind them with the horses. The slavers looked askance at Vahanian, clearly fearful of the smuggler, who grinned wickedly, making sure his lips drew back to expose his teeth. The two slavers recoiled, and Vahanian chuckled.

Vakkis stopped in front of Vahanian, who looked up and met the bounty hunter's eyes defiantly. "Well, well," Vakkis gloated. "Look what we've caught. I wasn't trolling for you, Jonmarc, but I won't turn down the bounty."

"Go to the Demon."

In response, Vakkis backhanded Vahanian and Tris could see blood well at the corner of the mercenary's lip. "I may go to the Demon as you say, Jonmarc," the bounty hunter replied, rubbing the back of his hand, "but I assure you, you will go with me."

Vahanian said nothing in response, but a killing chill came to his eyes as Vakkis moved a step to stand before Tris. "Ah, good. You've followed instructions well, Tarren," Vakkis said. "This is exactly the one I was looking for." Vakkis looked him over carefully, and Tris had the uneasy sense of being merchandise, appraised for the sale. "We have a common... friend... who will be very glad to see you again," Vakkis said. "You have much to account for."

"I'd watch my back if I were you," Tris replied evenly, although his heart pounded. He hoped he could replicate Vahanian's defiance. "After all, I've seen your... friend... in action. Don't count on living to spend the money." Tris thought that Vakkis would cuff him, too, for his insolence but the bounty hunter seemed to think better of it and merely folded his arms.

"I'm not concerned," Vakkis brushed off the reply. "But you should be. Better to be the hunter than the prey."

"It's not over yet."

"We shall see," Vakkis replied. The bounty hunter looked over to Tarren. "Guard them well. Double the guard you have posted. Bring them back to Shekerishet, and your company will be rich. Fail, and you will all die."

The threat did not seem to faze Tarren. "Those were our terms," Tarren replied. "They'll get to the palace."

"Good," Vakkis said, looking around the camp for the first time. "Now, come with me. We have much to discuss."

Tris watched the two men walk away, waiting until they were out of sight before he glanced over to Vahanian. "Looks like we know all the right people."

Vahanian managed a crooked grin. "Yeah, imagine that. You can take it as kind of an honor that your brother sent Vakkis after you," the mercenary added. "He's the best in the business. I've ruined his perfect kill record for quite a few years," he said. "Guess everything has to end sometime."

"That's one record I'd like to see stay ruined," Tris replied.

Before long, Berry began her rounds again, bringing bread and water to the prisoners. "You're the ones Tarren's been after, aren't you?"

she asked Vahanian as she fed bread to Tris and held a cup for him to drink from.

"Looks like it," Vahanian replied. "So why are you here?"

Berry shrugged. "Wrong place at the wrong time. Ambushed."

"Have you heard them talk about where we're going next?" Tris asked between bites.

Berry nodded. "Back into Margolan, toward the palace. Tarren had an argument last night with his lieutenant about the road to take. Vakkis wants them to go the straight way, but that runs along the Ruune Videya forest. Tarren doesn't mind, but the men are superstitious," she added, as Tris finished his bread and gratefully accepted another drink. "They don't want to go near the forest."

"So which road are we taking?" Tris asked thoughtfully.

Berry moved on to offer a crust to Vahanian. "The one Vakkis wants. But it doesn't mean the slavers like it."

"That might be just the break we need," Carroway hissed. "You know the stories."

"Anything else?" Tris pressed.

Berry shook her head. "No. I'll keep listening. In the meantime, here's this," she whispered, and just then, appeared to stumble. As she recovered, Tris saw her drop something into Vahanian's bound hand. "It's not much," she said, and Tris caught a glint of metal before Vahanian concealed it in his fist. "But it's sharp."

"Thank you," Vahanian replied. "You're in."

Berry grinned. "Good," the girl replied. "Oops," she said suddenly, "Got to go." And she moved on to Carina with a glance over her shoulder.

The next day, the slavers woke the prisoners at dawn. The camp was alive in the chill morning as the slavers took anything of value in the caravan's belongings and readied themselves for the march. Tris and the other captives were loosed from their stakes, dragged to their feet and bound together with lengths of rope in single file, then herded onto open wagons, where each end of the tether was tied securely to the wagon's supports.

With the gray dawn, a chill had settled around Tris's mood. The vow he had sworn to Kait and to the Lady rang hollow in his memory, and the possibility of fulfilling it seemed as remote as the Border mountains. Perhaps Harrtuck had been right, Tris thought. The road and its hardships had finally begun to make a sheltered prince into a king. Tris lifted his face into the wind and begged the Lady that those lessons would not come too late to save his friends, his kingdom and his sister's soul.

"I've always liked carriage rides," Vahanian muttered to no one in particular. Carina glared at him, but said nothing.

"This isn't looking good," Carroway whispered from behind Tris. "I'm in no hurry to get back to Shekerishet."

"Especially not like this," Tris replied.

They traveled until dusk. After camp was made, a rider was escorted directly to the tent where Tarren and Vakkis conducted business.

When the supper fires were darkened, Tris heard a rustle behind them, and caught a glimpse of Berry out of the corner of his eye.

"You've got to make a break for it when we reach the forest tomorrow night," Berry whispered urgently from the shadows.

"Why?" Vahanian hissed.

"I heard Vakkis and Tarren talking with the rider who just came in," Berry whispered. "Word from the buyers. They will only pay for the good-looking women and the strongest men." She paused. "And of course, you and your friend," she said with a nod toward Tris.

"So?" Vahanian replied.

"That means Tarren will kill the rest as soon as we get through the lowlands tomorrow," Berry whispered, her fear evident in her voice. "He needs help to move the wagons through the swampy areas. But he won't want to spare the provisions to take 'cargo' through the forest if he won't be paid for it."

Vahanian frowned. "What about the healer?" he asked, glancing toward Carina.

"No good," Berry hissed urgently. "Tarren said he can't sell her because no one will trust a captive healer without hostages. Might not try hard enough, I guess. They'll start the killing as soon as we reach the forest," Berry repeated. "I hope you have a plan."

"Sure we do," Vahanian replied confidently. "Just keep us in view."

"We've got a little extra time," Berry added with a self-satisfied snicker. "I added some wild mushrooms to their stew tonight. I don't think they'll sleep well," she said, and in the distance, Vahanian could hear the sound of a man retching.

"Berry," Vahanian said.

"What?"

"I'm glad you're on our side."

"Look sharp!" she warned, and disappeared into the shadows.

Vahanian looked over to Carina. The healer was quiet and distant, as if she remained silent long enough, she might hear Cam calling for her. "Now is a good time to say a few prayers, priestess."

Carina looked at him, but did not meet his eyes. "I'm not a cleric," she murmured. "Can't help you there."

"Might not be a bad time to think about a switch," Vahanian quipped. But Carina looked away, unwilling to be drawn into the banter.

"So tell me about this plan," Tris whispered.

Vahanian scowled. "We get to the forest and you use that spook stuff of yours to make them all disappear."

"That's the plan?" Tris asked skeptically.

"Got a better one?" Vahanian shot back.

"You know," Carroway said, his voice barely audible. "That might just work."

Tris turned as far toward Carroway as he could. "How do you figure?"

Carroway paused. "I'm not quite sure where we are, but I know that there are places where the forest runs along cliff sides with lots of caves.

They could make it impossible for the slavers to follow us once we get loose."

"Uh, you're forgetting something important," Vahanian replied. "The getting loose part."

"Ask the spirits for help," Carroway replied. "They would listen to Tris. The ghosts of the Ruune Videya were slaughtered by an unjust king." Carroway shrugged. "Maybe they'll be sympathetic."

"Or we could end up as dead as the slavers if the ghosts aren't of a mind to listen, assuming I could even get their attention," Tris whispered.

"Let me get this straight," Vahanian muttered. "Our only hope of getting out of this rests in Spook here calling up a bunch of ghosts, setting them on the slavers, and hoping to hell that they don't turn on us while they're at it?"

"You've got the main points," Carroway replied.

Vahanian groaned and leaned back against the post. "Great," he muttered, "and the only thing worse is that I can't come up with anything better."

Tris shut his eyes. *Grandmother. I need you. Please*, he begged the spirits. *Show me what I must do.*

Trust your instincts, came the memory of Bava K'aa's voice. *When the time comes, you will know what to do. Doubt, and all is lost.*

But how will I know? he asked.

You will know, the old sorceress's voice replied, *when you are too frightened to do anything else.*

CHAPTER TWENTY

TRUE TO BERRY'S whispered warning, the slavers began to move toward the forest the next day. Hanson's Bog lay between the road to Dhasson and the southerly, more direct road back into Margolan. The wagons began to roll more slowly from the time they left the Dhasson road, and within two candlemarks, the slavers emptied the wagons of any cargo that could walk.

By midday, the road was so soft that the captives and the slavers frequently put their shoulders against the wagons to force them onward through the mud. Tris felt his mood darken. As Berry suggested, it would truly take the slavers and all of their captives to reach the southern road. Once there, the slavers could easily rid themselves of any cargo that could not be sold, lightening their load for the perilous trek through the forest. Time was running out.

From the time they entered the bog, Tris tried to sense whether Carroway's tales of restless spirits in the forest were correct. A desperate plan to win their freedom had been forming in his mind, but it would depend entirely on the nature of the forest's spirits—if there were any—and whether or not they acknowledged his power. For most of the day, Tris tried in vain to sense any revenants, peaceful or not, and began to despair that the tales were merely stories to keep youngsters from venturing far afield. But as they reached the nether end of the bog, the spirits began to call him.

The initial contact staggered him, nearly causing him to fall. Carina helped him to his feet, watching with concern as if she suspected that more than slippery mud caused him to lose his footing.

Why have you come? A cacophony of voices howled in his mind.

Tris strengthened his mental shielding, knowing that without the training from Alyzza and Carina, the contact would have overwhelmed him. *I am a prisoner,* Tris replied to the howling voices. *Who are you, and whom do you serve?*

We are the lost, and we serve vengeance! howled the voices. Now, he could feel them present in the glade, beyond all but mageborn sight. *Who are you?*

Kin and heir to Bava K'aa, replied Tris, struggling to push the wagon so that he did not attract the slavers' attention. It was getting more difficult to split his concentration, since the ferocity of the spirits required him to keep conscious control of his shields.

Bava K'aa... Bava K'aa... Bava K'aa. The name echoed among the hundreds of voices, until it became a moan like the sound of the wind. *Free us, kin of Bava K'aa*, the voices wailed. *Give us our vengeance!*

Tris felt the anger of the revenants at their long-ago betrayal and murder, their jealousy of the living, and their deep desire to right the generations-old wrong. Yet he could sense no evil, though the spirits grieved their loss with such intensity that, in their mourning, they struck back at any living being that came within their boundaries.

You are a summoner! The voices returned. *Give us our justice. You may enter our forest, but the others are not welcome.*

My friends and I are prisoners, Tris repeated, hoping that the gambit beginning to form in his mind would work. *We were taken by slavers. We have no choice but to enter your forest.*

Slavers... slavers... slavers. The word repeated through the voices, and Tris felt gathering anger. *Give us the slavers!*

Free us from the slavers, promise me safe passage for the captives, Tris commanded, *and when we reach the forest, I will give you rest.*

Rest... The voices stretched out the word in a long, sibilant howl. *We cannot rest.*

Give me your promise that the captives won't be harmed. Free us and I will help you pass over, Tris bargained.

Rest... the voices hissed. *We will accept your bargain, kin of Bava K'aa. But our power dwells in the forest. Come to the edge of the forest, and we will set you free.*

Give me your promise, Tris repeated, *your oath that the captives won't be harmed.*

We want only the slavers, the voices howled. *Free us, and you may pass through our forest in safety. But if you cannot pass us over to the Lady, you and your friends will join us forever.*

It was a fool's bargain, Tris thought, but less certain a fate than what awaited them at the hands of the slavers come nightfall. *Accepted,* Tris pledged.

At the edge of the forest... when darkness falls, whispered the spirits as they drew back. Their sudden departure left him out of balance, like a man braced against a strong wind that suddenly failed. His shields, reinforced against a power no longer present, flared in his magesight as he tried to dispel them.

"You there, put your back into it," shouted a slaver, bringing a whip down hard across Tris's back. Already off balance, the blow drove him to his knees, and he struggled not to cry out in pain.

Carroway helped him to his feet with a worried glance, and Tris shouldered his portion of the effort with the bulky wagon once more.

"Are you all right?" Carroway whispered, an eye on the glowering slaver and his whip.

"Not really," Tris replied through gritted teeth. The lash burned, and he could feel blood mingling with sweat running down his back. "But I think I've got a plan."

"We need one."

"Let the others know. Come nightfall, I'm going to call the spirits."

"That's the plan?" Carroway hissed. "We get killed by the spirits instead of the slavers?"

"We have an... arrangement. I think," Tris replied under his breath. "Whatever you see, whatever happens, just get to shelter. Leave me to handle the ghosts."

"Gladly," Carroway murmured. "But that's not exactly the kind of plan I was hoping for."

"It's the best we're going to get," Tris said, fervently hoping that his reading of the spirits' intent was correct.

"Much more of this, and it won't matter that Carina healed Jonmarc," Carroway whispered. Tris followed his gaze. Vahanian was obviously not fully recovered from his injuries. Twice, the smuggler stumbled and fell. Only the slavers' fear that Vahanian might be vayash moru spared him a beating. That fear was waning, Tris thought, as the slavers' anxiety grew about entering the forest.

Tris groaned as he shouldered their wagon through a particularly sticky patch of mud. Beside him, Carroway cursed creatively in the many dialects of the Margolan court. At the opposite corner, Vahanian and Carina strained against the mire. Vahanian was pale with the effort, and Tris noted that despite their frequent sparring, Carina extended her fierce protectiveness over her patients to include the injured smuggler. She slipped beneath Vahanian's shoulder, steadying him with her own thin, strong frame.

"In another minute, Tarren's going to send one of his bully boys over here to find out why we're not moving," Carroway hissed, warily keeping an eye on the slavers, who were cursing another group of captives whose wagon, mired to its axles, refused to move. The slaver, twice the bulk of any of the straining captives, lashed the nearest man viciously with a riding crop, but did nothing to add his own strength to the effort.

"I know," Tris murmured. "Let's try rocking it this time."

Alyzza, still feared by the slavers, sat hooded and bound on the wagon. She had remained motionless throughout the trip thus far, but now, the old witch slowly scooted herself down the bed of the wagon to be closer to where Tris and the others struggled with the mired vehicle. Following their voices, she stopped just an arm's length from Tris and Carroway, and began to hum softly, swaying with the melody.

"Look!" Carroway breathed. As Alyzza sang, the wagon began to rise, just enough to get it over the ridge. Carina and Vahanian exchanged glances with Tris and Carroway, then lunged against the wagon to seize the opportunity. With a lurch, the stuck wagon came free, nearly rolling out from under them as they scrambled to catch up. Alyzza stopped humming.

"Thank you," Tris whispered as they pushed the wagon past the glare of the slaver with the whip. Alyzza inclined her head, just barely, in acknowledgment.

Twice more before nightfall, Tris and his friends were obliged to depend on Alyzza's help to move the obstinate wagon through the rutted road. By sundown, the worst of the bog was behind them, and Tris felt a chill fill him that had nothing to do with the evening's cold. The end of the marshy ground meant the end of the captives' usefulness, he thought, as the slavers lit the supper fires and staked the captives at the edge of the camp. If Berry's warning was correct, it would be killing time very soon.

The slavers camped at the entrance to the forest, where the trees met a large, vertical cliffside pockmarked with shallow caves and shifting rock. As the camp bustled with its preparations for supper, Tris shut his eyes and tried to concentrate.

When darkness falls, kin of Bava K'aa. When darkness falls.

Tris watched the supper preparations with a leaden feeling in his stomach. The slavers' hushed conversations and furtive glances only confirmed Berry's warning. Tris glanced at Vahanian, who struggled with the small blade Berry had given him, working to weaken the ropes that bound his wrists.

Tris knew the day had gone hard on all of them, with a forced march and exhausting physical work. It looked to have been hardest on Vahanian. Before the march, Vahanian might have held his own in a brief battle. Now, Tris doubted Vahanian could do more than skirmish.

Carina appeared lost in thought. Annoying as the constant sparring between the healer and Vahanian had been during the caravan's trek, now that the healer did not respond, Vahanian seemed to miss the challenge. The double blow of her brother's disappearance and their own reversal of fortune seemed more than Carina could bear.

Carroway was the most visibly nervous. If Berry's warning was correct, then of the five of them, Carroway, Carina and Alyzza would die. As Tris watched, he realized that Carroway, too, was preparing to fight. Hidden in the folds of his tunic was one small dagger that the slavers had missed. Carroway jostled the blade into his numb fingers. He caught Tris's glance and shot a daring grin. If there was to be a battle, the minstrel was going to give the slavers a good fight.

At dusk, as the supper fires burned down, Tarren and his lieutenant walked toward the prisoners. The lieutenant shook his head. "Are you sure we can't find buyers for the rest?" he asked, struggling to reconcile orders with his own business sense. "They aren't the best lot we've taken, but there are mines in the East that would take the bunch of them, no questions asked, so long as they're breathing."

Tarren shook his head. "I know, I know," he said. "Can't say I like it either, but there's the forest to contend with, and I like that less."

The lieutenant eyed the trees once more and nodded. "Aye, I'll agree with that. Well, then, best to get it done if there's no getting around it."

He walked toward where Tris and the others were staked, and Tris watched as he strode down the line. "This one," the slaver said with a flick of his blade toward Tris, "is the one Vakkis sent for," he confirmed as Tarren nodded. "And this one," he said, with a gloating grin toward Vahanian, "is the bonus to sweeten the pot." He looked to Tarren once more. "The others?"

Tarren shook his head. "The thin one," he said with a nod toward Carroway, "couldn't do a day's work in the mines. The others are worthless. Kill them."

The lieutenant stroked his blade along his finger thoughtfully as he took another step toward the bound captives. He stopped a pace in front of Carina, and only then did the healer look up, her dark eyes unreadable. "Maybe I'll start with you, pretty lady," the slaver chuckled coldly. "I don't imagine you remember, but you rapped me pretty soundly with that staff of yours. Time to pay the debt," he said, advancing, as Carina shrank back against her post.

Vahanian's wrists were raw as the obstinate ropes frayed. "No!" he rasped. As the lieutenant bent, blade ready, Vahanian's bonds gave way and he sprang like a coiled snake, tackling the lieutenant and grasping for his knife hand.

Vahanian pinned the lieutenant between his knees, wresting the knife free and tossing it into the darkness, then swinging with all his waning might with clasped fists at the slaver's jaw, until the man fell slack. Boot falls warned him of another opponent, and Vahanian tore the lieutenant's sword free of its scabbard, dropping and rolling to come up in a crouch.

Tris lurched forward, straining against his bonds, one word in his mind. *Now!* he cried to the dark presences just beyond the forest's edge. A chill wind swept through the clearing, and the ropes that bound his wrists dropped away, sending him sprawling as a damp fog suddenly rolled in around them from everywhere at once.

"I'll cover you!" Carroway hissed, rubbing his newly-freed wrists. The force of the spirits' rage buffeted Tris like an unseen windstorm as he staggered to his feet, struggling to maintain contact with the onslaught of ghosts that swirled thickly around them in a heavy fog enveloped the clearing.

"Get to cover!" Tris shouted above the wind.

The camp erupted into chaos. Out of the corner of his eye, Tris glimpsed Vahanian intent on his next opponent as the swirling fog started to take human shapes, twisted, pain-wracked shapes with gaping, open mouths—the stuff of nightmares. It took all of Tris's strength to continue his link with the ghosts, and as their numbers grew and their keening wails shrieked louder, he felt his control begin to slip.

Protect! Tris cried in his mind, summoning the spirits around him. He could feel their anger, their vengeance so long denied, and the malevolence he sensed grew like storm clouds. Carroway set about with a stolen sword, driving back the slavers that launched themselves at Tris. Vahanian, who was doing the lion's share of fighting, was tiring fast. The slaver fighting Vahanian seemed to sense the mercenary's weakness, and doubled his offense, driving Vahanian back toward the cliff face with wild blows that could have split a man from shoulder to hip.

The slaver scored a shallow cut on Vahanian's shoulder. Sure that he had the upper hand, the slaver beat forward with all his might, leaving Vahanian parrying wildly for his life. Then, just as Tris was sure that Vahanian could hold the slaver off no longer, a rock the size of a melon fell hard from the ledge above, striking the unsuspecting slaver cleanly on the top of his head and dropping him without a word. From above Vahanian on the cliffside came a mischievous giggle, and Tris glimpsed Berry leaping from ledge to ledge, ducking the slavers' arrows, hurling a rain of boulders and large rocks down on their heads.

Tris returned to the spirits with an abrupt wrenching, as the malevolence of the dark cloud grew stronger. He intended for the ghosts of the forest to drive off the slavers, but, as the spirits massed around him, Tris knew that they had other plans. The winter wind cut though the glade in an icy blast, chilling Tris to the bone and whipping his hair into his eyes. Beside him, Carina seized one of the stakes from the ground and was using it as a makeshift staff, holding off a slaver who threw himself at Tris, half-mad with terror.

Vahanian sprinted back to them, breathless and pale. "I can help cover," Vahanian said, relieving

Carina. "One of these days, you've got to start using a sword."

"Can't," Carina breathed as she used the staff to trip a passing slaver and then thump him heavily on the head. "Healers may not use blades."

"Dumb rule," Vahanian shouted back, engaging a slaver who made a run toward Carroway, giving the bard a chance to lob a dagger and drop the man in his tracks. "Must make for a lot of dead healers."

"I didn't expect you to understand."

"Someday, you'll have to explain how whacking a man on the head is better than just running him through," Vahanian retorted.

Tris struggled to retain his concentration as the effort drained him and he began to tire. It was almost impossible to see in the fog, which had almost obscured the moon. Even the moon seemed cursed tonight, glowing with a strange light as darkness began to blot out its light, casting the orb in eerie colors. Deep in the miasma of the fog, Tris could hear the frightened screams of the slavers and the clang of battle. The other captives, freed by the spirits, took up arms or fled. A few of the slavers ran from the fog wraiths into the shadowy forest, and their bloodcurdling shrieks attested to worse than specters awaiting those who copied their folly.

The fog was churning, punctuated now and then by balls of the mage fire that Alyzza threw at the few slavers who remained to fight. An instinctive warning prickled at the back of Tris's neck. The fog became more dense and the revenants easier to see. Their contorted faces would haunt his nightmares for days to come, Tris was sure, and he knew, as the wind howled louder, that he was no longer in control.

"Get to shelter!" Tris shouted to his friends. "I can't control them any more!" From their ashen faces, Tris knew that his friends suspected as much. "Go!" he cried above the wind. "I'll keep them away from you. Head for the caves!" Vahanian and Carroway grabbed Carina by the arm and started toward the meager cover of the cliff. She pulled back.

"Tris, what about Tris?" she shouted above the howling wind.

"Get out of here!" Tris cried, raising his hands in warding against a gust that nearly took him off his feet. He could feel the spirits' malevolence, and it took every shard of power he could summon to hold a protective aura around his friends.

"Tris can take care of himself," Vahanian assured her, dragging her with him toward the cliff. He stopped just below the ledges. "Berry, jump!" he urged, holding out his arms. Her weight nearly drove him to his knees, but he staggered and held his feet, dragging both Carina and Berry toward a cleft in the rock. He thrust Berry in first, then Carina despite her protests, then Carroway, and sealed the opening with his body. His sword was ready in his right hand, and his left arm shielded his face, instinctively protecting himself against the spirits in their murderous rage.

Tris opened himself to the spirits, staking his waning power and his soul to hold a faint blue shield of power over the crevice where his friends sought refuge.

And then, the moon went dark.

Tris knew the sounds of pitched battle, had heard the cries of dying men before, but what erupted around him in the glade was far from human, and the torments inflicted by the spirits upon the slavers surpassed any artist's fancy of the Place of Darkness. Bitter cold, the vengeful spirits hunted their prey, toying with the desperate raiders. The shrieks of dying men mingled with inhuman wails until Tris longed to clap his hands over his ears and dared not open his eyes to guard his sanity. The metallic tang of blood was heavy on the wind, and Tris felt the graze of spectral teeth against his flesh, shuddering as the revenants passed over him and through him, unwillingly linked to their gory vengeance, unable to pull himself free from the force that was determined to cleanse the glade and extract revenge.

The darkness seemed to last forever. At last, Tris felt the spirits wane, sated with their kill. He chanced a look skyward, to see the bright disk of the moon obliterated by a dark orb, which gradually slipped sideways, until at last, after what seemed an eternity, the moonlight shone again. The fog, its bloody work complete, rolled reluctantly back toward the forest.

We have kept our bargain, kin of Bava K'aa, the voices howled. *None held by force were harmed. Now, give us our rest.*

Gathering the last of his remaining strength, Tris stretched out his arms in blessing. As he began to murmur the words of power, he felt the spirits swirl around him, but their mood was longing, grieving, lonely. He drew strength from the compassion that welled up in him for the spirits' long exile, their betrayal, their loss and grief, and wove that strength into the final blessing, working the passing-over ritual. In the plains of spirit visible only to the mageborn, Tris could see the souls that awaited release, and in the distance, at the edge of darkness, felt more than saw the presence of She Who Rules the Night.

Her call to the lost spirits was the sweetest thing his soul had ever heard, although he could never utter it in mortal tongue. Even his own spirit yearned toward it, though his body anchored him from following.

Rest now, Tris said in benediction as the revenants began to slip free of the bonds that held them to the forest. *Rest forever.*

As if he were suddenly released from the clutch of strong fingers, the spirits left him, and Tris fell to his knees, too spent to feel the ground rush up to meet him as everything went black.

WHEN VAHANIAN DARED to open his eyes, the glade was still. The ghosts of Ruune Videya had taken their vengeance well. Strewn about the camp like broken dolls, the slavers lay in contorted heaps, faces twisted with fear. Heavy wagons were upended like toys amid shredded tents. Tris lay face down in the midst of the wreckage, motionless. Of the captives, there were none in sight, save for Alyzza, who stumbled toward Tris, her eyes bright with madness.

Vahanian signaled cautiously for the others to leave their hiding place, and he heard Carina gasp as she spotted Tris. The healer broke into a run to reach him and gently turned him over.

"Is he—" Vahanian started.

"Alive," Carina nodded, tears in her eyes. "I don't know what he did, or how he did it, and I don't think I want to. But he's drained himself badly," she said. "He's going to have one hell of a headache when he comes around."

"What about the rest of the captives, are they dead like the slavers?" Vahanian asked as Carroway and Berry spread out among the fallen bodies.

"There is no need to fear for the safety of the other captives," a voice said from behind them. Vahanian wheeled, sword in hand, then stared in astonishment at the flaxen-haired man who emerged from the darkness. "They are safe. They have scattered, but nothing your friend summoned will harm them," the newcomer vowed, walking closer with an uncanny gliding step. The aristocratic man stopped an arm's length from Vahanian and then bowed low in respect.

"Who are you?" Carina asked, although Vahanian would have bet the healer could guess the nature of their visitor.

"I am Gabriel," the vayash moru replied. "I serve the Dark Lady, our mistress," he said as if it were a common introduction. "I have been sent for you."

"Why?" Vahanian asked suspiciously.

"The spirits of the forest obeyed your friend's command," Gabriel said smoothly, "But there are other, less natural, beings that serve the Darkness. My Lady has sent me to guide you safely to a place where you might spend the night and attend to your needs."

"Ah, Jonmarc," Carroway said, his eyes never leaving Gabriel, "Tris and I had really bad luck the last time a ghost found us a place to stay—"

"You do this a lot?" Vahanian questioned, and Gabriel turned his unreadable eyes on him.

"The Lady watches over her own," Gabriel replied.

"You know him?" Carina exclaimed. Berry, wide-eyed, shrank between Vahanian and Carina, wary but fascinated.

"Uh, we've met," Vahanian managed, and Gabriel's thin lips formed a faint smile.

"Your companions are known to my mistress," Gabriel replied in a courtly tone. "Their quest is familiar to Her."

"We can tell by how easy it's been," Vahanian muttered.

Behind them, deep in the forest, there was a rustling noise, and a howl not made by any creature Vahanian could name.

"Come," Gabriel said. "Dawn is not far off. Follow me." He leaned down and lifted Tris's motionless body as if he were a sleeping child, carrying him effortlessly at a brisk stride.

They followed in silence down a path all but obscured by the thick branches of the forest. Without prompting, the group packed closely together in the center of the trail. It was as if the forest itself were watching them, Vahanian thought. He was as relieved as any of them when they finally emerged and saw a crossroads ahead, and just past it, the welcoming lanterns of an inn. Gabriel led them up the back stairs, to a room large enough for the group, and laid Tris on one of the beds.

"I will make arrangements with the innkeeper. You will be safe here," Gabriel said.

"Just like that?" Vahanian asked. "You're going to leave us here?"

Gabriel nodded. "We will meet again. You have far to travel before your quest is complete. But this message I bear from the Sisterhood. Tris must not pass the Dhasson border. Arontala spelled the border, and called the beasts that threaten the northern kingdom. The spell is particular. Should Tris try to cross into Dhasson, the beasts will mass. He will not survive."

Unbidden, memories of those beasts came to Vahanian, far too real. "Then where—"

"You must travel to the Library at Westmarch," replied Gabriel.

"I was supposed to get paid in Dhasson," Vahanian said levelly.

Gabriel slipped a signet ring from his left hand and gave it to Vahanian. "The ring alone is worth your trouble," the vayash moru said evenly. "Consider it a downpayment. After Tris has gained what he needs at the Library, you will go to Principality City. There, my accounts—and King Harrol's—are more than sufficient to pay what you were promised."

"We weren't going to Principality City," Vahanian said edgily.

"No?" Gabriel said with an unsettling smile that showed the tips of his long incisors. "The bounty on your head in Margolan rivals even the royal bounty for your life in Eastmark," Gabriel replied, "and you are... shall we say, 'unwelcome'... in Nargi. The border of Dhasson swarms with magicked beasts. Where would you hide, Jonmarc, except in Principality, with its mercs and its hired swords?" At Vahanian's stare, Gabriel chuckled. "Do not marvel that you are known to the Sisterhood. For now, at least, Tris's road and yours is the same."

Vahanian turned away with a curse, slipping the ring onto his left hand. Gabriel looked to the others. "I will aid you were I can. But now, rest. You need fear no more from the slavers."

"Milord," Carina interjected, addressing Gabriel. "Please let me add something. I am called Carina Jesthrata, and my brother and I were also heading to Dhasson on an urgent mission," she continued, her voice fervent. "We traveled from Isencroft, where I was... am... healer to King Donelan. The king lies under a wasting spell, and he is dying. Kiara Sharsequin, his heir, sent us to find the cure. We know that the Sisterhood has a great citadel in Dhasson, near Valiquet, where some of their best healers are said to be. We were traveling there to see if they might have a cure."

Gabriel looked thoughtful. "The Dark Lady indeed has her hand in this," he murmured. "M'lady," he said respectfully, "I am sorry, but I cannot assure your safe passage to Valiquet." He paused. "There is, however, a smaller holding of the Sisterhood in Principality City. If you traveled with the group, perhaps the Sisters could advise you."

Carina looked crestfallen.

"There is something more to consider," Gabriel went on. "The Library at Westmarch is renowned for its books. You may find some healing knowledge in the wizard's library."

Carina nodded slowly. "If the Library is controlled by the Sisters, perhaps I can find someone there who can help me, or get me to the Sisters in Dhasson."

"There is one more thing," Gabriel continued. "The beasts hunt the forest between here and Westmarch." Gabriel looked at Vahanian, and his gaze implied more than the mercenary cared to acknowledge. "They fear only fire. Take pitch and make torches and arrows that can be lit at a moment's notice. Only then can you turn the beasts."

"Easy for you to say," Vahanian murmured acidly.

"Thank you," Carina replied. But without seeming to pass among them, Gabriel vanished.

"Does it matter if I don't like this at all?" Carroway groused.

Berry bounded up beside Vahanian, and he marveled that after everything they had survived, the girl was actually skipping. "Do you believe that?" she exclaimed. "A real vayash moru, and he knew Jonmarc, and he didn't eat us or anything!"

The girl's open excitement brought a tired smile even to Vahanian. "Stick with us, Berry, you'll be amazed," he quipped. But the smile faded and as the fighter looked at Tris's still form.

"What are you going to do?" Vahanian had taunted not long ago. "Darken the moon? Tame the vayash moru? Raise the dead?" Tonight, Tris had done just that. Come their arrival in Principality City, that knowledge would force a choice. If, as Vahanian had sworn so many times, he truly wished for his vengeance on Arontala, committing his loyalty to the young exiled mage might give Tris a fighting chance. Vahanian looked away, not yet ready to make his decision. It might, he thought darkly, be made for him, and for all of them, if the will of the Lady was not to be denied.

CHAPTER TWENTY-ONE

JARED DRAYKE REINED in his skittish stallion, jerking back on its bit so hard that the animal reared. Around them, the smoke from the burning village hung in a haze over the winter afternoon, and the fires that still flamed high above the remaining structures made the courtyard unnaturally warm.

"That's the last of them, Your Majesty," the captain reported with a crisp bow.

"Are you certain?" Jared asked, surveying the destruction.

"Yes, Your Majesty," the captain repeated. "There'll be no vayash moru from this village to plague the rest of us, you can be sure of that," he said with a satisfied smile.

Jared watched the thatched roof of one of the buildings give way in a shower of sparks. "Good work, captain."

"Thank you, Your Majesty," the soldier replied, bowing once more. "Orders, Your Majesty?"

"You know what to look for," Jared replied, bored with the charade he was committed to maintain. "Burn the monsters out, and any who give them aid."

The captain nodded. "Yes, Your Majesty," he answered, then turned to round up his scattered soldiers as Jared wheeled his horse and re-joined his bodyguards.

"A good day's work, don't you think, Your Majesty?" asked his companion, a baron recently come into his title.

"Just a drop in the bucket," Jared replied ill-temperedly as they rode toward Shekerishet. "You should hear the petitions that come pleading for my help," he said, watching the credulous baron out of the corner of his eye. "Filthy monsters stealing children, slaughtering livestock, laying waste to entire villages. And all with the help of that shadowy Sisterhood," he added.

"Never trusted them," the baron added fervently. "Probably spirit the children away themselves for blood rites or some such thing."

"Would you like to see one put to the test?"

"A Sister?" the baron gasped. "You've captured one?"

"I'll be interrogating her when I return to the palace. Care to join me?" Jared enjoyed the look of utter anguish on the baron's pudgy face, torn between the request of his king and his own fear.

"If it would please my king," the baron choked out finally, his jowls atremble.

Jared turned to hide the amusement that curled his lip. "You may find it... enlightening," he said, spurring his horse on faster so that his guards rushed to follow.

The baron followed Jared hesitantly into the stables, and remained as far behind as protocol would allow as they made their way down the sharply twisting stairs into the lower regions of the palace. Carved into stone with solid rock jutting high overhead, Shekerishet was built into the cliffs, and its dungeons descended into caves deep beneath the mountain. For almost five hundred years, Shekerishet watched over Margolan, a brooding, silent fortress, unbreached by any enemy.

It was to its deepest regions that Jared led the baron. This was the realm that Arontala claimed as his own. It was here that the most useful captives were brought for interrogation—those suspected of magecraft, or the unfortunates truly likely to be genuine vayash moru.

The pudgy noble was white with fear, his hands trembling so badly that he was forced to hook his thumbs in his belt. Jared admitted to himself that he had more than an inkling of the same uneasiness. A good deal more, he thought, given that he alone knew just how powerful Arontala had become, growing stronger with every wretch he tortured and killed. Arontala was adept at dampening the powers of his captives, preferring most often to drug them with wormroot—a potion that disassociated their powers.

So it was that their captive awaited them. She knelt, bound hand and foot, bent over at the waist so that her forehead nearly touched the ground, resting or asleep, or perhaps just drugged beyond the point where she could hold herself upright. Matted brown hair spilled from beneath her cowl, and the brown robe that marked her as one among the Sisterhood was torn and muddy, testimony that her capture had not come easily. Nor cheaply, Jared thought with a frown, as he recalled how many guards had died in the attempt to breech the mages' stronghold.

Arontala waited for them, greeting them with the barest nod of his head, almost one the shadows that danced along the cold stone walls in the torchlit chamber. Around them, the instruments of inquisition littered the benches and tables, stained dark with the blood of past victims. Another figure, the inquisitor, stood silent and formidable in his dark tunic. Jared saw the fat little baron swallow in fear and step backward, until the solid wall blocked his way. This one doesn't even require a hostage to know his place, Jared thought with a smile. A glance from Arontala would have him groveling for an easy death.

"Ready, Your Majesty?" Arontala asked, in the self-confident tone that Jared knew paid only lip-service to the rank and power of a mortal king.

"I am," Jared said, managing just the right note of ennui to impress the hapless baron, who hugged the wall so closely as to resemble a tapestry.

"Then begin," Arontala instructed the inquisitor, who stepped toward his subject and jerked her upright.

The baron fainted.

In all, the interrogation went on for more than two candlemarks, and even Jared was surprised at the victim's single-mindedness. Battered beyond reasonable hope, bearing the wounds of the inquisitor's craft, the Sister remained mute, fixing Arontala with a steady gaze that infuriated the dark mage.

"You don't seem to be getting anywhere," Jared observed dryly, as the inquisitor tried yet another instrument of his trade, inflicting its measured agony to no avail, as the Sister remained silent but for her screams.

"She is obstinate," Arontala fumed, and Jared hid a smile, enjoying the mage's frustration.

"Perhaps," Jared replied, "she is the first real mage you've questioned, instead of those hedge witches with whom you so enjoy toying."

"Even mages have a breaking point," Arontala replied, setting his teeth, and gesturing for the inquisitor to try yet another set of tools.

"And their failures," Jared said, relishing his first opportunity to best the dark mage in quite some time.

"As do kings," Arontala replied evenly. "Your Majesty," he added, barely bothering to veil the sarcasm in his voice.

"The fact remains that you have yet to find and destroy the remains of Bava K'aa," Jared pointed out. "Until you do, we are at risk."

"We have destroyed every citadel from here to the Principality border, and west to Isencroft," Arontala replied tightly.

"You just haven't looked hard enough," Jared replied, stepping over the prone noble and walking toward the stairs. "I've had enough amusement for tonight," he said dryly. "I'll be in my rooms."

"As you wish, my lord," Arontala replied, his voice tight with barely restrained anger. As Jared turned the first corner of the stair, he glimpsed Arontala wheeling on the hapless captive, snatching away the tools from the inquisitor and advancing on the drugged mage. Her screams echoed the length of the twisted stairway.

Jared had barely reached the main hall before the captain of his guard caught up with him. "If it please Your Majesty," the man interjected, bowing.

"It does not," Jared snapped irritably. The man clearly had come from a long ride, his clothes splashed with mud and bearing the dust of the road. "Well?" he growled. "What is your news?"

"From the Principality border, Your Majesty," the flustered captain replied. "There's been a report that a swordswoman on a great steed drove off two of our guardsmen single-handedly and took a group of peasants across into Principality."

Jared frowned. "A woman, with a sword?"

The captain nodded. "Aye, Your Majesty. And not a dabbler, either, from the report. A trained blade, and a good one."

Jared cursed. "What else could your men tell you after they failed to hold the road?" Jared snapped. "I'm amazed that they didn't dream up a giant ten feet tall!"

The captain fidgeted, clearly uncomfortable with his role as the bearer of bad news. "I couldn't say, milord," he replied nervously. "But they've stuck to their story, even though they took not a little ribbing from their mates about being driven off by a doxy. They've said she was a pretty lass, excepting for her travel clothes, which were more suited to a man."

"What did they say she looked like?" Jared asked, his suspicions growing.

The captain gulped. "Auburn hair, quite wavy, and tied back in a queue. A pretty face, if she weren't of a mind to chop you in two," he added.

"On a warhorse, you say?" Jared asked carefully.

Once again, the nervous captain nodded. "Yes, Your Majesty. A big horse, trained to kick and rear, and she knew how to ride it well, they said. Nearly kicked their heads in with its hooves, she did, until she ran them off."

Jared's eyes narrowed. "Send your best men into Principality after her," Jared ordered. "Have them go in twos, armed with bows, and bring the horse down first. But I want the woman alive, do you understand?" he barked.

"Aye, Your Majesty," the captain assented hesitatingly. "But sending troops, into Principality, suppose they should be discovered? A war—"

"I haven't asked you to think, I've asked you to fetch the bitch and bring her to me for questioning,"

Jared snarled. "Do you think you can handle that, or should I send someone else?" Just then the mage's anguished screams sounded again, and the captain's face went paler than moonlight.

"No, Your Majesty," the luckless man gulped. "As you request, Your Majesty."

"And be quick about it," Jared snapped, turning, his mood even more foul than when he had left the catacombs.

"Yes, Your Majesty," the man answered, his voice trailing off as Jared began to ascend the broad main stairs to the king's quarters above.

The captain's report could mean only one thing, Jared knew. Kiara Sharsequin had begged off from traveling with his emissary only to slip out of Isencroft, through Margolan. Her betrayal meant nothing to his heart; he had met her once, years ago, and had no interest in a wife beyond securing his dynasty. For those practical uses, he admitted, a more pliant partner would certainly be less trouble, more likely to know her place. No, the only reason to suffer the tempers of the Isencroft princess were the lands that would come as her dowry, rich farm lands that would more than double the size of his holdings.

If, once the wedding was past and an heir was delivered, his queen were to die in childbirth, well, such things were common. And practical. But now Kiara added an affront atop her veiled rejection, slipping through his hands and running off his soldiers like errand boys. That a few peasants had found their way into Principality did not bother him in the least. More troublesome, he thought, as he reached his chambers and secured the iron-wrought door behind him, was the notion it might put in others' minds that the troops and, therefore, the king, of Margolan was easily bested. For that, Jared sulked as he poured a large goblet of brandy, she must be punished.

The fire in the hearth had burned down to embers before Arontala joined him. Jared was used to the mage's silent approach. "Well?" he asked without looking away from the fire. He was well into the brandy, soaking up its warmth as he basked in the glow of the flames.

"The mage is dead."

"And what you have learned?"

"That mages of the Sisterhood are not made of iron and rock," the dark sorcerer replied evenly, refusing to take the bait. "That they can be killed even if they cannot be broken."

"So you failed."

In the blink of an eye, Arontala traversed the room, to lean against the large hearth, watching Jared with his expressionless gaze. "Failure depends upon the goal sought, My Lord," he replied, here in private making no attempt to veil his scorn. "Another of the Sisterhood is dead, a message that will not be overlooked by the group. Another of their citadels has been abandoned. Word comes from the king of Nargi that he would be more than happy to loan his troops should the uprisings along the river need a strong hand to settle. Dhasson is too busy with the beasts on their border to come to the traitor's aid. And I have fed... quite well," he said, his tongue darting at the corners of his lips as they drew back, just barely, to expose the elongated teeth within. "We advance our cause."

"Advance!" Jared roared, sending the table at his side to the floor with a crash as he rolled to his feet. "My brother remains at large, despite your 'best' efforts. The Sharsequin bitch has slipped the net. And the Sisterhood you are so proud of destroying has merely gone underground. Tell me those aren't failures!"

Arontala regarded him unemotionally, his chalky complexion almost glowing in the firelight. "It is still too early in the game to know," he responded, shrugging away from the hearth. "You hold the throne. Your coffers have never been more full. And whatever the people may think of your methods, they now fear the vayash moru even more than they fear their king." He smiled. "We have given them a common enemy, and eliminated my rivals, all for the good of Margolan. Quite ingenious, don't you think?"

Jared wheeled on the slender mage and made a drunken roundhouse punch. He would have missed a mortal man by a fair distance, but the vayash moru traveled across the room before the punch was completed, and watched the king stagger. "Temper, Jared," Arontala clucked. "I shouldn't like to have to remind you about the terms of our partnership," he said smoothly, circling the enraged king just out of reach. "But if I must, I will... how shall I say it?... 'nip' the behavior in the bud?" he smiled, his teeth the grimace of a predator.

With a howl of rage, Jared lunged at the mage, only to fall flat on the chamber floor while Arontala affected a bored pose against the opposite wall. "Really, Jared. This is pointless. What do you propose if you got your hands on me, hmm? Are you going to kill me?" he taunted. "You're too late. Someone did that for you a long time ago. And you're forgetting something quite important."

"What is that?" Jared snarled, having unsteadily regained his feet to glower impotently at the smug mage.

"Before too many more months, the Hawthorn Moon will come," Arontala replied. "When it does, nothing else will matter. I've bound the spirits of the mages we've killed, along with Kait and Serae and more than a few of the palace ghosts, in the Orb as an offering," he explained in a self-congratulatory voice. "As a meal when the Obsidian King awakes from his slumber. I will hold the power of rebirth over the greatest mage that ever lived," he went on, "and you," he added with a hint of acid in his voice, "you hold power over me. We both get what we want, isn't that true, milord?"

"Get out!" Jared shouted, trembling with a drunken combination of rage and fear. "Don't come back until you've something to show for it. Bring me the body of Bava K'aa, or the head of my brother, or that Isencroft trollop in chains. I will not be mocked!" he bellowed, hurling a pitcher at the mage, who moved aside faster than the mortal eye could follow, and watched with a trace of disapproval as the pitcher's contents dripped down the stone wall.

"As you wish, Your Majesty," Arontala replied, completely unflustered. In the blink of an eye, he stood by the chamber door. "And I'll have someone sent to clean that up," he said as the door shut behind him against another shouted oath, and a piece of crockery slammed against the heavy wood.

Jared, out of breath and hoarse with shouting, leaned on his thighs and stared after the mage. Somewhere, somehow, he thought, this entire thing had gone drastically out of hand. And come the Hawthorn Moon, it was likely to get worse.

CHAPTER TWENTY-TWO

Martris Drayke awoke—and regretted it. His head pounded and every muscle in his body protested. Resolutely, he opened his eyes to find himself staring at a strange ceiling. With even more effort, he managed to sit up, then grimaced and shut his eyes again as the scene swam and his head throbbed.

"Welcome back," Alyzza rasped from nearby, pressing a cup of steaming tea into his hands and helping to hold it to his lips. For a moment, he focused on nothing except the smell of the hot liquid, feeling it burn its way down his throat. Then he opened his eyes once more to find himself the center of attention of the small group gathered in an unremarkable tavern room. Vahanian sat in a chair near the fire, his sword nearby, looking not much better than Tris felt. Berry was sitting on the table, her legs crossed under her, playing an animated game of tarle with Carina while Carroway looked on in amusement.

"Where are we?" Tris asked, his voice sounding strange as it croaked from his dry throat. He drew another draught from the cup Alyzza offered, then refused to lay back down, although Alyzza had to prop him up with pillows to keep him from swaying.

"You're just across the river from Principality," Vahanian replied. "A little north of the forest and a little east of where we left the slavers. A few days from the Dhasson Pass." He paused. "Gabriel brought us here. And he warned us again that there's a spell on the Dhasson border, so if you try to cross it will call every one of those magicked beasts. Now you're supposed to go to the Library at Westmarch and then on to Principality City—and the rest of us are along for the ride."

Bits and pieces of the flight from the slavers returned to Tris's memory, the thrill of his power as it filled him, and the terror as the angry spirits worked their long-awaited revenge on the slavers. Beyond that, Tris remembered nothing. "You'll have to fill me in," he said, chagrined. "I don't remember anything after the ghosts in the forest left us."

"Not much to tell," Vahanian replied. "Gabriel found us in the forest and brought us here—he seems to have an arrangement with the innkeeper to cover anything we need. You've been sleeping for the last two days.

Can't say I objected to the chance to rest, myself. Carina's earned a little travel money healing some poor unfortunate, Carroway's been playing for coins in the common room, and we've all been getting the crap beat out of us at tarle by Berry," he summarized, and the girl grinned her satisfaction.

"What about the other captives?" Tris managed, sipping at his tea.

"We've seen nothing ourselves," Carroway said soberly. "Gabriel told us that they all escaped. They weren't among the dead in the glade, although how they fared if they fled into the woods, I don't know."

Tris nodded. "I made a bargain… with the spirits," he said, quietly. "Their vengeance in exchange for our lives—all of the captives. I hope they… kept their part," he rasped, finishing the brew and returning the cup to Alyzza, who skittered off to fetch another cup from the kettle that boiled next to the fire.

"Take it," she pressed. "You worked yourself past reason back there. More than one mage has drained himself to death by pushing too far," she chastised. "Now you feel why even strong mages must rest after such a working," she cackled. Tris glimpsed a new respect in her eyes, and the realization frightened him. *Sweet Chenne*, he thought *what did I do back there? And if I couldn't control it, how will I ever face Arontala?* The implications of that last question were entirely too large just now, and so he focused resolutely on the steaming cup in his hands.

"How is everyone?" Tris asked, glancing around at the group.

Vahanian shrugged. "I've been worse," the fighter replied. "Didn't take any new damage, so I'm ready whenever you want to move on."

Tris looked from one face to the other, receiving a nod or a shrug that indicated readiness. He remembered nothing clearly after he had summoned the spirits back at the glade. He recalled the flash of a slaver's knife, Vahanian's shout and then the howl of the spirits, turned loose to work their vengeance. The rush of the revenants' emotions—overwhelming sadness, longing and rage. There was terror, too, Tris remembered, his own terror as the winds of vengeance swept around him, utterly out of control. He could still hear the screams of the slavers and smell the tang of blood, and the shame of having called down that horror warred in his soul with the relief that they were free.

They know I called the spirits, Tris realized as he looked at his companions' faces. And that I lost control. Something was different in their eyes, just like old Alyzza. Perhaps not fear, but not quite comfort either, even in Carroway's face. As if, Tris thought, your familiar riding horse awoke one day to be a battle steed, or, perhaps, a demon mount, able to fly on moonlight and kill with its eyes. They aren't sure what I've become, Tris thought, uncomfortably. They don't know if it's what they bargained for. Perhaps for all of them, he thought, the stakes of the game were frighteningly real.

"Well," Tris began, knowing that they were waiting for his decision, "if you all think you're up to the ride, let's start out in the morning. The sooner we get to Westmarch, the sooner we can rest a little easier."

"Come on, Berry," Carina said. "Why don't you help us get the horses ready for the ride and pack the bags." Berry willingly went with Carina, Tris suspected, more from boredom than for any other reason. Alyzza followed them, pulling the heavy door behind her.

"The innkeeper's been quite good about running us a tab," Carroway said, perched on the corner of the table. "For someone who doesn't eat... at least not regular food... your friend Gabriel found us a place with a good kitchen." He grinned. "Best of all, the whole place didn't vanish into smoke when we woke up, so I'm happy."

"You've got a strange way of selecting an inn," Vahanian replied, turning back to the fire.

"I'm not sure I'll ever think anything's strange again," Carroway said fervently. "But when we're safe—whenever that is—I'll have my pick of courts and noble houses with these tales." His grin broadened. "Thanks, Tris."

Tris rolled his eyes. "Don't mention it." He finished the last of the tea and eased himself back down. To his surprise, he was hungry. "So if this place has great food, where is it?"

Carroway jumped to his feet with an exaggerated bow. "You have only to ask," the bard said, straightening. "I'll let the two of you plot the route north. I'll go see what my friend Shaia in the kitchen has in the pot for tonight," he said, with a knowing raise of his eyebrows.

"Whatever she's got, see if they can water the ale less than last night," Vahanian called over his shoulder as the bard headed for the door.

"As you wish," Carroway said, slipping out and closing the door behind him.

There was an awkward silence after Carroway left. Tris lay staring at the cracked inn ceiling, while Vahanian did not move from his place by the fire. Finally, the mercenary spoke.

"What happened back there?" Vahanian asked, his voice roughened by the damp weather. "You called them?"

Tris paused before answering. "Yes."

Another silence, broken only by the pops and hisses from the fireplace logs. "And what came— you controlled them?"

This time, Tris paused longer. "At first," he answered truthfully. "Later, I don't think so."

Vahanian turned in his chair to look at Tris. "Think so?" he questioned incredulously. "Those demons wanted to kill every living thing, and you aren't sure whether they were listening to you?"

Tris swallowed. "They weren't demons."

"They looked like demons."

"They weren't," Tris replied. "For one thing, no Light mage will call a demon."

"At least, not on purpose."

"And for another, I don't know how even if I wanted to," Tris continued, ignoring Vahanian's comment.

"So what you're really saying is that as far as you know, those things back there weren't demons, and you're pretty sure you had them under control, at least some of the time."

Tris sighed. "I guess that's right," he said. "But it sounds worse when you put it that way."

"You didn't see what you called."

"No," Tris admitted. "I guess I didn't. But we're free."

Vahanian drained the last of his mug. "That we are," he replied. "And I don't think Principality City can come soon enough for me."

IT WAS SEVERAL hours later when Vahanian finished with the horses and the preparations for their departure in the morning. Carroway, true to his word, supplied them with an ample supper. Everyone seemed to be feeling the strain. Berry hung on doggedly, but at last she fell asleep on Carina's cloak by the fire. As they banked the fires, Carina needed to fetch a powder from her saddlebags to ease Tris's headache, and Vahanian ill-humouredly consented to escort her to the stables.

"You could walk a little slower," Carina complained, hurrying to catch up with him. Her borrowed cloak nearly enveloped her, and she lifted its hem to keep it from dragging on the ground.

"Look, you're the one who needed some damned potion," Vahanian groused, slowing only a bit. "Why don't you just ask your Goddess to fill up the bottle for you?"

Carina gave him a dour look. "I thought I told you. I'm not a cleric."

"Oh, that's right," Vahanian replied with a sidelong glance. "You just bash the poor bastards over the head instead of really hurting them with a sword."

"You're impossible," she retorted, hustling past him and into the relative warmth of the stable. Their horses, curried and fed, nickered in recognition.

"I've been called worse," he remarked. "Too damn many coincidences going on for my taste. Tris was headed to Dhasson—now it's the Library. And since the witch biddies are there, that just happens to be helpful for you, too."

Carina shrugged. "What the Lady wills, She directs," she replied.

Vahanian looked at her sourly. "Tell me, priestess, who are you... really?"

Carina stopped abruptly and looked at him, then ducked her head and went back to examining the contents of her bag. "I don't know what you mean."

"Don't you?" Vahanian walked a few steps closer and leaned against the wall. In the moist night air, the stable was redolent with the smell of barley and half-eaten apples, and the warm, sweet scent of the horses. "I think you do. Never try to bluff a man who's made his living gambling. That last name you gave, 'Jesthrata,' it's a highlands word. 'Wanderer,' isn't it?" he pressed. "Not a family name. More like a trail name, the kind you give yourself when you're in a hurry to leave something else behind."

"You seem well versed in that sort of thing," Carina murmured, apparently engrossed in her task. "It's a fascinating theory."

"I've just got to ask myself, what's a court healer doing giving a trail name?" Vahanian continued, well aware of her discomfort. "Not that I know much about how things are at court, but I always imagined that most of the folks there were those useless younger brothers and sisters that the other royal houses didn't need any more."

"How interesting," Carina observed acidly, without looking up. "Do go on."

"I know all about wandering," Vahanian continued, ignoring her sarcasm. "And you're a little too fine-blooded."

"You've got a great imagination for a guide," Carina retorted, finally looking up to fix him with an angry stare. "Why don't you pretend that I'm just along for the ride, and keep your mind on guiding?"

"Well, there's one little problem with that," Vahanian said with an off-hand gesture. "See, I get shot at by people who do know who you are, and I don't like that. So as I told your friend Tris, I either know the whole story, or I don't guide."

"Fine," Carina replied, gathering up her cloak and her potion. "Don't guide. Go wait for us in Principality City. We'll find what we're looking for just fine without you."

"Maybe," Vahanian said equitably. "Maybe not. 'Course, that's not a very civil way of looking at things, after I saved your life—"

"What?" Carina exclaimed, her eyes bright with anger. "You ungrateful wretch! You would have been dead a week ago if I hadn't healed you!"

"And you'd have been dead, too, if I hadn't tackled that friendly slaver," Vahanian replied. "So we're even. Now," he said, moving another step closer so that the angry healer was barely a hand's breadth away from him, "I'll ask again. Who are you, really?"

She was standing so close to him that she had to tilt her head to glare at him, and for a moment, he fully expected her to hit him. Then suddenly, the flash in her eyes clouded over with something else, and she turned away. "All right," she said in a flat voice after a long silence. "Have it your way." She paused, then drew a deep breath.

"My father is a minor noble in the highlands on the eastern border of Isencroft, a cousin of the king," Carina said quietly. "It's a long way from the city, and they keep their own ways, have their own ideas. There's only one thing they like less out there than twins," she said, her voice just above a whisper. "And that's magic, of any kind."

Vahanian frowned. "Every place wants healers."

Carina shook her head. "Not there. It's harsh country, and they have no patience for anything weak. 'Better to die than hold back the herd,'" she quoted softly. "Healers just slow down the process." Another pause, longer this time. "They might have suffered the lord's twins, on account of his being the lord. But even he couldn't tolerate magic, once he knew it for what it was." She looked up at him, and angry tears glistened in her eyes. "I found out I could heal when I was twelve. And when they caught me at it, the next year, they decided to 'foster' Cam and me out. Only they never wanted us back." She looked at him defiantly. "So I took a name I chose myself, since I had no family, and no home. We made a good living, Cam and I, with one merc group after another until Kiara caught up with us and gave us a place to live in Isencroft. There. That's the story. Got what you came for?"

Vahanian held her gaze. "Yeah," he said finally, as she turned away. "I did." He paused. "So they don't like healers, huh?" He shook his head. "That's about the dumbest thing I've heard of, next to bashing people over the head with a stick."

"You really are impossible," she repeated, but this time, her voice lacked its edge. Vahanian was suddenly aware of just how warm the stable had become. She stood only a few inches away, and wrapped in the oversized cloak she looked small and vulnerable. He could smell the scent of herbs that clung to her robes, aware all at once that his heart was hammering in his chest. The attraction he felt was not new; it had been building now for weeks despite his barbs. The peril in the slavers' camp only served to heighten it, although until now, Vahanian had been able to force it out of mind. But here, in this moment, alone with her and close enough to touch, he felt it fully, enough to know its danger.

"That's what they tell me," Vahanian said, turning away with effort and feigning interest in the straps of a saddle that hung along the wall. "Come on," he said a little more abruptly than he intended. "We've got an early morning ahead. Let's get some sleep." She followed him back inside the inn without another word, and all the way, Vahanian cursed himself silently for being a fool.

Those slavers must have addled your brains when they ran you through, an inner voice castigated. *First, you're fool enough to take on a job with no money up front. Then you stick around when they're even hotter than you thought. Now, you start noticing a paying customer. Exiled or not, one that's the wrong side of the blanket for being noble. Don't fool yourself, Jonmarc,* the voice in his mind warned. *Chummy as your passengers have gotten, they'll remember their place as soon as you're back to the City, and they'll remember yours. Hired help, and don't forget it.*

By the time they reached the rooms and found the others asleep or dozing by the fire, he found that his mood, sour to begin with, was considerably worse. Half a bottle of brandy did nicely to remedy that, and he settled down a candlemark later to enjoy the last safe night's sleep he was likely to find for at least a fortnight.

CHAPTER TWENTY-THREE

MORNING FOUND THE group in surprisingly good spirits. Gabriel had already settled up with the innkeeper. Alyzza informed them that she would be heading in a different direction, and took her leave just after sunrise. Gabriel's purse outfitted them all amply with horses and tack, and the innkeeper, grateful for paying customers, found clothing to replace the group's tattered outfits. Homespun, plain and scratchy, they were suited to the cold and would pass unremarkably among the other travelers. Their disguises from the night of Haunts had worn off long ago, and they did not continue to dye their hair or alter their appearances the further they got from Shekerishet. Tris's white-blond hair was most likely to attract attention, and he usually wore it in a queue, covered with a hat.

So they headed north once more, choosing a different route from that which either the caravan or the slavers followed, mindful of ambush and anxious to reach Westmarch before the early snows made the roads impassable. The snowfall grew heavier with each hour, and as the road wound north, drifts filled the ditches and edged the fields. In the month since Haunts, the days had grown shorter and the winds colder. This far north, snows came much earlier and stayed longer than in the plains of southern Margolan. While the Library was in the same general direction as Principality City, it was further northeast, in the foothills of the mountains. An early winter was even more likely there, and Tris wondered if they would be able to leave the Library easily.

It took more than an hour before Carina felt like talking, and Vahanian's mood remained dark even longer. At Gabriel's suggestion, each of them carried a bundle of torches soaked in pitch and a tinderbox, along with buckets of a sloppy, thick pitch mixture that could flare into fire at the barest spark. Tris found that he could call a spark to hand as quickly as he could strike one with a flint, and agreed to carry more than his share of torches for ease of lighting, should they encounter the beasts.

"Skrivven for your thoughts," Tris said to Carroway as he rode beside him. Vahanian took the point position this hour, with Carina and Berry in the middle, and Tris taking his turn in the rear. Every few candlemarks, Tris and the other fighters exchanged positions, giving each a turn on watch.

Carroway grinned sheepishly. "If you have to know," he admitted, "I was thinking about the menus at Shekerishet at this time of year. Roast mutton, potatoes and leeks and warm puddings." He sighed. "And those end-of-the-season-at-court parties before the outlying nobility go back to their lands for the winter, all of them needing a bard and feeding me well for my trouble!"

Tris smiled, savoring the memories for a moment himself. He had learned quickly to make do with hard biscuits and sausage on the road north, and to be thankful when they weren't moldy or full of maggots. Memories of a warm banquet hall filled with the delicacies of a court kitchen seemed increasingly like a half-remembered dream.

"You might find the social calendar altered a bit with Jared in charge," Tris remarked, shaking himself from the reverie. "And Arontala put a damper on any event if he walked in the door. I wonder if the nobles feel as much like celebrating, now that Jared is king."

"I wonder, sometimes, what will be left, by the time we can go home," Carroway said, sobering. He stared out toward the gray, barren tree line that marked the uneven horizon. "Whether we winter at the Library or in Principality City, we'll have to stay somewhere over the worst months. If the Sisterhood is sending you to the Library, then there must be something there you need, maybe books or spells or who-knows-what."

"I wondered about that myself," Tris said. "I'll need far more training before I can hope to defeat

Arontala. But I don't have years… at best we've got months."

"Then there's the question of raising and outfitting an army," Carroway supplied. "That won't happen at a library. We'll have to spend time—months—in Principality City to do that. It won't be cheap, either. It's a good thing you've got your uncle's accounts there; and having him vouch for you doesn't hurt, either. Then we have to get back down into Margolan—no small trick."

"By the Hawthorn Moon next summer," Tris added, feeling hopeless. "Grandmother's spirit came to me in a dream," he said quietly. "She told me that Arontala means to work magic on the Hawthorn Moon to free the spirit of the Obsidian King from where it was bound at the end of the Great War. If he does that, and gains even more power—"

"There won't be any way to stop him, without another great war, even worse than the first," Carroway finished his sentence for him. "That isn't leaving us a lot of time, Tris."

"I know," Tris replied. "Believe me, I know."

The weather turned colder, with a gray, overcast sky that bode darkly for the days ahead. Tris moved up to ride his turn at point, leaving Carroway and Carina to talk as they rode about the legend of the Library and what a healer might find useful there.

Tris tried to shake free of the brooding mood that settled on him with the coming of the autumn weather. He thought through the timeline Carroway put into words. No matter how

he worked it—and even without the unantici-
pated detour to the Library—it left precious
little time.

I can't face Arontala the way I called the spirits
in the forest, he thought. Arontala is vayash
moru—only the Lady knows how long he's been
a mage. Between what little grandmother taught
me and what I have time to learn, how can I hope
to defeat a mage like that?

Yet his grandmother's spirit had told him of lessons that would come back to him when the time
was right. He could not imagine the time being
more right than this, but although he tried to
recall any forgotten lessons, both awake and in a
trance, nothing beyond the most basic workings
came to mind. How can I ask an army to follow
me when a fool can see I haven't got a chance?
He had more questions than answers, and as the
clouds darkened and the day wore on, he found
his mood grow bleaker until they reached a protected, level place, and set up camp for the night.

They camped by the side of the road near a
dilapidated well, and that night, they kept close
to the fire, watchful for enemies both human and
magic. The snow stopped but the wind was bitter, and the ground beneath them was already
frozen. The innkeeper sent with them generous
provisions of crusty bread, dried and salted
meats, wedges of cheese and wineskins—more
than enough to keep them going for several days.

"So where is this Library, anyway?" Vahanian
asked, poking at the coals of the fire with the toe
of his boot.

Tris leaned forward, looking into the glowing embers. "I'm not quite sure. The legend says it's upstream on the Nu, where the waters cry."

"Cry, huh?" Vahanian said skeptically. "Great. Nice directions. Anything else helpful?"

"If the Library is near the river, then traveling upstream should bring us there eventually." Carina said.

"Well, now that we've got that taken care of, I'm going to get some sleep," Vahanian said, standing stiffly. "Wake me when it's time for my watch."

Tris found his dreams were far from peaceful. The ghostly faces from the forest howled around him, draining his life and defying his control. Then, amid their keening, he could hear Kait's voice, distant and plaintive. *Tris, help me!* Again he glimpsed her face, pressed against a transparent barrier, her eyes frightened and desperate, one hand outstretched. He lunged for her, but as his fingers were about to touch hers, the image receded, her voice growing fainter and fainter as the memory of the forest ghosts closed in around him again, only to be replaced by Kait's falcons, screeching in anger and flying at him from all quarters, their talons open and their sharp beaks hungry for the kill. He fended them off but they kept coming, their wings stirring a storm around him, ripping into his skin with their claws.

Tris woke, shuddering, to find himself sitting bolt upright, his blankets fallen away. He caught his breath raggedly and closed his eyes, but the dreams were gone.

Milord, a word with you, if you please? a voice said as a sudden cold surrounded him, and it took Tris an instant to realize that he heard the words only in his mind. He opened his eyes to find the spirit of a young woman standing in front of him. She looked to be in her late teens, a beautiful girl with long, dark hair and a slim frame. Tris was unsure whether the sadness in her eyes or her extreme deference to him troubled him more, and exhausted as he felt, he was moved with pity. A glance around reassured him that he had indeed awakened, for Vahanian sat his watch, oblivious to Tris's ghostly visitor.

What is troubling you? he asked silently.

You are a Summoner, the ghost said, and Tris nodded. The spirit smiled and clapped her hands. *Then this is the day I have waited for! Please, milord, hear my story. I was betrothed to a young man from the next village, but my father would not allow us to marry. One night, we agreed to run away, and so I stole the dowry and slipped out to meet my lover here at the well.* The spirit's face grew troubled, and Tris saw anger in her eyes beneath the sadness. *When my lover came, he had been drinking, and he was angry that the dowry was so little. We quarreled, and he knocked me back against the well. I fell, and as I died, I could hear him laughing as he gathered up the dowry,* the spirit recounted sorrowfully.

I can bid you peace, and free your soul to find the Lady, Tris offered, moved by her story.

You are a Summoner. Bring me back, the girl insisted, her eyes bright with hope. *Let me have my vengeance on the one who killed me and make peace with my father.*

Tris shook his head. *I cannot*, he replied. *It is forbidden to bring the dead back among the living.*

Forbidden by whom? the ghost argued, and Tris could see that the brightness in her eyes was not hope but vengeance. *You are a Summoner. I can feel your power. It calls to me. Give me my due!*

Again, Tris shook his head. The longer the spirit remained in his presence, the more uncomfortable he became. There was a darkness about the girl that chilled him.

Surely this is not too large a thing for such a mage as yourself, the girl begged. *I died not two days ago. See, my body lies under the snows just beyond the well. My father is a wealthy man. He will reward you well for returning his only daughter.* She looked to him entreatingly. *Only last night my mother passed this way, calling for me. I did not have the strength to answer, and so she passed on by. They mourn me, milord. Let me return to my home.*

Only the Lady herself may reanimate a corpse, Tris replied. *It is forbidden.*

The ghost's eyes flared in anger. *You are no better than my lover*, she said scornfully. *I have begged you, pleaded with you, and you turn me away.* The darkness that first tinged the specter now limned its outline, and Tris instinctively called a warding around himself and his friends, driving the ghost back outside the circle.

How dare you! the ghost shrieked in a wail that echoed deafeningly in Tris's mind. *I'll show you just like I'll show him!* she swore, *I'll find my way back, if I have to bargain with the Crone herself!*

The image dissipated in front of him into a swirl of mist, but the chill he felt remained, even as he went back over his warding to assure himself that he had done everything possible to guard his friends. Finally, exhaustion overcame him, and he drifted into fitful sleep.

Berry's scream awakened them all a candle-mark later, in the darkness just before sunrise. She was standing at the edge of the warding, pointing.

Staggering to his feet, Tris saw Carina by the well. She stood rigid and still, outside the wardings had Tris set. Vahanian lurched to his feet, sword ready, as Carroway scrambled from his post.

"I thought you were on watch," Vahanian grated.

"I was, I swear," Carroway breathed, eyes wide. "There was a noise over there," he pointed in the other direction, "and I went to check it out. There was nothing," he recounted, "and then I turned, and saw Carina at the well. I thought she might have needed a drink, but she moved like she was still asleep, and I was just about to go after her when Berry screamed."

"Something's been out here," Vahanian said, walking around to the other side of the well. He pointed at the body of a young woman, half buried in a drift. On her temple was a dark bruise and around her neck, the marks of a belt or rope. One hand stretched out, claw-like, from the drift, in a final grasping gesture. But it was the corpse's face that held Tris's gaze, for though it was contorted in fear and anger, the dead girl's features were those of the ghost who had sought his help.

Tris turned back to Carina and gently called her name. The healer's eyes were glazed, her expression astonished, still standing rigid as death.

"What's wrong with her?" Carroway asked, not attempting to hide the fear in his voice. He reached out toward her, but Tris caught his wrist.

"What are you doing?" Carroway protested.

"That's Carina's body," Tris said quietly, stretching out his mage senses, "but there's another spirit in control."

"What the hell are you talking about," Vahanian snapped, his hand on the pommel of his sword.

"Last night, while Jonmarc was on watch, a ghost came to me," Tris said, staring at Carina's motionless form.

"I didn't see any ghosts," Vahanian differed.

Tris shook his head, staring at Carina. "She wasn't strong enough for anyone but me to see her," he said quietly.

"She?" Carroway said breathlessly, stealing a look at the corpse. "That she?"

Tris nodded, and told them the dead girl's story.

Vahanian looked at him skeptically. "So this ghost thought you could snap your fingers and bring her back from the dead?" he recapped incredulously. Unspoken, the next question seemed to hang in the air. *And could you have?* Tris knew they wondered, though they did not dare to ask, and Tris, remembering the fiasco with Alyzza and the field mouse, was grateful they did not.

"Even if I could," Tris said, "it is forbidden by the Lady. I had to turn her away," he recounted. "That's when she swore she would find a way back on her own," he added in a voice just above a whisper. "I set a warding over us. I thought we would be safe."

"Yeah, well it didn't work," Vahanian clipped.

"The warding was breached," Tris replied. "Carina stepped outside the circle. The ghost must have called to her."

"Can you bring Carina back?" Berry whispered, a dagger clutched in her fist.

In answer, Tris laid a hand on Carina's shoulder and closed his eyes. He stretched out his senses, searching for Carina's life force, the glowing thread he had felt the night they saved Vahanian's life. To his relief, it burned—dim but present—within her form, but it was not Carina's spirit that rose up to meet him.

Instead, heady laughter greeted him. *I told you I would find a way,* the ghost's voice mocked. *Look what I can do!*

"Look what I can do," Carina's voice shook him from his trance. Tris's eyes snapped open to see Carina's mouth moving, her voice flat and toneless, her eyes still staring sightlessly ahead.

As they watched in horror, Carina's form began to tremble, and then one arm jerked up, suspended as if by a puppeteer's string. It fell to her side as the other arm rose, and then awkwardly the healer shuffled forward, bumping into the well without reaction before blindly turning toward them.

Vahanian, his face contorted with rage, stepped forward, sword drawn. "By the Whore!" he cried. "Let her go!"

"What do you expect to do with that sword?" Carroway said quietly. "That's still Carina's body."

Gathering all his courage, Tris moved to block the shuffling form. "By all the faces of the Lady and all the power of the Goddess," he swore in a low, still voice. "Return her spirit and go your way."

"Not yet," a voice replied, emanating from Carina's mouth though it was not the healer's voice nor did Carina's lips move. "Not until I have what I came for."

"You cannot take this body," Tris replied steadily, holding his ground. "It is not yours."

A chilling laugh broke the moonless night. "It is mine now."

Tris lunged forward, wrapping Carina in a tight embrace as the spirit made the healer's form buck and struggle. On instinct, Tris held on as he called together all his strength, and breathing a prayer to the Dark Lady, closed his eyes and plunged into the darkness.

Down, down he traveled, just as once before, when Vahanian lay dying, he and Carina had taken a similar inward journey. The healer's body convulsed in his arms, trying to tear itself from his grip as he drove resolutely onward in his mind. Just as Carina nearly wrenched herself from his grasp, Tris felt powerful arms encircle both of them.

"Whatever the hell you're doing, we won't let her get away," Tris heard Vahanian swear, his voice distant, as the mercenary and Carroway tightened their grip.

With a scream of rage, Carina's form went slack, and Tris dove downward, pursuing the spirit of his ghostly visitor. *Give her back,* he commanded as he hurtled through the darkness of the pathworking.

Take her if you can, Lord of the Dead, the ghost taunted. *She is mine now.*

It seemed to Tris that he and the ghost reached the glowing life thread in the same instant, and in a sudden flash of horror, Tris realized the ghost intended not to break the fragile strand, but to stretch out her own presence along it, driving out Carina's spirit and replacing it with her own.

Lady of Darkness, hear me! Tris cried as he made his desperate gamble. Once before, he'd borrowed from the glow of his own thread to hold Vahanian to life. Now, Tris threw himself on the blue-white thread, overlaying it with his own life's strand, and with all of his will, drove back the ghost in the brightness of its glow.

No! the ghost girl screamed, and Carina's body contorted wildly. Hanging on with every bit of power he could summon, Tris held the image of the two glowing strands in his mind as he felt his friends' arms tighten around him, holding fast as Carina convulsed and beat at them with her fists. The glow grew stronger, pushing back the darkness, and finally, as a cry tore from Carina's throat and stabbed through Tris's mind, he hurled the darkness from them, leaving only the glow behind.

For a heartbeat, everything was silent. Then Tris felt the glow of Carina's life strand pulse stronger and, gently, he drew back, relieved and amazed, to see the healer's thread glow steadily on its own. As Tris came back to himself, Carina sagged against him and would have fallen except for the support of the arms that encircled them. Tris felt his knees buckle, and it was sheer willpower that kept him on his feet as the fatigue swept over him, leaving him utterly spent.

There was only the crunch of snow behind them as a warning, and then Carroway staggered as something struck him from behind. Tris glimpsed one clawed hand over the bard's shoulder as Vahanian released his grasp and reached for his sword.

"Look… at… me…" Words rasped from the corpse's mouth as it clawed at Carroway. The bard, eyes wide with terror, beat back the lurching form, tripping over himself in his haste to break free. Vahanian stepped forward, sword drawn, interposing himself between the reanimated corpse and Tris and Carina, who slumped together behind him.

"Dark Lady take my soul," the mercenary breathed. "Get back!"

The thing lurched toward him, once again. Just as the first light of dawn broke over the horizon, Vahanian's sword swung down with all his might, glinting in the pink glow of morning.

"No, please!" came the strangled cry from the dead girl's unmoving mouth as the blade connected with a sickening thud, and as the sun glistened on the snow, cleaved through the corpse with a mighty blow. The body fell at Vahanian's feet, once more silent and lifeless.

"What happened?" The voice that broke the stillness was Carina's, and from the baffled look on the healer's face, Tris was sure she had no idea of what transpired, nor why she found herself in his arms.

"What do you remember?" Carroway breathed, rejoining them. His face was ashen and his eyes wide.

Carina pushed back a little from Tris, then a look of complete exhaustion crossed her face and she did not struggle to break away. "I heard someone calling me," she said, looking at Tris searchingly. "Maybe I dreamed it, but it seemed so real. I got up and walked over to the well, but no one was there." She shuddered, remembering. "I looked into the well and saw a face staring back at me." She paused. "That's all I remember," she said, leaning hard against Tris as Carroway helped them to their feet. Reflexively, Tris put his arm around her, and patted her hair as if he were comforting a small child. A strange look crossed Vahanian's face in the instant before the fighter turned away.

"Let's get out of here," Vahanian said roughly.

"Tris, what happened?" Carina asked once more, stepping back and looking at him searchingly. Berry ran to her and flung her arms around the healer, burying her face in Carina's robe.

Tris glanced away, unsure how to answer. "A ghost called you," he began, telling the tale as best he could with Berry jumping in from time to time to fill in the gaps. Vahanian and Carroway loaded up the horses as they talked, refusing resolutely to look over to where the sundered corpse lay in the morning light. A look of horror crossed Carina's face as she looked from Tris to the body of the girl, then to the well, and for a moment, she was silent.

"But how—" she started and stopped. "How did her body come back to life?"

Tris forced himself to stare at the corpse. "I don't know for certain," he admitted. "When I pushed her spirit away, all I cared about was throwing it clear," he said in a hushed voice. "They say that at dawn, the spirit world is closer to our own. Maybe it was close enough for her to try to take back her own body, and close enough for Jonmarc to be able to strike her down."

"Thank you," Carina managed finally, looking first to Tris and then to the others. "Thank you so much."

"All in a day's work," Vahanian replied sarcastically. "Now can we get the hell out of here?"

Tris took a step toward the camp, felt his knees buckle, and stumbled. Carroway caught him as his head swam, pounding with a headache from the working.

"What damn good is magic if you feel like shit after you've used it?" Tris swore under his breath, struggling to walk with Carroway's assistance.

"If it's any consolation, Carina doesn't look any better. Can you ride?" Carroway asked.

"Give me a cup of kerif and a candlemark to collect my wits," Tris asked as Carroway helped him to a seat by the fire. "And then we'll ride, even if you have to tie me to the horse."

Vahanian went to calm their mounts, and Carroway pressed a cup of the strong, bitter drink into Tris's hands, then made sure Carina had a warm cloak and a cup of her own. Tris could feel the way they were staring at him, as if he had suddenly become nearly as strange and fearful a thing as the corpse in the glade behind them. Carroway went to help Vahanian, and Carina settled into a seat beside Tris, saying nothing for a while.

Mercifully, Carina did not ask the questions he knew she must be thinking. With the headache that pounded behind his eyes, Tris doubted he could supply more than one-word answers. He had only been partly joking about the need to be lashed to his horse. While Vahanian might have had the experience of riding back from battle more dead than alive, Tris felt as spent as if he had completed an exhausting day's labor without food or a night's sleep.

Sweet Lady, if this is what a real working takes, then I better get it right the first time when I take on Arontala, because I'm hardly likely to survive it, Tris thought. For the first time, he considered the possibility that magic and not battle might kill him before he could take the crown. Even if I don't live to be king, they can hardly find someone worse than Jared if I can just take down Arontala, he thought, before the pounding in his head made thinking too painful.

Though no one mentioned the incident for the rest of the morning, of one accord they rode more slowly. Tris managed to stay seated on his horse without lashing himself to the saddle, but only just, and he doubted that he could have kept his seat at a gallop. Carina was too unsteady to ride unassisted, and accepted Vahanian's offer to share his horse without her usual barb. They rode as hard as they dared, anxious to put as much distance between themselves and the haunted well as they could.

By late morning, when Carroway's time riding point was over, he let his horse drift back to match the stride of Tris's mount. They rode side by side in silence for a while, until Carroway finally spoke.

"Are you all right?" he inquired awkwardly. "You look a bit worse for wear."

Tris managed a haggard smile. "I'll get over it."

Carroway looked as if he were about to say something, thought better of it, and began again. "Tris," he started, "before your grandmother died... did she ever tell you that you were—"

"Her mage heir?" Tris supplied with a hint of bitterness in his voice. "No. But then again there are things I see in dreams, workings that I did with her that I didn't remember at all." He paused, staring at his hands.

"Are mages born or made?" he continued. "You know, I've been able to see the ghosts at the palace, talk with them—not just on Haunts, but all year— ever since I can remember. But this..." his voice drifted off, lacking the words to continue.

"Your grandmother was the greatest summoner of the age," Carroway replied thoughtfully. "I often wondered why no one in her line seemed to have her talent. I guess we have our answer."

Tris's head still ached, but he could sense that Carroway needed to understand. "When I was little, grandmother let me tag along, watch her do her workings. When I got older, she let me help—simple things like calling a flame to light a candle or the fireplace, small workings. There were some that she let you help with, too," he said, and Carroway nodded.

"I always thought it was her way of giving me something special, since I was the second son." Tris gave a lopsided smile. "We all know second sons are only spare parts," he added. "When she swore us to secrecy, I figured that was because Jared would pitch a fit if I got to do something and he didn't."

Tris paused, waiting out a stab of pain from his throbbing head. "Then right before I went for fostering, she brought you in on more workings, and we did some complicated magic. When I came back from fostering, grandmother was ill." He looked off at the horizon, remembering. "Don't you remember? She asked that I be the one to serve her. I guess they didn't have any better use for me, so they let me. I was with her when she died."

"Did anything... unusual... happen?" Carroway pressed gently.

Tris looked at him, frowning against the headache, and against the blank in his memories. "I don't remember. That's the problem. I never noticed before, but there seem to be whole stretches with her that I don't remember. Goddess, I've tried! But I can't." He looked down at the reins in his hands. "Back with the caravan, Carina and Alyzza helped me with some basic things. Grandmother came to me in a dream, told me that I would remember the training she made me forget—for my own safety—until it was needed." He gave a sharp, mirthless laugh. "Well, I can't think of needing it more than now, but so far, I still can't remember."

Carroway listened in silence, as if he were carefully weighing what Tris was saying. "Perhaps," he said finally, "things will seem more clear when we reach the Library."

"I hope you're right," Tris said fervently, closing his eyes as his head throbbed again, "because there's far too much at stake to try to make this up as I go."

Breakfast was eaten cold as they rode, and they would have done the same for lunch had Carina not begged them to stop. For once, she and Vahanian did not spar the entire morning. The morning's battle had cast a cloud over all of them, Tris thought as he sat by the small fire. He was thankful when the evening came with no further surprises awaiting them, and they made a cold camp that night, just a few days' journey from where the river set the boundary between Dhasson and Principality.

CHAPTER TWENTY-FOUR

TRIS AND THE group rode in silence as the road wound toward Westmarch. A cold rain fell. It was Tris's turn to ride point, and he found himself jumpy and irritable. Neither Carina nor Carroway were talkative, and twice, Vahanian waved the group ahead while he waited, sword ready, sensing something that did not materialize. At least, Tris thought moodily, he was not the only one with a feeling of foreboding.

Westmarch was near the borders of three kingdoms—Principality, Margolan and Dhasson. Mindful of Gabriel's warning about the magicked beasts, the group chose a more northerly route, one which took them further from the Dhasson border. Unfortunately, Gabriel's warning did not indicate just how far Arontala's border spell extended. Though it was still daylight, each of them rode with a torch. A bucket of pitch hung from each saddle. Carroway carried two quivers of arrows with burlap-covered, pitch-soaked points. Carina wrapped the tip of her stave in burlap and pitch, and Tris counted on his ability to conjure fire. Berry, riding close to Carina, had her own weapon. She had tinkered with the bard's recipe for the pellets he contrived for smoke and colors to accompany his tales. A slight adjustment to the proportions yielded small balls that burst into flame on impact. Armed with a slingshot, Berry had a surprisingly accurate aim.

Vahanian, the only one with actual experience with the beasts, was clearly the most nervous. He rode with a crude lance, fashioned from a sturdy pole, its tip wrapped in pitch-soaked rags. It was longer than Carina's stave and sharp-ended. From the fighter's grim expression, Tris knew Vahanian felt the same foreboding. The further they rode, the darker Vahanian's mood grew and the shorter his temper became.

At this rate, we'll all be wrecks by the time we reach Westmarch, Tris thought. By agreement, they rode as hard as their horses could tolerate, stopping only when the animals needed food, water or rest.

"Do you hear that?" Vahanian asked.

Tris frowned. "Hear what?"

"Exactly," the mercenary said, settling his lance in front of him. "It's too quiet." They passed no one on roads that should have been well traveled by traders and farmers. "I don't like this."

Carroway brought his horse up closer. "I couldn't catch what you said," the bard interjected, "but it's too damn quiet out here."

Tris smiled tightly. "Looks like we're all thinking the same thing." His horse nickered, reminding Tris that a stop and some water was overdue. He sighed and patted his mount's neck. "The horses need to rest," he said, and looked around with concern. "The problem is, where?"

"Over there," Carroway pointed toward a village at the crest of the next hill. "I smell supper fires. Maybe we can buy a hot meal for us and some food for the horses."

"Look sharp," Vahanian warned.

They approached the village cautiously. As they drew closer, it became clear that supper fires were not the source of the wood smoke. The village lay in smoldering ruins, its buildings blackened shadows.

"There!" Carroway pointed. A body lay crumpled beside a burned-out tavern. Tris nudged his horse closer, then dismounted, sword in hand. He rolled the corpse over with his foot. Whatever had killed the man, it was not flame. Great gashes rent the man's face and tore open his throat.

"What creature hunts like that?" Carina exclaimed, reining her horse closer.

"I've got something over here you need to see," Carroway called. Tris and Vahanian joined him, with Vahanian in the rear, warily eyeing the streets, his weapon ready. Carroway pointed at a heap near the door of one of the burned buildings. Tris realized that the body was not human. Tris rolled the thing over and gasped.

The beast would have stood taller than a man. Its hind legs were strong, and thin arms ended in wicked talons. Its thickly muscled legs attested to speed, and its massive shoulders spoke of inhuman strength. But it was its face, if one could call it that, which took Tris's breath away. The gray-skinned creature's face was a fearsome thing. Huge, sunken eyes were located on the sides of its head, above a large, snout—its mouth filled with rows of glistening teeth. Tris swallowed. The beast was obviously burned, and a warning tingled in Tris's mind. Perhaps it was not the beasts who had burned the village, he thought. Perhaps it was the work of desperate villagers, who even with their sacrifice were not able to save their lives. Vahanian said nothing, but for the first time, Tris thought he saw a flicker of fear in the fighter's eyes.

"Let's get that water and get out of here," Carroway said, swinging back up on his horse.

"I think that's a good idea," Tris replied. He turned, and stopped short. In the center of the street, between them and the village's well, stood a man.

Carroway's bow was raised, trained on the man's heart, as Tris took a step forward. "We mean you no harm," Tris said, advancing open-handed.

"Have you come for the fire?" the man shouted, drawing a few steps nearer. He was old, with wild white hair framing a gaunt face, caked with dirt and blood and streaked with the spittle that drooled from a corner of his mouth. The stubble of a white beard shadowed his face. Torn rags hung from his body, which bore the marks of an encounter with the beasts in the long claw marks that raked across one shoulder and down his chest—claw marks that unmistakably resembled Vahanian's scar. His dark eyes were bright with madness. "Have you come for the fire?"

"What happened?" Tris asked. Behind him, Vahanian cursed under his breath.

The man spread his arms wide. "The spirits came," he said, turning to take in the village with his gesture. "They came for us, only we hadn't been good. No," he said, shaking his head, "we hadn't been good. So they weren't good spirits. Dark spirits, they were, with wings of fire."

Tris looked at the man with a mixture of horror and pity. "The fire," he said slowly, trying to reach through the man's madness for answers. "What started the fire?"

The man brightened. "Oh, we did," he replied. "To see them better. Because fire sends them home, don't you know?"

"How did you survive?" Tris pressed.

The old man began to laugh. "I'll tell you a secret," he whispered, one filthy, gnarled hand reaching beneath his tunic. Vahanian and Carroway readied their weapons, but when the man withdrew his hand, he held only a charm on a worn leather thong. Behind him, Tris heard Vahanian gasp a potent curse.

"I wanted to die, but it wouldn't let me." Grief overtook him and he began to sob as he tore the talisman from around his neck and threw it at Tris's feet. "I tried. I attacked them with my bare hands, ran at them with swords, walked among the flames," he sobbed in a singsong voice. "But it wouldn't let them take me, and now I'm all alone," he repeated. His hand slipped to his belt and drew a dagger, raising it purposefully. "But I'm going now," he said, his mad eyes clear with purpose. "I'm going home," he said, and before any of the three could stop him, he plunged the dagger deep into his chest. A smile lit his ravaged features as he stiffened. "There are no fires," he whispered, "no fires at all," he rasped as he fell dead and his hand slipped away from the knife hilt.

"Leave that cursed thing and let's get out of here," Vahanian cried as Tris bent to pick up the talisman. It was a small, simple design worked in a burnished gray metal with a pattern of parallel and perpendicular lines, a circle embedded within them. As they sprinted for their horses, Tris slipped it into his pocket.

"Look!" Carina warned as the things came into view. Tris scrambled for his horse and Carroway moved into position, his bow at the ready. Three of the gray beasts loomed just beyond the well, their heads inclined to scent out living blood. Carroway held steady until they ventured closer, then lit and loosed a flaming arrow. His aim was true, and the missile struck its target. The thing howled as its claws tore at its own chest while dark ichor flowed from its gaping mouth. It fell forward, dead. Carina cried a warning from behind.

"Carina and Berry, stay between us," Vahanian shouted as the group retreated. Their horses whinnied, terrified by the smell of the beasts. Carroway picked off one more of the beasts. Carina and Vahanian lit their weapons, and Tris lobbed a fireball toward the lead creature. Two more staggered from the wreckage toward them.

"We can't hold them at bay for long," Carroway shouted, loosing another arrow. Although he dropped three of the beasts, two more appeared from the shadows to take their places.

"Ride for it!" Tris commanded. "I'll hold them as long as I can, just get out of here!" Carina wheeled her horse and the others followed, their panicked mounts pounding down the village street as Tris lobbed fireballs.

Behind him, he heard a horse's terrified cry and Berry's scream. "Berry!" Carina shouted. Berry's horse reared and bolted, leaving the girl on the road.

"They're gaining!" Carroway shouted, firing off two more arrows.

Vahanian leaned into his horse and kicked its sides, riding down on Berry, his lance leveled. He snatched the girl up by her cloak with his left hand and she clambered onto his horse behind him, hanging on for her life.

A guttural howl split the twilight as two more of the beasts appeared, blocking Carina's path. As Tris flung fireballs and Carroway fired arrows, the beasts began to circle.

Carina screamed as one of the beasts lunged for her horse. She poled it in the chest with her flaming stave, but her mount reared and nearly threw her. With a battle cry, Vahanian leveled his lance and rode for the thing at full gallop. Berry ducked her head and clung, white-knuckled, to his back.

Vahanian's lance scored a direct hit on the beast closest to Carina. His lance impaled the writhing creature, enveloping it in flames as it shrieked, charring with an acrid stench. He shook the dead thing free of his weeapon and wheeled his horse, wrestling it against its fear, rearing on two legs to bash his lance down on another beast.

"Those were my last arrows," Carroway breathed.

"I'll make an opening," Tris shouted above the din. "Ride for the road and don't look back."

At that, he dug his heels into his mount, crouching low, and bolted toward the center of the cursed village. Heart thudding, Tris realized that the beasts followed his sudden motion, whether from predator's instinct or Arontala's curse.

"Now!" he shouted, as the beasts—nearly a dozen of them—started after him. From the scrabble of their clawed feet behind him, he badly misjudged their speed. His ruse might have only a few seconds to play out. He heard the thunder of hoof beats and knew the others were making for the road. Barely ahead of the monsters, Tris suddenly wheeled his mount.

Tris opened himself to his power, and his mind formed the image faster than the words could reach his lips. Summoning a shielding over himself and his panicked mount, Tris called a curtain of fire that sprang up from the village earth, enveloping them. Even within the warding, he could hear the death cries of the beasts as the flames incinerated them.

It was over just as quickly as it had started, leaving Tris and his horse standing amid a blackened circle and the remains of the cursed beasts.

A cry cut through the silence. At first, Tris thought it was Carina—then he realized that the sound came from a grove of trees near the other side of the village, opposite from the direction in which his friends had fled. He turned his horse toward the sound, and although the mount was trembling, it obeyed, carrying him toward the crossroads.

A lone traveler, stalked by one of the beasts, was running out of time. The traveler was capable with a sword, but the beast was implacable, and Tris knew he had only moments to intervene.

"Stand clear!" he shouted, spurring his horse toward the traveler at a full gallop. Calling down a curtain of fire here was impossible—in the wooded area, they would be killed along with the beast. Tris stretched out his hand, and the image of Vahanian's lance came to mind. As his horse closed the distance, Tris willed both force and flame and a streak of fire shot from his outstretched palm. It struck the beast in the chest and engulfed it. Fire crackled in the dried brush.

"Get out of there!" Tris shouted to the traveler. The traveler dismounted and ran into the thicket, emerging a moment later with a small bundle before swinging back up onto the big stallion. "This way!" Tris gestured, and the traveler rode toward him, glancing backward several times at the fallen beast.

Together, Tris and the traveler thundered down the roadway until the smoke of the village was far behind them. When they finally slowed, he realized that the rest of his party—if they had survived—were on the far side of the village. A bad headache had begun to build in reaction to his working, and he struggled to clear his thoughts. He resolved to ask for some of Carina's headache tea, assuming his friends had also made it to safety.

"Are you all right?" he asked breathlessly as he reined in his horse.

The traveler did the same, and sheathed the sword still clutched in hand. "Thank you," the traveler said, and the heavy cowl fell back to reveal a woman, close to Tris's own age, her auburn hair caught back in a braid and the glint of a studded mail breastplate unmistakable beneath the neckline of her cloak. "We never had a chance," she said ruefully. "That... thing... came out of nowhere. I couldn't hold it off."

"We?" Tris asked, hearing the note of sadness in her voice.

"I had a tame fox, and a hunting gyregon," she said quietly. "The fox tried to attack when we were surprised. I saw him die," she said with a catch in her voice. "The gyregon is badly wounded," she continued, and only then did Tris see the bundle that she held on the saddle in front of her. Tris saw the head of her gyregon loll to one side. He brought his horse alongside hers and dug into his pack. Tris shook free a piece of cloth and offered it to her.

"It smells of cheese," he said with a smile. "But you might make a sling to carry him."

"Thank you," she said with a note of surprise. Only when she winced as she reached for the cloth did Tris see the deep gash in her shoulder.

"Night's a dangerous time to ride alone," he said. "My companions should be on the other side of that small village. We were also ambushed, but we drove the beasts back," he said, omitting just how that was accomplished. "We have a healer with us. Perhaps she could look at your shoulder."

He saw the wariness in the traveler's eyes. "You're welcome to camp with us for the night," he offered. "Be on your way in the morning. We'll all be safer with another sword," he said with a nod toward the weapon she sheathed. "I doubt any of us will sleep this night,"

He paused. "By the way, I'm Tris."

Whether it was the promise of healing or the fear of camping alone, she seemed to come to a decision, and a faint smile came to her lips. "I'm Kiara." She paused again. "I was sent on a Journey by the priestesses," she admitted, letting her horse fall into step with Tris's as they rode, warily watching the bushes for signs of other beasts. "It's a... rite of passage... among my people. A way to test what you're made of, I guess."

"Sounds like a good way to get killed."

Kiara smiled. "Maybe you're right." She looked off into the distance. "I had the choice between that and an arranged marriage, so to tell you the truth, I thought I'd take my chances."

"Someone must be disappointed."

Kiara looked at him as if trying to discern whether his comment was sincere. "Angry, yes," she sighed. "Disappointed—not really." She adjusted the gyregon in its makeshift sling. "He's got quite a few things in common with that... thing... you just killed, to tell the truth," she said distastefully.

"Then I hope the Journey is successful."

She looked at him as if taking his measure. "What you did back there—you are a mage?"

After the display at the crossroads, it would be futile to protest, Tris thought. "Mage student might be more accurate," he said uncomfortably. He stopped and rose in his stirrups to take his bearings.

"Right now, I'd like to know whether this road meets up again with the road on the other side of the village," he said. There was a waxing moon, which saved the need for a torch, but the rolling hills made it difficult to gauge the lay of the land. "I have no desire to ride back through the village."

"I have a map," Kiara offered. She dug the map from her pack, grimacing with the movement. Tris guessed that the wound was deeper than she let on.

When Kiara unfolded the map, Tris called a small ball of cold handfire. That Kiara did not seem afraid of his power impressed him. That she was able to hold her own against one of the beasts, however briefly, intrigued him more. He chanced another glance at her. From the way she sat her horse and held herself—as well as the stoic way she bore her wound—he guessed that she was military-trained. Her brown eyes were intelligent, and her manner spoke of education and means. She wore no ornamentation, and her cloak and tunic were those of a man. In the dim glow of the handfire, it was her face that caught his attention. *How is it that a beautiful woman— trained at war or not—rides alone into the wilderness to escape an unwanted suitor?*

"Look," Kiara said, pointing at a spot on the map. "If that's where we are, then the roads should meet not far from here."

Tris nodded. "Let's go. The sooner we find my friends, the safer we'll be."

KIARA LAPSED INTO silence as they rode. She felt Greyfoot's absence keenly, but lacked the words or the will to share the loss with her riding companion, who might think her mad for mourning a fox. She glanced at him as they rode. Shoulder-length, white-blond hair was caught back in a queue. His manner and his speech suggested status that his calloused hands contradicted. *What is a mage doing riding around the countryside,* she wondered? Although grateful for his intervention, the sudden rescue made her suspicious. *Lady and Childe! I could be getting myself into* more trouble, but I don't think I'll live long riding alone!

Jae shifted in his sling. She stroked his scales, and the unexpected kindness Tris showed made her look at him again. Though close to her own age, she guessed, he looked weary, as if he had been on the road for quite some time. His cloak was of common cloth, and his breeches of homespun fabric. But his blue eyes had a haunted look to them, and she wondered from what, besides the beasts, he might be running. Something about his face, his high cheekbones and his profile, looked familiar.

She had not traveled long before she learned that out here, everyone was running from something. There's more he's not saying, she thought. She sensed no threat from him, something rare given the other soldiers she met on the road. Her obvious skill with a sword and her warhorse did not seem to bother him. I wonder where his party is going, she mused. Perhaps they'll turn off before I head north to Westmarch. I'd hate to explain why I'm traveling to a library that doesn't exist any more!

They rode barely half a candlemark before a man dressed in riding leathers stepped out from the bushes. Kiara's hand fell to her sword, but Tris reined in his mount.

"You waited for me?" Tris called in recognition. The swordsman, a lean, fit man with dark brown hair and a hunter's tan, nodded.

"Took you long enough. I was just about to ride back to find you," the man replied, in a tone both relieved and annoyed.

"I ran into another one of those friendly little beasts," Tris replied sarcastically. "And drove him off before he could eat a fellow traveler," he added, indicating Kiara.

Just then, Jae popped his head out of the makeshift sling and flicked his tongue. The swordsman's expression moved from annoyance to concern to resignation. "Picking up strays?" he asked with an edge, directing the comment to Tris.

"She took a bad gash and needs a healer. So does her gyregon."

The swordsman held his ground for a moment, then shook his head and turned aside. "Hey, it's your party," he said, turning his back and starting up the road. "The more the merrier."

The obvious play of wills between the two men left Kiara wondering even more about her new companion. The swordsman was clearly used to being in charge, and seemed to consider himself master of the excursion. But there was an air of command to Tris that won out over the head-strong swordsman. They had not gone far before the swordsman signaled them to dismount, and Kiara slid down from Wraith as best she could without squashing the gyregon, who protested ill-humouredly. Tris took the reins from her and led Wraith over to a small stand of trees, where he tethered the horse with the other mounts. That Tris did not insult her by trying to help her down from her horse made yet another positive impression.

"Careful how you split up that food. There's another mouth to feed," the swordsman called as they approached the camp.

"Glad to see you back in one piece," called a tall, black-haired man who rose from near the fire. He was strikingly handsome, with blue-black hair framing his face. When he moved, it was with a dancer's grace more than the stride of a fighter.

"So am I," Tris replied as he tethered his horse. Beyond them, a thin, brunette woman hunched next to a fire, and a young girl assiduously cut a loaf of bread with a knife.

"She's been hurt," Tris said as they drew closer. "I told her we had a healer with us."

At that, the woman looked up and froze as her eyes met Kiara's. Kiara felt breath leave her as if she'd been poleaxed, as she met those eyes in startled recognition.

She wasn't even sure she had choked out Carina's name before the dark-haired healer was in her arms, both of them talking and crying at once.

"Did you get this kind of greeting too?" the swordsman asked dryly as the others looked on in amazement.

Kiara dragged her sleeve across her eyes. "I'm sorry," she said, finding her voice. "It's just, oh Goddess! We're cousins, and Carina's been on the road for so long—"

The black-haired man stepped toward them. "Then you must be Kiara Sharsequin."

"How—"

"It's all right, Kiara," Carina said, collecting herself with a deep breath and wiping the tears from her eyes. "They're friends. Come on. I'll take a look at that shoulder and at Jae. We've got a lot of catching up to do."

Carina introduced Carroway, Vahanian and Berry, then went to retrieve her healer's bag from the satchels on her horse while Berry pressed a hunk of bread and chunks of meat and cheese into Kiara's hands. Jae's head thrust out of the sling, surprising the girl, who laughed and then reached for the gyregon. Kiara expected a hiss of annoyance, but to her surprise, the gyregon accepted the girl's gentle touch. Kiara carefully removed the sling, leaving the gyregon wrapped in the cloth bandage and handed him to Berry, who put a pot of water on the fire and then settled down cross-legged where she could hear Kiara's story and feed niblets of cheese to the gyregon.

When the healer finished with her shoulder, Kiara found that it no longer throbbed. Jae hissed in recognition as Carina took him gently from Berry, and let the little gyregon flick his tongue along her hand in acknowledgment. After a short while, the cut along Jae's belly looked nearly healed. Between healings, Carina mixed a tea which she presented to Tris, who looked as if he were in pain. He accepted the tea gratefully.

Night had fallen by the time Carina had recounted their escape from the slavers, and the detail she provided about Tris's role in obtaining their freedom confirmed that the young mage had considerably more power than he let on. She explained how circumstances had changed their course, directing them all to the Library at Westmarch instead of Dhasson. Carina even managed to tell of Cam's disappearance with a fair amount of control, although Kiara was unashamed of the tears it brought to her own eyes. Of the others' stories, Carina offered little. While she talked, Tris and Carroway made rush torches and arrows to replace the ones they had used and Vahanian refilled the bucket with pitch, ready for another encounter.

"I hate to break up the story," Vahanian said from where he leaned against the trunk of a tree, "but if we're riding out tomorrow, do we have some idea of where this Library of yours is?" He stretched up and back to flick off a loose piece of bark before looking at the group once more, glancing from Tris to Carina and back again.

"Would it help if I gave you my map?" Kiara offered. Briefly, she explained her quest, and the Oracle's directive that she seek out the fabled library.

"Now we're getting somewhere," Vahanian replied, accepting the old map.

"If this relic is true," he said after a moment's examination, "then we're within a day's ride. Of course, that assumes the Library is still there. Spook here," he added with a nod in Tris's direction, "can tell you I'm more of a seeing-is-believing kind of guy."

"Maybe we should get some sleep," Tris interjected. "We'll have our chance tomorrow to see if the Library is real or not."

Kiara nodded, suddenly aware of just how exhausted she was.

"I'll help you find a spot for your bedroll," Carina offered. "We stay pretty close together." She managed a tired smile. "We decided that we'd give up a little privacy to stay out of the slavers' hands."

"Good idea," Kiara agreed. She looked from Tris to Vahanian to Carroway. "I expect to take my turn on watch," she said.

"First night's free," Carroway smiled. "Tomorrow, you can take your turn, and mine too if you'd like," he said. Kiara tended to Wraith then carried her blankets to where Carina cleared a space for her. After so long alone on the trail, she was surprised at how great a comfort it was to fall asleep with the sounds of other people nearby.

MORNING CAME ALL too quickly. Carroway warmed gruel over the small fire, which they washed down with water from a spring beyond the hill. The small group had been together long enough to have a routine for getting on the road, Kiara noted, and tired as they were, they packed up the camp in record time.

Kiara felt a tingle of excitement as they took to the road. Finding the Library had become a quest in itself, and she sensed the same anticipation among the others. For a while, Kiara rode with Carina, enjoying the familiar companionship. Jae hopped from her shoulder to Berry's, and let the girl stroke his scales as he made contented chirps.

Mid-morning, Kiara found herself riding alongside Carroway, and enjoyed his songs and tales. By the good-natured ribbing, she gathered that his stories were familiar to the others, and Carroway explained that he often earned their night's keep by entertaining in taverns.

Most interesting was the time she rode next to Tris. Taciturn at first, he opened up a little when she revealed her own limited abilities with magic, and they talked of magecraft, both experienced or rumored. She was surprised when Carina drew her away privately as they made camp that evening. "What were you and Tris so deep in conversation about?" Carina asked.

Kiara shrugged. "We were trading theories about magic more than anything, comparing the few mages we've met, that sort of thing."

"I'm amazed you're so open with him," Carina said. "Considering."

Kiara frowned. "Considering what?"

Carina looked at her carefully. "You don't know, do you?"

"Know what?" Kiara asked. "Would you please stop talking in riddles?"

"I didn't introduce him because I assumed you'd covered all that," Carina replied. "Did he tell you who he is, or why he's out here?"

Kiara shook her head. "It's never really come up. I've gotten used to not asking that sort of thing on the road. I assumed you trusted him."

Carina nodded. "I do, completely. But there's something you need to know. Tris and his friends saw King Bricen's murder, and the murderer wants them dead. Tris was told he'd find his answers in Westmarch."

"There's something else you're not saying."

Carina met her eyes. "Kiara, he's Martris Drayke. Of Margolan. Jared Drayke's younger brother."

Kiara exhaled sharply and glanced back at Tris, who was standing near the fire talking with Vahanian. "Sweet Chenne," she said.

The resemblance she noted now made sense, Kiara thought, looking at Tris from a distance. While Jared was as dark as Tris was fair, there were similarities, around the eyes, in the high cheekbones, although Tris had a kinder turn to his lip and his stance revealed none of Jared's casual arrogance. Her revulsion and anger at what she had seen on the Margolan road swept back over her, equal to her fear of what an arranged marriage to such a king would mean, for her people and for herself. Could two brothers be so truly different? Yet, she genuinely liked Tris and found herself more comfortable with him than with most men. He showed no need to best her at sword skills or patronize her. He did not ask her rank at all, nor allude to any royal blood of his own.

"He means to find a way to unseat Jared," Carina continued. "King Harrol of Dhasson may be prepared to stake a fortune behind him to do it." Her dark eyes were worried. "There's going to be war, Kiara, and we're smack in the middle of it."

Maybe more so than you think, my cousin, Kiara thought, looking again at Tris. Best to keep her own counsel for a while, and as she did, to put some distance between herself and Tris, at least for now.

"Thanks for the warning," she said in her best off-hand voice. "While they're rooting around for supper, why don't you fill me in on the others? Starting with him," she said, with a nod toward Vahanian.

CHAPTER TWENTY-FIVE

They rose earlier than usual, eager to get on their way. They left the main road within a candlemark and headed off on barely passable trails. This area was dotted with tumbledown cottages and barns, and then, as they rode further north, these gradually thinned out until there were no signs of recent habitation at all.

This land was rocky, without good planting or pasturelands, and its hillsides offered neither minerals nor gems. Here the tributaries to the Nu River trickled down from the mountains, too shallow for commerce. They rode without encountering another soul. Even better, Tris thought, they saw no more beasts, though they still rode with torches and pitch at hand.

They spent part of the morning following a trail that ended in a wall of rock. Another old trail stopped in an empty field. Dust-covered, hungry and restless, they followed a barely visible third road. Vahanian dismounted to clear away the underbrush. By the time the sun was high in the sky, they had reached a small stream.

"Well, this should be it," Vahanian remarked, holding the map in front of him.

"I don't see anything," Kiara said, sidling her horse next to Vahanian. Tris noted that their new companion, so friendly the day before, grew more withdrawn as they rode.

"Over there," Carroway pointed to the overgrown ruins of a stone building.

"Not much of a library, but let's go see," Vahanian said, urging his horse on.

Amid the scrub trees and the low bushes, the remains of a tower rose from the ground. A tangle of vines and brambles obscured the building. Broken slates led up to what once were sweeping front steps. An iron gate with a solid door blocked their entrance. Although badly damaged, the wall was still intact.

"This can't be the right place," Kiara said in a hushed voice. "The Sister and Sakwi, they seemed so sure..." she drifted off, staring at the scene in disappointment. Carina, who rode up beside her, looked equally desolate.

Tris swung down from his horse and began to pick his way through the scrub toward the gate. Carroway dismounted also, and joined him as they headed toward the ruins. "What do you think you're going to find?" Vahanian called to them, as the others tethered their horses.

"Don't know," Tris called back. "Maybe nothing."

Something felt wrong, Tris thought as he made his way toward the ruins. Not dangerous, but strange, as though his senses were in conflict with something his inner sight knew to be amiss. There was magic here, old and strong. Something urged him to turn away. A spell? he wondered. One that would cause enough discomfort to make casual passers-by choose another road?

"What's left is too high to climb over," Tris observed.

"Take a look at this," Carroway called. Tris looked up to where the minstrel was pulling at loose vines covering a large seal on the iron gate to reveal an inscription.

"What does it say?" Tris asked.

Carroway ran his fingers lightly over the dark metal surface, squinting. "I'm not sure. It's written in a language I don't recognize," he said, bending closer. And there's a spot down here," he said, touching an indentation, "where something's been prized loose."

"Let me see," Carina said, and Carroway stepped aside. Carina bent to examine it then stood. "It's Nargi," she said.

"Can you read it?" Tris asked, crowding closer.

"I'll try," Carina replied, and leaned toward the plaque once more. "*C'sque nu osir, a'tesyr ja kescue*," she read slowly.

"*Kuscue*," Vahanian corrected, turning toward them. "*A'tesyr ja kuscue*," he repeated in perfect Nargi. "It means, 'I bar this gate.'"

Carina looked up, surprised. "Nargi's not an easy language. Do you want to take a look?"

Vahanian made his way through the scrub. Tris and Carroway stepped aside, and the mercenary brushed some dirt from the seal. "*Ib vossir, e diselon, vi fosset a'ysse, c'sa.*" Vahanian read fluently, continuing down several lines of the strange, mellifluous language. "'With my hand, I bar this gate...' there's a date here, back about fifty years ago, I think."

"The Mage Wars," Tris said looking up.

—"That none should despoil this place of learning," Vahanian translated. "Only the seal of the Lady may pass."

Carina looked at Vahanian. "The Nargi don't teach their language to outsiders," she said skeptically. "Where did you learn that?"

Vahanian shrugged and turned away. "Spend two years as their prisoner and see what you learn."

"The seal of the Lady," Kiara murmured. "The star pendant," she said, reaching inside her tunic for the pendant which glowed brightly as she drew it out, shining on her palm. She stepped forward and fitted the star into the indentation.

Around them, everything changed.

Beyond the gate was a massive stone building, four stories high, with a tower that stretched toward the sun. Gone completely was the overgrowth of vines and brambles inside the fence. The lawn around the Library was neatly tended, surrounded by ancient trees and a small, well-planned garden around a placid reflecting pool. The iron gate creaked inward on its massive hinges and the front door of the tower opened. A sprightly white-haired man nearly danced to the opening, his arms spread in greeting.

"Come on in," he said, welcoming them. "You're late, quite late, but we've been expecting you." And then abruptly, as if interrupted by a tap on the shoulder, he turned peevishly to one side to address empty air. "I've had enough of your silliness for one day. Now off with you!" He turned toward Tris and the others again. "Don't let him bother you," he said, with the air of an embarrassed parent. "He's really quite harmless. Do come in."

Tris moved forward, but Vahanian placed a hand on his shoulder. "I'm not sure 'harmless' is the right word," he cautioned. "He's talking to thin air."

"Not exactly," Tris said, chuckling. "There's a ghost, just off to his right. It's been poking him the whole time, rather pesky."

The man in the doorway brightened. "Goddess of Light! Someone else can see him! Please, please come in," he entreated, gesturing in welcome. "I'm Royster, a keeper of the Library."

Tris led the wary group into the darkened hallway. Jae squawked nervously from his perch on Kiara's shoulder. As they stepped inside, torches flared into brilliance on both sides of the passageway. Brown-robed figures assembled in the hallway, until a company of about twenty stood before them.

"These are my brothers and sisters," Royster introduced, then laughed aloud. "No, no—not blood family. We are acolytes to the Sisterhood, and our charge is to protect and maintain all this," he said with a grand sweep of his hand. "We are the Keepers."

Tris bowed in greeting. "I am Martris Drayke, grandson of Bava K'aa, the sorceress," Tris introduced himself, "and these are my companions," he added, introducing each in turn. "I've come to find a way to defeat a dark mage who killed my family. Carina seeks a cure for King Donelan's mage-sent illness. Kiara must speak for her own Journey, but the Sisterhood itself sent her here. Can you help us?"

Royster jumped as if poked and scowled at the empty air on his left. "Now stop interrupting!" he admonished the ghost. "They'll get to that. Don't be so impatient!" Exasperated, he turned his attention again to Tris. "Perhaps," he said, with a cunning smile. "Mageborn, are you?" he asked, peering closely at Tris.

"Just learning," Tris admitted.

"Don't let him kid you," Vahanian muttered under his breath. "If he's just practicing, I don't want to be around for the real thing."

"At the doorway, you could see Kessen," Royster said. "You are a spirit mage?"

Tris nodded. "Both the Sisterhood and the spirit of my grandmother believe you can help me with my training."

Royster stroked his beard. "You stay out of it," he snapped to the ghost. "You're just partial to him because he can see you. Well you're no treat to look on, let me tell you." He looked back to Tris, his blue eyes twinkling.

"I bet I can," he said spryly. "Make yourselves at home," he said, with a spring in his step as he turned and beckoned them to follow. "Plenty of room for all. First a room and a bed, then some food, then more than enough time for the books. You, hush up," he snapped as an aside to the ghost.

"Do you see anything?" Tris heard Berry ask Vahanian as they followed the sprightly librarian deeper into the huge building. Jae squawked nervously. The other Keepers melted into the shadows as silently as they had emerged, and Tris might have wondered, without his mage sight, if they were also ghosts. Royster, on the other hand, was definitely mortal. He was a thin, slightly built man barely taller than Carina, with unruly white hair and a full beard. What he lacked in size and bulk, he made up for in energy, since he seemed always in motion and moved with a sprightly glee that made him seem younger than his years, although Tris guessed him to be nearing his sixtieth summer.

"Just trouble," Vahanian admitted. "I've seen enough ghosts already for a lifetime."

"Me, too," Berry agreed. "Do you think there are vayash moru here?"

"Now that's a pleasant thought," Vahanian replied darkly.

The rooms that opened off the hallway were dimly lit and cavernous, filled with towering shelves of ancient tomes, leather-bound volumes, carefully wrapped bundles of scrolls and sheaves of flattened parchment. The wisdom of the mages, Tris thought in awe. Hidden for a lifetime. His curiosity drew him toward those ancient volumes, and Kiara, Carroway and Carina looked as excited as he did, while Vahanian appeared decidedly uncomfortable. Berry fairly bounced with enthusiasm.

Royster led them to a dormitory-style group of rooms, each with a stiff bed, a chair, a nightstand, a fireplace and a small table for study. There were enough rooms for them all, but Berry gratefully accepted Carina's invitation to share.

When Tris headed back into the corridor after washing up, Carina was just starting down the hall. "Cat got your tongue?" she asked, falling into step beside him.

Tris smiled. "Amazed by all this, I guess."

"Me too. Compared to this, the library in Isencroft is a sitting room," Carina agreed.

"Are you coming?" Carroway called from a few steps ahead. "Unless I'm mistaken, that's food I smell. Good food."

Tris grinned. "I keep thinking about that first inn where we stayed. It looked solid and disappeared in the morning. Now we've got to the Library that didn't look like it was here, and turned out to be solid after all."

"Just as long as the food is real," Carroway quipped. "I've learned to do without on this trip, but I'll always appreciate good food and a crowd with an ear for stories."

The aroma of fresh stew led them to the tower's kitchen and dining hall. Rows of tables and chairs filled the large chamber. Several of the brown-robed Keepers were busy fixing supper. Royster, bent over a large cauldron, looked up as Tris approached.

"We don't often get company for dinner. The soup should be ready, and there's bread and cheese enough." Royster looked to the side in irritation. "Hush. You're a ghost and ghosts don't eat, so what do you care?" he said to his unseen companion.

"I think that sounds wonderful," Tris admitted gratefully. "We've been living on trail meals."

"Bring your plates up, all of you," Royster called, beckoning to the others.

Royster seated himself across from Tris and Carroway. Carina and Kiara found seats with them, while Vahanian took his food to the other side of the table and Berry followed. Jae found a spot on the edge of the table, settled his leathery wings contentedly, and pulled at a piece of cheese. In turn, the travelers told their stories to the librarian. When they finished, Royster nodded.

"If the knowledge you seek exists anywhere, then you will find it here," he said. "That is why the Sisterhood took such care to hide this Library. In the right hands, the knowledge stored here can do great things." He paused. "After the Mage War, the Sisterhood could not bring themselves to destroy the Library, so they hid it, so that its secrets might not be abused." He looked

around, as if imagining the dark building
bustling with students.

"Only the most senior and trusted of the Sisters
have access," Royster explained. "That pendant
is not given lightly. There have only been a few
outside the Sisterhood who are so honored, and
as for the Sisters," he continued, "they most
often come by transport spell." At that, Kiara
shivered.

"No thanks," she said, setting down her drink.
"The Sister who sent me on my journey used a
spell like that to take me from one place to
another. It was… unnerving."

Royster smiled indulgently. "It does take some
getting used to. Fortunately, the Sisters come to
us, so we Keepers have no need to travel." He
finished his food and mopped up the last drops
with a sop of bread. "Vayash moru who are long
known to the Sisterhood bring us provisions and
news of the outside," he continued. "Some of
them have studied at the Library for hundreds of
years. Their loyalty to the Lady is absolute." He
paused. "I have been told to expect the Sisters.
They will sense your coming. I believe you will
have the first of many tutors, my lord Summoner,
come morning light."

"Aren't the Sisters taking a chance leaving you
here?" Vahanian said, leaning back. "I mean,
you've got all the time in the world. What's to
keep you from being the next Obsidian King?"

Royster chuckled. "I imagine the good Sisters
had that very thought." He jumped as if poked
and glared to his right. "Yes, of course I was

going to get to that," he scowled. "Be quiet." He looked back to Tris and the others. "I believe, in this case, I was chosen as much for what I'm not as what I am. And I am not a mage."

Vahanian looked skeptically at Royster. "Let me get this straight. We've come all the way so that Tris can be tutored in magic by a librarian?"

Royster chuckled. "Basically—yes."

"Maybe you'd like to take over the sword training, while you're at it?"

"Nope. But you're missing something."

"What's that?" Vahanian asked, annoyed.

"You could never be sure that mages weren't trying to gain power for themselves, with all this knowledge and lore. That is why the Sisterhood have permitted so few to enter. But me," he shrugged. "I can't take it, and I couldn't use it." His eyes narrowed, like a card player going for the big bet. "On the other hand, we've had a life-time among these books. We know them all. Each of us," he said, gesturing to include his silent companions, who filed in to take their own dinners, "has a specialty, an area of magic we have studied most of our lives. Healing," he said with a nod of his head to Carina, who looked up sharply, "battle magic," he said, catching Vahanian's eye, "spirit magic," he added, looking to Tris. "Just like your own walking, talking index. Memorized quite a bit, too."

Vahanian shook his head. "I don't understand. Why would you memorize what you can't use?"

Royster leaned forward and tapped the merce-nary on the forehead. "Knowledge. That's why."

"Because it's there," Vahanian mumbled, rolling his eyes.

"Exactly," Royster replied with a satisfied smile, sitting down with a thump. "And, for another reason. The good Sisters feared that the Library might one day be destroyed. My life's work has been memorizing the books as well as keeping them."

"But how did you get to be the librarian?" Berry piped up. "The Mage Wars happened a long time ago. You don't look that old."

Royster chuckled indulgently, then looked sharply at his side and scowled. "You be quiet," he snapped at the ghost. "She's a sweet thing and she didn't mean it that way. You old coot!" he retorted to his unseen tormentor. Smiling once more, he turned to Berry.

"Oh, I'm old all right, but not quite that old," he admitted gamely. "But you're right, the Mage Wars were a long time ago. Pity," he said, stopping to pick a particle of food out from between his teeth. "No decent chroniclers in the lot. Haven't got an account worth reading of the whole war."

He paused for a moment. "Ah, but you asked a question," he replied with a grin. "When I was five years old, Kessen came to my village. He gave a test to all the children. He told them a story and they had to repeat it. Of them all," he said with a hint of pride, "only I could say it word for word." He shrugged. "I was an orphan, so Kessen took me with him right then. I have lived in the Library since that day." He looked around at his robed companions. "So it was with each of us," he said. "Now, one of us journeys with a Sister to do the same. To be a Keeper is a calling of the Lady."

"Kessen... is the ghost that bothers you?" Berry asked.

Royster chuckled, then poked a finger at the air beside him. "Did you hear that?" he challenged. "She said 'bothers.' 'Bothers' you foggy old spirit! She's being polite, you know," he said, then smiled sweetly at Berry. "Yes, Kessen the ghost was Kessen, my teacher," he said.

"But why?" Berry asked.

"Why does he hang on here, looking to pester me day and night?" Royster said with overblown exasperation. "I'll tell you. Because I could never organize the bloody books quite to his liking. 'Royster,' he used to say, 'I'll see you get the knack of this if it takes to my dying day or beyond,'" Royster quoted, "and even by the time the old coot died, I still wasn't doing it up to his standards." He sniffed. "Serves me fine. I can find anything I need. But he's elected to plague me, anyway." He leaned forward as if to impart a secret, and Berry bent to hear him. "You know what?"

"What?" she whispered conspiratorially.

"I really don't mind. Gets a bit too quiet here, what with fifty years come and gone. But don't tell Kessen," he warned. "It'll go to his head."

Berry pantomimed sealing her lips. Royster patted her hand. "That's a good girl," he said.

As Royster talked, Tris closed his eyes, focusing on the ghostly librarian. He called the image to mind, envisioning its outline with increasing clarity. When he opened his eyes, Kessen's ghost was clearly visible.

"Look, there he is!" Berry gasped.

The librarian began to chuckle. "Serves you right, you old coot. Now you won't be able to sneak up on people." Royster paused and looked to Tris. "That's your doing, isn't it?"

Tris nodded. "And I'm afraid he can't stay that way," Tris replied. "It's hard to explain. I don't think he likes it. But he doesn't mind that we've met him," he added.

"Do as he bids," Royster agreed. "It's nice to see there's still someone there," he added wistfully. "It's been so long, sometimes I feared I was talking to myself."

Tris closed his eyes once more. Kessen's relief washed over him as the revenant vanished.

"You know all of these books?" Kiara asked, picking up the conversation once more. She looked unnerved, and Tris realized that it was the first time she had witnessed his magic beyond fire starting.

Royster nodded. "Every one." He chuckled. "I'm the index. After dinner, I will introduce you to the specialists."

"Do they talk?" Vahanian asked irreverently, washing down his bread with a mouthful of ale.

Royster laughed, and they could hear a murmur of amusement pass among the figures at the other tables. "Oh yes, we talk," he said. "But after so many years together, we often have little new to say to one another. Be careful what you wish for—now that we have guests, our curiosity might give us more questions than you want to answer!"

"Could you show us the healing guides?" Carina asked. "Especially about mage-sent illness? Oh, I'd like to see all the texts!" She looked at Kiara, her eyes shining. "What an opportunity!"

"I'll be glad to help Carina," Kiara put in, "but the Oracle sent me here to find a way to save Isencroft. I'm not sure what to ask you to look for," she confessed. "The servants of the Lady said I would find what I needed here."

Royster considered her request for a moment. "Perhaps a place to start is with the histories of Isencroft and the stories of her kings. You may find something to be of help."

"You wouldn't happen to have any histories, would you?" Carroway asked, looking up as he finished his dinner. "Some nice volumes set in interesting times?" He glanced at Tris with an apologetic shrug. "Not that you haven't given me enough to write songs about, but as Carina said, this is quite an opportunity."

Royster's eyes twinkled. "You're a bard?" At Carroway's nod, Royster grinned. "I've got histories you've never even heard, about warrior mages whose songs have been forgotten. Musical instruments, too," he said, and Carroway's eyes lit up. "You'll find that many of the Keepers are accomplished players and storytellers. We have much time to pass, and many winter evenings. You'll have your songs, bard, I promise."

"Can I come with you?" Berry asked excitedly. "I'd like to hear some of those stories." She looked at Royster. "Do any of them have princesses in them? I like stories about princesses. Especially ones that get into trouble and get rescued."

Royster smiled paternally and chuckled. "Aye, you'll find more than a few of those. I'll pick out the best for you myself... if you can read," he said, narrowing his eyes quizzically. At Berry's decisive nod, he brightened. "Good girl. That's rare for a girl." He turned to Vahanian. "How about you?"

Vahanian put up a hand, "I've seen all the magic I want to see for a while. Just give me a nice empty room and let me get the weapons ready. You wouldn't happen to have a salle here, and a blacksmith's shop, would you?" When Royster nodded, Vahanian smiled. "Well now, that's different. I'd like to have a look at that. I'd rather not train in the snow, and there's work to be done with the horses and weapons."

Royster turned to Tris. "You've been quiet, son. What can I find for you?"

"I'm not quite sure," he said. "If there are books about summoning and spirit mages, perhaps I can find out why the magic works and what I'm really doing." He grinned sheepishly. "It's been rather trial and error so far," he admitted. "I've had dreams, visions of my grandmother. She tells me that I will remember her training when the need is great," he said, spreading his hands with a shrug, "but I can't seem to remember any training." He paused, "And the Obsidian King," he went on, "if you have histories about him and about how my grandmother helped defeat him." He paused, longer this time, "We may have to face him again."

"At your service, my lord," Royster said, in all seriousness. "I suspect that perhaps for this need we have trained all our lives. I will find what you require." He gestured toward a gray-bearded man at the next table. "Devin is our Summoning expert. Maire," he said, and nodded to a white-haired woman, "knows all about the meaning of dreams and unlocking memories that do not wish to be found. And I," he said with a twinkle in his eye, "have always been partial to stories about the Obsidian King, so I shall work with you on that."

"Thank you," Tris replied.

"I take it these are the guests you were expecting?" A voice came from behind Tris, startling everyone but Royster. Tris turned to see a thin, dark-haired man who looked scarcely older than himself—until he met his eyes. Lifetimes, not a mere two decades, haunted those eyes, set within the pallor of a fine-featured face. The man held himself like a soldier, and his dark hair was close-cropped, as if for a helm.

Royster smiled. "Yes indeed. Mikhail, let me introduce Martris Drayke and his friends," he said, introducing each in turn. Royster looked back to Tris. "This is Mikhail, from King Harrol's court."

Mikhail made a courtly bow. "I am honored," the vayash moru said. "King Harrol sent me to Westmarch since Dhasson's borders are—difficult— for mortals to pass."

"We've noticed," Vahanian muttered.

"I was sent to learn how to dispel the beasts that plague Dhasson," Mikhail went on. "The king also asked that I watch for you, should the fates bring you to Westmarch. I will be pleased to report success in both matters."

"You've found a solution to the beasts?" Tris asked.

Mikhail shook his head. "Unfortunately, all evidence points to the work of one mage—Foor Arontala. Whether he created the beasts I cannot tell, but it appears certain that he called them. Until he is destroyed—or you are dead—they will not disperse."

"Gabriel warned us that the border was spelled against my crossing," Tris said. "Otherwise, we would have headed for Valiquet. Did Harrol have any other news?"

Mikhail withdrew a pouch from his pocket and handed it to Tris. Inside was a letter, and a seal. Tris scanned the letter, then looked up. "He pledges what military assistance Dhasson can provide, given the siege of the beasts. And he's given me his seal as a bond to his exchequer, to help us raise an army—and pay our debts," he said with a glance toward Vahanian, who shrugged.

"King Harrol expected, I am sure, that what I found here would confirm his suspicions. He believes that to defeat the beasts, the power of the beasts' sender must be broken," said Mikhail. "It makes Margolan's troubles Dhasson's business, until the mage Arontala is destroyed."

"Good luck," Vahanian muttered darkly.

"Now can we get the stories?" Berry interrupted. They chuckled as they rose from the table. As they were about to leave, a cool breeze blew past them and the crockery rose, piece by piece, suspended in midair.

"Kessen," Royster sighed. "It bothers him to no end if I don't tidy the table the minute I'm through." He planted his hands on his hips. "Leave the dishes!" he shouted at the empty room. "Fifty years, you've done the dishes. The grandson of Bava K'aa comes for training, and all you can think of are dishes!" With a gesture of dismissal, he turned and motioned the others to follow. Behind them, the dishes crashed to the floor.

"He always had a bad temper," Royster muttered without a backward glance at the pile of broken crockery.

CHAPTER TWENTY-SIX

WHEN THEY AROSE the next morning, a brown-robed visitor awaited them. A spare-framed, tall woman with close-cropped white hair and piercing blue eyes stood in the main hallway. She took a few steps to stand in front of Tris, and looked at him as if she were taking his measure and weighing his soul.

"You are Martris Drayke?"

"I am."

"What do you seek here, son of Bricen?"

Tris held her gaze unwaveringly. "To understand my power and control it. I have to find a way to defeat Arontala and unseat Jared."

The sister looked at him appraisingly. "Very well. Our time is short, and the quest is great. At the coming of the Hawthorn Moon, Arontala will attempt strong magic—blood magic—to free the soul of the Obsidian King. If he succeeds, we will see conflict and darkness greater than in the time of the Great War."

"Can't the Sisterhood stop him?" Tris asked. "I mean, you are experienced mages—"

"Only a Summoner can stop him." She met Tris's eyes. "And you are the only Summoner in the Winter Kingdoms." She paused.

"Teach me," Tris said levelly. "We came here to find out how to overturn the darkness, in Margolan, Isencroft and Dhasson."

"It is the same darkness, and the same quest," she said. "Your paths are woven together by the hand of the Lady. I have come to be the first of your teachers. I am Sister Taru."

Tris began his lessons with Sister Taru and Maire right after breakfast. As Vahanian headed for the salle, and Carina, Kiara and Carroway—with Berry at his heels—paired up with keepers and headed into the depths of the Library, Taru guided Tris to a sparsely furnished study. Maire lit a fire and set a pot of tea to boil. Finally, Taru motioned Tris to sit. She and Maire sat down to face him.

"So you are the grandson of Bava K'aa," Taru said. "My Sisters believe you are her mage heir. What say you?"

Tris met her gaze. "I have always been able to speak to spirits, call them, see them—even when others couldn't. Not just on Haunts. I remember some lessons with grandmother, when I was young. Simple pathworkings, warding spells, household magic. But since the murders," he said, and his voice caught. "Since the murders," he repeated, willing his voice to hold, "I feel power I've never felt before—in me and around me. Sometimes, like with the slavers, it flows through me, past what I can control." Taru and Maire listened as Tris recounted the story of their journey, the ghosts he had encountered and those he freed, and finally, the spirits of the Ruune Vidaya.

When he ended his tale, Taru and Maire exchanged glances. "In the years since Bava K'aa died," Taru began quietly, "mages have been sent to the Ruune Vidaya to quiet the spirits. None succeeded and none returned. Yet you have lived to tell the tale, you, barely twenty summers old, a fledgling mage, and you have bent the forests' spirits to your cause, bargained for the safety of your friends, and then given them their rest!"

Tris flushed and looked down. "I know it sounds hard to believe."

"Except that we have confirmed it," Taru said evenly. "The Ruune Vidaya is no longer haunted. I believe that any mage of power could feel the wrenching of the currents that night. I felt it myself, although I did not know the cause. Wild magic, barely still within the Light," she said, fixing Tris with her stare.

"I felt pretty awful for quite a while," Tris admitted sheepishly. "If you could, please, teach me how to stop passing out every time I do a large working. I can't fight Arontala if I keep doing that."

A faint smile came to Taru's lips. "Trained mages have died amidst that kind of storm," she said. "Yet you did not."

"Help me," Tris said. "I'm acting on instinct, and it isn't enough. If Carina and Alyzza hadn't shown me how to shield back at the caravan, I'd be mad from the spirits by now. That night, in the forest, the shields almost didn't hold. I thought—" he started, and then stopped, afraid to put into words something he only felt. "I thought," he started again, "that I might lose my soul there. It felt as if... I was being pulled to pieces—by the power, and the spirits."

Taru was watching him closely. "Your instincts are correct," she said. "You were closer to death—and your soul's destruction—than you may realize. An untrained mage could not have managed what you did. That is not instinct," she said, leaning forward, "and that is not talent. That must be training, deep training, that someone wanted you to forget."

"Look at me, Tris," Maire said, and Tris shifted in his chair. From the folds of her cloak, Maire withdrew a crystal carving of the Lady with her quatrain icons. "I want you to focus on this," Maire said, her voice soothing. "We're going to do a pathworking, and I'm going to take you deep into your memories. It will be as real to you as when it occurred. The way may not be easy."

"I'm ready," Tris said.

Taru set a warding around them. Then, within the warded circle, she set another warding, this one separating Tris from herself and Maire. "I cannot gauge your reaction or your control," the Sister said. "This is for your protection as well as our own."

"I understand."

Maire set the focus icon on the table in front of him. "When do you remember first working with your grandmother?"

Tris thought for a moment. "Grandmother always let me follow along with her. She taught me to call handfire the same summer I started my schooling. I was five or six," he recalled. "I don't think I helped with her pathworkings until I was eight or nine."

Taru nodded. "That is the age when a child with promise would begin serious lessons. Take him back to his tenth year," she instructed Maire. "And let's see what he knew."

Maire met his eyes. "Focus on the icon, Tris," she said, "and listen to my voice. Fix the icon in your mind. Memorize it. Make your picture detailed, as if you have it in your hands. Weigh it. Feel its texture, how cool it is to the touch, how smooth. See how it shines. Smell the incense that clings to it. Taste the incense in your mouth. Once it is real, hold that image. Hold it. Now, make it disappear. Hold the emptiness. Hear nothing but my voice. Hold the empty space. Close your eyes. Breathe deeply. Again. You are present in that empty space. You are ten summers old, with your grandmother in her study. What do you see?"

Tris opened his eyes, and looked around him at Bava K'aa's rooms in Shekerishet. The familiar smell of her candles mingled with the scent of wood smoke and incense. Summer sun streamed through the mullioned windows, casting a parquet of shadows on the floor. On the table lay the instruments of a pathworking—a bit of parchment, her athame, a candle, some herbs. Near him, his grandmother bustled about, moving between the table and the fire, where a small pot simmered on the hearth. He could feel the energy of her warding, creating a sense of safety around the perimeter of the braided rug she used as her workspace. Tris heard himself describe these things aloud, as if in a dream, separate enough from himself that he did not wonder at it.

"What do you know of magic, Martris Drayke?" he heard a distant voice ask. Bava K'aa continued her work, as if the voice spoke to him alone. Here within the warding, he did not fear the voice.

"I have completed the first level of wardings, and the second level of workings," he replied, his voice thinner and cracking on some words, in the way of a youth on the verge of manhood. "I'm not permitted an athame yet. I can summon the spirits and dispel them. I have watched grandmother bless their passing over, joined her in the spirit plains, to feel how it is done. We practice many hours each day."

"Good, very good," the voice soothed. Now close your eyes. A year has passed. You are eleven. What do you know now, Martris Drayke?"

The boy looked around himself at the familiar workroom, at the goblets and half-burnt candles, at the worn mortar and pestle, at the vials and boxes. "Grandmother says we must hurry," he replied. "Sometimes, Carroway helps us. I have set wardings, and used her scrying ball. We have gone to the crypts and summoned the spirits of my fathers, and once, we turned a demon." The boy shuddered. "It came in the guise of a spirit, begging a favor. It asked for harm to fall on the living, which is not permitted. I refused, and it showed its true nature. I fought it and turned it without her help, but only barely. I was sick for three days and mother was afraid I'd taken a fever." He paused. "We are at the third level of wardings and the fourth level of workings."

"You are a clever boy," the voice responded. "Now, close your eyes once more. It is the summer before your fostering. You are fourteen. What of your mage studies now?"

The boy's voice was deeper, no longer a child's. "I have walked among the vayash moru and I can work fifth-level pathworkings. I have helped grandmother with battle scryings, and I have called spirits. I have intervened between the living and the dead, and made the passing for those who wish to seek the Lady. Grandmother is worried."

"Why?"

"Because I go to my fostering, and she has not finished my training. We work dawn to dusk. I am tired. She has gotten mother to postpone the fostering twice, and without explaining the true reason—she cannot sway father again. She says I must not show my powers, not even to mother. But she is also anxious to send me away."

"Why?"

The boy paused. "She is afraid for me. She fears Jared will harm me."

"Tris," a voice called. "Come back. Breathe."

Just as quickly, the scene left him. This time, the memories remained—of Bava K'aa and of the workings.

Maire and Taru were watching him with concern. Maire fetched Tris a warm cup of tea, which he accepted with shaking hands.

"If I knew how to work magic then," Tris asked, his voice unsteady but once again his own, "why didn't I use it against Jared? Lady and Whore, if I could have used magic, why didn't I?"

Taru considered for a moment while he struggled to steady his nerves. "I believe your grandmother knew of your situation, and did what she could to arrange the 'fortuitous accidents' that intervened on your behalf. But Bricen would not hear her about Jared. To protect you, your grandmother buried the memories of your training deeply. Tell me, what specifics did you remember, of all the time you spent with her, before this working?"

Tris thought hard. "Just that she wanted me around, and I was happy to be there." He frowned. "I know that it kept me busy, but before this, I couldn't have told you how."

Maire nodded. "I suspect that even before Jared brought Arontala to Shekerishet, he was coming under Arontala's influence. Bava K'aa would have sensed that. She must have known that if Jared—and Arontala—suspected that you bore any magepower, they would have killed you." She paused. "Perhaps, she also knew that her own time was growing short. She could not protect you for much longer—at least, not as a living mage. Hiding your training was her best hope of preparing you to protect Margolan someday."

"Then why did I begin to use my power after the murders?"

"Sometimes, those with magegift do not know their power until there is a great shock, a fear so deep and so complete that it opens all channels and frees whatever blocked the flow of power," Taru said slowly. "I do not know what trigger your grandmother intended," she added. "Perhaps your power would have come at a certain age or in a certain place. But the grief and fear and anger you felt the night of the murders were strong enough for you to use the most primal instinct to survive." She paused. "For you, that meant triggering your gift."

She sat back and looked at Tris. "What do you remember now?"

Tris thought for a moment, and stared at the tea in his cup. "A lot," he said quietly. "It's like someone opened a door to a room in my mind that I never knew was there before."

Taru nodded. "Your grandmother pushed you hard. By your account, you reached the level of a fifth-year student. It is a solid beginning."

"But Arontala is a full sorcerer!" Tris protested. "And the Obsidian King the greatest mage of his time. How can I hope to defeat them?"

Taru considered carefully. "With mastery comes arrogance. It is in your favor if they underestimate the strength of your power. Your gift is very great," she said, "but I am not yet sure you can control it. Which means that it might be wrested from you and used against you, or—"

"Or?" Tris countered. "That's not bad enough?"

"Or it may take over, as it did in the forest, blasting through a channel that cannot contain it, destroying both you and everything around you." She paused. "First, we must prepare you to win back the sword of your grandmother from the spirit of King Argus who guards it, here in the catacombs below the Library. For good reason have you come to Westmarch."

"I don't understand," Tris said. Who is King Argus? And why must I win his sword to defeat the Obsidian King?"

Taru and Maire exchanged glances. "King Argus was the king of Principality during the Mage Wars. He fought beside your grandmother against the Obsidian King."

"He was a friend of my grandmother's?"

Taru frowned. "An ally, it might be more truthful to say. Argus's first and only allegiance was to Principality. He could be a ruthless enemy. He kept his own counsel, and fully trusted no one, except perhaps Bava K'aa. But one thing was unquestionable—Argus was the sworn enemy of the Obsidian King. Truly sworn, because in the last, darkest days of the Mage Wars, when all seemed lost, Argus swore Istra's Bargain to offer his life for that of the Obsidian King. The Lady granted his oath. And it was the sword Mageslayer, ensorcelled at its forging with great power, that Argus and Bava K'aa wielded to strike the deathblow to the Obsidian King." She paused.

"Even were you a fully trained mage, there are some among the Council who do not think you could succeed without Mageslayer. Therefore, we must risk retrieving it."

"Risk?"

Taru met his eyes levelly. "So great was Mageslayer's reputation—and perhaps, its power—that Bava K'aa and Argus determined it must be guarded. Some argued that it should be destroyed, but perhaps Bava K'aa feared that we might one day face another threat. So Argus, who was himself a Summoner—though lesser in power than Bava K'aa—agreed to stand watch over Mageslayer, in a crypt below this building." She took a deep breath. "None may retrieve the sword, except it be won in combat. Many have tried. None have returned. To fail means joining Argus on his watch. Argus's spirit is bound here by strong magic, because he fell not a day's ride from these walls, at the foot of Gibbet Bridge."

"We've only got until the Hawthorn Moon."

Taru shook her head. "Less than that. You must reach Principality City before the snows set in, when the best armies are to be bought. And we are still too close to the Margolan border for you to stay here."

"Could Jared really reach us here in the Library? Isn't it spelled?"

Taru nodded. "You are safe from his armies within these walls. But we cannot allow him to cut you off from Principality City, and every day that passes makes that possibility greater. Our time is short."

CHAPTER TWENTY-SEVEN

KIARA WAS THE first to reach the salle the next morning. Morning light was just beginning to fill the large room. Jae found a perch on one of the equipment racks. Kiara began to stretch, slowly at first, then with long strides and high kicks.

It feels good to do something familiar, she thought. She whirled and arched into first-level kada, then on through the progression, each level growing increasingly more complex and potentially more lethal. She saw Vahanian standing silently along one wall, watching.

"You're good," he said sincerely. "Want to try that with a real opponent?"

"Swords or small blades only?"

Vahanian raised an eyebrow as if he had not expected such a challenge. "Small blades, if you think you're up to it. Street rules."

"You're on," she said. Taking a fighting knife in each hand, she straightened and faced Vahanian as the rising sun beyond the windows cast a game board of light and shadow on the wooden salle floor. They circled warily. She watched Vahanian's footwork and the way he held himself. Eastmark trained, she thought, like Derry, and mother. This should be good.

Kiara lunged first, and Vahanian parried, catching her blade on his own and pushing her back. He wheeled, coming close with his blade, but she bent away from him, gracefully eluding his thrust and using the momentum to come up behind him, scoring a nick to his shoulder. "Quit it!" she snapped as he circled.

"Quit what?"

"Quit taking it easy on me."

In response, Vahanian lunged, and this time, his blade sliced the cloth on her sleeve, raising a small cut. Jae screeched from his perch but did not intervene as the two circled and parried. The scrape and clang of their steel blades echoed in the empty salle as they exchanged blows and Kiara sensed the change in Vahanian's manner, the force of his strikes, which told her he judged her worthy of an all-out press.

He swung into a high Eastmark kick. She blocked him, although the force nearly knocked the air from her. It was worth it, she thought, to see the surprise on his face. She used the momentum of his strike to wheel into a kick of her own, and grazed his ear with her boot. At that, she saw the glint in his eye that said the fight was on. She was barely aware of the others who made their way into the salle, watching the combat silently from along the walls. Vahanian kicked again and she caught his leg, using his momentum against him. He went down, but scythed his legs to take her with him. In a heartbeat, the point of his knife was at her throat.

"Yield?"

She saw it register in his eyes as her own knife came up below his breastbone. "Draw."

A grudging smile hinted at the corner of his lips, and he helped her to her feet. Both looked a little chagrined at the applause that greeted them from Tris and the others, who awaited their morning training.

Vahanian leaned forward with his hands on his thighs to catch his breath, and Kiara noted with satisfaction that he was sweating. "You're good," the mercenary acknowledged. "Damn good. Where'd you learn that?"

Winded, Kiara used her forearm to clear a stray lock of hair from her face and realized she was bleeding. "My armsmaster came from Eastmark. He left there during the Troubles. My mother was also Eastmark born and raised. In Isencroft, two years of military service is required of everyone—even the king's own."

Vahanian noted the shallow cut on her forearm and went to fetch a strip of cloth and a bit of salve. The cut she had scored on him was bleeding through his shirt, but he did not seem to notice. "I imagine you can get Carina to heal that if you want," he said, with a cynical smile. "You likely won't get the lecture that comes with the healing I get."

The others crowded around them with appreciative comments, until Vahanian raised a hand for silence.

"Now that we've got a salle and not some Goddess-forsaken clearing in the woods," he said, "it's time to get down to real training. We'll also train with a bow and crossbow. It might not be a bad thing for our bard there," he said with a nod to Carroway, "to enlighten us about throwing knives. I'll keep working you on swords. And since there's been interest in footwork," he said, with a glance toward Kiara, "perhaps Kiara would help me work with anyone who thinks he's up to it." He straightened his tunic. "To fit that in means double practices," he said and Kiara chuckled at the reaction. "If you're going to start a war, you're going to need all the practice you can get."

A candlemark later, Kiara dipped a cup from the bucket by the window when Tris approached. "I'm impressed," he said. She searched his expression for any hint of sarcasm and found none. To her chagrin, she could feel the color rise in her face.

"Thanks," she murmured. "I guess that's one of the good things about my Journey," she said, meeting his eyes and looking away. "I can actually use my training out here. There wasn't much call for it with the ladies at court."

"The ladies at court are overrated," Tris replied evenly. "At least, I always thought so."

Kiara turned to look at him. His eyes were absolutely serious, and she saw nothing in his manner to suggest that he felt any distaste for her skill. She offered him the water cup. "I thought I was the only one who didn't care for court."

"If you two are done at the water barrel—" Vahanian interrupted, calling them back to the group. Tris flashed a mischievous grin and sauntered back to the group, and she followed a step behind, lost in thought.

AFTER ARMS PRACTICE, Tris found Sister Taru waiting for him. With her was Keeper Devin, a man of middle years with a close-shaved tonsure of white hair and a salt-and-pepper beard. His dark brown eyes were uncomfortably perceptive, and he had a swarthy complexion that suggested blood-lines from Nargi or Trevath. Tris followed them to a study room and was grateful to see a mid-morning snack of bread, cheese and dried fruit set out on a table. Taru handed him a warm cup of tea from a kettle on the hearth. The fire barely drove back the autumn chill.

"I have shared with Devin what we learned yesterday," Taru said. "He has many questions for you."

Tris took a seat near the hearth. "I want to understand this... gift. And I'd like to stop being knocked flat on my back every time I do a major working."

Devin chuckled. "Such is the price of magic, I fear. But with practice and skill come resilience. Now, tell me about the spirits of Shekerishet and your experiences on the journey north."

It took a candlemark for Tris to answer Devin. The Keeper made him go back over the encounters with the spirits on the way from Margolan, quizzing him on how it felt when he used his power, and what—specifically—he did in each situation. Devin was most interested in the encounter with the evil spirit who possessed Carina and with the spirits of the Ruune Videya. Finally, when Tris could tell him no more, Devin closed his eyes.

After a moment, he looked at Taru. "He is indeed the heir of Bava K'aa. A spirit mage with less power would not have survived these tests."

"It was a little too touch-and-go," Tris replied. "Even now, I can feel the spirits out there, the ones who want intercession, or justice, or simply the freedom to pass over. How can I keep them from driving me mad?"

Devin considered in silence for a moment. "That is one of the burdens of a Summoner," Devin said finally. "You are the mediator between the living and the dead. When your power becomes known, the living will seek you out as well, hoping to receive final blessing— or pardon—from the dead, wishing to calm angry spirits or cast out evil spirits. To be Lord of the Dead and Undead is not a ceremonial title. It holds all of the responsibilities, in the shadow realm, that a living king bears in the day realm. It is necessary to bring the realms into balance."

"If it's so important, why are there so few spirit mages?"

"Mages are made at the choosing of the Lady," Taru replied. "Perhaps there are times when Summoners are more common. In our time, Land and Water magic is the most common gift, and to our good fortune, less so Fire."

"Arontala is a Fireclan mage," Tris murmured.

"Arontala aspires to become a Summoner," Devin replied. "He believes that when he frees the Obsidian King, in return for permitting the spirit to use his body, he will also gain the mage gifts of that spirit. Those gifts together would bring ruin."

Taru nodded. "We can help you gain the stamina you need for strong magic. You will have to work hard for it."

"I'm ready."

"I will bring you the texts of the spirit mages," Devin promised. "Two of the Obsidian King's journals are here at the library. The third has been missing for many years. It is wise to know one's adversary."

"Spirit magic is the rarest of the gifts," Devin continued, "and the most dangerous. Only the spirit mage, the necromancer, may blur the line between life and death. It is the province of the Goddess herself. Only a few in a generation receive the gift, yet without an intercessor between the living and the dead, we are not complete. Many of the great spirit mages were destroyed because the temptation of their gift is the strongest."

"Like moths to light," Taru said, "your power draws the dead and the undead. Most pass without need for a mediator into the realm of the Lady. But those who are bound by guilt—their own or that of the living—those whose purpose is unfinished, and those who do not have their vengeance, remain. Those are the souls that seek you out, some for honest reasons, and some less so."

"Many mysteries of the spirit mages died with Bava K'aa and the Obsidian King," she said. "You must never assume the intentions of spirits are as they seem."

"I don't understand."

Taru shrugged. "Spirits see much more than the living can imagine. They have a way of ferreting out the weaknesses of the living to use against them."

Tris shut his eyes. The image of Kait from the dream came unbidden. "I would give everything I have to save my sister's spirit," he whispered.

"Then you are already lost," Devin replied. "For what harm can you do to Arontala, who holds her spirit?" Tris said nothing, staring at the shadows. "To defeat Arontala, you must be willing to give up what you hold dearest," Devin pressed. "Your companions, your sister's spirit, those you love most. Your grandmother could not," Devin said sadly, "and that is why the Obsidian King may rise to threaten us again."

"But why would she hold back against such evil?"

"The Obsidian King was not always evil," Taru replied. "Once, he was a good man. Some say he became impatient with the ways of the Lady and bitter about the randomness of fate. Bava K'aa believed that he was possessed by an ancient and evil spirit. He began to take the course of life and death into his own hands, to punish and forgive. He took on the role of a god," Taru said. "And the power seduced his soul."

"But if grandmother knew him, why didn't she stop him?" Tris asked.

Taru shook her head. "Many were the times she tried. You see, before she was a sorceress, or he a wizard, they were in love. But she saw the bitterness growing in him and the longing for power. She was the last to truly believe that he was evil, and her loyalty nearly cost this realm its freedom," she continued. "She and your grandfather, once the Obsidian King's dearest friends, were forced to bind him," she said sadly. "Even so, she could not bring herself to completely destroy him."

"Your way is perilous," Taru went on. "Never may you bind a soul that wishes to be free. Never may you reanimate a corpse. And never may you bend a spirit to do your will. Never, even when to do so might seem to serve the greatest good," she cautioned. "Heed well, or we are lost."

"I will help you defend yourself better in the ways of magic," Sister Taru continued. "It will soon be time to journey to Principality City, where there is a citadel of the Sisterhood. You can continue your training there."

Tris met her eyes, knowing that she understood what was at stake. "I will do whatever it takes to free Margolan," he vowed.

"I believe you will, Martris Drayke. Let us pray to the Lady it is enough."

CHAPTER TWENTY-EIGHT

INSIDE THE THICK stone walls of the Library there was no sense of time. Engrossed in their separate studies, armed with parchment, ink and quills, the travelers had to be reminded, usually by Berry, of the passing hours and approaching meal times.

Vahanian spent his days in the salle. He found the promised blacksmith's quarters behind the Library, and fired it up to fix their weapons. Mending armor and saddles, re-shoeing the horses, exercising their mounts and keeping the weapons honed kept him busy as the late autumn days grew shorter. The others would not have ventured outside the Library at all had Vahanian not insisted that sword practice be augmented with archery lessons. When the first practice of the day had ended, the researchers disappeared into the Library until it was time for the evening practice session. Vahanian seemed content to fade into the background.

After morning arms practice, Tris headed for training with Taru, Devin and Maire. After evening sword training and supper, Tris plunged into the dusty volumes assigned to him for his studies. He found a quiet chair in the Library and settled in with a sack of cheese and bread. Yet for all his reading, not one mention of a "Soulcatcher" came to light.

Tris also noticed that Kiara kept her distance from him. She remained close to Carina, giving him no chance to inquire as to the sudden shift from her friendliness on the road. Tris found that the absence of her conversation bothered him more than he expected, and he resolved to find an opportunity to question her.

That chance came sooner than he expected. As he readied himself for sword practice in the first light, Tris stepped outside the Library to get a breath of fresh air. The cold, crisp morning air snapped him awake—a welcome change from the mustiness of the old leather volumes and the dusty Library.

In the garden, he saw Kiara. She sat alone on a small bench, wrapped in her cloak and deep in thought.

"Hello."

"Oh! Hello, Tris," Kiara replied. "I didn't hear you coming."

"Has Carina found a way to strengthen your father?" Tris asked, taking a seat at the other end of her bench.

Kiara shook her hair, her auburn braid coming loose from her hood and spilling down her shoulder. "I don't think so. Not yet." She looked away.

"Carroway tells me you've been looking for other ways to help your kingdom."

Kiara brushed back a lock of hair. "Things haven't been good for Isencroft for a long time," she said quietly. "If we can't turn the situation soon, Isencroft will not survive."

"Mikhail means to ask my uncle's advisors for whatever help they can provide," Tris said, and she looked up at him. "I can't even promise that I'll live to take the throne, but if I do, Margolan will pose you no threat."

He saw tears start in her eyes, and she looked away. "Thank you," she said softly.

"I've missed talking to you," Tris said after a pause.

"I've had so much on my mind."

"I don't think that's it," Tris said gently. "Did I say something to offend you?"

"No, not at all."

"Then what's wrong?"

Kiara looked down at her hands, silent for so long that Tris feared she was not going to speak. "Do you remember what I told you when we met?" she said finally. "About why I left Isencroft?"

Tris nodded. "For your Journey."

"And something else," she added.

Tris paused. "You were avoiding an arranged marriage."

"Did you ever wonder with whom?"

Oh yes, Tris thought. Many times. It surprised him just how much he enjoyed Kiara's company. In Margolan, Tris had his choice of companions. He found that few could converse on anything of interest and fewer still could carry an interesting conversation more than once. Bored with the available company, and sickened by Jared's indiscretions, Tris had kept to himself, much to the consternation of ambitious fathers at court. Kiara was different. Her retreat bothered him more than he expected.

"What does it matter?" Tris asked. "You're not in Isencroft."

"I have to go back," she said softly.

"Do you love him?"

"No!" she protested. "And I never could."

"Is your father the sort to force you into a marriage you don't want?"

Kiara shook her head. "Father won't. But circumstances may. If father dies, we will be vulnerable. Another poor harvest, and I won't have a choice. I'll have to make the alliance, just to keep the people fed."

"Is he a stranger, or truly a bad man?" Tris asked gently. The dim light set Kiara's face in shadows. Even the heavy cloak could not completely hide the strength of her shoulders, the fitness of her body. Her independence intrigued him, as had her skill with a sword. He was acutely aware that this journey was no place to form an attraction, that he stood little chance of living through his quest. But denying that attraction would also be futile, Tris thought, although the best he might hope for would be her friendship.

Kiara looked at him for a moment before speaking, and he could see the conflict in her eyes. "I'm betrothed to Jared Drayke of Margolan."

Tris felt the force of the words like a physical blow. "No."

Kiara looked away. "It was an old pact, made long ago. Father wanted more security for Isencroft, and he liked and trusted your father. It seemed logical to unite our kingdoms and so they made a pact that I should wed the heir to Margolan's throne."

"You can't marry Jared," Tris protested. "He'll never honor the pact. He'll tear Isencroft apart to feed Margolan and leave the rest for bandits." But the image that came to his mind was not about kings and treaties. The image was of Jared, the night of the coup, and of the rape Tris interrupted. And when his mind supplied Kiara's face in place of the terrified servant girl's, his blood felt turned to ice.

"Don't you think I know that?" Kiara cried. "I've already eluded his ambassador twice. And if I had any doubts, I don't any more. Not after riding through Margolan."

"Tell me, please. What did you see?"

Kiara recounted the tales of the refugees and her flight from the border guards. Tris felt his anger rise as she described ruined villages, murders and rampaging guards. They sat in silence when Kiara finished, the weight of the matter between them.

Finally, Tris spoke. "You know that I'm going to have to kill him."

"I know."

Tris reached out to take her hand. "Listen to me," he said. "If I live to rule Margolan, I swear to you that nothing will ever be required of Isencroft by force. You have my word."

"Thank you," she said, so quietly that the words were nearly lost on the wind. She squeezed his hand before she pulled away. "You can't imagine how much that means."

They were silent for a few moments. "Where will you go, when it's time to leave here?" she asked.

Tris looked away, to the cold horizon where the first light of dawn was fading. "First, to Principality City. Uncle Harrol's accounts are there. We'll need them to pay Vahanian. And then there's Berry. I was hoping Carina could find a safe place with the healers for her.

"Then, we raise an army and plan the assault on Jared," Tris continued quietly.

"You'll have to kill Jared's mage first, won't you?"

"I don't know if I can," Tris admitted. "But I swore to the Lady on the souls of my family that I would do it, and I will."

Kiara's smile was bittersweet. "Then you'll find a way."

"Quite an errand for a prince who never wanted to be king, don't you think?" Tris mused aloud. "I guess they're right when they say the Lady chooses our path."

"She does," Kiara agreed, and told him of her vision on the battlefield. "Ever since then," she admitted quietly, her breath freezing in the chill air, "I've known that there was something She meant for me to do." She shrugged. "Only I still don't know what it is," she admitted. "Maybe that's why She gave me the Journey."

Footsteps on the dry leaves startled them both and they turned to see Vahanian. "There you are," he said, planting his hands on his hips like a schoolmaster. "They've turned the Library upside down looking for the two of you. It's practice time."

When practice had finished, Tris headed back, anxious to resume his studies. His aching muscles told him that Vahanian had put him through a particularly grueling session. Inside, the smell of stew and baking bread greeted them—testimony that Royster was already at work on supper. He took a platter of bread, fruit, dried meat and cheese with him, along with a pitcher of water, and headed up the stairs to the tower for his lessons with Devin and Taru. They were still at work when Berry scampered up hours later, to remind him of evening arms practice and dinner.

By the time Tris and the others had finished their work in the salle with Vahanian, Royster and the others were already gathered in the dining hall. The group became accustomed to unseen hands setting the table for dinner as Kessen helped with meals. Royster kept up a one-sided banter with Kessen's ghost the whole way through the meal, ending in the shattering of a goblet when one of Royster's barbed comments annoyed the spirit beyond restraint.

"I wish I could see Kessen all the time," Berry said, reaching for another piece of the warm bread. "I haven't met any ghosts at all, other than the nasty-ones with the slavers." She bit off a large piece of bread and chewed it hungrily.

"Royster," Mikhail said, "are there any books I haven't found yet about the beasts?" He paused. "Short of burning down the world, there seems to be nothing about how to turn them."

Royster drained the last of the ale from his mug. "Well," he said, licking his lips, "the only way to get rid of them is to destroy the mage who sent them." The old librarian looked thoughtful. "The last time, ten years ago, it was the same way."

"Ten years ago?" Vahanian asked, leaning forward with sudden interest. "Where?"

Royster pulled at his beard in thought. "Up north, along the border between Isencroft and Margolan, just below the great sea. Terrible things got loose up there."

"What do you know about it?" Vahanian pressed.

Royster paused again, staring at the ceiling as he thought. "Haven't thought about that in years," he mused. "I lose track of things a bit here in the Library." He frowned, thinking. "Ah, yes," he said, brightening. "There was a dark mage who called himself Lustari, 'the fearsome one,'" he recounted. "He raised the beasts to keep his rivals at bay. They did some awful damage until he was destroyed."

"By the Sisters?" Vahanian asked intently.

Royster shook his head. "No, no that was the odd thing about it," he remembered. "Fallon said that the Sisters hadn't found a way to destroy him. But someone did," Royster said, nodding. "I guess he underestimated one of his rivals."

"Royster, have you ever seen this?" Tris asked, sliding his hand across the table toward the old librarian. When he lifted his palm, the dull metal talisman lay before the librarian.

"Why did you bring that cursed thing with us?" Vahanian demanded.

"A madman gave it to me in a burned-out village," Tris said to Royster. He told the story while Vahanian listened, white knuckled and tight-lipped.

"That thing calls those monsters," Vahanian said in a rough voice. "You should have left it with the madman."

Tris shook his head. "It turned the things, not called them." He paused and glanced from Mikhail to Royster. "But would it have been powerful enough to get me across the Dhasson border?"

"Nothing turns those things," Vahanian retorted. "Nothing but fire."

"Tris is right, Jonmarc," Royster replied quietly. "Here. Let me show you." The white-haired man sprang up from his seat, disappearing into the stacks to emerge a few minutes later with a dusty, leather-bound tome. "Look here," he said, as they gathered around him. His gnarled finger moved down page after page of yellowed parchment, along lines of carefully inscribed manuscript in a language Tris did not recognize.

"It's an old Eastmark book," Royster said, answering their unspoken question, "from before the days of the Obsidian King. It details the rise and fall of a dark mage, and all of the damage he inflicted. But look here," he said, his finger pointing to an illustration. He slid the metal talisman over the page until it lay over the drawing—a perfect match.

"See," he said, and began to read from the text, interpreting as he went.

"'But in the days of the final battle,'" he read, "'the mage fashioned a metal working with the power to protect its wearer against beasts born of magic. The king took the talisman, and none of the beasts harmed him. The king smote the beasts with fire, and they were destroyed.'" He looked up. "There you have it," he said with a shrug. "Doesn't call them. Protects the wearer. Handy thing." He thought for a moment. "As for getting across the border—I don't know that I'd trust my luck if Arontala's spell called hundreds of those things. Amulets have their limits. And there's no protection for the rest of your party. Me, I wouldn't chance it."

"I've got some work with the horses," Vahanian mumbled, and with barely a nod to the others, walked out of the room.

Royster looked after him. "Odd," he mused.

"You know fighters," Tris said, attempting to hide his concern. "I don't know if they ever get comfortable around magic."

"While we're comparing jewelry," Kiara said dryly, "have you ever seen anything like this?" she asked Royster. From a pouch beneath her tunic, she withdrew the spelled pottery chit. Royster held the flat clay circle gently, turning it against the light. Tris leaned forward to get a better look. He could feel the magic in the simple oval, but try as he might, he could not make out the runes stamped on its surface.

Royster motioned to one of the Keepers, a woman in her middle years with short dark hair. The plump scholar hurried over, and exchanged an excited glance with Royster.

"This is Ystra, whose expertise is talismans," Royster said.

"You are indeed favored by the Sisterhood," Ystra said appreciatively. "I've never actually seen one of these, just sketches in books."

"What does it do?" Berry asked, elbowing forward.

"The Sister told me that it could transport people from one place to another," Kiara said, carefully tucking it back into her pouch.

"It will move them magically," Ystra agreed. "Such magic comes at great cost to the mage who sets the spell," he added. "It is not lightly that the Sisters give such a powerful token. Use it only when no other power can suffice. Strong magic has its consequences," she warned.

When the group had dispersed and Tris was certain no one would follow, he headed down to the stables to find Vahanian. He found the mercenary practicing his kicks against a stack of hay bales, jumping and wheeling until he raised steam in the chill night air and sweat soaked through his shirt. Tris stood in silence for a few moments until Vahanian finally paused and leaned against the bales to catch his breath.

"What do you want?" the mercenary said.

"I came to talk."

"I've talked enough for one night."

"What if I could prove to you that Royster is right about the talisman?" Tris said, walking closer.

"How are you going to prove that?"

"Maybe it's time you stopped hanging yourself for something you didn't do."

The words hung between them for several moments before Vahanian spoke. "What are you proposing?"

"Let me call Shanna's spirit," Tris said, meeting Vahanian's gaze without flinching. "Royster is right. Your village got caught in a war between two mages. I believe Arontala was the one who destroyed Lustari—that's why he wanted the talisman. Only Lustari struck before Arontala could come for it. You got caught in the middle. But it wasn't your fault."

Tris had never seen the look in the mercenary's eyes that transfixed him, and he wondered if any other man lived who saw that anger burning there. "How sure are you that you can do it?" Vahanian growled.

"I'm sure," Tris replied. "I suspect she's bound here by your guilt. Maybe I can free both of you."

Vahanian swallowed hard, his eyes conflicted. Then he nodded. "Do it if you can," he said quietly. He looked at Tris. "But I swear by the Dark Lady, if this is any kind of trick, I'll rip your heart out."

"No trick, Jonmarc. I swear."

At Vahanian's nod, Tris closed his eyes, and found the center of his magic. Then, he let himself flow out, searching among all of the lost and disquieted souls that roamed the hidden places until one spirit stirred to his call. He opened his eyes to find the ghost standing before him, a young blonde woman who would have been pretty in a common place way, were it not for the sadness in her eyes. One glance at Vahanian confirmed his success, for the mercenary was pale as death and speechless.

"Hello, Jonmarc," the spirit said. "I've missed you."

"I've missed you, too," Vahanian replied in a strangled voice. "Oh Shanna, I'm so sorry!"

The spirit moved a step closer. "You fought bravely, Jonmarc. You were fearless."

"I wanted to die with you."

The spirit shook her head. "The Lady's hand is on you. It was not your time." She glided closer and Vahanian stretched out his hand, palm first. Her image stopped and she did the same, reaching out for him and through him. "What happened was not your fault," Shanna said earnestly. "There was nothing more you could have done."

"I could have given the necklace to you," Vahanian replied, heedless of the tears that streaked down his face. "I could have saved you."

The spirit smiled sadly. "You tried, my love. Now please, let me rest. Let me go." Her image flickered and dimmed.

"Stay with me," Vahanian begged, his voice raw.

"I cannot, except in your memory. Please, if you loved me, forgive yourself and let me rest." The image faded. "I will always love you," she whispered, raising her hand in farewell. "Goodbye."

Vahanian mouthed the words in response, but his voice failed him as the ghost faded and disappeared. Tris murmured the passing over ritual and felt the presence slip away. With wrenching clarity, he returned to himself. As the ghost disappeared, Tris's head began to throb.

Tris stood in silence for a moment watching the weeping mercenary with compassion, and then left Vahanian to his private grief and quietly slipped from the stable, using a flicker of magic to drop the bolt behind him so that no one might intrude.

He barely made it back up the path to the Library when he encountered Carina. "Where have you been?" she asked. "Kiara and Royster sent me to find you. They think they've found something in one of the books. Come on!" she said, and frowned, looking past him. "Is Jonmarc with you?"

Tris shook his head. "He's busy in the stable. He'll be along in a little bit."

Carina looked skeptically at him. "I suspect he'd seen that bit of jewelry before?" Tris drew a deep breath, decided against a lie, and nodded. "I'm amazed he wins at cards at all if that's his best betting face," she replied, but the comment lacked her usual barb. "You don't have to answer, but from that reaction, and the way he acted at the village, I'd bet he didn't have much success fighting off the things the last time." Tris hesitated again, then nodded. "Do you think he'll really leave, once we reach Principality City?"

Tris shrugged. "That's what he says and he's a man of his word." He looked at Carina. "I thought you'd be glad to get rid of him."

It was her turn to shrug. "He's a good sword," she replied noncommittally. "And having patched him up twice, I hate to think what he'll do to himself back on his own."

Tris chuckled. "You may have a point there. But you and Kiara will be going back to Isencroft once we get back to Principality City."

"I know," she replied. "And as homesick as I've been, I'm not looking forward to it."

CHAPTER TWENTY-NINE

WHEN TRIS AND Carina reached the third floor of the Library, they found Kiara and Royster bent excitedly over a massive book. The yellowed pages were dusty and brittle, and the old ink of the fine handwriting took a bright lantern to decipher.

"Tris, you've got to read this!" Kiara called excitedly, beckoning him to stand beside her. He bent over her shoulder, following her finger as she traced the lines while Royster read.

"'For three days, and three nights, the battle arcane raged between the Obsidian King and the sorceress Bava K'aa,'" he read. "'"Yield to me!" the Obsidian King demanded, "and I will grant you a painless death."

"'"I will yield only with your death," the sorceress replied.

"'Believing she was wounded mortally, Bava K'aa loosed her last, most potent spell—a gray magic which would bind both of their souls. The Obsidian King had wrought a magicked sphere, which opened into the Abyss itself, with which to catch and bind souls to strengthen his power. Into this Abyss Bava K'aa thought to seal the Obsidian King, even if she must forever stand guard.

"'As Bava K'aa spoke the words of binding, there appeared a great light, and the image of the Lady appeared with them within the warding, between Bava K'aa and the Obsidian King, so that when the final words of power were spoken, the spirit of the King was bound to the crystal orb, but the spirit of Bava K'aa the Lady did not permit to pass. We blinked, and the light and Lady were gone. Bava K'aa fell to the floor. We lifted her up and bore her away, as her wounds, though grave, were not mortal. And the orb was given to the sons of Dark Haven to guard, where it remains to this day.'"

"That's it," Tris breathed. "The Soulcatcher."

Kiara looked to him, puzzled. "Soulcatcher?"

Tris told her of the pulsing orb in Arontala's quarters. "I've been afraid that somehow Arontala found a way to bind Kait's spirit," Tris said. "I keep seeing her in my dreams, pressed against a glass prison, calling for me."

Royster was deep in thought. "Dark Haven is a holding on the Principality border of Margolan," he mused. "Foor Arontala came from there."

"Foor Arontala was one of the sons of Dark Haven," a familiar voice said from the shadows. They looked up to find Gabriel standing in the moonlight that streamed through the mullioned windows. "He betrayed us, and stole the orb."

Tris felt a chill that had nothing to do with the winter night. "Can he free the spirit of the Obsidian King?"

"He will try," Gabriel said. "At the Hawthorn Moon. He has great power, and the blood magic he works has strengthened him even further. You must stop him."

"That's half a year away," Tris replied. "The summer solstice."

"When our world and the spirit world have few, if any, boundaries," Royster said quietly.

"I remember the misery that dark wizard brought. This land cannot sustain another mage of his evil," Gabriel replied.

"You knew my grandmother?" Tris asked. The vayash moru nodded.

"She was a great woman," Gabriel said. "And a trusted friend."

"Who are the sons of Dark Haven?" Kiara asked.

Gabriel looked at her, his dark eyes luminous against his pale skin. "The sons of Dark Haven are Those Who Walk the Night," he replied. "Long has Dark Haven been a refuge for our kind. Longer still has the temple to the Dark Lady in those hills been sanctuary."

"If Arontala was one of the sons of Dark Haven," Kiara said, "then he is—"

"He is vayash moru," Gabriel confirmed.

"But that doesn't make sense," Kiara argued. "The refugees told me that Jared Drayke was trying to exterminate all vayash moru."

"It is the truth," Gabriel replied. "Arontala is a traitor to his kind because he fears us. He believes that were we to act together, we might be successful against him. There is one more thing he fears, even more," Gabriel said, looking at Tris. "He knows now that you are a spirit mage. He, too, would have been able to feel the power you wielded in the Ruune Vidaya. Arontala fears that we would follow you, should you rise against him."

"And would you?" Tris asked neutrally.

"I believe so," Gabriel replied. "Never have my people sworn allegiance to any mortal ruler. We are a solitary lot," he said, licking at his thin lips. "But I have been to Margolan, and I have seen the burned bodies and severed heads of my kind, and of mortals, killed like vayash moru to feed the fear of those around them. If there are any left when you return, my lord, I believe they will follow you."

"I thought Dark Haven was abandoned," Kiara said.

Gabriel shrugged. "When Arontala stole the orb, he rent the foundations of the great house. In the chaos, the lord of Dark Haven died. Since then, the great house has been empty, awaiting the will of the Dark Lady. But what is ten years out of the course of hundreds?" he replied. "There will be another lord."

"What brings you to Westmarch?" Tris asked.

"I came to speak with Mikhail about some dealings in Dark Haven."

"And I imagine you'll want to do some reading on your own," Royster said with a grin. Gabriel smiled, a disquieting expression that made his sharp teeth more obvious. "I once thought that immortality would answer all my questions," he said in a voice laced with ennui. "Now, I learn that it only disproves my answers, and replaces them with more questions."

"If vayash moru are immortal," Carina said slowly, "how can they be destroyed?"

"Immortal is a relative term, my lady healer," he replied. "Years alone will not destroy us. Nor will disease. But immortality is not the same as godhood. I and my kind can be destroyed, by fire and stake and magic, just as all those the Lady names immortal have some weakness, unless they truly be gods."

"So Arontala can be destroyed," Carina said.

Once more, Gabriel shrugged. "I believe so. That he is vayash moru I know without doubt. But what abilities his magic gives him, and what protections his blood rites have wrought, I cannot say. One thing I do know. The power of blood magic comes at a terrible price. Those who use it to gain strength often become quite vulnerable, if a mage knows where to look."

"Before we leave this place, I will make sure you've seen every text that could serve your need, my lord," Royster said to Tris.

"We?" Kiara asked.

Royster grinned. "Of course. I've been waiting for something like this to happen for fifty years.

I intend to tutor him in Principality City." He looked at Tris. "Not being a mage and all, I'd do you no good in battle," he said apologetically. "Kessen chose me well—I'm not suited to work that strains the heart. But the head," he said, tapping his forehead, "now that's where I can help. I always had a weakness for the stories of Bava K'aa," he admitted. "I've been scribe to every Sister who has wanted to add to the record over the years. So having me along is just like packing up a good bit of the Library, and a whole lot easier to carry," he said with a wink.

"We would be honored to have your company," Tris replied. "Although I can't promise that the road to Principality City will be safe."

"That's an understatement," Carina murmured.

"I must take leave of you now," Gabriel said, with a courteous bow. "I will see you again. Mikhail is a servant of the Lady; he will be of great help to you. But I warn you," he said gravely, "there are traitors among my kind. Trust no one who is vayash moru unless I send you to them. Arontala's reach is far. Those he has made, and those he has bound, will do his bidding. Do not travel lightly by night."

Then with a rustle of wind, the vayash moru was gone.

ONE EVENING AT the start of their second month at the Library, Tris was working his way through a stack of books in the third-floor study. He glanced up when the door creaked open. To his surprise, Kiara slipped into the room with a teapot in one hand and a small cloth sack in the other.

"May I come in?"

Tris smiled and set aside his book. "Please," he said with a gesture that welcomed her to a chair near the fire. Kiara brought the teapot over and set the cloth sack down on the table, out of which tumbled a piece of crusty bread, a wedge of cheese and a sturdy mug.

"Carina sent me up with some of her headache tea," Kiara said. "Since I was headed this way, Royster added the food—seems he and Kessen got into a row in the kitchen and dinner will be late tonight," she added with a chuckle. She sank gratefully into a chair, and declined his offer of food.

"No thanks. I grabbed a bite for myself while I was in the kitchen," she confessed. "Although I might take a sip of that tea—I have been reading until my eyes feel crossed!"

She paused. "Sister Taru says that Cam and two friends of yours reached a keep of the Sisterhood in northern Margolan."

"They're alive? That's the best news I've heard in a long time," he said.

"Carina was so relieved, I thought she'd never stop crying." She paused. "Taru says that your friends will meet us in Principality City," Kiara added. "She sent them on to start recruiting troops. Cam rode for Isencroft with an elixir to keep the illness from getting any worse. But they can't heal father while the mage lives who cast the illness."

"Do you know who sent the spell?"

Kiara met his eyes. "Arontala. He wants father dead—that way, we have no choice but to ally Isencroft with Margolan to survive."

"I'm sorry," Tris replied.

She looked away. "You're doing all you can. The elixir buys us time. Carina has found some other things in the books that may also ease his suffering and give him strength until..."

"Until I can destroy Arontala," Tris finished her sentence.

She met his eyes, then looked down and nodded. "Yes." She was silent for a while longer. "I want to do a scrying," she said finally. "To see if Cam arrived safely and see if father is doing better." Tris poured a cup and slid it toward her. She took a few sips, and closed her eyes.

"I never had the chance to ask you more about your magic," Tris said, watching her in the firelight. Jae hopped down from his perch on her shoulder and Tris offered him bits of cheese. Jae snapped up the treats before curling into a ball on the edge of the desktop.

Kiara shrugged. "It's not really sorcerer-caliber talent," she admitted. "The gift is very limited. Scryings, some battle divination—things directly related to the safety of the kingdom," she said. "It shows only snatches of information, out of context." She sighed. "On the future of Isencroft, it has been silent."

Tris sipped his tea. It began at once to ease the tension in his shoulders and the reaction headache that throbbed in his temples. "Maybe the future is yet in motion," he said gently. "Maybe we alter it, even now, by what we do."

"Perhaps," she said. "I'd like to think so."

Tris slipped another crumb of cheese to Jae, who gobbled it then stretched out lazily, lolling to one side to invite a belly scratch. "He isn't like that with just everyone," Kiara observed. "You've made a real friend."

"I hope so," Tris said, meeting her eyes. She looked away, her cheeks coloring slightly, as if she caught the full intention of his comment.

"Thank you," he said. "For the tea. And the company. It gets too quiet up here."

"You're welcome," she said, daring a glance back at him. She held out her arm, and Jae waddled toward her, making a gurgle of protest as he lighted on her shoulder.

"Kiara," he said seriously, "please don't scry without me. Just a feeling I've got... Taru went back to the citadel to confer, Gabriel is gon I wish you'd reconsider."

Kiara shook her head. "How could we be any safer than here, behind all of the Sisterhood's spells? Carina's desperate to see that Cam is safely home, and I'm as lonesome for a glimpse of father as I am anxious to see how he's doing."

Tris sighed. "We're probably as safe as we'll ever be. But please, wait for me."

"All right," she said, "you've got a deal."

AFTER SUPPER, CARROWAY favored them with several new stories; then three of the Keepers joined him for a candlemark of chamber

music. Tris drank another mug of the mulled
wine and breathed deeply, enjoying the first
chance to relax. He was enjoying Kiara's company as much as the entertainment, and could
see that Carroway was relishing the opportunity to entertain with the lute the Keepers had
given him.

When the program ended at the tenth bell,
everyone congratulated Carroway and the other
musicians. As the group filed from the room, a
handful remained behind.

"What's going on?" Vahanian asked as he
passed Tris.

"Kiara wants to do a scrying to see how her
father is doing," Tris replied. "She'll need a few
of us to hold the circle, but we've got enough that
you're off the hook."

Vahanian gave him a sideways glance. "I think
I'll stick around outside the circle and watch your
back, if it's all the same, Spook," he said. "After
all, if you get your royal ass fried to a crunch
with some magic-gone-wrong, the rest of us have
a one-way trip to the hangman's noose."

"I want to watch," Berry chirped.

"No," Tris said.

"Absolutely not," Carina echoed.

"Isn't it late for you to be awake?" Vahanian
asked. Berry made a sour face.

"I don't have a bed time," she announced. "I've
never seen a scrying. It will be fun."

"It can be dangerous," Tris said.

Berry dismissed him with a gesture that looked
oddly like one of Vahanian's mannerisms. "I'm

not afraid. I've fought slavers and seen ghosts and vayash moru."

"She's actually handy in a fight," Vahanian said off-handedly, and Berry beamed. "All right—I'll let you stand behind me, on one condition."

"All right!" Berry agreed enthusiastically.

Vahanian fixed her with a steady gaze. "No matter what happens, you don't get in the way."

Berry gave him a smug look. "Of course I won't get in the way. I wasn't in the way at the forest throwing rocks, now was I?"

"It's possible that you pair are two of a kind," Tris observed dryly as they followed Kiara into the parlor.

Fresh torches burned in the sconces and a fire blazed on the hearth. In the room's center was a small table surrounded by six chairs, and on the table sat an amber scrying ball the size of a melon, on a stand of tangled bronze dragons. "It's beautiful," Kiara commented, reaching toward it and pulling her fingers back just before they touched its smooth surface. Jae flapped nervously on her shoulder, hissing.

"I'm still not comfortable about this," Carina said. "At Isencroft you had the chamber, and it was spelled and warded. When Alyzza and Tris tried a scrying with the caravan, there was... something... out there looking for him," she recounted with shudder.

"You are in a fortress of the Sisterhood," Royster interrupted. "It, too, has safeguards." He jumped as if jabbed from behind, and glared at the empty air. "Did we ask you?" he snapped at the ghost. Tris saw Kessen tugging at Royster's shirt, for once completely devoid of mischief.

"I think he's trying to tell you something," Tris said. "I don't think he's joking."

Royster stopped in amazement, unused to others seeing his ghostly companion. "All right," he said abruptly to the ghost. "What, then?"

"What did he say?" Carina and Kiara asked in one breath.

"Did you just talk to him, Tris?" Berry asked excitedly.

Tris nodded. "He doesn't think it's a good idea."

"I have to know," Kiara persisted stubbornly. "I'll be all right."

"But Kiara—" Carina protested.

"I'm going to do it—alone if I have to."

Carina finally nodded. "All right." She looked at the others. "Once everyone is seated, I'll begin the warding," Carina said.

Vahanian and Mikhail stood near the door as the others found their seats. Kiara stood before the scrying ball, with chairs for Carina to her right and Tris to her left. Devin was next to Tris, then Maire and Royster to complete the circle. Kiara closed her eyes and stood in silence for a moment, readying herself. Carina moved slowly around the room, setting the wards into place. Silently, Tris repeated the warding ritual in his mind to add his strength.

"Powers that be, hear me! Goddess of Light, attend!" Kiara recited, her eyes still closed. "I am the Chosen of Isencroft, the line of the blood. We gather to invoke the ancient Powers."

"Spirits of the Land, hear me!" Kiara said, laying a hand on the amber globe in its dragon-winged holder. "Winds of the north, obey! Waters of the southlands, bend your course to the will of the Chosen. Fires of the eastern sun, be bound by my command. I compel you by the right of the heirs of Isencroft to reveal what is hidden and find what is dear. Let it be so!"

A glow began deep within the heart of the scrying ball, a swirling mist that sprang from its deepest center. Slowly, the glow grew brighter and brighter. Kiara stared intently into its depths.

"Look! There!" Carina whispered, bending as close as she could without breaking the circle of hands. Tris let his own mage senses stir in sympathetic union.

"Father," Kiara breathed. "Dear Lady, he's looking better, Carina, can you see?"

Carina nodded, wide-eyed, her smile joyous. "He does look better, though not his old self. Oh! Kiara, look!" she cried, tightening her grip painfully hard on Kiara's hand. "Cam is with him!"

"Wait, it's shifting again," Carina said.

The mist closed over the globe like a coming storm. All at once, the temperature in the room plummeted, and from the depths of the globe, a blood-red glow began to stain the mist, until out of its depths burst a ray of brilliant crimson light that struck Kiara full in the chest.

Kiara sagged to her knees. "Break the circle!" Carina hissed to her. "You have to break the circle!"

Kiara, unresponsive, stared straight ahead, her eyes fixed and her form rigid.

"Wind and Fire, Land and Sea, I release you!" Carina commanded, her voice just shy of panic.

"Those are not your powers to command," a deep voice boomed from Kiara's open mouth.

"Kiara!" Vahanian shouted, diving toward her. Mikhail pulled him back.

"You can't stop it," Mikhail said. "Leave it to Tris."

Tris released the hands of those sitting next to him and took a step around the table toward Kiara. "Let her go," Tris said evenly.

The light pulsed and Kiara shuddered, her face contorting in pain as Carina and Berry screamed.

"Let her go!" Tris commanded once more, focusing his power and his will. "What do you seek?"

"I seek Martris Drayke," the voice rasped, tearing the words from Kiara's throat. "And a bargain."

"What bargain?"

"Surrender yourself, and I will not kill your friends."

"We've got our own scores with this one," Vahanian growled. "No bargains."

Tris took a step closer. "If it's me you want," he said evenly, "here I am. Let her go."

"We have sought her the length of Margolan for her treachery," the voice rasped. "She is ours."

"She is her own. Let her go."

"I'll let her go," the voice boomed. "Into the arms of the Dark Lady." A burst of light streamed from the orb and Kiara convulsed, held suspended in its blood-red glow.

"Not if I can help it," Tris grated, diving for the globe. He gasped in pain as his body cut through the crimson light. "Shield!" he cried, summoning his power, and a blue glow rose to envelop him, blocking the light from its target.

Behind him, Kiara slumped to the ground. Carina rushed to her side, placing her own body between Kiara and the globe.

"You have grown stronger," the voice boomed. "I should have killed you when I had the chance. Give up your foolish quest now, and I can cut short your sister's torment," the voice baited. Within the globe, Kait's face, twisted in fear and pain, pressed against the inside of the glass.

"Go to the Whore!" Tris rasped as he summoned all of his power to make one great push against the crimson light, forcing it back toward the nexus of the scrying ball. A scream, Kait's scream, tore through the chamber as Tris gave one final effort, hurling all of his strength against the crimson light.

The globe flared like the sun, blindingly bright. The ball exploded, raining fragments that glowed like embers. Tris fell forward and the blue glow vanished as the others crowded around.

"I think we can all agree—no more scrying," Vahanian said, getting his shoulder under Tris's arm and helping Tris into a chair.

"Agreed," Carina said from where she and Devin and Royster knelt beside Kiara. She lay still on the floor and like the rest of them, bled from the shards of the scrying ball.

"You're not going to hear any arguments from me," Tris said weakly, sagging back against the chair, his head throbbing. "How is Kiara?" he managed, proud that he was still conscious.

Carina looked up. "Alive. Unconscious. I'd like to get her to bed so she can sleep it off." She looked at Tris. "That was Arontala, wasn't it?"

Tris nodded, then stopped as his head pounded so hard that he nearly blacked out. "It was the same thing I felt back with the caravan." He paused. "Jared wants Kiara," he said quietly. "She's defied him and he knows it. He won't stop until he has her under his control."

The worry in Carina's eyes showed that she had reached the same conclusion. "Then we really have no choice, do we?" Carina said. "We can't break the wasting spell on King Donelan while Arontala lives. Nowhere is safe for Kiara while Jared rules. We must help you defeat them, or Isencroft and Kiara will never know safety again."

"I agree," Mikhail said. "To destroy the beasts that plague Dhasson, we must destroy Arontala." He met Tris's eyes. "Even Dark Haven is no longer safe," he said. "I will help you."

"Thank you," Tris whispered, feeling the last of his strength fading.

Mikhail bent to gather up Kiara in his arms. Carina gave Devin and Berry a list of herbs and items from the kitchen.

"I'll get Kiara back to her room," Mikhail said. "You look like you've got all you can handle just getting back upstairs," he added, appraising Tris's condition.

"Here, lean on me," Vahanian said as Tris managed to stand up, then stumbled. "Carroway, come around on the other side, he's going to need some help."

Maire looked at Tris worriedly. "I will bring up some hot tea and something to clean those cuts."

Carina looked back at Tris, as she headed for the door behind Mikhail. "I'll be up as soon as I get Kiara taken care of," she promised.

"I'll send up Seldon," Royster said, promising the herbalist's help. The librarian looked scared.

Carina turned to Vahanian. "What about you?"

"What do you mean?"

"Where do you stand? Arontala has to know you're with us. You don't think he's going to let you off any easier than the rest of us."

"Right now, my job is to get you to Principality City alive. If we live that long, I'll worry about it then," Vahanian said. Carina turned on her heel and followed Mikhail.

"I should have stayed in Margolan," Tris said quietly as Vahanian and Carroway helped him toward the stairs. "If I'd killed Jared right then, none of this would have happened."

"We carried you out on a stretcher," Carroway reminded him. "Did you forget that part? We were outnumbered. We'd all be dead by now. There would be no one who could stop Jared."

"I'll go back alone, I'm the one Arontala wants—"

"Your friends have their own reasons for choosing to go with you," Royster said from behind them. "Their quests are as important as your own."

"This is exactly the kind of stunt I warned you about," Vahanian grumbled as they worked their way up the stairs. "I've a mind to lock you in a cell somewhere just to make sure you live long enough to get to Margolan."

Tris found that he was too exhausted to reply. He managed to stand long enough to wave off further help once they reached his room, but halfway to his bed his vision blurred, and the last thing he remembered was grabbing at a chair to break his fall.

CHAPTER THIRTY

TRIS OPENED HIS eyes slowly. His head pounded hard enough that everything he saw was surrounded by a nebulous glow. Even the light from the fireplace was far too bright. The skin on his hands and face burned as if from nettles, and he felt as if he had been thrashed.

"Glad to have you back." Taru's voice came from the shadows beside his bed. He managed to turn his head to see her. The effort made his head swim.

"I made it as far as my room before I blacked out this time."

Taru sniffed. "As soon as your friends let go of you, you fell face down in the middle of the floor." She smiled slightly. "At least they pulled off your boots before they put you to bed," she added. "But you are correct. You stayed conscious after the working, you got up the stairs without being carried—so they tell me—and you have been out only a few hours. Your training is paying off."

Tris closed his eyes. "Not good enough."

Taru stepped closer, and laid a hand on his shoulder. "No, not yet," she said, her voice a little gentler. "But there are months yet before you must face Arontala. This is promising."

"How is Kiara?" Tris asked, realizing that if he whispered, it didn't hurt quite so much to hear his own voice.

"She's sleeping it off," replied Taru. "Carina tells me that scryings have always gone hard on her. The attack was intentionally meant to be both terrifying and draining. Had you not intervened, she would not have survived." She paused. "Which reminds me," she added, her voice taking on an irritated edge, "what were you thinking to attempt this when I was gone?"

Tris sighed. "Kiara said she did it many times before, and since I wasn't the one doing the scrying, I really didn't think it would attract attention. We were wrong."

"You might as well have lit a bonfire." She bustled with some objects on the stand next to the bed and Tris opened his eyes again. He lifted his hands and saw that they were covered with fine cuts. "Here," Taru said, taking his hand. She smoothed ointment over the cuts, reducing their sting. Tris gratefully allowed her to do the same with his neck and face.

"Forcing power back through a breakable object isn't the most efficient move," Taru said.

"You were fortunate. If the power truly concentrated in the ball itself, and not in the sender's channel, you might have had a nice explosion on top of just spraying the room with shards of glass."

"Understood," Tris replied, abashed.

Taru's expression softened. "Don't be too hard on yourself. You did the right thing, in an unorthodox manner. It worked. However, there are reasons for the methods we teach you. Things mages have learned the hard way—like exploding scrying balls. Devin and I will confer. Your level of power creates dangers at this point in your training that would not normally pose a hazard until much later. We must reconsider."

"We can't stay here much longer," Tris said, as Taru helped him sit up and pressed a cup of Carina's headache tea into his hands.

"No, you can't," she agreed. "You cannot afford to be snowbound here. That is one of the reasons I went to confer with my Sisters. They have been monitoring your lessons from afar. They agree that you have completed nearly all that is possible here at the Library." She paused. "All but Argus."

"Now, there is a new danger," she said, drawing up a chair and settling herself. She poured herself a cup of the tea, and from her reaction as she sipped, Tris realized she was pushing her own energies as well.

"Because of what happened tonight? Can Jared reach us here? We're not in Margolan."

Taru shook her head. "That is true. But we are not yet far enough into Principality for the king's troops to patrol this area heavily. Arontala will not have a precise bearing on your location, but it will be close enough. The vayash moru tell us that there are already small squads of Margolan soldiers, traveling out of uniform beyond Principality's borders, searching. If they comb this area, it will make the road to Principality City more dangerous for you."

She paused again, deep in thought. "The most dangerous section will be the first day's ride, from here to Gibbet Bridge. Beyond the crossing, the king's soldiers patrol the riverbank. I do not think even Jared would dare send troops that far inside another sovereign state. It would mean war.

"Royster will come with you. Given the... unusual circumstances, I have gained the Sisterhood's permission to take texts with us, so that they may be used in your training. But you have one more task remaining."

Tris leaned back on his pillow, feeling the full fatigue from the last many weeks. "Mageslayer."

"That, also, was a part of my consultation with my Sisters," said Taru. "We are in agreement that you are the rightful bearer. But you must still win the sword."

"What makes you think that I can succeed?"

"None who have challenged Argus were Summoners."

Tris thought about that for a moment. "Is it worth the risk? As Jonmarc pointed out, getting myself killed before the main event accomplishes nothing," he said with a lopsided smile, thinking of Vahanian's original wording.

Taru must have realized the paraphrase, because a smile hinted at her lips. "Your friend hides his skills well, but there is good reason that the Lady chose him for this purpose."

"Don't tell that to Jonmarc," Tris said, sipping the rest of his tea. "He thinks he makes his own decisions."

Taru smiled. "The Lady permits our self-deceptions where it suits Her purpose," she replied. "But to your question, we believe the answer is 'yes.' I raised that point with the Sisterhood, and there was... debate," she allowed. "While I do not have great faith, as a general rule, in talismans and amulets, it is not wise to discount their power. Rarely are they sufficient by themselves; yet, the right tool in the hand of the Lady's chosen becomes a powerful weapon. We believe that Mageslayer has a role in your quest. The risk of failure in Margolan is greater, my Sisters believe, than the likelihood of defeat by Argus." She paused. "However..."

"However?"

"It would be unwise to underestimate the threat. Once you are rested, it will be time. If all goes well," she said, "we will leave for Principality City when you return."

If all goes well, Tris thought, thinking about all that Taru left unsaid. She's not completely comfortable with this, he thought, watching Taru. She's not sure that I'm up to it yet, but we're running out of time. We could go to the city, train further, but there's the risk we couldn't get back here. And if we can't go on without it, then there's no option. He watched Taru drink her tea. She's starting to feel boxed in, and the Sisterhood doesn't like to have their hand forced. Welcome to my world.

"Please don't tell the others about the risk," Tris said, leaning back into the pillows as he felt a wave of vertigo wash over him. "Whatever happens is beyond their control. They've come so far, risked so much—I don't want them to worry."

Taru removed the extra pillows so he could lie down. "I have already spoken with Carina and Devin. Their assistance may be required. But I will honor your request, although I suspect your companions will figure it out for themselves."

She might have said more, but Tris could no longer resist sleep and he let it take him, hoping it would be dreamless.

THE NEXT EVENING, Kiara and Carina took dinner in the former's room. Kiara was still recovering from the scrying, which had left her badly drained. Taru went to bring more herbs for Carina's salve to soothe the small cuts from the shattered orb. As they waited, Kiara and Carina sipped their tea, lost in thought.

Finally, Kiara spoke. "Taru says it is almost time for us to leave the Library. Then I guess we go on to Principality City." She saw a look of discomfort cross her cousin's face. "I know you'd rather avoid that if you could," she continued, quietly. Carina hesitated, and then nodded.

"It's just that it… brings back a lot of things I'd rather not remember," the healer said quietly. "It's been seven years since Ric died. I should be over it by now," she said in a voice above a whisper.

"You know," Kiara said gently, "even after all this time, you've never really told me what happened."

Carina was silent for a moment, staring into the fire. Finally, she spoke, almost too softly for Kiara to hear. "When we were sixteen, Cam and I signed on with an Eastmark mercenary troop. He was so big, no one even asked our ages. They needed a healer and were happy to get Cam in the bargain. We made a good living."

She smiled faintly, her gaze far away. "Ric was the troop's captain. Best swordsman in the company. He was five years older than we were, and a bit of a rogue," she chuckled sadly. "He took good care of us. He broke a lot of rules, but he looked out for his men. We'd have gone to the Crone for him." She paused again, longer this time. "I fell in love. The next winter, he asked me to marry him. I said yes. And then word came that there was some trouble on the Dhasson border. Raiders. It was supposed to be an easy skirmish. Only it wasn't," she said, looking down.

"They brought Ric back with a bad belly wound. I tried to save him," she said, her voice thick with self-condemnation. "I ignored everything I'd ever learned about healing, about going too deep, hanging on too hard. When he died, I nearly went with him." She looked up at Kiara, tears bright in her eyes. "And I don't remember a thing after that until I woke up in the citadel of the Sisterhood in Principality," she said.

"Afterwards, Cam told me it was like I was dead and alive at the same time. Said I couldn't hear, couldn't speak, couldn't see. He was desperate," she said, looking down again. "The only place he could think to go was the Sisterhood, and he begged them to take me in." She shrugged. "He said they sent him away and told him they would find him if they succeeded."

Kiara knew the rest of the story. With nowhere else to go, Cam rode for Isencroft, where Donelan welcomed him. A year later, the Sisters summoned Cam back to Principality City. Carina was healed, but Cam said that she was changed, distant. Kiara suspected that was the reason her cousin had managed to elude any potential suitors—at least, until Jonmarc Vahanian.

"It's been a long time," Kiara said quietly. "Things are different now. You're not alone. You know we won't let anything happen to you... especially Jonmarc." She paused. "Don't tell me you haven't noticed the way he looks at you."

Carina blushed and turned away. "You know," she said, "in the slavers' camp, when they brought Jonmarc to me and he was so close to death, it was like having it all happen again. If it hadn't been for Tris, I would have lost him. I felt him slipping away. Tris anchored him. I was scared that if Tris went too deep to hang onto Jonmarc I'd lose them both."

"But you didn't."

"But I could have," Carina replied softly. "It's just so much safer not to care."

Kiara got up and walked over to stare out the window for a few moments in silence. The sky was gray and the trees bare. Deep snowfalls would come soon. They were silent for a while, each lost in thought.

"I can't believe I've come this far, only to fail at my Journey," Kiara said quietly.

"What are you talking about?"

"The Oracle sent me to the Library at Westmarch to find out how to save Isencroft. Everyone else has gotten what they came for. You found out that Cam reached father with the Sisterhood's elixir, and you've found more information to help father recover."

She sipped her tea. "Tris seems to have found what he needed, even if he will need to study with the Sisters for the rest of the winter. Mikhail found out more about the beasts, Carroway has his tales and songs and legends, even Berry has gotten the stories she wanted. Jonmarc's had a proper salle to train everyone and some time off the road. But I'm no closer to saving Isencroft than I was when I left," she said, looking out the window at the barren landscape.

They heard the door latch click as Taru closed the door behind her. "Tell me, Kiara Sharsequin, what you have learned on the road from

Isencroft?" the Sister asked, and Kiara was chagrined that the mage had overheard her lament.

"I saw the bloodshed in Margolan and the dispossessed farmers," Kiara said quietly, remembering. "I've seen just what kind of king Jared Drayke is. I've met vayash moru and fought magicked monsters and discovered that the Library exists."

"And your companions? What have you gained from them?"

Kiara thought longer this time. "I've certainly had a good brush-up on my sword skills from Jonmarc!" she said with a rueful smile. "Mikhail has promised to ask King Harrol for advisors." She paused. "He's also offered to introduce me to King Staden, and help me make a case for Principality's assistance."

"And what of Martris Drayke?" Taru pressed.

Kiara looked at her cup as she thought about that answer. "Tris promised me that if he takes the throne, Margolan will pose no threat to Isencroft," she said softly. "And that he will send whatever help he can."

Taru nodded once more. "You did not completely answer my question. What have you learned about Martris Drayke himself?"

Kiara blushed and looked away. "He is an honorable man, a brave man, a man of his word. He would make a good king."

Taru fixed Kiara with the considered stare of a teacher. "Would you have believed those things possible of Jared Drayke's brother, had you not traveled beside him?"

"No. I don't think so."

Taru looked at her appraisingly. "And what of your other reason for making the Journey? Your private reason?"

Kiara exchanged glances with Carina, embarrassed. "You mean to avoid the arranged marriage?"

"Yes."

"I know for certain just what a demon Jared Drayke is, and what forces are aligning against him," Kiara said quietly. "I have Tris's promise that nothing will be required of Isencroft by force."

"What did you think to find here, Kiara of Isencroft?" Taru said, gently reproving. "Were you expecting a talisman or a magic book?" Kiara blushed scarlet and said nothing. "You gain pledges of alliance and protection for Isencroft from Dhasson and Margolan, and likely Principality. You are at the center of the effort to bring down Jared Drayke and defeat Arontala—which must succeed to save your father. And you have won a chance for freedom—both for Isencroft and for yourself."

Taru's expression softened. "I am not unfamiliar with the language of kings. There is something more you might consider. Such an arrangement may be referred to as between Kiara and Jared, but the formalities would have matched the daughter of Donelan to the heir to the throne of Margolan. Once Jared Drayke is deposed, that heir becomes Martris Drayke," she said, amusement in her eyes at Kiara's surprise. "You are now free to follow your heart."

"We're really just good friends," Kiara stammered, embarrassed at Taru's insight.

"The Oracle told you that from Margolan comes source and solution, did she not?"

"I just never thought that it would be the people and experiences of the Journey that would matter more than what I found at the end," Kiara said.

"You are not at the end, although your time in the Library is drawing to a close," Taru replied. "The Sisterhood is agreed that there is some role the Lady would have you play in the defeat of Arontala. Signs suggest that the effort will be more difficult—or perhaps fail entirely—if your part goes unplayed."

"Sweet Chenne," Kiara whispered. "I thought about going on to Margolan with Tris and the others—Carina's resolved that she must. I wasn't sure whether I could leave Isencroft that long."

"Isencroft cannot afford to have you leave this thing undone," Taru replied.

"I heard Mikhail and Jonmarc talking with Tris," Carina told Kiara. "They want to get on the road before the snows fall. Mikhail says there are Margolan troops within a few candlemarks, in small groups. Assassins."

Kiara shuddered. "We're getting boxed in. I'm surprised we haven't left before this."

"There is one more thing Tris must finish, before you can leave," said Taru. "He is ready to enter the crypt of King Argus. Argus's sword, Mageslayer, must be won in combat."

"Taru has asked me to be on hand, when he goes," added Carina.

"To put him back together again if he fails?"

"If he fails, he won't come back, Kiara. That's the price," said Carina. "No one who has sought the sword has ever returned. Taru wants me there because we don't know what kind of shape he'll be in if he succeeds."

Kiara could think of no reply, and so she looked back out the window. Carina's words echoed in her mind, even after the healer and the sorceress had said goodnight and left her to her thoughts.

CHAPTER THIRTY-ONE

Although Tris said nothing to his companions about the quest for Mageslayer, he suspected that Carina had told the tale. On the day he was to go into the crypt, his friends lingered with him at lunch, as if unsure of what to say. Berry kissed him on the cheek for luck. Carroway looked sober, clapping Tris on the shoulder and wishing him the favor of the lady. Carina reassured him that she and Royster would be waiting, then took leave to gather up her medicines.

Kiara hung back, as did Vahanian. "Carina told us... about Mageslayer," Kiara confessed, avoiding his gaze. "Please be careful."

Tris dared to take her hand, and lightly kissed it. "I have a lot of reasons to come back," he said, meeting her eyes. She blushed and murmured a blessing before leaving.

There was silence for a moment between Tris and Vahanian. "Stupidest thing I've ever heard— a duel without taking a second with you," Vahanian said finally. "I can't be much of a body-guard from up here."

Tris smiled wanly. "I have a favor to ask," he said, and dug into his pocket. He withdrew the pouch with King Harrol's seal, and to Vahanian's amazement, handed it to the mercenary.

"If I don't come back, I'm counting on you to get the others to safety," he said soberly. "I need your word that you will see them safe."

Vahanian turned the seal in his hand. "What makes you so sure I won't just take off and col-lect my pay?"

Tris met his eyes. "You won't."

Vahanian said nothing for a moment. "You have my word," he said finally. "But you'd better come back in one piece," he warned.

Tris chuckled. "Believe me, that's my plan." Then he offered Vahanian his hand, in the fore-arm clasp of brothers at arms. "Thank you," he said.

"We've got a long road ahead. Thank me when we're done."

From there, Tris made his way to the Library's small chapel, sacred to Principality's favored aspect of the One Goddess, in her guise as Lover, and her dark reflection, the Whore. As he had seen Soterius do on the eve of battle, he offered his sword for blessing before the flickering can-dles of the altar, and awkwardly made his peace. Although he hoped against hope that the Lady might favor him with some sign, as she had done in the crowd the night of the coup, no supernatural presence touched his magesense.

Sweet Lady, he prayed. Honor my quest and let me win the sword. But if you will not, then honor the cries of your lost children in Margolan, and bring some other justice.

He waited, but the chapel remained silent save for the sound of his own breathing. Finally, he sheathed his sword, and made the sign of the Lady as he rose, hoping for a few hours' sleep before it was time to go.

TRIS, TARU AND Royster made their way at the eleventh bell to one of the small parlors on the first level of the Library. Royster tied a rope to an iron ring set into the massive stone fireplace, then let the rope out as he moved to the right of the hearth. His hand slid along the wooden paneling until they heard a faint click. A panel in the wall slid back, revealing stairs descending into blackness.

By torchlight, they went down a steep and crooked set of stone steps. As they descended, Royster let out the rope. They made their way down to the bottom of the stairs, into a small antechamber, at the end of which was a massive, ironbound door. Royster stopped. The darkness smelled of moldering cloth and wet ground, and the remnants of old magic prickled at the back of Tris's neck.

"This is the entrance to the tomb of King Argus," Royster said. "We can go no further." He paused. "One of us will watch for you at all times. If you cannot make it back up the stairs, pull on the rope. We will come for you."

Taru raised her hand in blessing, and murmured a prayer to the Lady. "Now go," she said. "And if Argus finds you worthy, return with the sword."

Royster and Taru turned and headed back up the steps. Tris set his torch in an empty sconce. Putting both his back and his magic into the effort, he inched the heavy door aside and called handfire, leaving the torch to light his way back. Royster's rope lay slack at the bottom of the steps. The crypt smelled of decay. Tris could barely make out two torch sconces on the wall just inside the door, and ahead, something massive and dark.

"Fire," Tris murmured, willing the torches to light. He stood in the tomb of a warrior king. To the right, finely wrought armor awaited its owner for eternity. To the left, a beautifully worked saddle sat astride a life-sized wooden horse. In the center of the room lay a catafalque with the likeness of Argus in eternal repose. Tris's heart thudded as he took a step toward the resting-place of the king.

A noise from behind him and a stirring of his magesense was his only warning. Tris wheeled, sword raised, as a warrior of sinew and bone lurched toward him from the darkness, its sword menacing. The undead warrior swung so hard, its blow nearly tore Tris's sword from his grip. Fighting back his own horror, Tris parried, even as he saw a second skeletal warrior rise from a heap of moldering cloth near the wall.

What gray magic is this? Tris wondered, parrying the shattering blows. It was clear that Argus played by no rules but his own. One thing was painfully clear, he thought as the third warrior struggled toward them. His mortal strength would fail long before the implacable warriors gave up their fight. Tris cut down through the first of the bony soldiers, only to see the bones rattle toward each other on the stone floor and sinew magically pull them into place.

A fourth and a fifth skeleton were starting from against the far wall. At this rate, Tris thought, breathing hard, the fight would be over before it began. Sweat poured down his back in the freezing chamber. One of the warriors slipped inside his guard and scored a painful gash. Then, as Tris made another stroke connect, splitting the skeleton from collar to hip, Taru's words sounded in his mind.

None has been a Summoner.

"Halt!" Tris cried out, even as one of the sword blows struck his blade so hard that it felt as if it might break his arm. "Fall back." As he spoke, he called forth his power, so that he saw the warriors in his magesight on the plains of spirit, where they stood with the appearance of living men, mortally wounded.

"By the power of the Lady, fall back," he willed, and the skeletal warriors lowered their swords and began to step away. Silently, the undead soldiers took up sentry positions against the walls, their swords lowered. But permeating the crypt, Tris could feel another magic, another presence, waiting to spring.

Just then, the torches winked out, leaving him in total darkness. The crypt door behind him slammed shut, although it had taken his full strength to push it open. A keening wail began, rising until it echoed in the stone chamber, as the temperature dropped until Tris was sure his breath fogged.

He called fire to the torches, but just as quickly, another power snuffed them out. Tris closed his eyes, relying on magesight, as he felt a presence, strong and dangerous, slip against him. His heart thudded, as the revenant turned on him, and in his magesight, he saw a hideous mouth lined with teeth, like the magicked beasts.

It lunged at him, and he felt its cold essence slide past him and through him as the wailing grew ear-shatteringly loud. Teeth snapped next to his neck, and he could hear the scratch of talons on the stone. Though his heart was pounding and every instinct told him to flee or fight, Tris struggled to find his center.

Protect! he willed, and his wardings rose, casting a pale blue light within the inky crypt and driving back the ghostly beast. It paced outside the shielding, more hideous in the faint light than the thought of it had been in the darkness. *Depart! You have no power here. By the Lady, be gone!*

The beast made one final lunge against Tris's wardings, flinging itself against the shields, which surged blue. Its teeth were only a breath away from him, its talons clawed vainly at the warding, and its keen shrieked until Tris thought it might split his eardrums. And then, the wraith vanished. Sweating hard, his heart in his throat, Tris fought to catch his breath as he warily lowered his shielding and willed the torches to light.

"None of your tricks, brother."

Tris wheeled at the voice, and felt his mouth go dry as a familiar figure stepped from the shadows. Jared stood just paces away, his sword in one hand, his left hand behind his back.

"You can't be here," Tris breathed, raising his sword.

Jared laughed coldly. "But I am. I've come to finish what I started—what I should have ended a long time ago." He advanced slowly. "And I'm going to enjoy it." He leered. "I could always whip your ass," he said, taking another step forward. "But I'm going to make sure that you've got plenty of time to think about how stupid it was to defy me," Jared grated. "Plenty of time while you're dying. You thought you could take my crown, my kingdom... and my bride. But I'll keep what's mine. You might be lord of the dead, but I am death itself," rasped Jared, as he withdrew his left hand from behind his back. Kiara's severed head hung by its hair, her expression frozen in pain and terror.

Every fiber of Tris's body and heart wanted to lunge for Jared, even as a cry tore from his throat. Jared chuckled. "I am as real as your nightmares, brother," he said, letting the head swing.

As real as my nightmares. Which aren't real at all.

"Dispel!" Tris screamed, hearing his own voice pinched with terror, as he held on to the center of his power. "You... are... not... real. Be gone!" And quick as thought, Jared's image winked out.

Without warning, unseen hands shoved Tris back so hard that he staggered. A mist coalesced above the catafalque until a stout, sturdy man stood at the foot of the tomb.

"Why have you come?" the specter boomed.

Tris bowed in respect. "I am Martris Drayke, son of Bricen of Margolan, grandson of the sorceress, Bava K'aa."

"Step closer," the ghost of Argus said. "Yes," he murmured after studying Tris for a moment, "I see your father in you. Why have you disturbed my rest?"

"By your leave, sire," Tris replied, "I have come for Mageslayer."

"Mageslayer may not be given," the ghost roared. "It may only be won in combat." At that, the force of the ghost's offensive drove Tris to his knees. Strong arms like iron bands encircled his chest, making him heave for breath. Tris thrashed, trying to break free, as the ghost chuckled and the grip tightened. "Too easy," he heard the ghost say behind his ear as the pressure increased. "Surely you are not the grandson of Bava K'aa."

Gasping for air, Tris struggled to ignore the ghost's taunts. He let his body go slack as he summoned his powers, then lashed back with all his might at the revenant now clear in his magic-enhanced vision.

"Well now, that's more like it," the ghost chuckled, coming at him again. Argus's spirit was as solid and real to Tris as any mortal opponent. Tris circled the catafalque warily.

Argus launched himself over the tomb in a leap impossible for a living fighter, driving Tris to the floor and knocking the wind out of him. "You've got to do better than this, lad," Argus said. Setting his jaw, Tris slammed forward with his magic and sent the ghost reeling.

They sparred for what seemed like eternity. Tris knew that Argus possessed one thing he did not—an immortal's tireless strength. Tris dodged and feinted, willing himself to ignore the pounding reaction headache and the crushing weariness that made every move ache.

When Argus leaped on him and sent them both to the ground, Tris could do no more than brace himself against the ghost, refusing Argus the upper hand although Tris lacked the strength to break free.

"Admit it, lad. You're beaten," Argus taunted, jerking his hold to make it hurt.

"I won't leave without Mageslayer," Tris grated between bloodied lips.

"You won't leave at all!"

Then, so clear that Tris could not believe he had not seen it before, the solution came to him and with a certainty driven of desperation, he closed his eyes and leaped along the inner path-workings, into the twilight of the spirit world. Down, down he dove as he had at the well, when Carina's soul was in peril, and before that, when

Vahanian lay dying amid the slavers. This time, the pathway was familiar, and Tris hurtled along it before Argus could adjust his grip, speeding like a falcon on attack, toward the blue life thread that was Argus. Heedless of consequence, Tris envisioned his own glimmering soul strand and began to weave it around Argus's in a complex, shining knot.

"Aye there, what are you doing?" Argus roared.

"If I cannot leave without Mageslayer, then I will not stay as your servant," Tris shouted. "We will spend eternity together, bound at the soul, closer than brothers. You will not think a thought without me, and I will not dream without you." He continued his weaving as the life threads glimmered and shone.

"Stop!"

"Yes?"

Argus loosened his hold. "I've no need for another infernal voice inside my head."

"But we have a stalemate," Tris replied. "I will not yield, although in time, you must win because my mortal body will tire. And if I must remain with you, it will be on terms of my choosing."

Argus released his grip on Tris with a curse. "Take the bloody sword," he swore. "No one in fifty years has fought me like that," he said, the gleam in his eyes making it clear that he relished the conflict. "'Tis a rigged game, that's sure, as you say. But I lose when I yield, and I can no more stand the thought of having someone in my thoughts than I can walk back among the living."

At that, the heavy stone lid of the catafalque ground open on its own accord, and the crypt door swung open. "Take the sword," Argus said, standing beside his tomb, "and with it, the blessing of Argus the king."

As carefully as he had woven the knots, Tris unraveled the glittering life threads, until the two strands glowed separately. And then, stretching out his spirit, he returned along the twilight pathway to sit up with a start. Doing his best to ignore the hammering in his head and his aching body, Tris struggled to his feet, feeling the long fight in every muscle. He staggered to the tomb and, with a nod of permission from Argus, thrust his hand inside. Cold steel greeted his touch, and he withdrew a sword of incomparable craftsmanship, its intricately wrought grip inlaid with gems in the crest of the House of Principality.

"The Lady's blessing upon you," Argus said, raising a hand in farewell as his image began to blur and fade.

"I can send you to your rest," Tris said, though his swollen lips slurred the words.

Argus shook his head. "Not yet. I made a vow, when I was mortal, that I would give my life to defeat the Obsidian King. He is not yet destroyed. Until then, I may not rest." He lifted a hand in salute. "You have earned my sword, and my blessing. My body and my army lie buried near the river. We are at your service, though we are bound to remain in these lonely lands."

The ghost shimmered and disappeared. The unlucky soldiers, one by one, winked out as a chill gust swept through the tomb, sending wild shadows across the walls. Mageslayer glistened in Tris's hands, unsullied by its years in the crypt, and from its rune-worked blade, he could feel the thrum of power deep within the ensorcelled steel.

"The Lady rest your souls," Tris murmured. With a thought, he snuffed out the torches, inched back the catafalque lid and staggered from the room. He felt a touch of pride that he did not fall to his knees before he reached the bottom of the stairs. The last thing he remembered was tugging on the rope and the distant sound of a bell.

When he opened his eyes, he lay on a couch in the Library parlor. Mageslayer lay beside him, and next to it, King Harrol's pouch. Royster dozed in a chair, but woke with a start, then grinned broadly at Tris. "I knew you could do it!" he exclaimed, jumping to his feet.

"Easy, easy," Tris murmured, his head throbbing. He wanted nothing so much as a hot bath and a soft bed. "I can't believe you couldn't stay awake."

Royster hummed an irreverent tune. "Oh I stayed awake for a long time, a very long time," he replied, fairly dancing in his excitement at Tris's triumph. "But after the first night, these old bones of mine needed some rest."

Tris found the energy to gape in amazement. "The first night?" he repeated.

Royster chuckled. "Aye. You were down there a night and a day, don't you know? Had to threaten the wrath of the Lady herself to keep that damn fool Jonmarc from charging in after you," he went on. "You've been out cold for a full day since we carried you up. But I knew you could do it, lad. I knew it!"

Tris looked around the room. Sprawled across chairs and library benches, Tris's companions slept in the parlor. Jae's startled shriek awakened the others, who crowded around Tris.

"Hold on!" Royster shouted. "Give him some room. There'll be plenty of time to tell his story," he said. "You there," he hailed Carina. "I suspect he's got a walloping headache that could use your touch. The rest of you, back to your rooms." Like a schoolmaster, Royster ran off the others until only Carina remained.

Tris could see a thousand unasked questions in Carina's eyes as she bent to her healing, letting her cool palms smoothe over his forehead and easing the pounding within.

When she was finished, Royster helped Tris to his feet. He leaned heavily on the librarian, and Carina slid under his other arm. Together they made their way to Tris's room, where Royster turned down the bed as if for a sick child while Carina heated a cup of tea by the fire. Against his weak protests, they pulled off his boots and trundled him into bed fully clothed, pressing a steaming mug of tea into his hands.

"Sleep," Carina instructed archly, supervising as Tris drank the tea. It smelled of herbs and honey and its steam soothed his pounding head. Tris handed her the empty cup and eased himself down. Sleep overtook him, and he remembered nothing else until morning.

CHAPTER THIRTY-TWO

THREE NIGHTS LATER, Tris and his companions readied for a hasty departure. Steam rose from the horses in the cold air, as they cinched their saddle straps and tied down their few belongings. Vahanian added a bucket of pitch to each rider's provisions, taking the torchlance for himself and passing arrows and bows to the other riders. When they were in the saddle, Mikhail and Gabriel stepped from the shadows.

"Remind me again why we're safer riding past magick beasts and assassins at night?" Vahanian snapped.

A hint of amusement curled Gabriel's mouth. "Because by night, we ride with you," the vayash moru replied. In the shadows beyond, Tris could see more figures stirring.

"Forgive me for noticing—but there aren't that many of you," Vahanian replied testily.

Gabriel shrugged. "These are of my family. Their loyalty is absolute. And they see that, in this, we have common cause with you."

"And they're real clear who's with us, and who isn't, right?"

Gabriel's disquieting smile revealed his incisors. "Quite."

"How does the road look between here and the bridge?" Tris asked, hoping his nervousness did not show in his voice. His mount nickered and pawed at the ground, as if it sensed both the undead and the looming danger.

"Clear when we passed," said Mikhail. "But we've seen scouts within a candlemark."

"If you saw them, why didn't you just eat them?" Vahanian growled.

"That would rather reveal our hand, wouldn't it?" Mikhail replied evenly.

"What of the beasts?" Kiara asked, and behind her, Berry edged her horse closer to Carina. Royster's eyes widened, and he clung more tightly to his reins.

"None sighted."

"The snows are getting deeper," Gabriel said, as two of the other vayash moru opened the stable doors. "We'd best be going."

Once on the road, the vayash moru slipped into the shadows. Vahanian rode point, with his lance lightly holstered and his sword close at hand. Tris rode behind him, while Kiara rode at the rear with Berry, Carina, Carroway and Royster in the middle. Each of them had a weapon at the ready—even Royster, who as it turned out, had perfected the use of a slingshot under Berry's tutelage.

"We've only got to reach the bridge," he heard Carina tell Berry comfortingly.

"Why is it called Gibbet Bridge?" Berry asked.

"Because they used to hang men from it," Royster replied absently. At the unanimous frowns he received from the rest of the party, Royster shrugged. "Sorry. It's the truth."

"If it keeps on snowing, we'll be pressed to make it in a night," Vahanian said, his sour mood clear in his tone. "Ride hard, but stay together."

Tris nudged his horse to pick up the pace, glad for the darkness. He hoped it would hide his fatigue from his friends. If they knew how much the working with Argus had cost him, and how drained he still remained despite Carina's best efforts, he was sure they would have postponed the journey. But the reports of Margolan scouts seemed to worry even Taru, who urged them to leave as quickly as possible.

Mageslayer hung at his belt, the finest sword he had ever possessed. Partnered with this, he amended his thoughts, because there was a sense of presence in the ensorcelled sword that was just shy of sentience. Taru had had little time to school him on the ways of enchanted weapons, but he had been able to glean three things about the sword. First, that it would temporarily enhance his magic in a battle arcane. Second, that it had some warding powers against poisons and venom and cursed objects, though Taru did not know the extent of its power, and cautioned against relying on the sword's protection. And third, that it was a masterfully forged and perfectly balanced weapon, which incited a glance of envy even from Vahanian, though no one dared handle it besides Tris.

They rode in silence, guided by moonlight, riding as fast as they dared over the snowy roads. No other travelers were about at this hour, and the inns were few in this sparsely populated corner of Principality. As the hours passed without incident, Tris began to wonder whether they had been worrying for naught.

"Not far now," Vahanian said wearily an hour before dawn. They could see the riverbank, and in the distance, Gibbet Bridge. Tris's imagination supplied dangling corpses, though he knew it was only the swaying of branches. A small hamlet sat to one side of the road, near a bend in the river. As they approached, the thatched roof of a house burst into flames, startling them and driving them back a pace with the rush of heat.

"Watch out!" Carroway shouted as arrows flew from the darkened houses.

"Ambush!" Vahanian yelled. "Ride for the bridge!"

Tris felt an arrow slice through his thigh, opening a gash. A rush of fire streamed from the darkness, averted at the last moment as Tris snapped his shields up, barely in time. Something was wrong, very wrong, he thought, as his heart began to pound and his blood thundered in his ears. The fire streamed brighter, as Tris fought to keep his seat on his horse. The fire pulsed once more, and Tris lashed out, on instinct more than plan, unsure later even of what power he sent in return. An explosion shook the night, sending a stream of sparks high into the sky and the blue light winked out.

"Ride!" Kiara shouted, as mounted men pounded from the hamlet's streets. Tris fell forward on his horse, gripping its mane, as vertigo washed over him. He heard the clang of steel and the swish of quarrels as his horse thundered through the snow behind the others.

In the moonlight, Tris sensed more than saw dark shapes, moving too swiftly for the eye to track. He heard a strangled cry from one of the archers, and then the panicked shriek of a horse as its rider was snatched from the saddle.

"Don't look back!" Carina shouted, grabbing Royster's reins and pulling the librarian's frightened horse along with hers.

Disoriented, struggling for breath, Tris held on to his horse with sweaty hands, feeling as if both sight and magesense were distorted by strong wine. He saw the spirits that rose up behind them as they neared the bridge, and knew by instinct that it was Argus and his routed men, risen to fight one last battle. The frightened cries of those few pursuers who remained assured him that the ghosts were not a product of his sudden delirium. He tried to raise a hand in warding, tried to work a simple spell to cover his friends, but found his power distant, unwilling to respond to his command.

The winter wind whipped their hair and stung their faces as they rode for the arched stone bridge. Their horses thundered across the roadway, over the dark, icy waters of the Nu River. Though they left behind both pursuers and protectors at the bridge, none of the companions slowed until the crossing was well behind them. Dawn was breaking as Vahanian, still leading, finally reined in his foam-flecked mount. The others nudged their exhausted horses to catch up. Vahanian rose in his stirrups and counted heads.

"Everyone's here," he said, fatigue clear in his voice. "Let's find somewhere to sleep."

The sharp staccato of quarrels hitting the ground rang out in the morning air. A line of arrows, launched at close range by crossbows, cut across the road in front of them. From out of the bushes, soldiers in the livery of the Principality army stepped into view.

"Drop your weapons," their captain grated.

By reflex, Vahanian reached for his sword, and cried out as a quarrel clipped his shoulder.

"The next shot finds your heart," the soldier warned. "Drop your weapons."

With a curse, Vahanian dropped his sword. Tris and the others exchanged worried glances, but did the same as more soldiers ringed them, crossbows raised and notched. Two soldiers came forward and gathered up their weapons.

"We have urgent business," Tris said, hoping he looked better than he felt. It was taking all of his concentration just to stay in the saddle, and he felt feverish. He felt suddenly worse as

Mageslayer fell from his grasp. His power still seemed out of reach, and it left a wrenching void that made him feel physically ill.

"I'll bet you do," the captain chuckled. "The king put a watch for a group with two swordsmen, a bard and a healer," he said with a nod toward Carina's green belt and the lute-shaped sack on Carroway's pack. "You can tell your urgent business to the general."

They rode for a candlemark in silence, ringed by armed soldiers. The gash on Tris's thigh burned, and he had begun to shake. Once, he saw Carina watching him worriedly. The soldiers led them to a small fort a few hours' ride from Gibbet Bridge. The captain motioned for them to dismount, and Tris fell rather than swung down from his horse, but managed to keep his feet.

"You'll wait here, until the general returns," the captain said, leading them to a large, sparsely furnished cell. Four soldiers with crossbows kept their weapons trained on the group until the door was secured, and two more remained on guard as the captain left.

Tris leaned against the wall and slid to the floor, as Carina rushed to his side. "What happened? Are you hit?" she said, and Tris wondered if he were as pale as he felt.

"Something's wrong," he murmured. "The magic... is out of reach."

"What does he mean by that?" Vahanian whispered, as Carina found the gash on Tris's leg. She frowned, and pressed one finger against the wound, then lifted it to her nose.

"Wormroot," she said, and looked through the pouches on her belt that the soldiers had permitted her to keep. "The arrow tips were poisoned."

"Wormroot?" Vahanian questioned. "It doesn't grow anywhere near here. And besides, at worst it causes a stomach ache—"

"That's because you're not a mage," Carina replied in a low voice. "I heard stories when Cam and I were with the mercenaries, here in Principality. They said to stop a mage, use wormroot. In large enough doses, over a long period, they say it will kill or drive a mage mad."

"Can you help him?" Carroway said anxiously. Royster kept watch for the guards, who stood at their posts, paying their captives no heed.

"I'll try," she replied. "But I never heard what the antidote was for wormroot, except that it should wear off over time. I'll start with rope vine," she said, digging in her pouch. "It helps with some of the poisons that fog the mind. The wound wasn't deep, so he can't have gotten much."

"He seemed to get worse when we were captured," Kiara mused. "In fact, he nearly fell when they made us drop our swords."

"Could Mageslayer have been absorbing some of the effect?" Carroway asked.

"It's quite possible," Royster said quietly. "Such powers are not uncommon for spelled objects, and it would be a handy thing for a mage's weapon to possess."

Carina rolled Tris over onto his back and ripped his pant leg wider to expose the injury.

Taking the hem of her cloak, she cleaned the wound the best she could, and made a paste of dried leaves from her pouch with the stale water Carroway fetched from a bucket in the corner. Within half a candlemark, the burning pain had stopped, and Tris felt the shaking cease.

"Thank you," he murmured to Carina, who was tending the gash on Vahanian's shoulder.

"Glad you're feeling better," Vahanian whispered in a low rasp. "Now, how do we get out of here?"

"Don't you think it's odd that the army was practically waiting for us on the other side of the bridge?" Carroway said. "Do you think the general is in cahoots with Jared? Think about it," the bard said tightly. "On the other side of the bridge, by night, at least we had the vayash moru and Argus. We lost both those defenses come dawn, as soon as we crossed the bridge. And that's when the army happened to be waiting for us." They exchanged worried glances as they considered the bard's scenario.

"But King Staden is a good king!" Berry protested. "At least, that's what everyone says," she added when they looked at her.

"Staden might not have anything to do with it," Vahanian replied, wincing as Carina worked on his shoulder. "Once this general gets us to the city, what he does with us is anyone's guess. Orders are easy enough to fake."

Kiara was on watch near the high slit that was the cell's only window. "Uh oh," she said. "Looks like the general has arrived."

Tris pulled himself into a sitting position and hoped he looked better than he felt. The Principality captain strode in, leading the way for a dark-haired man in a cloak. "These are the foreigners we arrested, general," the captain said as he stepped aside to give the general a look through the bars. "Came across Gibbet Bridge like the demon herself was after them. There are a couple extra, but four of them fit the bill."

Tris heard Carina gasp. Kiara glanced at her cousin, who had gone quite pale and stepped toward the back.

Kiara stepped forward. "Sirs," she said, making a perfunctory bow. "My companions and I were beset by highwaymen, which accounted for our haste last night. Two of my party are injured. We were traveling on business to Principality City. We have harmed no one. Please, let us be on our way."

The general looked them over. He was of medium build, with dark brown hair and intelligent eyes. But for the hard set to his mouth and a tightness around his blue eyes, he might have been considered handsome. That he was likely no older than Vahanian and held the rank of general spoke to his competence, and Tris guessed by his manner that he was accomplished with the sword that hung at his belt.

"I'm afraid that's impossible, m'lady. I have my orders from the king. What he seeks with you, I do not know, nor do I care. We will leave within a candlemark for the city. You can make your case there."

He was about to go when Carina stepped forward. "Gregor," she called softly.

The general turned, and his eyes widened when he saw the healer, as if he had seen a ghost.

"You?" the general breathed. "But I saw you die... with Ric... what magic is this?"

Carina bowed her head and stepped closer to the bars. "No trick, Gregor. Cam took me to the Sisters. They brought me back, from the very arms of the Lady."

Gregor's face hardened. "More than you could do for my brother."

Carina flushed. "Please Gregor, listen to me. Our mission is urgent. Please, let us go."

"I have my orders."

"Then give sanctuary at least for the girl and the old man," Carina begged. "Send them to the Sisters. The king said nothing of them."

"How dare you beg a favor of me?" Gregor demanded. "Why should I?"

Carina looked up at him, and her face was wet with tears. "For Ric's sake," she said quietly, "for what was before. Please, Gregor. Please."

Gregor looked at her in silence for a moment. His face was unreadable. With an oath, he turned away. "Take the child and the old man to the Sisterhood," he commanded the captain. "Make it clear they are to be kept there until the king gives permission for their release." He turned back to Carina, and looked at her coldly.

"All debts are paid," he said. The venom in his voice made Vahanian start toward the bars, but Kiara laid a warning hand on his arm, and he stayed where he was. Tris felt his own anger bristle, and saw fire glint in Carroway's eyes.

Carina looked at the floor. "Thank you," she whispered.

"Most people treat a healer with respect," Vahanian observed acidly from where he stood. His hand fell from habit to where his sword should have rested in his empty scabbard.

Gregor regarded him icily. He glanced at Carina. "Two of a kind, Carina?" he said with an edge, and the healer turned scarlet. Gregor looked back to Vahanian. "I had the utmost respect for my late brother's betrothed, until she failed to save him. To think she died trying made the memory bearable. Knowing she survived and he did not is a different matter entirely." He looked at the group. "I do not know what the king requires of you, but I am a willing instrument of his justice." With that, the general turned on his heel and left.

The cell door opened, and the captain gestured for Royster and Berry. Carina hugged Berry tightly.

"It will be all right, Carina. You'll see," Berry said with a child's certainty. Carina managed a smile.

"You'll be safe with the Sisterhood," she said, her voice tight.

Royster laid a hand on Carina's shoulder. "I'll see to the girl," the librarian said. "Thank you."

Carina nodded as the two were led out of sight. The guards returned to their post, and Carina buried her face in her hands. Kiara knelt next to her cousin and waved the others away, wrapping her arms around Carina as she sobbed. Vahanian turned away from the cell bars with a potent curse, and kicked at a rock. Carroway sat down next to Tris.

"At least we're headed in the right direction," the bard observed, with as much hope as he could muster.

Tris closed his eyes and leaned back against the wall. "The question is—do we get to stay?"

"It's nearly two days' ride into the city," Carroway said quietly. "Do you think... tonight... that Gabriel...?"

Tris shook his head. "Doubtful. Their fight is with Jared, not this king. And the vayash moru decide their own schedule. Technically, we're not in danger—at least, not yet. They won't risk reprisals here killing mortals."

"If the witch biddies are as smart as they look, maybe they'll figure out something's wrong when Royster and Berry show up on their doorstep," Vahanian said, leaning against the wall. "Although they don't ride to the rescue very often." He cursed again. "Which means, we're on our own."

The captain returned in a candlemark with six armed men to lead them to their horses for the ride into the city. He stood before Vahanian, fists on his hips. Vahanian's eyes narrowed and he spat just shy of the captain's boot.

"You will be taken for questioning," the captain announced. "Cooperate, and no harm will come to you," he advised. "Get moving."

* * *

THEY SPENT THE night under heavy guard at another outpost, and woke at dawn for the ride into Principality City. The roadway grew wider, leading to the castle. Merchants and beggars moved aside to let them pass. They reached a heavily gated entrance in the base of the castle, and as they entered, the massive iron portcullis creaked back into place behind them.

"I don't like this," Vahanian muttered.

"For once, I think I agree with you," Carina murmured.

Tris's imagination supplied many possibilities during their march, none of them pleasant. When they reached the castle, he expected to have the party split up, searched for the rest of their weapons, and locked—perhaps chained—in dungeon cells, awaiting an escort to Margolan.

The king's guardsmen met the captain at the inner bailey. "We'll take the prisoners from here," the guardsman said.

"General Gregor gave me orders to deliver them personally," the army captain countered.

"You may give the general the king's thanks. But we will take the prisoners from here."

The army captain's displeasure was clear in his face, but he gave a bow and signaled to his men to retreat.

"You will come with us," the captain of the guard said expressionlessly, as the liveried men-at-arms formed a column on either side of the prisoners. The captain of the guard marched them past the cells, and Vahanian and Tris exchanged puzzled glances as they climbed

up a winding stairway toward the higher levels
of the palace. They emerged behind a heavy
wooden door in a well-appointed room.

"You will wait here," the captain said. He drew
a dagger from his belt and split the cords that
bound them, then gave a crisp bow and retreated, leaving only enough guards to block each
exit. The prisoners looked at each other warily.

"Do you know this king, Tris?" Kiara asked.

"I've never met him. But perhaps Jared has,"
Tris replied. The reception hall, while not opu-
lent, was quite comfortable, with a fire blazing in
the hearth. A large, stern portrait glowered above
the mantle, a strapping king dressed for a hunt,
his trophy fox kill hanging from his grip, one
black leather boot poised in triumph atop a
downed stag. Finely woven tapestries covered the
other walls.

"I'd say we're going nowhere fast," Vahanian
said, rubbing his wrists. "I don't get it. First they
march us here as if they've got a gallows waiting.
Now it looks like they're going to serve dinner."

"Maybe they are," Carroway replied uneasily.
"Question is, are we the guests or the peace offering?"

Just then a door burst open. A streak of green
brocade, the rustle of taffeta and running footsteps caught them all off-guard as their visitor
lunged at Vahanian, nearly carrying him backward. Caught by the fighter's sharp reflexes, the
newcomer beamed at them, a bright-eyed girl
with a cascade of auburn hair braided with pearls
on strands of gold.

"I told you I'd be all right!" Berry exclaimed, and before Vahanian could react, she threw her arms around his neck and kissed him on the cheek.

"I see I have no need to inquire which of you might be Vahanian," a deep baritone voice said from the door, and the astonished group found a bearded, sturdily built man watching them, powerful arms crossed across his chest, his expression no longer stern as in the portrait above the fireplace, but mirthful and indulgent.

Berry released Vahanian, running with undignified joy to greet each of the travelers. Gone was her tattered tunic, replaced by an ankle-length gown of Mussa brocade, its bodice alight with small gemstones and pearls. The unruly auburn curls were tamed into a dignified braid that shimmered in the firelight, plaited with gold. Scrubbed clean, perfumed and powdered, the tomboy had disappeared, replaced by a beautiful young girl too excited by her guests to worry about her finery. "And this is Carina," Berry concluded her introductions.

"I have heard much concerning each of you," the king said, stepping closer. "Forgive the... irregular greeting," he said with a smile and a perfunctory bow. "I am King Staden of Principality. I believe you already know my daughter, Berwyn."

Behind Staden, Soterius and Harrtuck crowded their way into the gathering room, followed by Royster. They greeted Tris and the others with hearty cheers.

Tris stepped forward. "Greetings, gracious king," he said with a bow. "Forgive our surprise, but we had no idea—"

The king chuckled. "Yes, Berwyn told me of her ruse. She has, I fear, her mother's love for a prank," he said with a twinkle in his eye. "And I believe her role-playing may have saved her life, for her captors might have gone harder on her had they known the truth," he said, sobering. "For that same reason, when her traveling party was beset by bandits, we did not publicize that it was my daughter who was captured."

"The noble's daughter," Vahanian said, and King Staden nodded in confirmation. "The one the travelers at the inn said had been taken by slavers."

"We knew she could not conceal her noble birth," the king replied, "but we hoped to make her less of a hostage." His eyes grew serious. "When Berwyn returned to me last night, she told me about your capture. Forgive my use of the guards," he said with a gesture toward the soldiers who now filed from the room, dismissed. "But your friends here," he said with a nod to Soterius and Harrtuck, "warned me that you might not answer my summons any other way."

Staden smiled. "I, and my kingdom, are in your debt," he said. He walked among them, and stopped in front of Vahanian. "Yes, you fit Berwyn's description of an adventurer," he said with a grin, extending his hand to the mercenary, who shook it dubiously. "She told me you were her special champion," he said. "Tonight, there will be a banquet in your honor," he proclaimed. "For all of you, and your bravery in returning my daughter to her home. You have only to ask of me, and it will be done."

"Your Majesty," Tris began, and King Staden turned to him, taking his hand in greeting and clapping him on the shoulder.

"Berwyn told me of your circumstances, Prince Drayke," the king replied. "I shared many hunts with your father, and found him a worthy companion. I understand the urgency of your journey."

"I am grateful for your hospitality," Tris said. "But I fear that an open welcome may place your kingdom in peril."

Staden dismissed Tris's warning with a gesture. "On the morrow, we will talk, and you shall have the resources of my kingdom, my best men-at-arms, and my wisest military strategists at your service," Staden announced. "I have no love for Margolan raiders within my boundaries and I have heard the tales of the refugees who crowd my border villages. We shall all be better off when Margolan answers to a fit king.

"But tonight," he continued, "we feast. I never thought to see my daughter again. You have returned her to me. Nothing is more important. Come, we must get ready," he said, clapping his hands sharply. Servants streamed from the doors, gathering around Tris and the others and moving them toward the exits. "My servants will help you prepare," the king called after them, as Berry stood beside him with her arms around his waist.

CHAPTER THIRTY-THREE

TRIS WAS LED to a room that rivaled the most comfortable in Shekerishet. One servant poured a steaming bath, laden with musky oils, while another laid out fresh clothing on the bed and a third prepared a respite of wine, sliced fruit and bread. Berry's presence enabled him to relax his guard. He removed his soiled and tattered traveling clothes and slipped into the hot bath.

I may have already learned the first lesson of kingship too well, he thought, forcing himself to relax as he sipped from a goblet of wine. I've started to expect a knife between my shoulders no matter where I go.

Whether it was Carina's antidote or the passage of several days, Tris felt much recovered from the wormroot. He shuddered as he recalled the empty feeling of having his power out of reach. Its absence felt as if something vital were pulled from the marrow of his very bones, and he did not doubt Carina's observation that a long, strong dosing of wormroot could indeed kill or drive a mage to madness. He resolved to take up the issue with the Sisterhood at the first opportunity.

Better to have run into it now, when I can figure out how to deal with it, than later, when I'm up against Jared.

He finished an unhurried bath to the obvious satisfaction of the servants assigned to his care. Tris wondered how much Berry had stressed that the servants were to see to his every need, for despite having grown up with valets and footmen, Tris could not recall being pampered so lavishly , even in his own kingdom.

The bells of the courtyard tower were ringing the supper hour as Tris straightened his tunic and paced in the reception room, awaiting his companions. Staden's servants had done remarkably well at finding clothes to fit, and he now awaited the banquet in a gray tunic and slacks of the finest satin, chagrined at the costumier who insisted on adding what he called a "wizard's cloak" to complete the outfit. Catching a glimpse of himself in a mirror, Tris had to admit that he looked the part of a Summoner, a spirit mage dressed in the color of shadows.

Carroway and Soterius arrived together. Carroway was obviously enjoying their first opportunity in nearly three months to dress for court. The bard wore a flamboyant tunic of gem-toned silks, with draping sleeves and bright colors. Soterius could not have appeared more different in a muted outfit of hunter's green, devoid completely of ornamentation, remarkable only for the luxuriousness of its brocade and the perfection of its fit. To their surprise, Gabriel arrived a few moments later, dressed head to toe in midnight blue.

"The Sisters told me that I might find you here," the vayash moru said off-handedly at his unexpected appearance.

"No! I won't do it. You can beg me all you like. Bad enough that I can't take my sword. Be off with you!" Tov Harrtuck arrived, still arguing with the valet who had been assigned to him, adamant that he would continue to wear his worn leather vest over a rich brown brocade ensemble.

The costumier pulled at the scuffed vest, attempting to wrest it away by force, but Harrtuck scowled and held his ground like a terrier with a bone, prompting chuckles from Tris and the others. "Please, sir, reconsider. You're to be the guests of the King tonight! Surely you can make an exception—"

"I like my vest," Harrtuck retorted. "And you've already gotten me into these... things," he said with a wave toward his fine clothes. Tris realized that in all the years he had known the armsmaster, he had never once, no matter the occasion, seen Harrtuck dressed for anything but the barracks.

"Sir, please—" The costumier was almost in tears, but Harrtuck was resolute, though it

appeared that the stolid fighter had availed himself of the proffered bath and made an attempt to
tame his unruly hair and groom his recently
regrown beard.

"No! I will not! Now go," Harrtuck said,
shooing his groomers away with a flurry of waving arms. "Go dress Vahanian. It'll take half a
dozen of you just to get his sword away from
him," he said, chasing the flummoxed servants
from the room. He shut the door soundly behind
him, standing hands on hips as if ready should
the servants return. He turned toward Tris and
the others, grumbling under his breath as he
scratched at his beard.

"Lady and Whore!" he exclaimed. "What's the
use of making a body miserable for a feast, I ask
you?" he continued, in such obvious distress that
Tris and Carroway burst out laughing.

"Oh yes, go ahead, have a good laugh," he said
as even Soterius joined in. "Our little peacock
finally has his finery back," he said with a good-
natured jibe at Carroway. "And Ban here was
thinking of nothing but the ladies when he
dressed."

"Now it's not so bad," Tris answered, trying to
keep his laughter out of his voice. "I didn't think
they did too badly with me."

Harrtuck paused and looked Tris over from head
to toe. "Aye, my liege, you're right. Anyone who
saw you would know you for a wizard, and a
king," he said, with unexpected seriousness. Then
he shook his head, returning to his self-pity. "On the
other hand, it's a waste of good cloth to dress up the

likes of me," he added, giving Soterius a scowl when the soldier vigorously agreed. Whatever more might have been said was lost as the doors opened to admit the rest of their companions.

Royster strode into the room first, a wide grin on his face and a bounce in his step. His wild, snow-white hair was trimmed and tamed under a scholar's cap, and the thin little man beamed with pride at the flowing academic robe that replaced his riding gear. He hummed a tavern ditty and executed a sprightly pirouette for his audience. "Not bad, don't you think?" he said with a broad wink. "Oh, it almost makes me wish Kessen were here!" He looked quickly at Tris. "Not that I'd want you to summon him, mind you, but it would make him pop to see me in this! Scholar's robes indeed! I hope we get to keep them," he said impishly. "I'll save them until I'm back at the Library and wear them every day, just to vex him!"

Kiara and Carina entered together, the Isencroft princess leading the way into the room, with Jae circling overhead. Gone were Kiara's riding leathers and breastplate, the solid boots and coarsely woven cloak. In their place was a copper-colored gown of silk that played off her auburn hair and enhanced the firm-toned contours of her body by its slim cut. Tris met her eyes across the room and blushed as a smile crept to her lips, realizing that his expression betrayed his appreciation. Jae landed lightly on her shoulder, and Tris noted that the little gyregon now wore a slim gold chain around his throat.

Carina was a step behind. A green gown of Mussa silk replaced her healer's robes, and a headband of pearls secured her short black hair. But where Kiara's ease was apparent as she teased with the others and glowingly accepted their compliments, Carina hung back, and Tris realized that the court healer was at a loss outside of her role of physician, without the barrier that the status of her robes made easy to enforce.

"You clean up well," Vahanian said from behind her, and Carina blushed scarlet.

"At least it's green," she managed, for once at a loss for words.

Vahanian chuckled. "I've always wondered what healers wore beneath their robes," he murmured. Carina feigned an outraged swing at him which Vahanian dodged easily. "Hey, take it easy. All I meant was that you give Kiara competition in that dress."

"Really?" she replied, with a glance toward Kiara, who was joking with Carroway about the brightness of his waistcoat.

"Absolutely," Vahanian replied, executing a courtly bow without a hint of mockery. He was dressed head to toe in black velvet, with just the lightest hint of gold around the collar and cuffs. It complemented his hair and complexion perfectly, and Tris decided that Berry herself must have had a hand in their wardrobe. The only items out of place were Vahanian's scuffed black boots and the absence of a sword belt around his waist.

The mercenary pulled at his collar uncomfortably. "I still want to know whose rule it is that we can't take our swords. Stupid rule if you ask me."

"You can't wear a sword in the presence of the King," Carina replied. "Everyone knows that."

"Excuse me," Vahanian retorted, returning to their usual banter, "but everyone doesn't spend their days at court. I don't go anywhere without my sword."

"Where you go, that's probably a good idea."

"There's one small piece of business that hasn't been taken care of," Tris said with a glance toward Vahanian. "We have a little settling up to do." He walked to the table, and from beneath it, lifted a brassbound chest, heavy enough that it shuddered the table with its weight. "I promised to pay you once we reached Principality," he said to Vahanian. "Here it is."

Tris released the clasp and flipped open the chest to reveal an ample mound of Dhasson gold. More than enough to let a man live well for the rest of his life. Tris looked at Vahanian, an unspoken question hanging between them.

The smuggler had not moved, and while his stance suggested that he, too, heard the challenge in Tris's tone, his eyes were unreadable as he stood silent for a moment, looking at the chest.

"I'm going to Margolan," Vahanian replied. "Why don't you put it somewhere safe 'til I get back."

Tris broke out laughing and slapped his friend on the back as Kiara and the others gathered around the fighter, expressing their pleasure at his decision. Vahanian shrugged, uncomfortable with the attention, then grinned his pleasure at their acceptance.

"The feast awaits, honored guests," intoned a servant from the main doors. They filed down the corridor, and Tris found that, despite the assurance of Berry's presence and her father's sworn assistance, he was holding his breath as the wide doors swung open.

Inside the banquet hall, heavily laden feast tables awaited them. The servant guided them to the head table, where they would be joined by Staden and the queen. A fire burned brightly in the massive fireplace, and the smells of roasting game and simmering wassail greeted them as they edged their way through the throng. Four musicians struck up a merry tune on lyre, flute, dulcimer and drum, while costumed performers delighted the group and cupbearers poured ale.

"Now that's a feast," Carroway said. They took their assigned places at the table, and Tris was delighted to find himself next to Kiara. Carina, on his left, found Vahanian to be her tablemate, and Tris decided that Berry had tried her hand at matchmaking with her instructions to the steward. Berry had reserved the seat alongside Vahanian, and next to her would be King Staden and the queen. To the queen's left were Gabriel, Soterius and Harrtuck, with Royster and Carroway at the far end, nearest the musicians.

With a stately trumpet fanfare, the doors at the far end of the banquet hall flew open and half a dozen liveried trumpeters heralded the entrance of the king. Staden was resplendent in crimson and gold. The queen walked beside him, an older reflection of Berry. Behind them, Berry walked with her head held high. The green dress from the morning was gone, replaced by wine-colored satin. Tris caught a mischievous wink from Berry, and all rose as the monarch moved through the room.

Staden took his place at the table and looked out over the assembled crowd. "Nobles and ladies, honored guests," he began. "There can be no celebration grand enough to welcome home my daughter, Berwyn, in safety," he announced, and paused as a cheer went up from the crowd. He raised a hand for silence. "For her safe return, we thank the Goddess, and these, our guests," he said, gesturing toward Tris and the others, "who have brought her home at no small peril to themselves." He paused once more as applause rang out. "In thanksgiving for our good fortune, let the feast begin!" he said, throwing his arms wide with the same mischievous grin Tris saw so often on Berry's face.

Carina clapped politely, but her thoughts were elsewhere. Tris noticed that Vahanian seemed determined to break through the healer's distraction.

"I'm sorry," Carina murmured. "I'm just not in a festive mood," she demurred as Vahanian's attempt to engage her in banter fell flat. "I don't mean to spoil the evening for everyone else. You have every right to celebrate. It's just that... being back here..."

"I feel the same way about the Borderlands," Vahanian replied quietly, unusually serious. "I haven't been back there in ten years, since I buried my wife."

Carina looked back at him, surprised at the admission. He leaned toward her, dropping his voice further, and touched her hand. "The dead forgive us. I know that now. They want us to move on."

Carina was quiet for a moment, but she did not look away. "I want to believe that," she murmured.

"I wish you could."

The silence hung between them for a moment, and then Vahanian lightened the mood by sliding his goblet in front of her. "Until then, the best way to join the party is with some strong wine," he said and motioned for the steward, who filled both their goblets.

"I should warn you that I'm never on my best behavior," Vahanian murmured to Berry, deliberately attempting to make Carina smile.

"I think that's why she sat me next to you," Carina replied, making an effort. "It would be impolite for her to douse you with her water if you get out of place. I, on the other hand..." she warned, and ominously fingered her goblet as her voice trailed off.

"I'm sure that wasn't it at all," Vahanian replied sportingly, with a conspiratorial glance at Berry. "She's noticed how smitten you've been with the tales Harrtuck's been telling about my adventures, and so—"

"Smitten?" Carina echoed, beginning to rise.

Vahanian caught her wrist and pulled her down into her seat. "With the stories," he added teasingly, grinning at her glare. "Smile. Everyone's watching."

"You're impossible."

"Now you're catching on."

Tris saw Kiara suppress a smile at the banter. "Want to take bets on a fight?" she whispered.

Tris chuckled. "Could be a close call."

"In a perverse way, I think he's good for her," Kiara replied as she tasted her soup. "I've never seen her notice someone enough to get angry before."

"Then maybe a fight would be a good thing," Tris conceded with a smile. "Although I don't know how we'll explain it to the court."

Course upon lavish course was laid in front of them, each preceded by a different entertainment. Principality, legendary for its rich gold mines, might not make extravagance a daily occasion, Tris thought, but its king certainly knew how to make an exception. Berry clapped in excitement at the veiled Trevath dancers, whose shimmering silks and belled wrists and ankles made an astonishing and exotic display. Singers and musicians, magicians and jesters followed, each attempting to outdo those who had come before. Tris guessed that it was only with difficulty that Carroway restrained himself from joining them.

Tris was surprised to find himself at ease for the first time since their flight from Margolan. He resolutely refused to think about the more solemn preparations that would begin in the morning, and focused instead on this opportunity to engage Kiara in conversation. She, too, seemed willing to steer clear of serious topics, and so they fell into a comfortable banter, comparing their experiences growing up at court, the intrigues and observations that only came with the overprotected, yet overexposed, life within a palace.

When the last course was served, Staden rose, holding up his hands for silence. With great ceremony, he left the table to cross to his throne, escorting Berry to stand at his side. "Before we lose ourselves completely in revelry," he boomed, "I must acknowledge my debt to our guests, and reward them for their service in restoring Berwyn to her home. Although there is no reward truly equal to the life of a princess, for their bravery, I beg them to accept this token, and to divide it among themselves as they see fit," he said, as four guards entered, pulling a heavy, wheeled cart draped with the banner of Principality. When they reached the front of the greatroom, they stopped and at Staden's wave, removed the banner with a flourish.

Tris gasped, and he heard his companions murmur their own astonishment. Loaded on the cart was a large chest, opened to reveal a literal king's ransom in gold and jewels. There was enough to set a man up as a noble, Tris thought, or buy the aid of troops to fight a war. Nor was Staden's generosity lost on his guests, for pandemonium broke out at the abundance, until Staden bellowed for silence.

"Thank you," he said simply, facing Tris and the others. "Principality is in your debt." His gaze stopped on Vahanian. "One more boon has yet to be granted tonight," he said with a smile. "Berwyn has told me of the particular valor one of your company displayed in her rescue, and for that bravery, I call Jonmarc Vahanian."

Out of the corner of his eye, Tris saw Carina elbow Vahanian to move from his seat, as the low buzz in the room made clear that even here, the mercenary's name might not be completely unknown. Vahanian squared his shoulders and sauntered toward the king, his manner making it clear to any who might have doubted that, even without his weapons, he was a swordsman and a man of war.

"My daughter informs me that you are liegeman to no king. Is that true?" Staden asked.

"It's true," Vahanian replied levelly.

"Today, in gratitude for your bravery on behalf of my daughter, I name you Lord of Dark Haven, master of its lands and manor. In return," Staden added cagily, with the look of a man who knows his cards well, "I do not ask your fealty," he said, and a gasp went up from the assemblage. He raised a hand for silence. "In return," he continued, "I ask only that you consent to be Lord Protector of my daughter, Berwyn of Principality, should ever she require your sword in defense of her life. How say you, Jonmarc Vahanian?"

Tris saw Vahanian look at Berry for a long moment in silence, meeting her eyes as if searching her soul. Then, when it seemed that the tension in the room could last no longer, the mercenary nodded.

"I will. But for her defense alone," he said to Staden. "Not lands or kingdom or wealth."

"Leave it to Jonmarc to bargain with the King," Kiara murmured to Tris, who chuckled.

"Does it surprise you?"

"I guess not. No matter what Carina says, I rather like him."

"Good," Tris chuckled. "So do I."

The consternation that Vahanian's bargain caused did not appear to concern Staden. Or perhaps, Tris thought, Berry had warned her father well. "Agreed," the king pronounced. "Now receive my blessing, kneeling not to me, but to Berwyn."

Vahanian paused again, and for an instant, Tris thought that the proud mercenary might balk. Then, stiffly, he lowered himself to one knee, and bowed his head. Staden took Vahanian's right hand between his own and Berry laid a satin mantle over their clasped hands.

"In the names of the Goddess and by all the power of her faces, I name you Lord Vahanian, master of Dark Haven and champion of the Princess Berwyn," Staden pronounced, and the room broke into loud applause.

"Rise, Lord Vahanian," Staden boomed with a smile. "May the hand of the Dark Lady protect you. Go now, with the blessing of our realm and the gratitude of our royal person. All greet Lord Vahanian, Master of Dark Haven!" Staden pronounced as Vahanian rose to his feet and the guests broke into cheers and applause.

Vahanian returned to his seat amid a press of well-wishers and dropped into his chair with a satisfied smile. He turned to Carina. "Go ahead. Say it."

"Say what?"

"I don't know," he jibed. "But you've always got something to say."

Carina gave a knowing smile. "Just expect to see more of Gabriel," she replied sweetly.

Vahanian frowned, looking cautiously at her. "Why Gabriel?"

"You'll have to ask Royster. He was telling us some legends from that region and they were fascinating."

"Oh really?" Vahanian replied skeptically. "I'll have to check on that."

"Do that," she said with a wicked grin.

"You always get to have the last word, don't you?"

"Not me," the healer chuckled, becoming intensely interested in her wine. "Never."

"You're doing it again."

Carina looked away innocently. "Doing what?"

"Don't you need to go pray or something?"

Kiara leaned over to Tris. "How long do you think they can keep this up?" she asked in a conspiratorial whisper.

He shrugged. "Probably all night. Care to wager on it?"

She chuckled. "Sure. Just take a little of my share of that pile," she said, nodding in the direction of their treasure.

The revelry continued well into the night, its formality gone completely once Staden took his leave, guiding Berry unwillingly from the room when the tower clock struck midnight. Carroway slipped from his seat to join the minstrels, and was gaining the respect of his fellow bards with an adroit show of juggling. Harrtuck and Soterius drifted over to the guards' table in the far corner of the room, and from the occasional guffaw, Tris knew that Harrtuck was well into his ale and deep into his stories. To Tris's amusement, Royster found himself the eccentric darling of the ladies, and passed the evening at the center of a circle of noble women, who vied for the chance to sit at his feet and listen to his tales of passion and valor. Jae, who had stuffed himself on the dainty morsels Berry had offered him, waddled over to Royster near the fire and edged himself as close as possible to the warm hearth, then snored contentedly, his back gently stroked by one of the more adventurous court ladies.

The musicians struck up lively dance tunes, and to Tris's surprise, Kiara pulled him onto the dance floor, urging him to join her in the spirited reels and circle dances that now crowded the open spaces. He had never considered himself more than an adequate dancer, though the duties of court had required him to learn the basic steps. Kiara, on the other hand, was an excellent dancer and he found himself caught up in her enthusiasm.

He exchanged a glance with Kiara when Vahanian pulled Carina to the dance floor for the circle dance that was forming.

"Really, you can ask Kiara," Carina protested. "I don't dance."

"Neither do I," Vahanian replied. "At least, not sober. But this isn't really dancing."

"It's not?"

"Uh uh. It's just like walking on a ship, only on dry land. And after a little ale. Like this," he said, pulling her into the circle and slipping an arm around her waist while Kiara, grinning broadly, slipped an arm around her shoulder. The music began, slowly at first, then gained speed as the circle wove and wound through the repeating steps. The formation split apart, and pairs of dancers whirled through the steps two at a time, keeping their feet only by holding on to one another.

Tris found that his own excitement had little to do with the pulse of the music. Kiara appeared to enjoy his company as much as he relished hers. And while he held no illusions about the future of his quest, for the moment, she seemed as content as he to enjoy this night. The music swirled around them, carrying the dancers faster and faster. Even Carina seemed swept up with the spirited tune, and once she let the music take her, she danced well, much to Vahanian's delight. The swordsman's natural agility served him as well on the dance floor as in the salle, and whether he knew the complicated pattern of steps before, he picked them up quickly, circling the floor with Carina as the music built to its crescendo.

Tris found himself out of breath as he caught Kiara in the final step of the dance, face to face, one arm locked around each other's waist, the other clasping hands in the air. Their eyes met, and she leaned into him, bringing her only a breath away from his lips.

"Do it again, faster!" a girlish voice cried delightedly, and Tris reluctantly looked away to find Berry clapping enthusiastically. The princess wore a plain spun shift and soft slippers which she had no doubt borrowed from her servant, escaping her father to rejoin the festivities.

"I'm out of breath," Kiara murmured, slipping from his grasp.

"So am I," Tris admitted. Out of the corner of his eye, he saw Carina beg off the next dance also, to drop tiredly into her seat. Berry intervened, grasping Vahanian's hand and tugging the mercenary back to the dance as the musicians struck up another lively tune. "I could use a breath of air," Tris said.

"Agreed," Kiara said, and followed as he slipped out the rear doorway into the long, torch-lit corridor.

They walked side by side in silence for a while, enjoying the relative coolness of the hallway after the packed greatroom. They wandered for more than a candlemark, enjoying an opportunity to live only in the moment. At the end of the west wing, they found a small temple to the Goddess.

"Isn't this beautiful?" Kiara murmured as they looked around. Dawn streamed through two huge panes of stained glass at the front of the small, octagonal room. Four red candles burned on an altar, one for each of the light aspects of the goddess. Above them stood an exquisite marble statue with four faces representing mother, child, lover and warrior. The statue overlooked a reflecting pool, where the four dark aspects returned her gaze.

The colors of the stained glass repeated the theme. Red, the fire of the warrior avenger, together with the amber of the Mother, deep blue of the lover and the rich green of the Childe filtered the light in a shifting spectrum across the small nave. To the right of the altar on a pedestal was a basin for an oracle's scrying pool, and to the left, on a stand of gold, a perfect crystal orb.

"Despite Staden's welcome, I don't know if I'll ever feel safe again," Kiara murmured.

"That would be a shame," Tris said. "I'd like to change that."

"You might be able to."

Tris's heart was thudding so loudly that he imagined Kiara must hear it as he bent to meet her lips. For an instant she hesitated, then leaned into him, slipping her strong arms around his neck as he pulled her closer against him. A moment later, breathless, he drew back and looked at her in wonder. "You aren't afraid I'll turn you into a newt?" he joked gently. "I'm a wizard, you know."

She chuckled. "Jae would enjoy the company. You're not afraid I'll challenge you to a duel? I'm a 'swordlady,' you know."

It was Tris's turn to chuckle. "I rather like that, swordlady," he said affectionately. "Some party, huh?" he asked, tangling his fingers in her hair.

She smiled. "It's been so long since I've had a good time, I was beginning to think I'd forgotten how."

"I won't let you forget."

"Is that a promise?" she asked, reaching up to touch his cheek.

"Promise," he said, folding her close. They stood in silence for a while, his cheek against her head, her face against his chest, as the dawn grew brighter through the window. Tris lifted his eyes to the light as it streamed through the faces of the Lady, and froze. Brilliant in the dawn, the face of Chenne began to flush as if alive, and the amber eyes met his with a clarity that seemed to see through his soul.

Do not doubt, he heard a voice say. *I ride with you.* And abruptly, the apparition disappeared.

"Tris, what's wrong?" Kiara asked, leaning back from him with concern.

Tris attempted to speak and found his throat too dry to yield more than a croak. He swallowed hard, staring at the window which was now once more mere glass, and managed a reply. "I think I need some sleep," he said lamely, embarrassed. "I'm starting to see things."

"What kind of things?" Kiara asked suspiciously. When he said nothing, her frown grew deeper. "You felt Her, didn't you, just now?"

Mutely, Tris nodded, looking still at the lifeless window. "I thought I saw Chenne," he whispered, the words sounding fantastic even to him. "But there's nothing there now."

"You did," Kiara said with conviction, resting against him and giving him a reassuring embrace.

"I didn't hear anything, but I felt... something. I know that feeling," she said self-consciously. "It was the same thing I've felt before, when She was near." She paused. "What did She say?"

"Not to doubt," Tris repeated wonderingly. "That She would ride with me."

"So will I," Kiara said resolutely. "You know that, don't you? I'm coming with you to Margolan."

Tris met her eyes, overwhelmed by conflicting emotions. Elation, that by some miracle she might return his feelings. Joy, that she would share his quest. Fear, at the risk to her that their journey would entail. "I don't want anything to happen to you," he said quietly. "I don't think I could stand that."

She smiled. "I didn't think you were going to try to coddle me," she reproved gently. "Don't disappoint me. I fight as well as you do—or better, you've said it yourself. And I'll never be able to turn my back until Arontala is dead. I'll never be free, and neither will Isencroft," she said firmly. "It's as much my quest as yours, now."

Smiling, she lifted a finger and laid it across his lips. "It doesn't need a vote," she said gently. "It's decided."

He kissed her again, longer and deeper this time, until finally it was she who pulled away. The light of morning filled the sacred space around them, reminding him of just how much time had passed. "I imagine Carina will send a search party after me if I don't go back soon," she said with a smile.

Tris grinned. "Maybe. Then again, Jonmarc looked determined to keep her out late."

Kiara chuckled. "In a wicked sort of way, I kind of enjoy seeing Carina look so unnerved around Jonmarc. She's usually so damnably in control. He's the first one she hasn't scared off."

"I don't think he scares easily," Tris replied, linking his hand with hers as they walked from the temple. He glanced back over his shoulder, but the image of the Lady remained mere glass.

"You're not going to find an answer that makes sense, Tris," Kiara said, guessing his thoughts. "Stop trying."

He smiled and sighed as they headed down the corridor. "I imagine not," he admitted. "Funny how, not too long ago, I didn't think there were any mysteries at all. And now..."

"Now you're one of the 'hounds of the Goddess,'" she finished.

He looked at her quizzically. "What?"

She shrugged. "I read that somewhere, in a book about a sorceress from long ago. She called herself the 'hound of the Goddess' because she came when the Lady called and did as the Lady told."

"Hound of the Goddess, huh?" Tris mused. He thought about the road ahead of him, the odds against them, and his friends' willingness to stake their lives on his magic. A good pack of hounds could bring down a formidable enemy, like a stag or a bear. Tomorrow, they would meet with Staden to talk of war, and the prince who never wanted to be king would recruit an army to

avenge his family and take back his kingdom.
Tomorrow.

But for tonight, he thought, holding tight to
Kiara's hand, he had already won more than he
ever dreamed possible. It was all he needed, for
now. Tomorrow would come soon enough.

ABOUT THE AUTHOR

Gail Z. Martin discovered her passion for science fiction, fantasy and ghost stories in elementary school. The first story she wrote—at age five—was about a vampire. Her favorite TV show as a preschooler was *Dark Shadows*. At age 14, she decided to become a writer. She enjoys attending science fiction/fantasy conventions, Renaissance fairs and living history sites. She is married and has three children, a Himalayan cat and a golden retriever.

You can visit Gail at:

www.myspace.com/chronicleofthenecromancer

www.chroniclesofthenecromancer.com

Read her blog:

blog.myspace.com/chronicleofthenecromancer

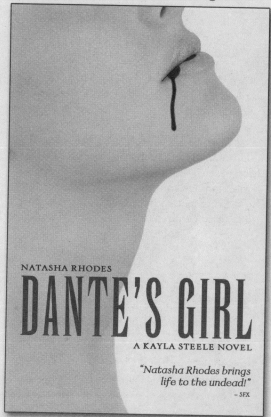

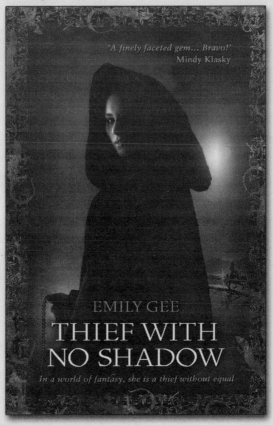